FLOTSAM

A DIVEMASTER RICKY MYSTERY

FLOTSAM

TRACY GROGAN

Cover by Damonza.

ISBN:
978-0-578-99867-1 (ebook)
979-8-9850140-0-6 (paperback)

To the thousands of bright, adventurous, driven women who teach, guide, and assist the world's divers—thank you for making our experience better.

Special thanks to the ones who manage all of that with a touch of quirkiness.

CONTENTS

1

EARLY MORNING – PALAU, MICRONESIA

I PAUSED, AS I always did, to reconsider my next steps. Then, having made my decision, I ran recklessly to the edge, feeling that mixture of faith and doubt as I committed to leaving solid earth. What followed was a full-on sensory assault: the final impact of my plant foot as I launched myself into the emptiness; the sight of nothing but a massive, empty horizon; the sound of air rushing past my ears, the sudden shift in smell as I plummeted; and then the quick nip of chill as my sun-warmed body plunged into the cool ocean thirty feet below the cliff. It never got old.

The sense of pressure rose as the water embraced me, enveloping me in a riot of bubbles, before the chaos resolved into a womb-like bliss. My descent slowed, the noise dissolved into silence, the water diffused the sunlight, and the current carried away the cocoon of bubbles. Gone was the world I'd awoken to that morning, replaced by my magical second home. And then, a few quick flutter kicks drove me toward the surface for a gulp of warm ocean air.

Popping up at the water's edge, I pulled myself onto the narrow, rock-lined shelf where my gear lay. Within minutes, I had rechecked my pressure gauge and diving computers, and pulled on my buoyancy compensator, tank, and mask. As I cinched up my straps, a flock of shearwaters flew by, gliding silently over the surface of the water. I noticed they were feeding—a sign there were baitfish near the surface, likely driven upward by predators below. Above me, beyond the top of the cliff, a noisy flock of dusky sparrows burst from the jungle hillside, then banked sharply and disappeared back into the canopy.

With fifty pounds of gear on my back, and an uneven, unforgiving surface beneath my dive booties, I didn't spend much time taking in the scene. Waddling the few feet to the edge, I tested my regulator for proper airflow, shoved it into my mouth, and leapt in. I was treated to another quick flurry of bubbles and then silence. Floating to the surface and drifting with the current, I pulled on my fins, dumped air out of my buoyancy compensator, and flipped upside down, descending farther away from the chaos of the world—weightless and free. Beneath me, the cliff plummeted almost straight down until it was swallowed by the shadows.

*

Ricky's Rocking Spot was my oasis. It wasn't perfect, and those imperfections added to its charm. For years, locals had used its crystal-blue waters as a dump site for things they couldn't reuse, repurpose, sell, recycle, or give away—castoffs that had outlived their utility and were viewed as just taking up space. I had seen a cockeyed Barco reclining lounger, a suitcase packed with still-sealed porn videos, and even a nearly new Camry, its Hertz bumper sticker just starting to peel. I had a hard time getting past the short-sighted, selfishness of it all—not just from the perspective of ruining natural beauty, but the very real destruction of the environment. The car, I was sure, was still leaching out petrochemicals that poisoned our fish and everything up the food chain. But marine life can be resilient, and it eventually embraces the surface world's jetsam—some of it had settled on the ledges and occasional slopes, providing new habitats. Most, though, just dropped down into the darkness of the sand bottom almost two hundred feet below. Still, it gored me that people could so casually choose to turn their problem into someone else's.

I dropped down to a sculpted coral reef one hundred feet below the surface and thousands of miles away from my worries. The diving was perfect, a virtual Zen state. I was flying. Spinning and somersaulting, I was transported back to a rare, carefree moment in my mid-teens when I was living with Mom. It was one of the good summers—she had enrolled me in a live-in circus camp for a month. I loved the aerial work, the liberating feeling of it, and here I was, fifteen years later, still getting off on the flying sensation like I had the very first time. The tights and tank top of the wannabe circus aerialist had been replaced with three millimeters of neoprene and a load of scuba gear, which made me feel a little less free, but, on the plus side, the consequences of falling were a lot less daunting.

A steady but gentle current had pushed me along a dramatic underwater cliff. Carried along like a leaf on a river, I did my underwater ballet, rolling and twisting in my weightless environment. Not a care in the world. Just the fish and me. A pair of bluefin tuna approached from down-current and sped by, scanning the depths for a quick meal. Although these fish were somewhere north of four hundred pounds, they were never a threat, feeding only on small baitfish. Sometimes the big fish had sharp teeth and a wider variety of dining options, but they didn't bother us nearly as much as we bothered them.

Although I dived the site solo, I wasn't lacking company that day. Besides the bluefins, a good-sized hammerhead shark was patrolling the depths. I gradually descended to a hundred forty feet to get a better look, something I couldn't do with most of our paying customers. We didn't take vacation divers anywhere near that depth... our reputation and bottom line couldn't afford a customer getting "the bends," a risk that increases as the dive goes deeper.

Contrary to their reputation, sharks are generally nonthreatening. Some can even be playful, but in a domineering way. Despite cable TV depictions and hysterical reports whenever there's a shark "attack" leading most to believe the worst, sharks tend to let people go their own way. We don't look or act like their normal food source, and we most certainly don't taste like it.

This hammerhead, though, had my attention. I figured

it was just curious and my mellow demeanor gave it the confidence to hang around, cutting tight 180-degree turns close to the reef wall. That, or it was agitated. It's always hard to tell, and I didn't want to be the blue-plate special should a shark decide it's dinnertime. They are deceptively fast and relentless when hunting.

As they weren't in the realm of the hammerhead's diet, the bluefins were still zipping about. Hammerheads favor meals on the sand bottom—octopus, rays, crabs, that sort of thing—so it was a perfect moment for me to be alone with some of the great creatures of the sea, coexisting in my private playground, its appeal ironically improved by the garage-sale look acquired over the years. The fish truly thrived in that environment as it provided an array of places to hide from predators.

After my time with the shark, I moved shallower, knowing it was best to avoid spending too much time so deep. Besides, the light was better in the shallower water, and the morning glow was beginning to bring out the marine wall's color.

Everywhere I looked there was a smorgasbord of fish. Many of the small ones were tucked into nooks and crannies, both the reef's natural ones and the new ones provided by the islanders' rejects. Some darted about from hiding place to hiding place, while others braved the open but stayed inches away from safety. At some point, though, even the well-hidden needed to emerge to eat, so a healthy population of larger predators patrolled the zone, waiting for one to make a mistake. Large cuttlefish blended into the scenery, changing color and texture to match their background. Schools of jackfish and barracuda flashed silver as they circled and waited. More tuna cruised through, turning on the afterburners as they pursued a mass of baitfish, and I could see splashes above me as the shearwaters dived into the ocean, attacking the school as it was driven to the surface.

With all of that rich soup of fish life buzzing about, this spot was ideal for predators, including any industrious spear fisherman willing to bypass the easy pickings of his local lagoon in search of bigger fish. So, as I drifted with the current, I wasn't totally surprised to see a man nestled down on a wide ledge a hundred feet below the surface of the ocean. The wall was concaved just below the ledge, so it was an ideal spot to look straight down to view prey. The local hunters picked spots like that where they could blend into the environment and lay there waiting for their prey to wander a little too close.

*

I was in awe of the locals. They'd been fishing beneath the waves their whole lives, often using homemade gear including their spears and masks. Most fished from shore or in shallow waters from dugouts and small runabouts—they seldom went deep and didn't need to. Ringed with over one hundred miles of reefs providing shallow, calm, clear water, the island chain was fringed with mangroves whose roots provided a sanctuary for the juveniles and other small fish.

Even so, a few special locals chose to go after the bigger prey like snappers, groupers, or the big wrasses, and did so with factory-made gear, usually purchased used, or accepted as gifts from departing visitors. Those were the free-diving ninjas. No scuba tanks for them. On a single breath of air, they kicked down to depths of a hundred feet or more, hovered motionless for a minute or even longer as they waited for their prey, fired the spear perfectly into the fish's brain, and then surfaced, ready almost immediately to do it again.

I was in no hurry and knew he'd have to surface soon, so I turned back into the current, swimming against it, putting some distance between us. There is nothing a predator, human or otherwise, hates more than an oblivious interloper spooking their prey. And I selfishly resented his intrusion into my space. Gently finning, I slowly pushed myself against the water flow and moved up-current about a hundred feet, deciding to take a couple of minutes to peek around in the coral. The metronome in my head clicked off the seconds.

*

Given the state of bliss I'd been in since hitting the water ten minutes earlier, I hadn't paid much attention to the smaller details of the reef. Normally I was deeper when I passed this point in the dive. I realized the interloper provided me an opportunity to chill and poke about—a good formula for centering myself, with the bonus of exploring an unfamiliar section of the wall. So much of the diving in Palau is spent drifting and looking into the blue for sharks and big fish—scanning the forest and missing the trees. It was easy to forget that some of diving's most joyful times were spent focusing on a tiny spot loaded with interesting critters.

I stopped to inspect an old kettle-style barbecue hanging lopsided on the slope. It was hooked by one leg onto an outcropping, slowly being enveloped by encrusting sponges spreading across its metal frame, gradually making it part of the reef. Soft corals in a kaleidoscope of orange, red, and yellow had taken root on the grill. An eel poked its head out of the metal bowl as I approached, and eyed me suspiciously, rhythmically opening and closing its mouth.

I drifted down-current a few feet, to a larger multicolored mound of sponges which I realized were part of a World War II army truck, one of many that had been abandoned as US troops moved off the island. The locals used them as workhorses for years after the war. Judging by the extent of encrustation, this one had been jettisoned long ago, but not before giving its all.

Over what was probably at least a decade, it had become a sponge-covered sculpture, although it was still recognizable thanks to its shape and a single headlight not being completely covered. What had looked like a small cave was actually an open or missing window. Schools of small baitfish no larger than tadpoles hovered inside the passenger compartment, sometimes moving out through the opening into less-protected water.

Having been finning into the current to stay where I was, I checked my status, time, remaining breathing gas, and depth displayed on my computer, then relaxed my rate of kicking to allow myself to slowly drift on.

A few feet past the truck, a school of baitfish darted into a refrigerator, its door slightly akimbo on one hinge, providing just enough space for their rapid excursions outside and even speedier retreats. Two lionfish hovered nearby, probably having just missed a prime feeding opportunity.

I figured I had given the spear fisherman at least three minutes—more than his lungs could handle—and stopped kicking, allowing the current to take me along the wall again. As I drifted around the corner and neared the concave, I was surprised to see him still there. Although I knew that some of the real hotshots in this area could stay down that long, and longer, something about him gave me the willies.

He was facing away from me in the classic hunting attitude, pointing in the direction of the current so that he could see the big fish swimming into it. They're slower going in that direction and easier to spear. But other than that, things were out of sort. First, he had no fins. Although a lot of spear fishermen swam without fins in the shallows, they all used them for these deeper ventures. Second, there was no visible spear. This didn't feel right at all. Drifting farther along the cliff to get a closer look, I realized the skin-tight black material on his body wasn't a wetsuit.

It was a business suit.

Crap!

As I hovered no more than ten feet from the body, trying to wrap my head around what I was seeing, that "crap" turned into a shitstorm.

*

For a reason still unknown to me, my attention shifted upward just in time to see a cartwheeling axle ricochet off the reef wall, passing far too close for comfort, with a chain snaking behind it pulling some new guy attached to its end. Unlike the first, this man was most decidedly not dead. As he shot past, I saw clearly his bugged-out, begging eyes as bubbles burst from his open, screaming mouth and his pawing, outstretched, mutilated hand.

As I instinctively reached for him, the whipped chain yanked him away from me. Jackknifing and kicking quickly, I started down into the depths, but he was almost immediately out of sight. At the speed he had passed, I was sure he was already beyond the range to which I could safely descend, so I stopped. And I began to shake.

Reflexively grabbing my regulator so I wouldn't spit it out, I vomited.

2

8:50 A.M. – DOWNTOWN KOROR, KOROR ISLAND

I ARRIVED AT the Koror Police Station in a less than flattering state. Actually, I was a mess. The Jeep was worse.

After seeing the body and watching the other guy disappear beneath me, I raced to my exit point, executed my prudent ascent and surfacing routine, and waded up onto the beach about a half mile down-current from where I entered. I searched fruitlessly for my cell phone, finally admitting defeat. I threw my dive gear in the back of my Jeep, then made a hasty retreat, sideswiping a tree as I peeled out and bounced up the jungle road. I hadn't even thought to take off my wetsuit. I puked twice during the drive—once while I was doing well beyond the 50 mile-per-hour speed limit. As gross as puking underwater can be, it's even worse at high speed in a convertible.

I parked right in front of Koror police station—a site of some prior unpleasantries. I hoped this time would be different. In, goodbye, out. I must have made quite the scene as I pushed the twin doors open, maybe a bit too enthusiastically, because heads immediately turned. I stopped to compose myself, but it was too little too late, giving everyone in the room more time to check me out. I probably didn't establish much credibility as I finally walked to the first available desk, which appeared to be home base for a pit bull with lipstick and one of those pullback buns that make it look like you've had a facelift.

Taking a moment to put on a calm, non-lifted, face, I announced in my best nonchalant divemaster voice, "I'd like to report a murder. Maybe two."

*

Although I had expected this introduction to result in an immediate call to higher-ups, my presence seemed to elicit the opposite response.

"Yellow line—scoot, scoot!" I followed the clerk's eyes to a worn painted line behind me at least five feet from her desk. It might have been yellow years before but was, by the time I walked past it, little more than a suggestion of color on the tan linoleum floor. I couldn't really blame her for putting some distance between us. The stench of salt water, sweat, and vomit that I carried with me may have been a bit overpowering.

Having established our pecking order, she paused, picked up a freshly sharpened pencil from a small tray, and—stretching out the word to twice its length—asked, "Name?"

"Ricky Yamamoto."

The receptionist eyed me with what I interpreted to be a mixture of disdain and confusion. "More slowly, please, this time."

I get this a lot, thanks to the gender confusion created by my first name and the mismatch of my last name and physical makeup – I'm tall, have long arms and legs, and am fair skinned, but I have black hair, brown eyes, and Asian facial features. I'm used to getting quizzical stares.

Patiently, slowly, trying to mask my tension and the immediate misgivings I was feeling being back in a police station, I said, "Ricky Yamamoto. I live here in Palau. I've just seen a murder."

"So you said. Have you been drinking?" Cranky and belligerent. Not what I needed.

"No, I have not; it's barely past nine. Why would you think I've been drinking?"

"Are you aware you are covered in vomit?"

She had a point. All I could do was shrug as I told her, "Yes, I saw a murder. I was pretty upset. I threw up a few times."

"You could have washed before coming in here, you know. We have to work here, and we don't have air conditioning."

Leaving the yellow line behind and leaning in, I dramatically reduced the space between us, knowing it was wrong but unable to stop myself. "It's freaking raining bodies out there. And you're worried about vomit?" Like a beach ball banging against a concrete wall, it seemed to have no effect. After a pause and a dramatic sigh, she shooed me back across the yellow line with a double-hand brushing motion.

"Well," she replied with a bit too much attitude for my state at that time, "one of us needs to worry about it and you don't seem inclined to do so."

Where do they get these people? Is every police station the same? There must be a training program for rude and oblivious front-desk staff. She could have been transported directly from the Hilo Police Department. Different island, different decade, different circumstances, same attitude.

"I'm telling you," I said, reverting to my calm divemaster voice, "that I've witnessed a murder, maybe two, here in Palau."

She wrinkled her nose and, in defiance of the skin-tightening bun, furrowed her brow. I wasn't sure if she was reacting to my news or to the rather unpleasant smell of drying seawater and vomit. "As you can see, we're quite busy here. We're dealing with a typhoon warning. We can't just drop everything when some vomit-covered, wild-eyed drunk staggers in here screaming of murder and raining bodies. Take a seat." She frowned deeper and pursed her lips. "Actually, there's a gardener outside. Have him hose you down. And don't come back in until you've stopped dripping. And wipe your feet. We just had the floor cleaned." That seemed to be true. Despite last night's rain, there were no muddy footprints on the linoleum floor—except for the small imprints of flip-flops that led to where I stood.

But that shouldn't have been an issue. I looked at her again, sizing her up. Mainlander. Deep tan. Local clothing. Another desperate expat trying to make it as an islander—and failing. A true Palauan would have looked right past the vomit.

The gardener was quite accommodating, and I must admit, it felt good to get hosed down. Tugging away at the neoprene wetsuit that had adhered to my skin as it dried, I stripped down to my swimsuit and kicked the wetsuit toward my Jeep, only then realizing my parking space was reserved for emergency vehicles. I figured my situation qualified. Relieved finally of my second skin, I asked the gardener to hose me down once again, peeling away the layer of salt and sand this time. A pair of layabouts, pressed against the wall near the entrance, cheered and called for more. They got a finger instead.

Checking the side-view mirror, I saw I needed to do something with my hair, so I pulled it out of its ponytail and combed out a few of the knots. And reminders of this morning's breakfast. I asked for and received another blast from the hose, this one drenching my head. After a brisk toweling off, which earned new catcalls, I swapped the neoprene for a knapsack I'd thrown in the back seat of the Jeep the night before, pulled out shorts and a T-shirt, and prepared to resume my attempt at being a good citizen.

Deciding not to tempt fate, I took the time to raise the roof on the Jeep and cover my gear with the towel before locking the doors and turning to join to my newfound friend at the front desk. The losers watched me intently as I skipped up the steps.

I noticed the pit bull wore no name tag, her desk provided no clue to her identity, and she didn't volunteer any such information when I returned. Perhaps, given her attitude, anonymity was a prudent measure. I did note, in her favor, that she had excellent posture.

*

Apparently, my new appearance and bouquet added substantially to my credibility, and I was soon seated with a uniformed officer, though his badge read "patrolman," which didn't suggest high standing in the peace officer hierarchy. Maybe my status still needed a boost. His name, according to his patch, was Idechong. I'd never met him, which was a relief. The less direct history the better. We were in a small, dreary interview room with a ceiling fan that produced more noise than breeze, and an overhead light fixture that threatened to overflow with dead bugs. The walls had probably originally been light tan, the default color for Palau government buildings, but they had since taken on a deeper hue that suggested years of cigarette smoke and limited janitorial service. The floor appeared to be bare concrete. He pointed me to a seat at the far side of the table, the only padded chair in the room. That was the upside. The downside was that, after a brief introduction, he documented my background information—name, age, occupation—and excused himself, taking the paperwork with him. This interview was clearly a low priority for the man.

By then I was hungry, irritable, and still quite tweaked by the entire episode. The room was stuffy and smelled of cigarettes. After what seemed an eternity, he returned, asked me the questions again, checked my replies against my previous answers, sighed, and looked up at the ceiling fan. Or maybe he looked past it for divine inspiration. Regardless, I took this as yet another negative.

I had sought assistance from this department before and had severe misgivings about their discipline and integrity. Of course, if he was familiar with that backstory—and perhaps he had checked on it when he stepped out—he might have similar misgivings about me. Suffice it to say, I might be remembered and viewed as a rabble-rouser and an irritant by higher-ups in the force. I also might, independent of that specific event, have a bit of a reputation as a wild one. Either of those pieces of information might explain the limited intensity of the interview.

We proceeded at the pace of a slug race. The entire concept of finding a body on a ledge a hundred feet below the surface of the water was, to say the least, foreign. The form the officer was trying to complete—a greyed copy of a copy of a copy, probably unchanged in decades—clearly had not been designed for this situation. That didn't stop Officer Idechong from faithfully working his way down the form.

"No, there were no signs, businesses, or landmarks nearby. Yes, that's correct, he passed me at about ten to fifteen miles an hour—it's hard to say."

He asked a follow-up question about the conditions, but at that point, my mind was pondering exactly how fast a person would descend when attached to a big hunk of metal. The note of irritation in my interrogator's tone as he repeated his last question brought me back to the moment.

"Sorry. I don't know if it was sunny or not. I was a hundred feet down. It's never sunny down there. It was cloudy when I entered the water and I think it was cloudy when I exited. There's a storm coming, you know." I realized I wasn't helping my case, but so far no one in the department shared my sense of urgency.

Gently sliding his chair back, he began to rise and wondered out loud if this was in his jurisdiction, suggesting it was the domain of the marine law enforcement division, the Rangers. That was the last thing I'd want—the Rangers were responsible for patrolling the ocean waters for illegal fishing, particularly the taking of sharks. They had a small force to cover a massive territory and, despite their best efforts, they were overwhelmed by the task. Diverting them to deal with a police matter was simply wrong.

"The initial crime probably took place on land," I pointed out. "I doubt that the first guy was lured to the ledge, a hundred feet deep, and then killed." I paused. "Also, neither guy seemed dressed for an oceanic excursion, what with the black suits and leather shoes they were wearing." He sighed and settled back into his chair. At least for the moment, it seemed I had thwarted his plan to pass the murder off to the Rangers, although his attempt at a steely-eyed squint suggested he appreciated neither my guidance nor my willingness to jump to conclusions.

*

The interview was torture. I hadn't eaten for hours, and what I had eaten was recently hosed off my wetsuit. I needed caffeine, and my bladder was at its bursting point. Fortunately, the patrolman suggested we take a break, and I agreed to come back in an hour. As the officer led me by the front desk, I smiled at the receptionist, but she seemed to be intently marking up a list with a yellow highlighter.

The Koror Police Station boasted two very convenient neighbors. The first was the prison, which adjoined the building. The trip from processing to cell was no more than a hundred feet. The second nearby point of interest is the Rock Island Café, a hangout for expats or expat wannabes. I could probably have gotten by for weeks at a time on their breadsticks, but at that moment I was thinking of pizza. The best pizza in the country, bar none. That might not sound like much, but it meant a lot if you were living in Palau.

I looked at my watch. It was 10:10. I had time for a piping-hot medium, maybe even a custom-made job. I decided to make it a large—pepperoni and jalapeno, a Rock Island classic. Paired with a diet cola, it was a meal that would prepare me to go again.

I was back by 11:00, my belly full but still slightly ill at ease. I had to wait only a few minutes to resume the interview. Officer Idechong returned promptly upon being paged, but the second round started out even more slowly than the first, and I had the distinct impression my story was being dismissed. They'd sent me the slowest of the slow and had probably told him to wear me down. He searched about for the earlier paperwork, a task that seemed to drag on forever, but couldn't find it. He pulled out a clean new form, and we took it from the top.

"Name?"

By the time we got back to where we had left off, I could feel the cola—and the free refill that followed—working its way through my system. My weak bladder was notorious among my friends and coworkers, but there was no way I was going to ask for a break and risk starting at the top again. This guy could have driven Sisyphus over the brink.

"Identifying marks or jewelry on the victim?"

"Jewelry? Yes, as a matter of fact, now that you mention it... he was wearing a truck axle."

He lifted the pen off the paper and raised his head to stare at me. Not a good sign. I needed to back off a bit.

"I'm telling you, he went past in a flash, and all I saw was his bugged-out eyes, his open mouth and his outstretched hands. It was creepy." I took a breath and swallowed, deliberately. "I think I might throw up again." As the words came out of my mouth, the image immediately came back with a clarity that intensified the nausea, then just as quickly distracted me enough to suppress it. I actually *had* seen more. "Wait, there was something. On his—" I held up my hands and looked at them to orient myself, "—on his right hand... he was missing parts from his pinky and another finger. Yes, that was it, his right hand."

That got his interest. Good.

He took some quick notes, then, without a word, he stood up and left the room, papers in hand. Not good. I thought about taking a bathroom break, but didn't want to risk him returning to find me AWOL.

I stayed. I tried to relax. I began to count the dead bugs in the overhead light.

3

10:45 A.M. – THE SAME CONFERENCE ROOM

He returned shortly after my bug count had reached one hundred, this time with another officer. The pit bull, who seemed to have abandoned her station, hovered in the background until the new officer swung the door closed rather emphatically.

*

A uniform was about all that these two had in common. The second officer had at least six inches and fifty pounds on the first. A well-formed fifty pounds, mind you. He passed through the door at least two paces ahead of the patrolman and immediately took charge. Idechong did his best to stay out of the way, but seemed ready to contribute. In the presence of this new officer, he seemed like an anxious lapdog.

"Sergeant MacArthur Uchel. Glad to meet you, Ricky." His voice was deep and gentle, with an air of confidence, and somehow, domination. He didn't wait for me to reply. "Is there anything I can get you? Coca-Cola? Coke Light?" He moved to the head of the table.

"No, no, I'm fine, thank you." What I really needed was a trip to the bathroom, but I'd committed to my plan to avoid asking for a break. This seemed like progress, and at Palau police headquarters, progress was a rare treat to be respected and nurtured.

"Officer Idechong tells me you believe you saw a body while diving." Sergeant Uchel seemed engaged, perhaps amused, but I sensed the source of amusement was the patrolman and his clumsy interrogation. Still standing, Uchel leafed through the report. He had a military bearing about him, not what I had come to expect from the national police.

"I'm quite clear I saw one body, already dead, and another on his way to being dead soon."

"He wasn't yet dead?" He was taking notes. Another good sign.

"No, it appeared he was still alive."

"Did you try to administer assistance?"

Officer Uchel put away the original notes and started taking notes on a lined sheet of paper. The level of questioning, now no longer tied to a form, gave me the impression he was taking this seriously.

"No, it was impossible. He was too far away."

"Yet," he said, making a show of returning to the prior notes, "according to Officer Idechong, you were close enough to see his hands clearly?"

"Yes."

"And he was missing parts of two fingers on his right hand?"

"Yes."

"But now you say he was too far away for you to render assistance?"

"Yes, he was near me for only a second and then he sunk away." As I replayed the moment in my head, it was all too vivid. For the first time, I clearly recalled the sound—not of the chain or the axle bouncing off the reef, but of his scream—at first shrill, but muffled, and then deeper and gurgling. It had lasted no more than a second or two, but I suspected it would stay with me for a lifetime. The officer's voice jarred me from my stupor.

"I'm familiar with diving, although I'm sure much less than you. But I am surprised. You should know that I'm familiar with you by reputation, so I'm trying to understand how someone could sink so fast that an accomplished dive guide couldn't catch up with him."

That made me a bit anxious. I had several reputations on the island, depending on who was talking, and they weren't all positive.

"I dumped air out of my BC and jackknifed to start down..."

"BC?"

"Sorry, buoyancy compensation vest. We use..."

"I know what a BC is, I just figured you for a backplate-and-wings diver."

Touché.

"Sorry, we tend to dumb down our terminology when talking to non-professionals."

"Of course, point taken. Please continue. You were explaining why you couldn't catch up with the victim."

"He was chained to a truck axle. It carried him down faster than I could swim."

"A truck axle?" Apparently, there hadn't been a check box on the form for that piece of information.

"A truck axle."

"Well, that's a new one." I thought I saw the corners of his mouth rise a bit. "How deep were you again?"

"At this point, around a hundred feet." I knew where this was going. He had probably gotten certified and done a few dives, and now thought he knew everything.

He pulled back a chair, its metal feet screeching across the floor, and settled in. It was a bit of a squeeze. "Let's start from beginning. And please, please don't leave anything out. Take your time because I want to make sure I have this right. How did you happen to arrive at the scene?"

*

He asked for all the details, and I left nothing out. My unwanted early morning wake-up. What I did on my way to the site. My entry. The hammerhead. Sponges and the abandoned truck. Then I got to what he really wanted.

*

"Is there any chance you might have been experiencing rapture of the deep?"

I laughed. I loved the term, though almost no one used it anymore. More officially known as "nitrogen narcosis," it was also frequently called the Martini Effect—something divers can experience during deep dives—a form of intoxication brought on by increased pressure as you go deep. I had been diving so long I'd conditioned myself to the changes and seldom experienced it.

"Fair question. We call it 'narced,' and no, I wasn't. I have too many hours underwater to get narced at that depth. I frequently go much deeper as part of my job and during my recreational dives."

"You do understand why I ask?"

"Yes, and there's nothing I can say that might convince you otherwise. It sounds like you're a diver. Maybe you want to join me to see for yourself." I didn't, for a moment, believe I had imagined the whole event. I had been completely aware and unimpaired. My job now was to make sure he took me seriously. Then I could be done with the whole mess.

"I've gotten wet a few times. But we have a team that can conduct a proper search." He jotted something down in his notes. "You have much cause to dive deep around here?"

I wasn't sure where he was going. Possibly he was intrigued, maybe he was testing me, but he definitely wanted to keep control of the conversation.

"Sure, not all the time, but we take folks to almost two hundred feet on Big Drop Off, also Siaes Tunnel, and Blue Corner. And for the ones who are qualified and interested, we go to a wreck called 'The Perry' at over two hundred and fifty feet. That requires special equipment and gas mixtures. I'm certified to train divers in that type of diving as well."

"So, you have no doubt about your report. A truck axle, a heavy chain, and two missing fingertips."

"Nope, no doubt. It's all way, way too clear in my memory."

"Did anyone know you were going to this..." he paused and checked his notes, "Ricky's Rocking Spot"?

"Yes—and no. A few people knew I was going diving. No one knows where my secret spot is."

He stared at me, obviously waiting for more details.

"My bosses, for sure. I told one of my neighbors. She asked if I was going to have any fish when I came back and I told her I was just going to a pleasure dive—no speargun. No other details."

The local scene wasn't like a commercial fishing operation; they didn't take until they couldn't take any more. The Palaun's lifeblood has always been subsistence fishing—enough food to feed family and friends for a day or two and then back out in the water again. So, on any given day, most would take one big fish, maybe two, and if they were lucky enough to get a really big one, they made their neighbors very happy. What they didn't eat the first day, they smoked and preserved. If they needed some cash, they might grab an extra fish to sell. In the afternoon, a small fish market would pop up, selling out within an hour.

"Anyone else?"

"My Dad. From Hawai'i. I'm not sure if I told him or not. He usually does all the talking. I was still half-asleep, so I'm not really sure. And, if I did, I don't know if he paid attention."

"Is that it? Any others?"

"Like I said, I went for a run this morning. With my friend Ruluked. I told her. Just the diving part, not the location."

"Ruluked?"

"Yes, Ruluked Reklai. She works with one of my bosses at the Office of the Attorney General."

"I'm familiar with her—by reputation."

He made an odd clucking sound and jotted down more notes, then he took out his cell phone, excused himself, and stepped out into the hallway. Hopefully, my answers were sufficient to trigger a turning of the wheels of justice. That was fine with me. I needed to pee. I wanted to hand this off and get away from this place. I wanted to go home. This was not my concern, not my job, and not how I wanted to spend my day off. Officer Idechong, by this time having been rendered irrelevant, stood by the door. He appeared to be counting the bugs in the ceiling light.

*

When he returned, Officer Uchel dismissed Officer Idechong. "Miss Yamamoto, I'd like to thank you for your patience. And for your cooperation and diligence. I understand this has been stressful. I'm going to, however, request a bit more of your time."

At this point, I began to reconsider the wisdom of getting involved in the first place. I could have just gone about my day without raising the alarm. It's not as if anyone else had seen me. I could, at that very moment, have been cleaning my gear and preparing for a return visit to the Rock Island Café. But I was kidding myself. It was no longer in my nature to turn my back on something like this.

Surprisingly, Uchel's only request was for more

specific details. He even offered to spare me the task of leading his team to the body. I gave a detailed description of where I had gone in, where I had found the body, and where I had seen the body-to-be. The officer, who I was beginning to like, knew the location well.

"I once 'misplaced' a couch over that way, in my younger years," he said with a slight twinkle in his eye.

Picking up the receiver from the ancient phone that was the only adornment, besides the table and chairs, inside the otherwise bare interview room, he said, "I'll get a team out to locate and secure the bodies. We can't do a formal recovery until we have a more complete description of the crime scene, and the coroner's approval to move the bodies."

Thumbing through a small notebook he had pulled from his shirt pocket, he stopped at one of the well-worn pages. Punching a smudged button labeled "outside," he dialed the number and waited. After what seemed an unusually long time, he smiled. "Bonjour, Monsieur Fontaine, this is Sergeant Uchel." For my benefit, he added a wink.

Of course. Pascal. I should have guessed that the national police wouldn't have an underwater recovery team. He had called Pow Palau Divers, an operation considered a competitor for my dive shop, but only in the loosest sense. Pow Palau catered to casual divers and, as a business model, took them to the closest sites possible. It was a winning formula for both. The dive shop saved gas and time, and their customers could brag that they'd dived the famous reefs of Palau, though in reality, they'd been to some of the least impressive and most crowded.

For some, that was enough, and they could be back in time for a game of cards and early cocktail hour.

Pascal was a good man and a great dive guide. He was just running the operation for pocket change and to pay his bills until he could get a job in a new locale. That's the life of an expat dive guide—you drift from one place to the next and do what you have to do to stay afloat. At least customers were safe in his hands, and he would find interesting critters and a few sharks that they could tell their friends about. I guess he was also enterprising enough to hire out to the police when situations required.

Unfortunately, that meant Pascal and Pow Palau would find out about Ricky's Rocking Spot. No way they would ever take their customers there—too hairy—but my secret would soon be out. *Crap.*

"Monsieur Fontaine," he said, in a slow, officious tone. "We have a body-location job. Should be pretty easy. We've got a general fix on where it went in, and it appears it won't be going anywhere. What? Car? No, no car over the edge. But a car part, it appears. I'll explain later. First," he said with another wink, which I found a bit off-putting, "I've got a young lady here who can give you directions. You may know her," he added and handed the phone to me.

"Hey, Pascal," I sighed into the phone.

"Ricky! Aloha!" shouted the island's lone French dive guide, always one for a friendly and enthusiastic greeting.

"Ok," I said, with resignation, "here's what you need to do..."

*

It was 12:30 by the time I briefed Pascal, finished my report, and was free to go home. I went out to my Jeep only to find that the driver's side window had been smashed and my dive gear stolen. All I could muster was a mild curse. Then I noticed I had also gotten a ticket for parking too long in a restricted zone and immediately found the energy for a much more colorful set of obscenities.

I was only halfway into the day and I was already feeling like a piñata at a little leaguer's birthday party.

4

EARLIER THAT DAY – BABELDAOB ISLAND

I SHOULD REALLY start this story with some relevant background information.

As you already know, my name is Ricky Yamamoto. I have made an interesting and sometimes comfortable living as a scuba diving guide. I've traveled the world, hiring my skills out to a range of dive shops and boats in exotic locales. At the time I watched a man plunge to a certain, watery death, I was working for a scuba shop just north of the equator and off the western edge of the Pacific Ocean. Oh, and lest there be any confusion caused by my name, I'm a girl.

The day on which this story began was my day off, doing my favorite R & R activity: diving. But diving with no responsibilities other than to myself.

It was my time and my space, both rare commodities for my profession. We're always hustling to make ends meet, frequently moving between countries and employers. Tenure is a limited concept in this industry; we're always proving ourselves to a new boss, adapting to new team members, and learning new locales. We measure free time in minutes, and space is scarce. We work in a massive ocean and yet are seldom alone.

For the first time in my diving history, I had settled down. I had laid my head on a pillow in a single locale for more than four years, in Palau, an island paradise in Micronesia, a pleasant 2,500 miles southwest of my home state of Hawai'i. If you're going to be a suddenly grounded nomad, Palau is a fine place to land. A friendly, sparsely populated nation of 21,000 people and around 300 islands, it was full of adventures, rich in marine life with lots of variety in its underwater playground, and off the beaten track. People arrived daily from all over the world to dive our most famous sites. As I said, I was a nomad, as are most folks who work at dive resorts and on dive boats around the world. As my friend Pascal once told me, "Most of us move around either because we're wanted, or we're not wanted." So true. In Pascal's case, the rumor was that he couldn't return home because he was wanted. In my case, I moved around, not because of any impending arrest, but because I liked to put a comfortable amount of distance between my family and myself.

Mind you, I loved my parents, but sometimes I found it a challenge being their daughter, an only child with all the baggage of that role. We've had our rocky times, and even moments where relationships appeared unsalvageable. And, although distance has become a relative thing in the modern world with the ease of e-mail, texting, and social media, I've found that my parents' ability to push my buttons is more limited with an ocean between us. And so, shortly after my twenty-seventh birthday, I ended up in Palau.

*

My day began with a reminder that physical distance isn't what it used to be. I'd set my alarm for five to get ready for an all-too-rare run for 5:30. But at 3:55 I woke to a familiar ringtone. I never answer the phone automatically and am even less likely to do so at that time of day or for that particular tune, but an unwelcome premonition pulled me groggily from my bed to the kitchen where my cell phone sat ringing away.

It was Dad. No premonition-worthy topic. Nothing urgent. As so often happens when my parents intrude into my life, the call was bizarre, badly timed, and disruptive.

By the time I was done listening to his latest rant, I had no chance of going back to sleep. I wandered into the living room and opened the sliding window facing the nearby coastline, breathing in the dark o'clock stillness. In the distance, I could make out the white foam of the waves breaking over the offshore reef, and I imagined the sounds as they crashed down on the shallow coral that surrounded the island. In the background was the early-morning buzz of bugs and birds. It was just after four. I had to leave in a little over an hour.

Although counter to my usual low-key approach to running, I decided to take advantage of the early wake-up to prepare a proper meal and do some stretching. As I lay on the couch, wiggling my toes in the air (which I'm sure is the prescribed first step in a proper stretching program), I considered my plan of attack and settled upon food first, then more stretching. I didn't want to tax my muscles too much.

After a quick search that went no further than a line of fruit on my kitchen counter and a machete on the cutting board, I set about assembling a tropical treat of coconut, mango, and pineapple—the result of friendly relations with a neighboring family with more trees than mouths. That, and a cup of freshly ground coffee chewed up and brewed in a fancy machine I barely knew how to use and certainly couldn't afford. With sugar. Lots of sugar.

By the time I scraped the last of the coconut meat away from the shell, cleared up my mess, and tossed a rotting mango into the yard where it would be eaten by that same neighbor's goats, I had run out of time for serious stretching. I rushed through a quick set to loosen up my legs and back, then grabbed my keys and headed to my Jeep.

*

The island was still dark, and the breeze was light, bringing to me the uniquely pungent blend of sweet blossoms and rotting leaves that hung heavy in the early morning tropical heat. Down the coast I could see dots of light as the few local fishermen who went to deeper waters outside the reef set out to get their morning catch. One, just leaving the protection of the fringing reef, cranked the throttle, sending the sound of his whining, undersized motor rising through the hills. As if in response, the birds and bugs intensified their screeching and buzzing. As I closed the Jeep door, it all became a subdued white noise.

I pulled onto the main road, splashing through a large puddle that marked the end of my dirt track. Passing a patch of grass that served as the site for our local market, I saw that several of my neighbors had already begun to set up their day's harvests. A few had tables, one had a wheelbarrow, and several had simply laid out tarps upon which they were arranging clusters of bananas, small piles of papaya or sweet potatoes, and a solitary pineapple. Most locals I knew grew enough for their own consumption, so the market was fairly sparse, offering only the surplus that their family couldn't use. I stopped for a quick chat with a neighbor, who was disappointed I wasn't going out to catch fish, and made a mental note to stop on my way home for the night's supplies. Or maybe just pick up a pizza. It would be a coin-toss decision.

*

I got to our meeting spot five minutes early, only to discover that Ruluked was already there, stretching and yakking on the phone. We had been friends since my early days on the island. We'd go running together when I showed the discipline. When I didn't, she ran alone. She was one of the most driven people I had met on the island, but also one of the most intimate. Being her friend meant letting her into your life. If you didn't, she'd be friendly, but she wouldn't consider you a friend. I liked that. Reminded me of my mom—in a good way.

"Well, gracious! Good morning," she sang out, in a voice far too perky for 5:30 a.m. She ended her call with a curt, "Later," then said to me, "You actually look alert."

"Four a.m. phone call from my dad. The discussion was no more bizarre than his typical call, but by the time we hung up, I was wide awake."

"And how is our buddy Sumo?" she asked with a perverse grin. Ruluked knew I was better at being friends with my parents than at being their daughter. She had heard my litany of childhood traumas and found them, for the most part, amusing, seeming to think they'd been only mildly damaging.

"Good," I said, diving into my stretching routine, partially in hopes of terminating the discussion through distraction. "Something about four galaxies colliding head-on and a lot of talk about dark matter." I turned away and executed a lackluster stretch. "Yikes, I'm tight. We'll need to take it easy for the first mile."

"I promise to start slow." She smiled and flashed what might have been the Boy Scout salute. "That'll give us a chance to talk about my favorite mad scientist."

The run was supposed to be for relaxing, not for picking at my emotional scabs. I intensified my stretching and responded with a squeak. One of the resident sparrows squeaked back in reply. The breeze pulsed with a wavelike ebb and flow, the puffs of wind sending leaves skittering across the asphalt lot.

"You know," she continued, "it wouldn't kill you to go visit him once in a while. I looked it up. Really. It's not considered a life-threatening activity."

As the island's "fixer", Ruluked was used to pushing people around on behalf of Palau's attorney general. If you wanted to make something happen, you made nice to Ruluked. She knew which buttons to push. She didn't mince words, and she seldom backed down.

"The subject didn't come up," I blurted out between toe touches. "Three. I promise to consider it. Four. After the tourist season. Six."

"That was five. And the tourist season," she scolded, "as you well know, runs year-round. There is no 'after' or 'before.'"

"I think I'm ready to run," I said, making one last attempt to stop the line of discussion.

"Honey, all you do is run. From your parents. From your ex-boyfriends. I swear you're the most conflict-averse person I know."

"Then, why," I called out as I took off down the stone-covered path, "do I hang out with you?"

*

Our starting point, a traditional Palaun village maintained as a tourist attraction but empty during our early morning runs, was always the same, although our route varied depending on the whimsy of whoever took the lead, which was usually Ruluked. She soon sprinted ahead of me, darting between thatched huts and past mock-ups of "typical" Palaun kitchens and workshops, taking the first available uphill path into the dense jungle that covered most of the island.

The first mile of the paths, snaking through the palm forest, designed for the more ambitious tourists and their guides, were well worn and wide enough for two walkers, but there was little room for passing on the run. Not that I was capable of that. After that first mile, by which time most tourists had turned back, it narrowed, making passing almost impossible. A healthy dose of hill climbing provided long stretches of concentrated effort, punctuated only by the slapping of our shoes on the muddy path and our heavy breathing—mine a bit more ragged and strained than Ruluked's. We finally took a turn onto a relatively flat trail that traversed the hill-side, providing a chance to change our pace. Occasional clearings that topped the ridgeline provided popular vista points for the few who'd made it that far, the worn spots widening where tourists had wandered about. They gave us a chance to run side by side.

"So," Ruluked gasped, which gave me a small measure of satisfaction, "how will you be celebrating this rare day off? Hair salon for a perm and pedicure?" I couldn't see, but I was sure she was grinning sarcastically. Personal grooming was, as she often pointed out, not my strong suit.

"Solo dive. My spot."

"Oh yes, THE spot. You ever going to tell me where it is?"

"Hell, noooo!" I wheezed and stopped dead in my tracks. Ruluked continued striding along, but I stood there, arms akimbo, sucking in a deep breath. "It's a secret—and it's going to stay that way. I don't want the other dive guides finding it and turning it into a new 'destination dive.' And don't you," I called out at the soles of her shoes vanishing around a bend, "tell anyone

I even have a secret spot. It's my, you know, sanctum." I sprinted after her, but it took a while to close the gap; she had picked up the pace.

The rest of the run took us past ancient stone monoliths and quarries, then down toward the shore where we wound through small gardens and working farms, keeping the talk light. Ruluked kept me up-to-date on the latest government gossip, a few new skeleton-filled closets she had uncovered, and who was getting paid off by whom. I reciprocated with a few juicy tidbits about a certain movie star who'd come out for a few days of diving with our shop.

About a quarter mile from the cars, we reached the savannah flats, striped with long shadows cast by palm trees in the early morning sun. Usually, I slowed down here to enjoy the ferns and flowers, but this time I reversed roles and took off at top speed. Long arms and legs pumping and flailing, I sprinted past Ruluked and began to put some distance between us. I suspected she let up a bit to ensure I won, but for once I think I earned it. I was blessed with limbs of unique proportion that would befit a sprinter and are capable of short bursts of speed. Ruluked had the endurance, but her compact body was no match for mine in the final push, and I had relative youth on my side. Well into her forties, she was older than me by at least fifteen years. By the time we reached the cars, we'd both worked up quite a sweat.

"Ricky, I swear, you're just a natural athlete. I can't believe you never played any sports."

I handed her my spare water bottle and waited as she took a deep draw. "Oh, you should have seen my

Rikidozen routine on the wrestling mat," I said mockingly, executing a clumsy karate chop that fluttered through the air. The hours of watching reruns of classic Japanese wrestling had given me an appreciation, if not a talent, for my namesake's signature moves.

My timing was perfect. Ruluked spit out the mouthful of water she had just sucked in.

"I never really went for the whole team concept," I continued. "Depending on others was never my strong suit, and when I got shipped off to Colorado and discovered soloing, I got all the exercise I needed without all the chatter. Solo climbing was like solo diving. It gave me time to work through things."

I stopped talking and glanced over at Ruluked. She was looking my way and waiting for me to continue. Immediately regretting bringing up the topic, I stood and shook out my arms and legs. It had felt good to test them with an all-out burst. I may have looked a bit comical, but I had gotten to the finish line first.

The silence hung in the air, interrupted only by our still-labored breathing and the background noises of island life. I took the opportunity to appreciate the morning as it began to settle over us. The sun was barely over the horizon, but the air was already warm and humid. The jungle was alive with buzzing bugs and chirping birds, and the mangroves that lined the shore were bustling with activity. Cormorants dived beneath the surface just offshore, more often than not coming up with a good-sized fish or crab that was unceremoniously swallowed. Herons paced through the shallows, pecking at treats in the mud between the mangrove roots. A pair of macaques sat low in a tree, grooming, while two others ran from branch to branch in some sort of early morning rush-hour routine.

Ruluked, compassionately, but uncharacteristically, didn't try to revisit the topic of my issues with my parents. Shifting gears, she adopted her own maternal attitude, nagging me over my delayed preparation for the impending big storm that had dominated the news the past few days. I finished my water and gave her a wet hug, offering her little more than, "Ok, will do, goodbye," before she dashed off to get ready for a day of keeping the people of Palau in line. Before she'd even left the parking lot, she was back on the phone.

I yanked down my Jeep's ragtop, made sure everything was reasonably secure, and climbed in for a quick run up-island on the new paved road, followed by a bouncing drive on jungle roads to my secret spot.

I was expecting a serene dive. What I got was anything but.

5

MIDDAY – NGERKEBESANG ISLAND

WHEREVER DIVERS CONGREGATE, at all the epic dive locales of the world, the iconic sites have dramatic, memorable names. Borneo has Barracuda Point. Indonesia has Cannibal Rock. Just a few miles from where I had been diving, Palau's most famous site is Blue Corner, a point of a massive limestone wall jutting out into the nutrient-rich, deep-blue sea, where hordes of sharks silently and ominously patrol the waters, watching for the fish that congregate there to feed.

In contrast, I had named my little patch of water Ricky's Rocking Spot. Maybe not the best name in the world, but it didn't have to be because I was the only one who knew about it. I consciously did not publicize the spot because it was mine. My place of refuge. My sanctum sanctorum. It was where I went for my own private dives. No one else dived there, probably because nobody else ever thought to check out the possibility of entering the ocean from a thirty-foot cliff. Sure, it wasn't exactly a secret location, just a secret point of entry to an otherwise inaccessible section of coastline.

A small beach was located a distance down the dirt road, where the rutted single lane dropped to meet the waterline. This was where I made my exit and where folks who fished the area entered the water. A few locals sometimes went there for spear fishing. The conditions were tougher than the more protected reef and the mangroves that surround the island, but the fish there were bigger. A successful day of hunting could feed a large family or a small village. On that day, though, I had followed a fresh set of tire tracks on the dirt access road, which was rare but not unheard of. I figured one of the local fishermen must have been eager to get an early start as they'd obviously driven through right after the prior night's rain. That hadn't concerned me. They didn't use scuba, so there wasn't much of a chance to run into them at the depths I dived. And I always had the place to myself. Until that morning.

*

I had done my part. Pascal and his team were already on their way to find the bodies. After filing the police report for my stolen gear and successfully appealing to Officer Uchel to get my ticket nullified, I headed to the office. By then it was after one and the day was essentially blown. I wasn't in the mood to work or even to interact with more humans, but the next day was a workday. I had to set up my replacement gear and needed to let my team know about the goings-on of the past eight hours.

As the receptionist had pointed out to me, the police

at the station were embroiled in preparations for a massive storm, which wasn't out of the ordinary. The storm, I mean. I'm not sure if chaos is a normal state for the station. Though we seldom got a direct hit, frequent warnings of impending or growing storms that might come ashore were common in Palau. After a few disastrous storms over the past thirty years, the government was taking no chances this time around. The local radio station was broadcasting weather alerts and the locations of buildings where citizens could seek shelter. It sounded like I might not need dive gear after all, given the increasing possibility we'd be canceling dives for the immediate future.

Our "office" was Palau Oceanic Scuba headquarters, one of the many small shops that serviced the diving needs of Palau's sizeable tourist population. For an island nation of 21,000, the 70,000 visitors who came each year—almost all from the US, Japan, and Taiwan, and almost all for world-class diving—were our main cash cow.

We were located on the neighboring island of Ngerkebesang, a quick trip on a short bridge from the island of Koror, and the country's largest city ("large" being a relative term for a nation whose population wouldn't fill a small town back in the States).

Palau Oceanic Scuba's dive shop sat on the edge of a small, manmade harbor on the southeast corner of Ngerkebesang, protected from the ocean wave action. It shared the harbor with two other buildings, all three constructed at the same time presumably as warehouses. Each had a dock that served a variety of vessels, from leaky fishing boats to expensive pleasure craft. They shared two parking lots, one running in front of the three buildings and the other in back between the buildings and the docks. Even from a distance, our sign stood out: POS.

I parked in the back. Usually, I parked in front in the customer parking area. It's never close to full. Most people who visited our shop either walked from one of the nearby resorts or came by shuttle from one of the more remote hotels. We seldom saw a local diver as they had their own gear and boats and no need for our guide services, so parking was not at what could be called a premium. Today, I decided the back lot was best—less chance of running into a customer and having to engage in idle chitchat. I wasn't in the mood.

*

Two other vehicles belonging to the bosses were parked in back. Both were beaten-up economy models, which meant they looked like every other Palauan car. There weren't many roads in Palau, and other than our new highway, most weren't in very good condition. Damage from negotiating the largely unmaintained roads was common, so every vehicle was scarred and prone to rattling. Most cars and trucks on the island were driven until the baling wire and welds no longer held the parts together. For some of them, their history could be traced back as far as World War II, like the truck I'd inspected at Ricky's Rocking Spot earlier in the day, but less soggy. My Jeep was about twenty years old, not particularly ancient, but it qualified as a typical beater. The broken window and stench, however, did detract from its prestige.

Checking the dock, I did a quick assessment. One fast boat was out, with either paying customers or the bosses. Perhaps both. Or our other divemaster was out solo on one of his recce trips—a pastime that we'd argued about, although I really had no right to complain about someone else diving solo on uncharted sites. The big boat remained tied up at the end of the dock. It had been booked by a group of eight, who'd cancelled, which was how I got my vacation day. It hadn't yet been battened down in anticipation of the storm.

The rear entry to POS was shut tight, so I unlocked the dead bolt and the spring lock and pulled back the heavy, reinforced door. The workshop was dark. In the tropics, you want to keep the heat as low as possible, so shutting off lights when leaving a room was standard procedure. With any customer out of the harbor by nine in the morning and whatever gear was rented not due back for another hour, the service bay tended to be pretty quiet by lunchtime.

We had no technicians on staff; the dive guides handled repairs and maintenance when we weren't out with the boats. Our small but mighty dive-guide staff numbered two: Justin, my partner in crime, and me. We did the heavy lifting, although the owners liked to go diving on the afternoon trips if their work schedules allowed, and they often did. It looked like I had the place to myself—and extra work prepping the big boat before I could go home. I hit the switch and the fluorescent lights hummed to life.

I moved quickly through the service area, where the workbenches were filled with odd bits of gear and tools, the shelves stacked with bins of equipment. Racks held wetsuits we offered for rental to our customers. This place was my home away from home. The bosses usually avoided the space out of concern they might be asked to do some actual work, but right now it wasn't very warm or cozy. Normally I enjoyed having it to myself; today I was on edge.

I was obviously a witness—not a great one, since I only saw the final scene, but a witness, nonetheless. Other than the police, no one knew that, so I didn't think I had much to worry about, but I still wasn't feeling great about the situation. The sooner I could extract myself from the investigation, the better, and until then my radar would be turned up high. Opening the door to the public portion of the shop, I left the service area, closing the door behind me and sliding the dead bolt into place.

Some moments of bad judgement come back to haunt you years later. Others bring more immediate regret. I should have just gone on home. As I turned the corner, I was set upon. There were three of them, and they hit me all at once. I didn't have a chance.

*

"Omigod, Ricky, are you ok?" squealed the short one.

"We've been out of our minds with worry," snapped the tall one.

"Don't you ever answer your cell?" nagged the obsessive one. "We skipped our dive trying to track you down."

Crap! My bosses—or at least three-quarters of the leadership team. The fourth must have actually been engaged at his paying job. These three, clearly, were currently focused neither on running the business nor on their own careers.

"We've gotten calls from the police, a Detective Uchel, and someone with the Ministry of Justice. They seemed interested in your mental health. Alcohol was mentioned. And then a different officer called about a police report. And then some guy came in here trying to sell some used gear. It was in his truck and he was too lazy to even bring it in. I sent the guys out to look and they realized it was yours. The guy said he bought it at a sidewalk sale. He might have already sold your fins. Are you ok?" My interrogator was Sarah Harmon, Columbia Law School Class of 2019. Second-year Palau Supreme Court law clerk, kick-ass diver, decent poker player—unless she was intentionally losing to make the guys feel good. Five feet nothing of pure bulldog, though pretty in a Barbie-doll way. Her nose might not have been original equipment, but by all reports, the rest of her was. A former law school buddy who came for a visit once told us she fought dirty.

"The officer, Uchel, intimated you've got a history with the police department. We weren't told anything about any problems when we bought you into the business. Is there something we should know? Is this a liability issue?" asked Dmitri Grafov. First-generation American, parents emigrated from the Soviet Union in the late eighties. A very nice guy, once you got past the paranoia. And the nervous tick. He finished his court clerkship last year but stayed on to run the operations side of the business. Still hadn't passed the bar exam. Didn't appear motivated to try again and seemed to be ready to settle down on the island. Said he had a few irons in the fire.

"That was your gear, wasn't it? Why did you sell it? Do you need the money for booze? I have lots. Come to my place, you can drink for free." And last but not least, Roland Marsh. Newest member of the team. Also a law clerk, and love-struck, which I wasn't above using to my gain. My rain gutters were cleaner than they'd ever been before, and that wasn't a euphemism. The guy would do anything for me, and he was really quite handy—and polished, the sort of guy you take home to meet the parents. Except I don't do that.

"No, no, and hell no. I haven't gone over the top, my experiences with the police department are completely legit, except for the topiary thing, and, ok, maybe that last one is a yes, I could use a drink. But I haven't been drinking, and, for the record, vomiting on myself is not a sign of an alcohol problem."

"Nobody mentioned puking on yourself," said Dmitri with an odd mix of disgust and awe. He stepped back just a smidge.

"Well, then, let's leave it at that. I've had a hard day. I ended my dive early due to a dead body and a soon-to-be dead body. I've been dealing with the national police. My hair is still salty. My Jeep now has flow-through air conditioning. And that pepperoni jalapeno pizza from Rock Island is repeating on me."

The ringing of the office phone interrupted my

diatribe, just when I'd gotten rolling. Roland answered on the second ring.

"Palau Oceanic Scuba, this is Roland, how may I help you?" he answered, sounding far too chipper for my current taste.

"Riccarda?" he replied to the caller with a slight grin. "Oh, you mean Ricky. Yes, she's here, and I'm sure she's anxious to speak with you—one moment." He completely ignored my hand signals and waving arms clearly indicating I was "not here" and definitely did not want to talk on the phone. Holding out the mobile unit with a quizzical look, he placed his hand over the mouthpiece and whispered, "It's the national police, that nice Detective Uchel. Are you sure you're not in any trouble?"

"Ricky," added Sarah, "do we need to talk about getting you legal representation? Whenever people use your real name, it means trouble."

She was right about that. I'd given Ricky as my first name at the station. Uchel had obviously been looking at my record. That probably wouldn't help matters.

"No, no, I'm fine. I'm just helping the police tie up loose ends." Taking the phone, I gave Roland my stern school ma'am look. "Hello, this is Ricky. Hi Sergeant Uchel. What can I... you're kidding? How long did they look for? Twenty minutes? They didn't find anything? Ok, then, I guess that's that."

Crud.

*

"Idiots. Blasted idiots. Morons." A swift kick sent a cardboard display for the newest trending dive computers skittering into the wall.

"Morons. Morons." Chimed in Ralph the parrot. "Bombs away." And with that she lifted her tail feathers and deposited a small drop of poop on the floor. Ralph and I had been together long enough that she mimicked too much of my vocabulary, but not all her training came from me. That last bit was a trick picked up long before I arrived on the island.

The shop was shoehorned into a building designed for utility, not for style. The floor was epoxy-sealed concrete complete with floor drains, which came in handy when cleaning up after sandy, wet customers and, perhaps more so, Ralph.

I smiled. Ralph had become a good friend. "Damn straight, Ralphie."

"Damn straight. Morons. Damn straight. Hubba hubba." Sometimes it was obvious that Ralph's grasp of the nuances of language was limited to some words from others in the office. One former owner in particular had invested significant amounts of time training Ralph to provide commentary on some of my more personal activities. Ralph offended more than one customer with her commentaries, though most found them mildly amusing.

Pow Palau had failed to find the bodies, so I wasn't yet off the hook. Either the police would continue to muddle along and there would be more phone calls from them and more visits to the police station, or they'd write it off as just another tall tale and file it away as a howl from the island's lunatic fringe. I wasn't sure which would be worse. I couldn't really blame Pascal for striking out. If they were diving on their standard tanks filled with air, twenty minutes was their maximum allowable time at one hundred feet. That should have been enough time to search the area I'd identified. Gravity was clearly dragging the second one to the bottom when we briefly met. At two hundred feet, the bottom was deeper than Uchel had authorized the guys at Pow Palau to go. And it was possible the one body on the shelf got pulled deeper by the current. They were probably fine with how it worked out. The dive team got paid for their time and got a story to tell at the bar. Win and win—for them. Me? I resigned myself to the fact that the only way to end this was to head back out to my spot and find the bodies myself.

Fine. There were worse ways to deal with problems than going for a dive. And where better than the local blue water and pale-yellow limestone walls? If Pow Palau and the national police weren't going to do what it took, I would have to do it myself. I wasn't about to let them take the easy way out and write this off as a hysterical rant. I had been written off before, and frankly, I wasn't willing to travel that road again.

*

It was almost 1:30. If things went by the book, the fast boat would return by 3:00. I had some time to spare, so I gave the bosses the abridged version of the story, making the puking-and-hosing-down part more prominent for the boys' benefit.

"You saw two dead guys?"

"One dead and the other definitely heading in that direction with little possibility of a cure."

"Did you touch them?"

"No, although one tried to touch me. Do you want me to vomit again or can we move off this topic?"

"I'm good."

"Me too."

"Sure... maybe more later?" Dmitri. *Such a boy.*

I shrugged them off, promising Roland I would join him, Dmitri, and Sarah at his place for drinks later that evening. At that moment, though, I had planning to do, and I did my best thinking without the hubbub that seemed to follow the owners. I mentioned the big boat and the need to get it ready, but they seemed oblivious to the thinly veiled hint.

6

EARLY AFTERNOON – NGERKEBESANG ISLAND

CHECKING THE TOTE board on the wall where we tracked boats, crews, and divers, I saw two paying customers listed. Fewer divers meant faster preparations and a quicker departure, which would translate into an early return and a quick wrap-up for Justin. Maybe he'd be back well before 3:00. That worked well because I needed his hands and head to be focused on my tasks.

Justin Barton and I had worked together for three years, and we had a comfortable, though not deeply engaged, working relationship. Justin was older than me—thirty-five or thirty-six to my thirty-one, if I calculated his life experiences correctly. A natural leader, Justin comfortably entered a scene and assumed it was his job to take charge. He exuded confidence and brought an excess of energy to any project he took on. I knew I could use a little of that for the day's duties.

To prove I hadn't imagined the whole thing, and to be done with any further exchanges with the police, I needed to find the bodies myself. To do that, I might need to go deep. Uchel had mentioned there were no obvious signs of a struggle or of a body being dumped along the cliff edge, though I assumed it would be hard, with any precision, to nail down the point along the road from which the bodies might have come. Too many tire tracks to draw any conclusions. All the evidence, it seemed, was below the waterline.

Who knew how heavily the first body was weighted—if it was weighted at all—and if he might have drifted? I didn't really care. I only needed to find one body to convince Uchel there had been a murder, and then I could walk away from the whole mess. The guy accessorized with the axle must have gone virtually straight down from the point I saw him. He was my target. Since he probably made it to the deep bottom of the channel, I was not going to be diving on standard tourist gear. Unfortunately, the bosses scared off the scumbag who "bought" my gear "at a sidewalk sale," so I wouldn't be diving with any part of my regular rig. That was unsettling, but not a deal breaker.

As if I had summoned it, the glass front door swung open, banging into the wall and derailing my train of thought. Someday, Justin was going to break it. This time he got lucky—it shuddered but stayed intact. Catching the door as it bounced back, Justin strode in, swiftly pirouetting to hold it for whom I took to be our two customers.

Justin was waxing eloquent about the wonders of Palau's deep wall diving and the world-class quality of our shark encounters. Obviously, they had seen quite a few. "Oh, crikey," he said with his best impersonation of that Australian who used to throw himself into bizarre wildlife situations. "You should see when the sharks really get going. You can see every muscle twitch as they power by. That one, I'll admit, may be the biggest I've seen and maybe the closest, but he wasn't in the mood for a meal. Mind you, if he wanted me for dinner, there wouldn't have been enough of me left to hose down this drain." He dramatically pointed at the floor drain, which handled plenty of Ralph poop but, to my knowledge, no human remains.

"But remember," he continued, holding a finger in the air and pausing for dramatic effect, "there have been no scuba diver deaths by shark attack in Palau in recorded history. On the other hand, humans kill over a hundred million sharks a year. Ask anyone here though, since Palau became a shark sanctuary, the harvesting of sharks by humans in this area has dropped to zero. Ricky here is not only one of our two best divemasters, yours truly being the other, but also a special advisor to our national shark preservation organization." He pointed at me and then at a section of wall displaying an oversized plaque of recognition and a photo of me with the President of Palau and a woman dressed as a "Happy Shark", our mascot. "She'll back me up on this."

The two customers, women I figured to be twins, glanced expectantly in my direction. I nodded my agreement, giving them my best all-knowing, Zen-goddess look. Adding a quick "Truth" to remove any doubt. The bosses, far less engaged in the project, suppressed a few smirks.

Justin was laying it on thick for the ladies, but he was essentially right. Sharks were definitely a low risk, and Palau was the world leader in shark protection. Regardless, I did a mental eyeroll. The shark sanctuary was a great start, and I was proud of Palau for leading the way, and happy to be in a position to influence policy, but we'd be naïve to believe the government's oft-repeated claim that Palau's shark killing had ceased. Anyone who cared knew it had merely moved farther offshore. It seemed like the ministry of tourism spent more money advertising our new law than the government did on the resources to patrol a vast expanse of water the size of France. And, even when they caught illegal fishing boats, enforcement of the law was, at best, haphazard. Without a significant investment, we'd never stop—or be able to document with any defensible precision—the ongoing slaughter. I didn't need to think of any more slaughter at that moment though.

Clearly, it had been a good dive. The ladies, two giddy sisters introduced by Justin as "excellent shark divers... from the States", were hanging on his every word and pulling out their credit cards to sign up for additional dives through the end of the week. I smiled politely. It's part of the job. Since he and I had been booked to spend almost a full week with the eight divers who'd cancelled, it was natural to chase a little replacement business.

It was at times like this I was in awe of Justin's people skills. He flowed from poetic stories of his favorite dives ("we'll have to get you out there before you leave... there are so many places I want to take you"), to praising their diving skills ("really, I thought you must have had many more dives than that... you dive like a fish"), to working them at the counter ("you know, we have a discount if you prepay for fifteen dives") with the ease of a Times Square hawker. The ladies were hooked. They giggled at all the right times, almost drooling in admiration of Justin's apparent mastery of the shark kingdom ("I don't know how you could dare get so close... he must have been ten feet long") and signed the credit card slip without even a glance. If they hadn't been twenty years his seniors, I might have imagined for a moment Justin was actually flirting with them. He was a rogue and a player, and would probably make a good grifter, but essentially benign.

I was feeling much closer to my natural, calm state. Justin had that effect. I had almost completely stowed away thoughts of bodies, cops, and puke, but had enough clarity of mind to realize I needed to get Justin away and focused on my plan.

Turning to Sarah, I said in my best divemaster's tone, "Honey, I need a few minutes with Justin to get briefed on tomorrow's dives—you know he's always got some new discoveries to share with me. How about you show..." I had to pause as I glanced at the tote board and quickly found their names, "Karen and Kate some hoods? They might be a bit chilled after a day of diving, and the weather report looks like water temps might drop a degree or two."

Although Sarah, Dmitri, Roland, and Ryan were the bosses, nobody had any illusions about who really ran the show. Unlike Ryan and maybe Dmitri, Sarah and

Roland were short-timers, while I had been with POS forever. (Well, four years is forever in the dive business.) And Justin and I had been the core of the operation for the last three. Ryan had been here longer than the other partners, but he had been less active of late. He had chosen residency in Palau for the long haul and took his government job seriously. It wasn't surprising he was the only one not skipping work that afternoon. He was a bit of a Boy Scout about his work hours and job commitments. He was less diligent about work around the shop, so I didn't have much use for him.

Sarah immediately dropped into sales-clerk mode, shooting me a look of gratitude that confirmed she didn't even mind that I had just pulled rank in front of partners and customers. Running customers out to dive sites pays the bills—equipment sales are gravy. There were whole cases and racks of dive gear squeezed into the place, just beckoning Karen and Kate to pull out those credit cards again. I noticed her guiding them toward the pricey boat coat rack.

Had I looked at the latest weather report, I probably would have suggested that Sarah just refund their money for their prepaid dives and send them packing to the comfort of their hotel for the next few days, but I was off my game and not paying attention to anything other than the matter at hand.

*

"Jus, I've got a problem and I need your help." I jerked my head in the direction of the service area, and he graciously told the ladies that duty called and swiftly followed me.

Once past the door, I provided a slightly more detailed version of the day's events, which he dutifully annotated with periodic gasps and exclamations of, "Wow", "No shit?" and "Holy moly." Despite his obvious theatrical skills, Jus also made a good audience, and I felt more relaxed just having him there to hear the story, particularly after the bosses' hysteria. He liked the puking part.

"Did the thief get your EndorFins?"

"Nope. Probably not a big resale market and they're so identifiable he probably couldn't unload them."

"Plus, they look goofy with that big, long fin and small foot pocket."

"Hey, a lot of trial and error went into those things. I'm always up for a challenge—want to try racing me... again? I could use the extra data when I start marketing EndorFins T dot M dot. Patent pending."

Justin had no immediate retort, so I finished with my reasoning about the follow-up dive, and that I was going to have to go deep, detailing what I needed. With no pushback or questions, he jumped to the task. Climbing up onto our workbench, he reached for the highest shelves and slid out the bins containing some specialty gear that we had, fortunately, assembled and checked a few days ago. He cleared a space on the workbench, careful to sweep away any stray bits of sand or metal, and began to set up a rig for a deep dive.

Justin was the only guy on the island I trusted to help me with such an important task. I hadn't met anyone else in my time here who could match his common sense and diligence. He could be headstrong and impetuous when at play, and enjoyed taking off on his reconnoitering trips in search of the next great site, but put him with a customer or the bench of the service bay, and he was all business. I knew the crew he had trained with back in Guam, and they were the best. Ex-military and totally anal-retentive, they were great divers and even better instructors – the best in the Pacific outside Hawai'i. It wasn't particularly complex, but this was the sort of thing that, if done incorrectly or even casually, could kill me. The last thing I wanted was a third dead body littering Ricky's Rocking Spot.

*

Palau's reputation as a world-class diving destination was well deserved. I had the privilege of diving its sheer underwater cliffs and deep-blue water almost daily, and the dramatic drops, bountiful fish life, and healthy, big-creature population still consistently blew me away. Above the surface, it might be even more enchanting.

The flight into ROR, Palau's international airport, takes your breath away. Even the most jaded travelers gawk from their window seats in awe of the landscape laid out beneath them. From above, the islands appear to be a cluster of mushroom-like mounds, dotting the deep-blue water with arching masses of green, bordered by bright, pristine beaches. The turquoise waters above the shallow reefs add a surreal look—the sort of stuff you would see in James Bond movies.

But most visitors don't come for the view from the air; they come for the underwater sights—the most prominent being our sharks. Divers come from all over the world for the opportunity to dive our famous limestone walls and watch sharks by the dozen patrolling the blue waters in search of a meal. To the pleasure of our customers, as Justin had so dramatically noted, neoprene-clad bubble-blowers aren't on the menu. As Justin had correctly pointed out, shark attacks on divers are virtually nonexistent, and there had been no recorded shark-related fatalities among any visitors to Palau.

That said, the deep submarine walls require respect and caution. In many cases, Palau's islands are mountains or volcanic craters rising up from the sea floor. With almost nothing to limit your descent, sometimes for thousands of feet, you need to be careful and use the right equipment.

I had no idea how deep I would need to go since Pow Palau hadn't found the bodies. I had given sufficient details; Pascal should have been able to find the shelf where I saw the first body. I knew that the chain guy had ended up much deeper, and I could imagine the currents ultimately moving the first guy on the ledge. It sounded like Pascal's team had merely gone to where I had originally seen the bodies and stopped the search at that point. The corpses had probably settled at the bottom—around a hundred feet deeper.

That meant planning on depths far beyond typical recreational dives, although I had the benefit of a sea floor at two hundred feet. If done by the book, the task wasn't risky. It took the right training and strict adherence to established protocols to prepare and use a special combination of breathing gasses, which was why I needed Justin to back me up as I prepared. This was the sort of thing you wanted to check and recheck, then have someone else check again.

We normally rigged our gear similarly to what our customers dived, which was a standard one-tank setup. This dive required a more complex setup, and with my own gear now in the hands of some miscreant, I needed a whole new one built from scratch. So, while I used tide and depth charts to plan the dive, Justin assembled a set for me. We all had our own unique aspects to our gear, but he was familiar with what I needed. Since it wasn't the usual setup, what would normally take less than ten minutes, took him almost thirty.

I waited until Justin had finished setting up the rig and testing the gauges before asking, "Hey, Jus, can you check my dive plan? I'm thinking I should be ready to go to 200 to find these guys... does my math check out? I'm kind of scatterbrained right now. I'd appreciate a second set of eyes. My slate's over on the workbench... the one with the drawing of the grim reaper." I cracked myself up, but Jus didn't seem to appreciate the moment as much as I did. That was ok. I preferred he took this seriously.

While he checked my math, I rechecked my tanks for gas mix and pressure. I was diving solo with little tolerance for error. Everything was perfect.

Justin was recently trained in deep diving using various mixtures of oxygen, nitrogen, and other gases, and though he was experienced in planning and prepping a dive, I wasn't about to ask him to do a search like this. I knew I would have to do this one alone. More than that, I needed to do it alone. I'd gone the good citizen route and got it thrown back in my face. Now it was personal. And when things got personal, I got focused. And perhaps stubborn. Definitely aggressive. Though he could only guess at most of the history and my motivation, Justin knew me well enough not to argue.

I had told Justin this was a body-recovery activity but technically that wasn't the right term... I had no intention of recovering the bodies. This was a crime scene, and I hadn't received an invitation to mess with it. Nor was I inclined to. My plan was simple: Locate one body and attach a line and surface marker to it. Or, in the case of the second victim, attach the marker to the axle. In either case, I'd shoot the inflatable marker to the surface, return to shore, call the police, make my point, and let them handle it. I had already invested too much time and lost too many meals over this. The last thing I wanted was for an arm to detach as I was swimming my mystery date to the surface. The very thought sent a new wave of nausea though my body.

"Hey, Rik?"

"You got something for me?"

"Yep," he said, returning my dive slate that contained my entire plan for gas mixes and depths. I used computers and gauges to help me manage my gas supply and depth for dives to recreational limits, but for deep diving this was my bible. "It's spot-on. Dive this plan and you're golden." He draped his arm over my shoulder and gave me a brotherly squeeze—perhaps more than brotherly, but I wasn't feeling receptive. Another time, another place.

"Roger, Wilco." Not the most natural response, but I was feeling a bit awkward about the display of intimacy. "Thanks, I feel a whole lot better having you watching over me."

"I've got your six."

"I know," I said. "Now take your hand off it and let me do my thing."

*

Before I even reached my Jeep, I realized my wetsuit wasn't the only thing that should have been hosed down. The warm sun and humidity had conspired to keep the mess on the floor both moist and aromatic. I had been too frazzled on my way back from the police station to even notice it, but now, after baking for a few hours, it was a tad overpowering. This made me thankful, for now, for the broken window. To complicate matters, the pizza in my stomach was kicking back something fierce. I tossed the floor mat out into the rear parking lot, hoping for a cleansing afternoon rainstorm. Removing the mat cleared up a lot of the mess and the smell, but not all of it.

Opening the rear gate, I loaded in my newly assembled gear, already missing my own stuff. I wasn't one for sentimental relationships, but some of the gear that got stolen had been with me for years. It wasn't just a matter of liking it; it was familiar. I could instantly find every single piece of gear in my rig, even in the dark. That familiarity could be the difference between life and death underwater. But I had no choice. *Crud.*

My eyes watered as I approached the front door and got hit by another wave of warm, wet odor, but I let myself in, belted up, and headed off.

7

LATE AFTERNOON – BABELDAOB ISLAND

Ricky's Rocking Spot was on the northwestern shore of Palau's largest island, the farthest diveable shoreline from our shop. The route was only about thirty kilometers, most of it recently paved, but it went through Koror which, for random reasons, has traffic jams that rival those in the States. It took me almost fifteen minutes just to get through town.

I experienced competing influences as I drove: the smell of the car and the indigestion from my early lunch, versus a gnawing hunger in my belly. Once I got out on the open, paved road, the top down and wind blowing, I was able to get past the smell of the car. That was enough to tip the scales. Steering with my knees, I unwrapped a couple slices of cold pizza—no jalapenos—I had rescued from the fridge at the office and wolfed them down. Wiping my hands on my seat, I made a mental note to give the Jeep a cleaning—or at least leave the top down during the next rain.

The dirt road was worse than usual, probably due to that day's inordinate amount of traffic what with me, the police, and Pascal's team, plus whoever had tossed the bodies, traveling on it. My stomach duly noted the bouncing. I finally arrived at three, and sunset would be around 6:15. I didn't want to be doing my exit in the dark, so I needed to hurry.

I stopped at the cliff top above my secret entry point. Nobody would ever think to start here, but two years of mountaineering and climbing during my exile with Mom in Colorado had provided me with a lot of experience and a few skills seldom found on tropical islands. Unfortunately, Pascal and whoever came out with him from his crew had learned about the place. I hoped they would keep it to themselves, though I doubted they actually accessed it through the secret entry. They probably entered down-current at the beach and used underwater scooters to pull themselves up to the site. Their operation was big on trendy technology. Their favored type of diver was the sort looking for maximum thrills with minimal effort. They catered to the more pampered, less technically skilled divers, and their equipment underscored that focus.

Opening the rear gate of the Jeep, I slid out my rig, then the rest of the gear. Normally I dived with one gas cylinder, but for this operation I was diving with three. I needed more air for going deep and a special gas mix to allow me to ascend with less risk of getting the bends. This was all part of the plan, but a new twist to my usual process for this dive. And I had a new rig to deal with. I don't like complications in my personal life or in my diving life, and the arc of this adventure had brought me both.

*

After making sure I had everything out of the Jeep, I hauled the rig, fins, and bags to the edge. The Jeep was facing the ledge, so it was a grind to haul it from the back. All the gear and tanks weighed in somewhere above one hundred and twenty pounds. I had parked facing that direction though, so the front bumper was nearest the edge. Unclipping the front-bumper winch hook, I laid out enough line to reach the cliff edge and attached it to my replacement rig.

My rig included the usual: buoyancy compensation vest, dive slate, depth gauge, watch and bottom timer, knife, signaling gear, and a spool of line attached to a surface-marking buoy. As we'd discussed, Justin had rigged two air cylinders on the back, each with a regulator and backup, pressure gauge, and a wireless pressure transmitter, as well as a third, smaller cylinder, complete with its own regulator and gauges, which I would secure by a sling under my arm. I had chosen two wireless dive computers, one on each wrist, and would carry a large spotting light. I'd also included in my bag a few more specialty items. It all added up to a very large package.

The next step was to get it to the landing spot below. The shape of the cliff was perfect for this—a concave that ended in a shallow rock and pebble shelf, no more than fifteen feet by ten feet, protected by a lip of fallen rocks. Easing my rig over the side, I felt the cable tighten. I walked back to my Jeep and started the winch. The rig slowly descended, and in just more than six minutes, it touched down. I wiggled the cable a few times, and the hook came loose. Normally at this point, I would drive the Jeep a half mile down the road, park by the beach, and hoof it back up. Then I would launch myself away from the edge, up-current from the rocky shelf. This had been a leap of faith the first time, but I had previously confirmed that the sheer wall continued to drop away beneath the water's surface. A quick swim to the rocks and I could don my gear to begin my dive.

With all this extra gear though, I had to send down a second load. I had squeezed the third cylinder, computers, and light into a mesh bag with the rest of my loose gear, the fins, and mask. This dive would be neither recreational nor relaxed, but the police and Pow Palau Divers had backed me into a corner. There was no way I was going to let their laziness and apathy derail a murder investigation. Not again.

After I dropped the last of my gear and reeled in the cable, I checked my watch. 3:50. Good. I figured I would have a decent current that time of day, probably over a knot, which worked in my favor. At the depths I was diving, I needed to minimize my bottom time. The more time I spent deep, the more time I would have to spend decompressing on my way up. So, less time spent in transit meant more time to find at least one of the bodies and secure a line and surface-marker buoy. I had enough gas and had calculated my decompression stops to support a planned thirty minutes at two hundred feet. After that, I would have to begin my ascent.

If by chance the bodies were shallower, I would have

had more time, but I wasn't counting on it. Logic told me they'd reached the bottom. Besides, Pascal hadn't found them when searching the shelf, so I had to assume the first body had drifted off the shelf and down. Pascal had never led me wrong before, although the rest of his crew were a bit dodgy. Really, I only had to find one of the bodies to make my case to the police, and I was thinking the one with the axle was the easier picking. He certainly had a lot of momentum going at the hundred-foot mark. I knew he probably dropped pretty much straight down and made it all the way to the bottom. Given the weight, he would have stayed where he landed.

The distance from the drop-in site to the beach was about a half mile as the crow flies. Underwater, where the terrain undulated and bent, it was more like seven-tenths of a mile, if my internal tape measure was right. My father once spent several hours trying to explain fractals and how they could help me understand the true length of shorelines and terrain, but I merely thought they were really cool-looking graphics. I smiled and listened but went right back to guesstimating, which Dad called a SWAG—a scientific, wild-ass guess. I'm cool with that. He's not. That's just one more trait we have in uncommon.

With a one-knot current, I could drift on the surface to a point up-current of the underwater junkyard. I wanted to drop in about two hundred feet before I got to that point. That way I could save my air and avoid an unnecessary buildup of nitrogen in my system to give me maximum time at depth for my search. If my guess about the axle not drifting was correct, sticking to where the bottom met the wall would allow me to find it without much effort. *Hopefully,* I thought, *the body is still attached.* And with that thought and accompanying vision, my stomach did a wild tango again.

I stripped down to my swimsuit and tossed my shorts and shirt into the Jeep. My wetsuit was still ripe from my morning's experience, which was probably why the thief left it behind. I pulled it on, yanked on a pair of booties, and walked about fifty feet to the right of the rocky outcropping below, where my gear now lay. I stepped back from the edge of the cliff, and like always, I ran madly, closed my eyes, and jumped.

*

Normally, I would swim to shore, don my gear, and then slowly descend as the current carried me. This time, though, I needed to stay on the surface until I was near the axle's entry point and then get deep as quickly as possible. Within minutes of swimming to the shelf, I had geared up, fully loaded and was doing it by the book. I looked a lot like Iron Man as I lumbered across the scattered rocks that comprise the shelf. A slip at that juncture would have been, at best, quite painful. Noticing the sky was darker than usual, I checked the time. 3:59. Perhaps the storm warnings were accurate this time.

Standing at the edge of the farthest rock, I jammed my regulator into my mouth, took one exaggerated step, and leaned forward. Gravity did the rest. I was carrying a lot of weight but had also planned for sufficient buoyancy—after my initial splash, a bit less graceful than usual, I bobbed to the surface and did one last check of my gauges. Confirming everything was operational, I slipped my fins off my wrists, secured them to my feet, and let the current carry me along the surface.

Though I had dived here many times, this was the first time I was viewing the terrain from this perspective. The water was crystal clear, so I tracked my progress by checking the reef below. I could tell, well before I got there, when I was approaching the abandoned truck. That was my target. I knew the body was down-current from there. When I was near, I released the air from my buoyancy compensator and settled beneath the surface. It was 4:02. I had thirty minutes before I had to begin my ascent. Dropping down the water column, I took a different tack than usual, swimming into the current. As long as I matched my swimming speed to the opposing pressure, I would be able to work myself directly downward, ensuring that I hit the bottom up-current from where I expected the body to be.

It took just a glance at either of my computers to monitor my depth, but I checked almost constantly, even though I had a good sense of where I was without electronic confirmation. You can't be too cautious when diving deep. Things can go wrong fast, and a change in current or too little air in your buoyancy compensator can make for a rapid—and dangerous—shift. At about one hundred and fifty feet I switched on my light. That late in the day, I was approaching the "twilight zone," that depth where rays of sun struggle to pierce the water. My eyes had adjusted and I could still see, mainly in black and white, but the beam lit up a decent patch of territory. Considering how much junk had been dumped over the years, I worried it might be tough to pick out my target.

It took about five minutes, but I reached bottom at about one hundred and seventy feet. The floor sloped gently away at that point, consistent with what I expected. I checked my watch. The time was 4:07. *So far, so good.* The five minutes was a bit longer than I had intended, but it made no sense to rush. Removing my waterproof pencil from my utility pocket, I made a note on my dive slate, marking the time at which I reached this depth.

The current was not as strong as I expected—in fact, there was almost no current—so I expended little energy kicking against it. That was good in terms of exhaustion and air consumption, but it also meant I needed to slow my kick rate to keep moving at the right pace. I passed right by the sponge-covered truck during my descent, so I knew that I was spot-on. For the last fifty feet of depth though, where less coral was growing, I had fewer visual clues to confirm I had been holding my own against the current, but I was reasonably sure I had. That, I calculated, put me about a hundred feet up-current from the spot where I saw my mystery men. By this time I had named them: the big guy on the shelf was Bachelor #1, and the smaller guy with the axle was Bachelor #2. It made it easier for me to think of them by those abstract names rather than envision their actual physical characteristics. I checked my watch again and let the gentle current push me along just above the seafloor.

I had never been this deep on this site. I was looking for the bodies, but I had to sort through the rest of the detritus as I went. The bottom was relatively flat, more rock than sand. Boulders, both large and small, were scattered about, the evidence of erosion and decomposition that created the cliff above the surface and the underwater ledge. There was even more junk at the base than on the wall. A car. A toilet. A couch. I wondered if it was Uchel's.

Stop, Stop. Focus. I pinched my fingertip, the pain clearing away some of the fog. *One job. No distractions.* This was neither the time nor place to be spacing out. When you're alone in the deepening darkness, sometimes it helps to talk yourself through the exercise. Even with my experience, I was deep enough that I began to notice the introductory pleasantness of what Officer Uchel called the rapture of the deep. I knew that confusion and disorientation were real risks and could sneak up on me at that depth, and when you're that deep, the margin for error is narrow and the stakes are high. At nearly two hundred feet deep, it's easy to mess up and difficult to recover, so I kept talking to myself. I had one reason for being down there and had to stay focused.

8

LATE AFTERNOON – DEEP BENEATH THE SURFACE

I KEPT THE wall between ten and thirty feet to my left, zigzagging back and forth to make sure I covered a sufficient area of the seafloor. I left nothing to chance. That cartwheeling axle could have pulled Bachelor #2 a distance away from the wall. For the most part, I stayed about ten feet above the seafloor, sometimes ducking between large rocks to make sure nothing was hidden there or behind them. Some boulders were the size of cars or small buses and required extra attention. Sometimes my light would catch a patch of color, but each time it turned out to be a sponge or a type of algae that was able to live in the near dark of the depths. Besides, I reminded myself, both men had been wearing black. They wouldn't be flashing colors at me.

I swept my light in a broad semi-circle as I went. Given the strong beam, I had an area of about twenty feet in front of me and to each side to scan. Theoretically, that allowed me to cover a forty-foot swath of bottom, but in practice, the rocky terrain limited my line of sight to less than ten. Beyond the reach of my light, I saw almost nothing. At nearly two hundred feet, regardless of the time of day or visibility, and particularly with the dark storm clouds, the sun didn't help much.

I had a limited sense of how much distance I had traveled, snaking through the boulders and moving both down- and cross-current. I had been going at a snail's pace to ensure I didn't miss my target. I had started at least one hundred feet up-current from where I saw the bodies, but was covering that distance slowly. I did know that my depth had been getting increasingly greater as I watched it creep down from a hundred seventy feet to a hundred ninety. I checked my watch. 4:14. I had been prowling the seafloor for almost seven minutes, which meant I had only eighteen minutes left before I began my ascent.

I maintained my pace, weaving among the boulders and scanning methodically from side to side. When I checked my watch again, I saw it was 4:17. I had fifteen minutes left. It seemed like I had probably covered at least a hundred feet of bottom. I noticed the boulders were getting larger, which meant the terrain above me was changing. Checking the wall to my left and above, I determined I had come to the area beneath the concave and the ledge where I had first seen Bachelor #1. The larger boulders had peeled away from that rock wall to form the concave.

My depth had been holding at a little less than two hundred—at the border of my planned range—since the time I noticed the larger boulders, probably the past two minutes. The boulders now ranged from the size of refrigerators to large buses. I had to work my way around each one, which slowed me even more as I kept my eyes peeled for the axle. Or Bachelor #2. At the base of the wall, under the overhanging ledges, there was almost no natural light. I could see only what my beam illuminated, and I worked methodically to make sure I checked every possible spot. Although normally I would have wanted to take in every little detail, for this task I was looking for a specific item. Everything else was just a distraction.

At times, I could see only three or four feet ahead of me as I worked between the rocks. Suddenly, at the base of the wall, my light caught a metallic reflection—something wedged underneath a small ledge. I eased around a boulder and dropped down several feet to get a better angle. As I trained my beam underneath the ledge, a large bolt of silver-grey shot right in front of me in an eruption of sand, grazing my shoulder as it passed.

Holy crap. My reflexes took over, and I awkwardly twisted away and down-current, banging my knee against a rock as I pulled myself into a tuck—no mean feat with three air cylinders and a mesh bag of goodies. Within seconds, it was gone. Just a shark, a grey reefie, its tail whipping in front of my face as it passed me. It was probably just resting on the bottom, and I had both disturbed it and been directly in its escape path.

My heart was racing, and stars flickered at the edge of my vision. I choked on a bit of water that had come in past my regulator as I twisted. I had to talk myself down, slow my pulse and my breathing. For what it's worth, the shark was probably as surprised as I was. That wasn't an attack, it was a retreat. My shoulder throbbed slightly, but the impact was minor and so was the outcome. But, yikes, that was a major pucker moment. No matter how passive they may be, when something that big flashes in front of you, it gets your heart pumping.

I paused and oriented myself to the wall to resume my search. The entire concept of looking for bodies had me rattled, and that was never a good starting point for a deep dive. The shark encounter had ratcheted up my anxiety even more. Between the exertion and anxiety, I could feel the fogginess of nitrogen narcosis creeping into my brain. I needed to slow my breathing. *Barney. Hum Barney.* My favorite purple dinosaur. *I love you...* Slow, measured breaths. *You love me...* Nothing to worry about. The shark was never a threat and wouldn't be coming back. *We're a happy family.* I slowly got my focus back.

But, because I couldn't help myself, I rolled to my left to see where my visitor had gone. Nothing. Not even a ghostly shadow in the distance. *Probably for the best*, I told myself. This was not a recreational dive, and anything other than a body was just noise.

As I turned back to continue my search, I felt a strong tug on my air hose, and before I could react, my regulator was pulled from my mouth and a brief explosion of bubbles poured from the open mouthpiece. Almost immediately, I realized I already had my backup regulator firmly in my mouth. My mind and training had gone into hyperdrive. Without my conscious awareness, my years of practice and regimentation took over and I had flipped my backup mouthpiece from directly below my chin into my mouth. But I wasn't out of the woods yet.

I struggled to work through my brain fog to process what was going on. Something or someone had snagged my regulator and hose, which were somewhere behind me. I was being held like a puppet by an unseen force. My body had rotated so my feet were down-current, and my head was up near what I assumed to be the snag. I was upside down, and my extra tanks were now dead weight and interfering with my ability to turn.

Paranoia threatened to take over.

I fought against it. I had trained for this. I knew what to do. But the rapid sequence of the shark encounter and then the loss of my regulator added to the tension of the search for the body and the increasing impact of the rapture.

It was a bad combination. I needed to begin eliminating distractions.

The shark was gone and had no interest in me. I just had to focus on what I could control, which was my ability to retrieve my primary regulator. I didn't know who or what had it, but given the pressure was steady and nothing new was happening, I dialed back the likelihood of "someone" and leaned toward "something." That meant the situation had stabilized.

Stupid! It couldn't be a person. Get a hold of yourself.

I reached up and behind me, blindly searching to find the hose where it connected to the cylinder. I found it and gently pulled but got only resistance. I pulled again, but all I managed to do was slightly rotate my body. I got the sickening feeling that as I struggled, I was actually wedging myself in deeper. I still couldn't see where the hose led. I knew that if I could follow the hose with my hand, I might at least feel where the regulator was stuck. But the hose was longer than my arm. With my own rig this would never have happened. I used an even longer hose but wrapped it around my torso.

I found myself cursing Justin, even though it was my fault. I had seen how he rigged it and figured the shop didn't have any spare long hoses. I also realized I couldn't waste time on the blame game. Stretching my long arm as far as I could, my wiggling fingers still could not identify the location or the cause. My first option was to turn myself so I could see it. I didn't really have a second option. I shifted my weight to the right but didn't move. I tried rolling to the left. Still nothing. *Crud.* My struggling had locked my tanks in tightly among the rocks and small boulders on the ocean floor.

My stomach started knotting up.

I had worked with hundreds of divers, some who were brand new and many who were unprepared for our sometimes extreme open ocean diving. In the intense currents that run past our island, the bad ones would flop and twist like newborn puppies struggling to get their first gulp of milk. Some would burn through their air, exhaust themselves, and need to surface early. Others would freak out. For the ones who would listen, I used a technique I learned at circus camp: I'd have them visualize their bodies as though they were Barbie dolls. I had them imagine working each limb, one at a time, to get their bodies in the right position.

I stopped moving and started thinking. One, by one,

I tested a different limb. Each time, I got more information. Finally, by pulling my knees up to my waist and then pushing with my left hand and dropping my right shoulder, I managed to get a bit of wiggle room and partially rotate my body. I still couldn't see the hose or regulator, but at least I had found the formula. With each repetition, I was able to free my tanks a bit more and get more rotation. Finally, on my fourth or fifth try, I felt my tanks break free from the obstruction. I twisted and spun myself around—and saw that my regulator was snagged in the spring of a large rusty axle, next to a pile of chain that was attached to Bachelor #2, who was now most completely and utterly dead.

As I stared at the face of the man I had seen plummeting down the wall just hours before, I felt the curtain lowering again on my brain as the overwhelming rush of revulsion hit. Forcing myself to look away, I grabbed the edge of a rock. It was slick with algae but jagged and easy to grip. I pulled myself into the current and wrestled the regulator out from where it was wedged. I pressed the purge button to ensure the regulator wasn't obstructed, and bubbles rushed out. Removing my backup regulator, I slammed my primary back into my mouth and allowed myself to take a gasp.

I was trembling, breathing way too rapidly, and getting tunnel vision. Not good. Not how I trained. I needed to relax and get myself right. I was tucked into a curl and clutching the axle, so at least I wasn't just drifting with the current. I continued to breathe heavily, but I slowly gained control of myself, exhaled deeply, and took a long, slow breath. I shook my head, trying to clear the cobwebs, then I eased out of my tuck and let my body stretch out in the current.

I looked at my watch. 4:20. All of this took, at most, sixty or ninety seconds. But as I replayed it in my mind, it was a slow-motion horror film.

Eighteen minutes at depth. Twelve minutes remained according to my plan. I checked my air gauge. I'd been sucking air at a quick pace the past two minutes, but I had planned a healthy reserve, so I didn't anticipate a problem with air supply. The thirty-minute mark wasn't about available gas—I was carrying plenty—but about how saturated my body would be with nitrogen. The exertion of struggling had increased my breathing rate and my saturation rate. It also increased my risk of narcosis, and even blackout due to carbon-dioxide buildup, though that clearly hadn't happened. I wasn't the sharpest tack in the box at that moment, but my training and practice had, to that point, served me well.

With the events of the past few minutes though, my training told me I should begin the planned ascent then and there. There were too many variables in play. I was dealing with risk factors with my exertion and depth that would normally cause me to abandon a dive. That was when being a trained expert and being Ricky came into conflict. Logic told me to abort, but the part of my brain that contained the stubborn reflex told me to finish the job. I decided to try to let them meet halfway. I gave myself six minutes.

*

As soon as I had the task in mind, things kind of slipped into place. I became focused. My breathing slowed and dropped into a measured cadence. My muscles relaxed, and my vision began to clear. I was once again in the here and now.

I needed a checklist to make sure I didn't miss anything. First, though, I had to manage the current, which was picking up. I slipped a short line and hook from my pocket and attached myself to a metal loop on the axle. (Being tethered to the axle was much better for me than it had been for Bachelor #2.) Then I wrote out my list on the slate. I had ten items to complete in less than six minutes.

I turned on a specialized LED light attached to my head so that I could have both hands free. Unstrapping my spotlight from my wrist, I laid it in the sand, wedging it up against the axle so the current wouldn't drag it away. Its broad beam, shining up from the seafloor, cast a long, eerie shadow along the sand and up the nearby reef wall. Then I detached the mesh bag from my belt and began to sort out the gear.

I had brought a special reel equipped with five hundred feet of line, which I attached to another loop on the axle with a brass clip on a swivel bolt. With my still limited alertness, sliding the clip open and working it onto the loop took longer than I anticipated, but I finally got it hooked. I attached an eight-foot-long inflatable tube to the other end. This was my surface-marking buoy, something I always carried but seldom used. It had been a while since I had last deployed one. They inflate using a standard regulator, and carry the line to the surface, sort of like an underwater kite. It was designed to bob on the surface and, in this case, serve as a guide for Officer Uchel and the team from Pow Palau to finish the job. I put in a couple puffs of gas, which is all it takes at that depth. The limp tube filled slightly and became buoyant.

I let the surface marker go, and it slowly rose toward the fading light above, picking up speed as it rose from the depths, expanding as the water pressure decreased, sort of like a helium balloon let loose into the sky. This one, however, was designed to release excess pressure so it wouldn't burst. As it rose, the current pulled it away on an angle. That was ok. I had five hundred feet of line to reach the surface two hundred feet above me, and despite the angle, they could just follow the line from the marker to the axle.

I unclipped the reel and thumbed the spool to restrict the flow of line and the ascent of the marker to make sure no snags developed. After about three hundred twenty-five feet of line played out, I could feel the tension diminish—the buoy had reached the surface. I reeled back in some line to ensure it stayed taut even as the current dropped, finally locking the reel and re-clipping it to the axle.

Glancing at my watch, I noted it was 4:24. Twenty-two minutes into my thirty, but only two remaining before my adjusted ascent time. I wasn't sure how much time I should have taken out of the thirty for those one or two minutes of thrashing, but I had to assume I was cutting into my margin of safety. Fortunately, we always planned for a healthy cushion, so I was not overly concerned. My computer, more liberal than the tables I had used for planning the dive, showed I still had more than fifteen minutes of available bottom time. I had been trained to be more conservative than that on deep dives though, and I intended to follow that training.

I stowed the mesh bag in my utility pocket. One more task and then I could go. I unclipped the compact underwater camera from my waist belt and went to take a few shots for the detectives. It would be hard for them to doubt me with one or two money shots, but the moment I looked through the viewfinder, I knew I was screwed. The blurred image told me what I should have already suspected. In all my twisting and banging, I had cracked the sealed housing, and the camera was flooded. Useless.

In a moment of pissed-off exasperation, I briefly considered taking a body part, but he was already missing parts of two fingers, and taking another just seemed wrong. Besides, odds were that would land me on the wrong side of a jail-cell door. The only thing left to do was return to the station and give them my update. I hoped it would be enough. Bubbles rose past my mask as I let out a sigh.

Checking my gauges and dive slate to reconfirm my safe ascent plan, I unhooked myself from the axle and quickly tucked the line and hook back into my pocket, as I held on with one hand. I checked the buoy line one more time and then released my grip, the current immediately pushing me away. That was fine with me. The more distance between me and the shitstorm, the better.

As I drifted down-current, rapidly moving along the sea bottom, I said a quick goodbye to Bachelor #2. I turned with the current to begin my ascent, and that's when I saw it—the other corpse, Bachelor #1, no more than ten feet from me. I was instantly struck by two facts. First, the small boat anchor handcuffed to his wrist had snagged in a gap between rocks and was sure to keep him in place until the police arrived. *A fur-lined handcuff? Sheesh.* The second thing I noticed put me instantly on edge.

As the body was caught in the beam of my headlamp, I realized I had seen those tattoos before.

I knew who he was.

9

DUSK – TWO HUNDRED FEET DEEP, BABELDAOB ISLAND

FORGET THE TATTOOS. Forget the tattoos. FOCUS. I punched myself in the thigh for good measure.

I'd done similar dives and ascents before. It was all mapped out on my slate. But this time was different. I was way outside my norm and having trouble concentrating. As I began rising through the deep darkness, I took another look at the slate for confirmation. In the glow of my headlamp, the plan seemed quite simple: two decompression stops totaling thirty-two minutes and then exit at the beach. Of course, I also needed to manage my ascent rate and my rate of drift in the current so that I didn't overshoot my exit point. I did not need to be thinking about what I just saw. And I did not need to be thinking about my next conversation with Officer Uchel.

I focused and tracked my progress against my plan. Maintaining my appropriate ascent rate, and facing into the current, I slowly kicked to counter the flow of water.

The surrounding ocean was busy with life, but I kept my attention mainly on my gauges and computer. The plan was simple but without tolerance for errors: slowly ascend to twenty feet, then hover at that depth for five minutes. Then ascend to fifteen feet and spend the next twenty-seven minutes holding at that depth.

When I reached twenty feet, I was at the thirty-five-minute mark on the dive, slightly better than planned. That was where the science got more complex. To shorten the time required before I hit the surface, I was carrying the third tank of gas. I turned the knob to begin the flow of gas and, releasing the regulator I had been using, swapped the new tank's regulator into my mouth, which provided a mixture far from normal air. In fact, it was seventy-five percent oxygen, almost four times as much oxygen as normal air. For the remainder of my dive, that infusion of extra oxygen would help clear the dangerous nitrogen out of my system at an accelerated rate.

Still finning into the current, I spent the next five minutes rigorously monitoring my depth, avoiding even slight drops and rises. During that time, my body rid itself of gasses that had become embedded in my muscle tissue and blood—gasses that were potentially crippling, or worse, if I ascended before they were released.

At the five-minute mark I ascended to fifteen feet.

The science of deep diving is subject to much discussion, and there is no consensus on how much time is right or even at what increments. There are, however, excellent guidelines for what constitutes a prudent dive plan. I always chose to dive conservatively because you never know what might happen. That final stop, for twenty-seven minutes, provided me with a safety margin that experts had computed to be reasonable. Very little real-world testing had been conducted, for obvious reasons, but there was general agreement on this protocol. I had been trained and certified in this, and I had trained others. I knew how to avoid problems and address problems I couldn't avoid.

The storm clouds above were blocking out the sun, and although the sun hadn't yet set, darkness underwater had already preceded it. My computer had illumination, but I relied on my headlamp to read my backup gauges, and checked them a couple times a minute.

Dive planning is a Rubik's Cube. With variables of time, conditions, and breathing-gas mixes, there are hundreds of possible answers when it comes to how long to stay at each increment of depth. We carefully planned the dive using our preferred method and then compared the times, depths, and breathing-gas mixes to computer-generated tables to validate our results. I had looked at sets of numbers dozens of times in the past few weeks as we'd prepared for a series of dives for roughly similar profiles, but the combination of exhaustion and anxiety was conspiring against me.

I knew I had enough gas, even if my breathing rate became elevated. I had just under fifteen minutes remaining, and my computer told me everything was fine. At that point, I knew I could probably handle anything that arose, but the warning bells in my head told me this was not the day to make that bet. I carefully watched the digital readout as it clicked off the minutes, obsessively holding my depth at precisely fifteen feet. Although it was too dark to see and I had no reference points, it felt like I was maintaining a constant distance from shore. My senses were definitely dulled though, and it had been a long, stressful day. I focused on my depth and time remaining—at least, I *tried* to focus.

Although this was a critical time, it was also a step I had done many hundreds of times before. Despite my training, I allowed my mind to wander. *I'd like to see the Pow Palau team pull off a trick like that.* Of course, with all due humility, it should have been expected that I could do what they could not. Given how long I'd been here, I was considered somewhat of an institution on the island. I had produced a lot of goodwill (though clearly not with the police force), and the owners of my shop loved me. I was a valuable asset both underwater and above—and actually a key marketing tool for them, though not necessarily for my diving skills. It just so happened I was originally hired in no small part because of my racial background. You see, a large percentage of Palau's tourism comes from nearby Japan. Palau Ocean Scuba wanted to pull in that market, and my heritage fit the bill.

As I said, my name is Ricky Yamamoto. So, first, how'd I get the name Ricky? My dad, as you might also have caught, is a geek. He named me both in tribute to his astronomer friend Riccardo, who won the Nobel Prize for some major achievement I've never been able to understand, and (I suspect more to the point) for Rikidozen, a famous Japanese wrestler of the theatrical sort. Kind of Japan's Hulk Hogan. I was, therefore, named Riccarda. Mom wanted to name me Jasmine, so all things considered, I lucked out.

Though my family name is Yamamoto, it would be a stretch to say that I'm Japanese. That part of my cultural upbringing was somewhat lacking. My father, whose real name is Otori, came from the Tottori Prefecture, home to sand dunes, big open sky, and not much else. He was named after a famous sumo wrestler (I guess it's a family tradition to saddle the kid with a moniker that invites trouble), which was ironic given his rather diminutive stature. That's not to say Dad is a wimp. He was a decent javelin thrower in college (he went to UCLA on scholarship), and to this day he maintains a set of muscles that my mother (to my revulsion—have I mentioned they're divorced?) describes as a "coiled python".

Mom—Ingvold—has her athletic chops as well. In her day, she was an almost world-class high jumper—and most decidedly not Japanese. She came from a suburb of Stockholm, Sweden, and looks every inch your stereotypical Swedish heartthrob. She was the dominant character in the family and the stronger influence in my early years. I'm not saying that's a good thing.

To the dive shop owners, though, I'm Japanese. I'm the best dive guide on the island, but my name is the big marketing draw. My father is a minor celebrity in Japan, and I bring some bragging rights with the business's Japanese customers. That I'm named in tribute to Rikidozen is a bonus. Sometimes I'm asked to show off a few wrestling moves, to which I begrudgingly respond with a few comedic, halfhearted swings and kicks that I learned watching mixed martial arts on TV at local bars. Truth be told, I had to take an intensive language course out in California in order to be able to speak even rudimentary Japanese. I was raised in California, Hawai'i, and Colorado, and frankly, the language used in my house was a strange blend that tended toward English unless there was an argument, in which case a whole range of languages (Mom favors Russian obscenities) were employed. Dmitri displayed appropriate awe the first time I let loose a torrent of Russian profanities in the workshop.

As I floated in the calm, dark water, my mind wandered into unwelcome territory: Dad. He never began a conversation with a greeting or a subject, he just started rolling before "hello" left your mouth.

Though it seemed like days ago, it was only a little more than half a day since we talked last, and I was still irritated. That call came hours before sunrise, and he was gushing about hot gasses and slingshots. As I fought through the fog of sleep interrupted, I began to hear the more familiar terms: *telescopes... celestial bodies... satellites*. The topic of the day was something called Pandora's Cluster, apparently one of those things Dad studies, not by what he can see but by what he can infer by the way light rays bend. Or something like that. My mind translated the concept into something akin to when Mom reads people's auras, something I could never tell him. It'd drive him crazy. He worries that I'm starting to think and talk like Mom. I actually share his concern.

Anyhow, all you can do when Dad starts on a roll is wait for him to stop to catch his breath and then try to apply a little focus to the conversation. On that call, the chance came about three minutes into his manic but eloquent exposition on the "totally and utterly awesome" collision of four galaxies and the unforeseeable chaos they created.

"Sumo." I began to count. *One, two...*

"You should see this, but of course you can't really 'see' anything... it's not optical..."

Three, four, five... "Sumo." Louder this time.

"But the images we've compiled... I can't even begin to fathom..."

Six, seven, eight, nine... I had no choice. I took a deep breath and yelled, "SUMO!"

"Yes?"

"Do you know what time it is?" I was staring at the readout on the answering machine, wondering where he got some of his ideas.

"Yes, it's just right now nine in the morning."

"In Hawai'i."

"Yes, Hawai'i, where else would I be?"

"Nowhere else. Of course you're in Hawai'i, but I'm not."

"But you're a morning person. You've always been a morning person."

He probably didn't hear my gentle sigh. "Dad, 4:00 a.m. is not morning. It's still night."

"Point taken. I'll keep that in mind. Anyway, I'm sending you a link and a password. You need to check out the wiki. Oh, and Falstaff and Waxer said to say hello."

That made me pause. "Waxer and Falstaff?"

"Yeah, they were on the island for a full-moon party

and dropped by. I'm taking them up to the telescope tonight for a tour and then we're going to catch some waves tomorrow. Loco Moco for breakfast."

Great. Dad's hanging with my surfing buds. The very ones he banned me from visiting back in the summer when everything changed. The guys who earned me my first "reputation."

"Cool. Give them a big Sumo hug for me. Good night, Sumo."

"It's not night, honey. It's morning. I've already had two cups of coffee. Maybe you should have some as well—you sound kind of sluggish."

"Good night." I hung up rather aggressively, for which I would need to offer an apology at some point, and then headed out for my run and my fateful dive. Replaying that call was not the best way to spend my decompression stop, but there you have it. Thousands of miles away, Dad was still in my head.

Twelve minutes of decompression time remained.

*

Checking my time, I noted that I was approaching my final countdown. It had been a long day—I should have known to go back to bed. It would have spared me the trauma of the dead bodies, vomiting all over myself and my Jeep, the dented fender, and the snippy receptionist. I also wouldn't be here now, trying to bail out the police and Pow Palau, finding the corpses.

As I hovered in the water, I began planning my triumphant return to the police station. It would be a quick in and out. I'd be done, and I could stop dealing with bodies. And truck parts. And mutilated hands. Finally, my computer counted off the final minute, clearing me to surface. I still had a healthy supply of gas—both the seventy-five percent oxygen mix and standard air—so I added five minutes to my stop for good measure. Then, kicking at an angle to the current and maintaining my depth, I started moving in toward shore and the awaiting beach.

I must have been farther from shore than I planned because it took me a few minutes longer than expected, but I soon reached the sand slope and worked my way up the incline. When my depth reached three feet, I twisted around so that I faced out into the ocean, planted my feet, and stood up. Looking back over my shoulder, I could see the beach. Pulling off my fins, I turned and trudged up the slope, the waves slapping at my legs. As I exited the water, the weight of my gear slowed my progress. The three tanks felt much heavier than when I began, though with less compressed gas inside, they were actually more than fifteen pounds lighter.

I had dragged myself through the surf just up-current of my planned exit point. Looking back up the shoreline, I saw in the fading light that my surface marker was bobbing prominently on the waves about eighty feet offshore. *Plan the dive and dive the plan. Damn straight.* The waves were larger than when I entered, and the wind was picking up. It seemed like a good time to wrap it up and head home.

It was 5:15, and the sun was peeking through the clouds near the horizon. I needed to close this out with the police, and I was expected for drinks at Roland's. A wave of unmitigated pride, along with a well-deserved sense of serenity brought on by exhaustion and relief, washed over me. Congratulations were in order. I had found not only one body, but both, and I knew the identity of one of the victims. *Yikes, I pity the cop who gets this case handed to him.*

My will, however, exceeded my capacity. As soon as I was past the high-water mark, I dropped my gear, literally incapable of carrying it, and collapsed in exhaustion. The sun was just dropping over the horizon, but it was still warm and humid. I was hungry, tired, and running on sheer adrenaline. Up since four that morning, I had barely eaten in the last twelve hours, and I had been down for just over an hour and fifteen minutes. The dive itself was not that demanding, but the mental stress of the last sixty minutes had been intense. And the soft sand was inviting.

*

I woke up almost two hours later to the buzzing of bugs. I had barely managed to shrug off my gear before I fell asleep. Now sticky with salt water, my wetsuit seemingly glued to my skin, I had somewhere north of a pound of sand sticking to my head – and my exposed skin had become a feeding ground for Palau's insect kingdom who seemed oblivious to the spray of sand being propelled by the intense wind. A large monitor lizard eyed me as it wandered along the beach looking for dinner, flicking its tongue at me, likely hopeful that I was an easy meal washed up on shore. I wasn't in the mood to field any further inquiry and tossed a shell at him. He seemed to take the hint and strolled on.

This was not the day off I had planned for my much-needed break after three straight weeks of work. We'd been managing full boats, intense diving, and festive evenings, but when a large group of tech divers that had booked us for the next two weeks bailed out at the last minute due to concerns over the weather, I took that as a sign it was time to take a break. I should have known from the moment I heard the phone ringing that my plans would go awry.

I was in a sorry state. I felt, looked, and probably smelled like carrion. To top it all off, I had a long uphill walk back to the Jeep. I turned on my LED headlamp and headed up the broken road through the fringe of jungle. About a hundred and fifty feet from the beach, the light began to dim, leaving me with barely enough artificial light to help negotiate the uneven surface. *Had I grabbed a depleted one instead of one from the "charged" rack? Justin?* Way too many things going on—mistakes like that can be fatal underwater. Whatever moon we had that night was hidden by the heavy clouds and overhanging branches. The walk required concentration that was in short supply, but I made it without major incident.

By the time I retrieved my Jeep, which I smelled long before I could see it in the near darkness, it was past eight o'clock. I drove to the beach, picked up my gear, tossed it in back, and headed toward town. My headlights illuminated a palm tree with a sizeable gouge in its trunk, and I recalled again, painfully, the significant dent in my Jeep I'd incurred as I peeled out earlier in the morning.

A drink with friends sounded better than just good.

Officer Uchel was long since off duty, and not wanting to start anew with someone else, I decided to wait until morning to notify the police that I had found my bodies. I might even tell them who Bachelor #1 was. That would give them a morning jolt.

I headed straight to Roland's, anticipating the evening's discussion would be rich.

10

LATE NIGHT - KOROR

DISTRACTED, DRIVING MORE slowly at night than during the day and dodging wind-propelled leaves, branches, and the occasional beach chair, I finally arrived at Roland's at 9:45 in need of adult beverages and juvenile humor. I fought the wind as I pushed the car door open, noticing aching muscles had settled in during the drive.

I'm not sure if it was a testament to the tolerance of my friends or a statement about their expectations regarding my hygiene, but when I walked in sandy, disheveled, and clad in neoprene, nobody mentioned it.

"C'mon in. Care for a drink?" Roland was a prince.

"Two of whatever you're having." *Perhaps I should have said three.*

"Four tequila shots coming right up." *Yep, I should have said three.*

I downed my shots in short order and headed for Roland's bedroom, tracking sand behind me. "I'm going to take a quick shower. Can I borrow shorts and a T-shirt? I'm going to peel this neoprene off me and I'm not planning on prancing around in my swimsuit all night long."

"Sure thing," Roland called out as I disappeared into the bedroom, "and if you need help with the neoprene..." Whatever came next was lost as I closed—and locked—the bathroom door.

By the time I returned from my shower, minus the neoprene and adorned in Roland's prized Beavis and Butthead T-shirt and baggy board shorts, the tequila bottle was almost empty. Before I even settled into the chair, I guzzled what remained.

"So?" Sarah asked, an edge to her voice that could have been either irritation or concern.

"Found 'em. Tagged 'em. Left 'em for the cops." For the first time since my morning dive was interrupted, I allowed myself to hope that this mess was over. A nagging voice in my head, however, told me such hope was folly.

"We were getting worried. It was getting way late. You should have called." *So typically Sarah.*

"My cell phone's dead. I can never get a connection. You had my dive plan. And I needed a nap."

"Still, we would have been a lot less worried if you had called." Behind her, Roland opened a new bottle of tequila.

"You looked pretty relaxed when I got here."

"We put up a good front."

*

I woke up on the floor at Roland's. My watch said it was a few minutes past seven, the heat and humidity already oppressive. The room was stuffy and smelled like a wet dog. My head was throbbing, my stomach growling. I realized I hadn't eaten since the pizza lunch.

Roland was already up. From my position on his woven bamboo carpet, I could see into his little efficiency kitchen, though everything was upside down. I saw legs—nice legs. I had never truly appreciated his sculpted calves up close. He was standing at the stove and appeared to be making food. *My prince.*

I scanned the room. It was still upside down, but it appeared Dmitri and Sarah had left at some point during the night. Or early morning. I couldn't recall much that took place after I chugged the last of the tequila.

Rolling over, I wiped a trickle of fresh drool from my face. Stiff and still itchy from the bug feast on the beach, I tried to greet him with a cheerful, "Morning!" What exited my throat, however, sounded more like a toad saying "mmmmm."

Roland turned and smiled. "Mmmmm, right back atcha, beautiful. Ready for breakfast? I've got Spam and duck egg scramble almost ready to go. I presume you could use a good meal. Unfortunately, this is the best I can do. You're probably anxious to get on with your Officer Uchel but I'm sure he's not in yet. You know the local constabulary—they do their best work between nine and nine oh one."

I wasn't sure how far removed from dear mother England Roland was, but his Oklahoma drawl was out of sync with his attempts at British lexicon. Still, the man was making me breakfast, so who was I to complain?

Roland was, as he might have put it, actually quite

the pleasure—wicked smart, though he always downplayed it, and quite easy on the eyes. His soft, round face was topped with a mop of reddish-brown hair and sprinkled with freckles. His disarming smile stood him well with both the Supreme Court justices for whom he and Sarah clerked, and with the steady stream of women who passed through his life. And he was charming to boot. He was, however, a wretched cook, as I discovered with my first bite of the runny eggs and undercooked Spam. As hungry as I was, the speggs disappeared quickly, and I even thanked him before accepting seconds.

Some aspirin and a glass of papaya juice topped off the morning. I decided, with mixed emotions, to forego the coffee. All that was available was instant, and he didn't have any sugar in the house. I could wait until I got home to grind up some real beans.

Roland was puttering about, cleaning up after last night's debauchery. The pounding in my head made it hard to track everything he was saying. "...and Justin's taking today's customers. We assumed you needed some time to recover from yesterday's trauma, and you didn't really get a day off. Besides, there were no other sign-ups beyond the sisters, who were obviously mad for Justin. I guess we might get some walk-ups—with the storm coming, people might try to squeeze in as many dives as possible today and tomorrow. Have you seen the reports? This might be a big one. The paper says it could be the storm of the century, but that weather reporter tends toward the dramatic. Nothing like we get back home, mind you. Hell, I don't even think of heading for the cellar for anything less than a hundred miles an hour.

Mind you, any good blow still gets the blood pumping. They're even talking about canceling court on Friday, although I think that may be inspired more by sloth than prudence. It certainly seems like the Supremes are willing to cancel sessions at the drop of a hat—but not today, so I should head off. How do I look? Have you looked at yourself in the mirror? You look rather peaked."

He stopped to take a breath, and I instinctively inhaled along with him. Because mine was more rapid, I was able to get in a few words. "You go. I'll finish cleaning up. Thanks for getting Justin to sub, I owe you both. Thanks for the warning on the storm—no I hadn't heard anything since yesterday morning. You look great. Nice shirt—I like the hula dancers. I'll be fine. Go."

"Thanks. It's a Mambo. By the way—hands off the rest. They're collector's items."

Roland and Sarah likely kept the staff and judges of the Supreme Court entertained. They both seemed to overflow with thoughts that needed to spill out lest they each burst. My alternate theory was that they subscribed to the belief the world might end at any moment, and like in Scrabble, you get penalized for any letters left in your tray.

*

By the time I'd finished cleaning up, and showered, it was almost 8:30. Time to go see Officer Uchel. I had no clean clothes of my own, and I had apparently spilled a variety of colorful concoctions on the Beavis and Butthead shirt—to Roland's horror, I was sure—so I looked around for a suitable replacement outfit. Houses in Palau didn't tend to feature closets, so he had devised a system of storing his clothes on the floor. He had told me that when he arrived on the island he planned to buy plastic bins in a variety of colors, but he quickly jettisoned that scheme when he visited Ben Franklin's and saw the prices. That worked well for me now. I didn't have to rummage through bins, I just eyeballed the stacks on the floor.

The Mambo collection, on padded hangers, was arranged on nails pounded into the walls, but I had already been denied access to those. I found a clean, substantially unwrinkled, light-blue oxford shirt and a clean pair of those Capri-style shorts that men seem to think look good on them. Although Roland was roughly the same height as me, our limbs were not proportionally matched. The sleeves of the shirt came nowhere near my wrists, and the pants barely extended beyond my knees. I looked freakish, with a slight element of ET going on, but I've gotten used to looking like an oddball.

You see, I am a mutt. Dad, a compact five feet, six inches with "chiseled muscles and classical Japanese looks"—or so it says on the self-authored biography he provides when speaking at conferences—wooed and married a lithe, five-foot-eleven blonde bombshell from Sweden, with total disregard for the genetic milkshake that would become their offspring. The implications of that recklessness were increasingly evident as I entered my teens. My facial structure is a mix: I have her dimples, and I have Dad's broad lips and wide nose. I have Dad's black hair and brown eyes but fairly light skin, and a short muscular torso like Dad's. Like Mom, I'm tall with long arms and legs that terminate at bizarrely small hands and feet.

This sort of genetic mash-up could only be the product of blind love. But for one chance encounter, my parents might have met and married mates who at least vaguely matched even a few of their physical characteristics, and the world could have proceeded normally. But they had to go stir up the gene pool.

Anyhow, that's how Ricky Yamamoto, she of all arms and legs, came to be. In the mirror I saw the reflection of the ill-fitting Capris and Oxford getup draped on my ill-fitting body and thought: *If I roll up the sleeves and legs enough, I can make this work.*

11

MORNING – KOROR

ROLAND'S PLACE WAS only a few blocks uphill from the police station, and walking with the increasing storm winds and airborne debris at my back, I made quick time. A garbage can lid barely missed me as it raced down the hill and through the red light of a traffic-free intersection. Though morning was well underway, the heavy, dark cloud cover made it look closer to dawn. I hadn't heard a single bird during my walk. They were smart enough to hunker down as the storm approached.

The locals, however, were going about their business. Fishermen were hauling their smaller boats out of the water, some stashing theirs under the pilings of waterside buildings while others dragged theirs as far above the waterline as possible. Some kids were flying makeshift kites. Another group merely improvised by tossing stray paper plates in the air and watching them fly up and away. Shoppers were heading to Ben Franklin's in droves and leaving with bags full of emergency supplies. I spotted more than a few cans of Spam poking out the tops of bags. The wind outside the station smelled sweet but greasy, likely due to the flood of old wrappers blowing along the street from Bem Ermii's toppled trash can, and from the pua leaves and flowers, stripped from the station's trees and swirling about the front lawn. The greasy smell made me wish for a burger, but the Bem's trailer was boarded up and loaded with sandbags. *Shame.*

I plodded up the stairs in the heavy morning wind, finding my friend from the day before there again and eyeing me warily as I approached the desk. Her eyes glanced down to remind me to stay behind the yellow line. I complied but wanted this over as quickly as possible. If she kept me waiting over thirty minutes, I would just leave Uchel a voicemail.

"Good morning. I'd like to see Officer Uchel. My name is Ricky Yamamoto. He'll know what this is about."

"You clean up well. Nice outfit. You make it work." There was a hint of a smile, and I wasn't sure if I was being complimented or if this was her way of dealing with a crazy person. I saw her hit a button beside the phone, so I figured it was the latter.

A uniformed officer in one of the glass-enclosed offices with a view into the lobby looked up and immediately rose. He checked his holstered pistol, which I took to be another bad sign, before coming to greet me.

"May I help you, miss?"

"She's here to see Sergeant Uchel. She says he knows what it's about. This is the young lady who reported the bodies yesterday."

"Ah, yes, we've met before. The sewage uproar. Ricky, right?"

Criminy, weren't they ever going to let that one go? Try to be a good citizen and report a sewage pipe leaking into the ocean, and suddenly everyone is blaming you for taking down two entire departments within the city government. Some people still think of it as a case of filing a false report, even though there were no such charges and no substance to the claim. In a small town like ours, a few whispered rumors can stay with you a long time. At least he didn't remember me for the topiary incident.

"Yes, I'm pleased you remember me. Always glad to be of service." Our prior meeting was far less pleasant than my smile suggested, but at that moment, the memory of my role in the scandal was probably a sore point and not likely to get me in front of Officer Uchel anytime soon. "I went back and found the bodies again. The divers from Pow Palau must have missed them." Probably not wise to criticize those in the employ of the police department, but I was just a bit tired of having my assistance dismissed. If I recalled the rumors correctly, this was the officer whose brother was involved in a pot growing operation on Peleliu. I'd keep my mouth shut if he did the same.

"Please be seated. I'll see if I can pry Sergeant Uchel away. He has a very busy calendar for the next few days. You are aware of the storm, are you not? Shouldn't you be home preparing?" *No, thank you, I'm not about to go anywhere.*

*

I sat on the bench facing the receptionist. Rigid. Breathing slowly. Staring at her. I believe I went at least two minutes without blinking. I read somewhere that if enough people stared at a glass of water, it would spontaneously boil. I was experimenting to see what one person could do. Finally, she picked up the phone, dialed a few digits, and whispered into it while covering her mouth and the mouthpiece with her hand. I believed I had succeeded in making her sufficiently uncomfortable.

There was a stirring at the other side of the lobby, and I spotted Ryan Ziegler coming my way, two cups looking tiny in his large hands. Ziegler, the one Palau Oceanic partner who I counted on to be working, even during storm preparations, was bumping his way through a crowd that had formed near a set of small cubicles used by patrol officers. Ryan sometimes had to deal with domestic disputes, and from the raised voices among the group, it seemed like this one might have needed arbitration.

Ryan handed me one of the cups. It was the local cola sweet even for my taste—but the caffeine was just what the doctor ordered. "I saw you coming in and you looked like you might need a pick-me-up. This was all they had in the break room. Jesus, Ricky," Ryan said, using what was probably the closest he ever came to bad language, "what have you gotten yourself into? I've heard your name come up at least four times in the last twenty-four hours. It seems like you're the topic of the day in every government office in Koror."

Well-practiced by this point, I gave him the quick version, which seemed to suffice. He was distracted by the appearance of an officer on the other side of the loud crowd, so I thanked him for his interest and sent him on his way. Before he left, though, he gave what for him probably passed as fatherly advice. "Keep your head down, lower your profile, and let people do their jobs. Best thing you can do at this point is to resist your natural inclination to butt in. Just go home and wait for the storm to pass." Then he gave me a punch on the shoulder and waded through the growing melee, speaking briefly with the officer and heading down a hallway that led to the bowels of the jail.

Police headquarters are an odd beehive. Everyone I'd been in had been the same. There is a clear divide between those who belong and those who don't. You don't need to see the badges to know the cast. You have those who wield the power and know it, and those who must almost inevitably submit. Ryan was in between, negotiating the choppy waters on behalf of his clients. I'd never been in the power position, and although I'd definitely been in the other, that never stopped me from trying to establish a degree of authority.

*

When I turned to resume my stare down of Miss Embry, I discovered she had slipped away from her desk. I assumed it was too much to hope that she had taken it upon herself to track down Officer Uchel, but to my surprise, the sergeant appeared almost immediately in the lobby.

"Miss Yamamoto, it's a pleasure to see you. Can I be of assistance?" He genuinely seemed pleased to see me, a reaction I hadn't historically gotten when dealing with public employees. "I'm sorry to have kept you waiting. Had I known you were here, I would have come out much sooner."

I shot a look at the empty reception and let out a grunt. So much for my ability to influence my friend at the desk.

"I found the bodies for you. I marked them. Your boys from Pow Palau can follow a line from the surface, I hope. They'll have to go deep, if they can. The bodies are both at two hundred feet." I wasn't sure why I was being bitchy to him. He was the only person who seemed to take me seriously.

He inhaled deeply and jotted a quick note on his report from the day before. He seemed to write emphatically and circled something with determination. Then he closed the file, shot a look that seemed to be either contempt or frustration at the empty reception desk, and said, "Come back to my office. There are some things I need to show you."

I had never been to the office portion of the police station, only the jail part. Clearly the real estate back there was reserved for prestigious members of the force and esteemed guests. The hallways were wider, the floors cleaner, the lighting brighter. For a big man, Uchel moved quickly, but he had a rolling gait that reminded me of a grizzly bear. He cleared the way, and I followed.

We passed a string of private offices, their doors closed, each bearing plates with names and titles for all the senior members of the Koror force. To my right, I noticed a conference room. The door was open, and several officers were huddled around the table involved in an animated conversation. The room looked as if someone had plucked it from the fancier governmental offices and dropped it down in the middle of the far dingier police station. It had matching chairs and a real ashtray. The floor was basic linoleum, like most of the rest of the building, but it lacked the wear, warping, and chips I'd come to know out front. Next, just past the conference room, we came to an office whose nameplate declared, "Sergeant MacArthur Uchel, Senior Detective, Palau National Police Force." *Impressive.*

As Officer Uchel opened the door, the aura of the "executive" wing took a nosedive. I was hit with the stale smell of an office long in need of renovation or at least a thorough cleaning. I couldn't place my finger on anything specific. He didn't seem to smoke. It was just years of accumulated life. Still, it was a whole lot better than the smell of sweat, tobacco, and bad perfume that filled the front lobby. Regardless of the smell, this was still a high-end office—it had a window. A window that obviously hadn't been opened often enough to freshen the room, but a window, nonetheless. Ribbons of light snuck in through the tightly shut blinds, likely as much to fight back the heat of the day as to protect the privacy I assumed Detective Uchel required to do his job. Against another wall were two guest chairs, mismatched but both rounded chrome with padded seats and backs, creating a nice place for a chat. Another chair—ancient, heavy, wooden, and low to the ground—sat near his desk. I guessed that one, designed to make you less comfortable and more subservient, was for interviewing.

I decided it wasn't time to sit. Uchel puttered about

with some paperwork that awaited him in his "In" box, which struck me as odd. He actually had an "In" box. At our office, we used an old turtle shell that someone found on the beach, and it was usually stacked with mail, receipts, and the odd note of some task that someone else needed to do. Uchel's appeared to hold only a few sheets of paper and a thin file folder or two. I tried to ignore him as I continued my inspection. He seemed content for me to take in the full extent of the room. I suspected he had invested time and thought into arranging it to create the impression he wanted. Sort of a peacock-tail display.

Lining the lower half of the walls on the last two sides were simple wooden bookshelves packed tight with an impressive display of books. Judging by the large "USED" stickers on the spines, many were textbooks purchased from a college discount bookstore in Guam. Above the shelves were a number of certificates from Palau Community College, documenting satisfactory or exemplary completion of a variety of courses.

POLICE AND COMMUNITY RELATIONS

PALAU GOVERNMENT LAW ENFORCEMENT AGENCY LAWS AND FUNCTIONS

POLICE REPORT WRITING

INTRODUCTION TO CRIMINAL INVESTIGATION

LEGAL ASPECTS OF EVIDENCE

INTRODUCTION TO CRIMINOLOGICAL THEORY

Our Officer Uchel was no slouch. But what really got my attention was the wall of photos over the comfy chairs. Officer Uchel with the President of Palau. Officer Uchel with members of the Supreme Court. Officer Uchel in full dress uniform at the dedication of the Koror-Babeldaob bridge with what appeared to be several Japanese dignitaries. Officer Uchel in a number of photos with whom I assumed were his wife and two young children. And Officer Uchel in dive gear—not just any dive gear, but a top-of-the-line wet suit and rig. Yet another photo showed him in a commercial diving dry suit complete with a high-tech diving helmet tucked under his arm. He saw me eyeing the photos, which was probably why he brought me in here. Yep, a peacock display, but it was well played. The photo with the President sort of trumped my "me and twenty-four other people with the President" photo that we proudly displayed at the shop.

When I finally settled into the guest chair, I was so low that my knees almost blocked my view. I got back up and looked at the undercarriage. The height could be adjusted by rotating the chair, so I began to spin it, raising it a bit higher with each turn. Uchel watched for a moment and then returned to his work. I didn't stop until the chair had reached its maximum height, enabling me to sit at eye level with him, perhaps even higher. He took another minute or two, pulling a few more forms out of his "In" box. He studied them thoughtfully and made a few notes on them before signing each, attaching a newspaper article he had torn out of the paper to the last one. They all went in his "Out" box. His "In" box was finally empty. In all my years at POS, ours had never been completely empty. I assumed the paperwork at the bottom was far more than four years old.

I could hear the voices in the conference room through the paper-thin walls. Although I captured only snatches, there was disagreement over how much overtime officers were going to have to work during the storm and who was going to pay for it. Nobody seemed happy.

Uchel still hadn't spoken a word since we entered the office. Rising out of his own chair, a newer and seemingly more comfortable chair than mine, he walked over to one of his shelves and picked up a copy of the local paper that was open to the comics and puzzle page. He flipped through, folded the paper in half, and slid it my way. "Did you happen to read yesterday afternoon's paper?" he asked, a hint of a smile barely turning the corners of his mouth upward.

I picked up the paper and scanned the section he'd turned to. It was the police log. Without looking, I knew that the upper half of the page was the weather section, probably filled with warnings and dire predictions. In a nation of 21,000, you don't get a lot of crime, so the lower half of this page was usually filled with fistfights, petty thefts, the occasional domestic violence incident, and minor drug busts. That day's paper was no different, except for the final entry, titled: "False report of bodies." It read, in full: "Sources within the Koror PD confirmed that a report filed today of two dead bodies had been dismissed as fantasy. No charges were issued for filing a false police report; however sources did confirm this was not the first false allegation from this source, a non-Palauan."

Criminy. Sometimes I hated the island and its parochial mentality. *Why take the time to attack the messenger?* I guessed it was good for business. At least they didn't mention me by name.

Detective Uchel smiled. "I appreciate your initiative in going back to find the bodies and your continued faith in Pow Palau, but I think it might be best if you and I did the recovery dive this time."

"Sorry, I've done my part. I'm not paid by the national police and I'm not the coroner. I've handed it to you and Pow Palau. All you have to do is follow the line to the bodies."

"Yeah, but is there a more qualified diver on the island?"

"No."

"Do you think Pow Palau can do it?"

"Probably. Maybe." I let out a big sigh of resignation. "I don't know."

As I pondered the implications of another deep dive—with an amateur diver—he reached into the top drawer of his desk, paused, and said, "I thought you might want to see these before we went to get your bodies."

He pulled out a plastic box held shut with a large rubber band. Perching on the corner of his desk, one leg on the ground, he draped the other, dominated by a rather meaty thigh, over the desktop. Peeling off the band, he popped open the box and began to sort through its contents—a handful of laminated cards and what appeared to be a diving logbook. He rifled through the cards, tossing his selections onto the desk in front of me like an experienced poker dealer. I recognized them as the standard issue from several dive-certification agencies. Basic Open Water. Advanced Open Water. Rescue Diver. Enhanced Air Nitrox. Then they got more serious. Master Diver. Instructor. Advanced Decompression. He saved the best for last: Trimix. He had done some serious training. But training and capability are two different things. He was asking me—or telling me—to take him on a deep, challenging dive. I wasn't sure. I had seen enough divers draped in certifications who didn't have the skills or experience.

Then he opened his logbook, flipping through thick sections of detailed notes until he got to the end, his most recent recorded dives. He flipped it around so that it faced me and slid it across the desk. The last fourteen entries were all deep dives from about six months before, all but a handful exceeding a hundred and fifty feet in depth. Not bad. He had been to Bikini Atoll, home to the remains of a fleet sunk during nuclear testing. He'd had the rare privilege of diving on the historic aircraft carrier *USS Saratoga*, as well as a half-dozen other great, heroic ships.

As I finished reading, he reached over and flipped back a few dozen pages until he reached another section. These dives were from several years earlier, but the numbers jumped out at me. He had been putting that Trimix training to work, diving with regularity in the two-hundred to three-hundred-foot range. I could see by the detailed notations he had been diving with complex mixes of gasses designed for those depths and used by only the most technically proficient divers. I was in good company.

I looked up at Detective Uchel and squinted. "How is it," I asked, "that I never met one of the most accomplished deep divers on the island?"

He pushed back in his chair, which I noticed strained a bit under his bulk, and smiled wistfully. "I haven't done as much diving in the past six years—probably twenty tech dives in a year. My two toddlers take up a lot of my time, but when I do dive, it's usually with a bunch of yahoos I met in Guam—retired US Navy guys. They schedule the trips, which are usually pretty exotic. We're able to hitch rides on military planes, so we save money that way. Lots of flights out of here to the way-off islands. I can't do many of those trips on a cop's salary. The cost of gas mix alone is too much. Besides, the free flights are on short notice—sometimes they get wind of a flight with available space and jump on it with just a day's notice—it's even dicier getting a return flight. They don't have regular jobs and can afford a few extra layover days. But back in the day, when I met those guys in Guam, we used to do some pretty hairy diving. My wife doesn't like to hear about it, so I tend to avoid the topic. It scares the hell out of her and when I talk about it, she can hear in my voice that I don't want to give it up anytime soon.

"But this—this—" he said, jabbing his finger at his handwritten note, which I now saw had "200" circled and underlined on the report from the day before, "this is police work. I can't say no to this." And then a grin spread across his big, round head like a wedge cut out of an orange. "How about we go for a dive?"

I still had nagging doubts about taking him that deep,

but knowing I didn't have much of a choice, I resigned myself to the inevitable. "Cool. Let's do it. Oh, by the way," I said as I prepared to lay down the choicest piece of news I had for Uchel, "care to know the identity of Bachelor #1?"

12

MID-MORNING – KOROR POLICE STATION

MASARU ISHIKAWA WAS a familiar figure among most of the populace of Palau, and a legend to a small few.

When he was facedown on the ledge, I didn't know who he was, but I couldn't help but recognize him the second time I saw him. At some point, maybe after the current pulled him off his precarious perch, his jacket and shirt had been shredded—and for the most part removed—as he slid down the jagged rock and coral wall. When I spotted his corpse at the beginning of my ascent, he was unmistakable. Once you've seen a yakuza tattoo, you don't forget it.

The yakuza are often referred to as Japan's mafia who make their living off the vices of others, from prostitution to gambling and extortion, and by inserting themselves into legitimate business enterprises, such as real estate, collection agencies, and private investigators. However, the yakuza operate much more openly than, say, the Cosa Nostra. They go out of their way to advertise their presence and membership. The elaborate tattoos that adorn their entire torsos, front and back, are common knowledge, though they are seldom seen by individuals outside the organization.

Ishikawa's tattoo, however, was hard to miss. It had been splashed on the front pages of newspapers and magazines throughout the US when I was a child. He had been caught in an FBI sting, and his booking photo, taken when he was shirtless, was everywhere.

He was already an established island icon by the time I arrived in Palau. The story I'd heard, in various shapes and forms, and from sources both trusted and otherwise, was he came to Palau in the early eighties to help support the Japanese whaling industry, in which the yakuza was heavily invested. The stories differed. In some, he decided to move out of mainstream yakuza life and viewed Palau as a nice, calm, backwater location where he could build a life but still keep his hand in the yakuza bowl. In others, he was party to some sort of disgrace, but in deference to his stature and his family standing, he was shipped out with instructions to never again set foot in Japan. Whatever. The bottom line was he had quickly expanded his business interests.

Within a year, he established himself as a force in Palau's backroom gambling industry, and in short order had driven out virtually all competition in a bloodless power play. The word on the street was he was also mixed up in the illegal shark fin trade. Rumors constantly flew about his involvement in various businesses—astute investments made at bargain-basement prices. If the stories were true, most small businesses in town were, in some way, connected to his little empire. His reputation was one of a ruthless sociopath, but he had stayed out of the hands of the law. No one had reported seeing him as much as swat a fly during his time on the island.

*

When I told Detective Uchel it was Ishikawa's body lying there on the ocean floor, the grin faded from his face. After hurriedly making a few notes on his report, he started a list on his notepad, then had me go back over what I had seen. Next, he made several calls, first to someone whom I could tell from Uchel's demeanor was a superior in the national police, and then to several contacts at what seemed to be other agencies. Palau may have the population of a small town, but it has the bureaucracy of a midsized nation.

Each call followed a script. Uchel would identify himself and his role, then explain he was investigating an alleged murder. More often than not, he would respond that, yes, this was related to the allegedly drunken report from the day before, but he had reason to believe it was legitimate and would be remiss if he didn't provide advance notice before proceeding. Finally, he called the coroner and requested permission to move the bodies, digging deep into the detail I provided and emphasizing that this was a "secondary crime scene" of a precarious nature. He took additional notes during the discussion and occasionally acknowledged what appeared to be a list of instructions.

After hanging up with the coroner, he had me provide a description of the beach location to another detective, and then he ushered me out to his SUV. Before opening my door, he wedged a hard-sided equipment case into the foot well behind the front seats. We pulled onto the main drag and stopped behind my Jeep, pulling out the gear I used the night before. I needed fresh tanks, but otherwise, it was pretty much ready to go. I had stupidly left it all in there the previous night and into the morning, but had not suffered a repeat theft. As we were getting ready to leave though, I noticed my car had yet another parking ticket. I knew people in medium-high places who could help me fix it later, so I tossed it on the floor before locking the car. It was only as we were pulling away that I realized, what with the broken window, locking the door was a bit irrelevant.

As I buckled myself in, the detective peered in the back. "What's with the fins?"

"EndorFins. Trademarked and soon to be patented. My invention."

"What makes them so special?"

"That's for me and the patent office to know. But they let me take off like a rocket when I kick hard enough."

"And your foot fits in that little pocket?"

*

On the way to the shop, Detective Uchel ("Call me Mac," he'd said, but that would take some getting used to) said he would need to make a few stops.

First was Ben Franklin's, and he told me to wait in the car. I decided to use the time to do some detective work of my own, but Mac returned before I could do much more than conduct a survey of the SUV floor. Clearly, the man liked his Bem Ermii burgers. As neat as his office was, his car was a mess. Burger wrappers everywhere. When he returned, he tossed a small shopping bag into the back on top of a discarded wrapper, and we headed off to the next stop.

"I've got a few things in my storage locker," he said. Rather than turning right and heading across the bridge to Ngerkebesang Island and our shop, he stayed left on Main Street and crossed over to Malakai, the other small island that, with Gerk and Koror, form the hub of Palau. Stopping at a small marina he asked me—ok, more like instructed me—to stay in the car. He went behind the car and lowered the tailgate, then let himself into the marina facility through a small side gate and disappeared between two industrial-looking buildings.

I passed the time by looking through his glove compartment. Finally, the gate to the marina was flung open, and Mac came backing out, lugging one end of something heavy. A man wearing a polo shirt with the marina logo, looking—at least physically—like he could be Uchel's larger brother, brought up the rear. Between them they carried a large duffel bag, which they lifted into the back of Uchel's national police SUV. Keeping my head up, I closed the glove compartment with my knee. As I did, I felt the SUV springs give a little as they put the bag down.

A quick broshake and a short discussion followed between the two men, then Mac was back in the car.

Pulling a quick U-turn, we headed back to Main Street and then on to the shop. Mac remained quiet, while I inspected the horizon through my open window.

The sky had cleared slightly, though the winds were stronger than usual. The ocean seemed a bit more active than the night before, but still there were only gentle swells, nothing too severe. I had never been through a typhoon before, but everything seemed ok to me. *Maybe*, I thought, *it will pass by.*

*

I directed Mac to pull into the back lot, even though there were no cars in the customer parking lot, and I let us in through the back door. The workshop, as was often the case, was unoccupied. The space Justin had cleared away the day before was still open.

I wrestled a cart for Mac out into the parking lot, the wind threatening to toss it into the water, and then I went into the workshop where weak light came in through the set of windows high along the back wall. Checking the front door, I was pleasantly surprised to find it locked—security wasn't usually a strength of our team.

A quick glance at the tote board confirmed what I had suspected—Justin was out with the sisters. Miraculously, he'd also picked up one walk-up customer. A couple coffee cups sat empty on the counter, waiting for someone else to clean up.

A receipt under one of the cups indicated they'd taken box lunches. I figured they would love an intimate lunch with their charming divemaster, but it also made sense. Justin had planned a trip to the farthest point in the islands. Not a choice I would have made, but at least he was headed to a protected side of one of my favorites.

Despite all the complications in my life, I stopped

and smiled. Lucky ladies, I thought. Diving at the southern end was going to be particularly sharky if the reef stayed true to form. They might even see whales, orcas, or manta rays. Even without the big stuff, they were in for some awesome diving and a tour of the jungle.

A branch banged against a window, jarring me from my reverie, a short reprieve from the matters of the day. Maybe the sisters weren't so lucky. Winds were picking up so there was a bit more chop, even on the leeward side that can change not only the dynamics of the fish life, but the mood of the guests. If the weather continued to degrade, they might be back in half an hour for a slide show and video in the front office.

Returning through the workshop to the back lot, I found Mac preparing to unload gear from the back of his SUV. I held the door open against the wind and, despite his protestations, helped him pull the duffel bag onto the cart, which had been shifted several feet by the wind. He stacked in my depleted tanks before I topped the pile off with my rig. Finally, he opened the side door of the SUV and retrieved the bag from Ben Franklin's, which he slung on his arm, and the hard-sided case, which he tucked into the pile on the cart. It took both of us to push the cart and its protesting wheels, into the workshop.

I pulled my rig and tanks from the pile, putting the rig on the workbench and the tanks in the refill rack, while pointing Mac to a clear section of the laminated countertop he could use. Neither of us seemed in the mood for conversation.

The hard-sided case came off the pile first. It contained a compact waterproof housing and lights for a video camera. I was used to seeing those from my customers, but it was a bit unexpected coming from a detective. He seemed to read the look on my face.

"This is a criminal investigation. We've got to record everything as we find it, even though we know the bodies were moved and the culprit was nowhere near where they currently lay. We call it a secondary crime scene." He had used that phrase before. Maybe he wasn't aware of how closely I had listened to his phone calls. Somehow, I doubted that. I suspected that he carefully regulated what I did and did not hear. "Pascal took it down yesterday but didn't use it, so it's all charged and ready to go." He took a few minutes to assemble the gear and put it to the side.

Unzipping his duffel, he began to pull out small plastic boxes and hand them to me. I don't recall him asking, but I dutifully took them and set them on the workbench. It was pretty high-end stuff, all boxed in clear plastic and labeled—*A bit over the top*, I thought, but I bit my tongue—and meticulously maintained. He had his regulator hoses coiled and tied off with zip ties, his regulators bagged, and his buoyancy wing partially inflated. I suspected I had latched onto an obsessive dive buddy. That is usually a good trait. His fins were enormous—too large for a box. Both of my feet could have fit into one of his foot pockets. I resisted the temptation to comment on how big they were.

True to form, his wetsuit (also not in a box) bore patches from a variety of certification agencies, dive clubs, and the US Navy. Peacock feathers. At least he was consistent.

Last out of the bag were several large nets and some bundles of rope. "I don't think my body bags can hold a body and an axle," he said with an air of resignation. "This is not going to be a by-the-book retrieval."

I had been placing each item on the workbench in a semblance of organization as he handed them up to me. We had quite a bit to add to what was already a complex set of technical diving gear.

The duffel bag now empty, Mac unceremoniously dumped the contents of the Ben Franklin's bag on the workbench. Out spilled six packages of women's nylon stockings, purchased, it appeared, from the plus-size shelf. "Don't get the wrong impression," Mac said, somewhat defensively. "I'm not planning on any date. For that I would bring chocolate too. These go over the arms of the victims... helps preserve any evidence that might still be under the nails or on the hands. That's if the cleaner shrimp haven't already picked it away. I got a few extra in case I lose one or two in the current. If I don't use them, I can always give them to my wife for her birthday."

Great, brine-soaked stockings. Too much information.

Finally, he pulled a pistol from his ankle holster. "Special Marine version of the Glock. Got it from one of my Navy buddies as a special gift. Shoots underwater... sort of," he said, placing it on a shelf out of the way. "Better than a spear gun at close range and shallow water. Say what you will about how sharks aren't a threat. When I'm on the surface and they're swimming around, they still give me the willies. Remember, we'll have been handling rotting flesh."

I decided I would have to check out those certificates on his wall a bit more closely. "Does Palau Community College have a course called James Bond 101?" I asked, laughing under my breath. Uchel shot me a stern look. I'm not sure everyone appreciates my wicked sense humor.

Suppressing my smile, I continued preparing our gear. I would let him worry about the forensics part; I would manage the diving. He might have brought a load of experience to the party, but I was the one with the license that said I set standards for leading deep dives, and I was the one carrying the liability insurance. We'd be using the same mix as the day before, and luckily, we still had three full sets of unused tanks from a prior canceled trip, so we were ready with that. I had residual nitrogen in my system and he didn't, so we'd be diving a profile aligned to my requirements.

As I went through the dive plan on my checklist, I swapped out my light with another fully charged LED and put it in my gear bag. I also grabbed three more lights, including a spotlight to wear on my wrist. I quickly mounted a smaller one to my shoulder strap using a couple Velcro straps. Not perfect, but it would hold. At least it was where I expected it to be if I needed it. I slid the other small one into a utility pocket on my rig. I went through my list a second time to confirm that my rig now matched my usual setup. I even found and attached a spare long hose for my regulator.

Mac handed me four glow sticks. "We'll want a lot of light," he said, "so we don't miss anything." They went into my utility pocket.

Squeezing past the bulky detective, who was making some adjustments to his own rig, I moved to the far end of the shop where we kept our seldom-used items. Kneeling, I set my feet, leaned back, and pulled out a box wedged underneath the workbench. The dust and shop grit that drifted off it suggested it hadn't been used in a while. Lift bags. You'd be surprised how many boaters end up with anchors on the ocean floor each year. Retrieving them was a profitable side business. I wasn't sure how much a truck axle weighed but guessed it was around five-hundred pounds—a lot more than most of the anchors we raised. With the axle and the bodies, I figured we'd probably need close to a thousand pounds of lift. That would mean at least five bags at two hundred pounds lift each—probably double that, for good measure. We only had eight. If I my weight estimate was off, we might be providing some of the lift ourselves. I glanced in Uchel's direction.

Uchel saw what I was doing and slowly shook his head, no. "I've got that covered. I arranged for a fishing boat to meet us. They've got a crane and a winch for pulling up traps. They can handle fifteen-hundred pounds easily—far more than the axle, anchor, and bodies weigh. We just have to get the hook down there and they'll do the rest."

Sweet.

We assembled the remainder of our gear and did a quick walk-through of the plan based on my recollection of the location. As experienced as Mac was, he and I had never buddied before, so there was a lot to discuss. With a dive of such complexity, problems can escalate quickly, and dive buddies need to be able to react with immediate precision. If you don't talk it through beforehand, your chances of a coordinated resolution drop dramatically. Mac then insisted on rechecking the dive plan I had developed. Once he'd reviewed it, noting that I had been conservative in planning our bottom time, he made his own copy on a new slate. We then exchanged slates and reviewed them to ensure they were identical. He was rigorous and detailed—I liked that in a dive buddy. I checked all the gases, had Mac do the same, then we were ready to go. We brought along two extra tanks to hang below the boat, just in case.

*

The boat with the crane left the harbor as soon as the detective I had briefed and joined them on board. From their dock to the site was about a two-hour cruise, maybe three. We'd spent a good hour and a half prepping, so we were pretty closely synchronized with them.

"Better grab some eats before we head out," said Mac. "You got a preference?"

Since it was a freebie and I was feeling a bit put-upon, I swung for the fences. "Sushi?"

Uchel's raised eyebrow told me he didn't think much of the idea, but he started up his engine and obligingly drove to the sushi restaurant just outside the marina. However, as we pulled up, it was obvious sushi was not to be. A worker from the marina maintenance company was boarding up the door, and there was no sign of life. "Braxton must have closed down for the storm. Naturally, first sign of trouble and he hightails it home, leaving someone else to take care of things. I miss old Hideo."

Crap. I had been looking forward to some free sushi.

I didn't know him by name, but I knew who the current owner was. American. Sort of a slacker type who showed up a couple years ago running the town's only sushi restaurant, which had been owned by a nice old Japanese guy named Hideo. That was the name on the sign. Kid took it over, did some quickie sushi chef course, and still called it Hideo's, but it wasn't as good. He still got the best fish in town, but he didn't have a gift for the art of preparation. I ate there every once in a while, but I missed Hideo too.

"Yup," said Uchel, "kid has never had Hideo's vision. Won the place in a poker game and it's been all downhill since. At least he didn't go through with his plan to name the place after his winning hand." He paused. Obviously, I was expected to ask.

"And what would that be?"

"Flush." Uchel flashed a satisfied grin. "Ok, we tried your choice. Now I get to pick." With that, he pulled a U-turn and headed downtown.

Based on my survey of his SUV, I had a pretty good idea what he had in mind, but he threw me a slight curve ball. Mac pulled in next door to the Rock Island Café, right in front of the entrance to the Coconut Hut Deli and Cyber Café in an area striped off as "no parking." It was well-known that national police plates provided a bit of latitude when it came to choosing parking spaces. I often wondered how far that privilege extended.

I didn't question his choice of eateries, even though

the smell of pizzas cooking up next door triggered a sudden urge for another jalapeno and pepperoni. But it was Mac's treat, so we went deli.

I ordered tuna fish from the menu board, but Mac engaged in intense discussion and supervision of the assembly of his sandwich. The giant stack that resulted from all this effort was tightly wrapped in plastic and dropped into a bag with two packages of chips. Two bottles of Diet Coke and four bottles of water were added to the growing pile on the counter. I grabbed two cups and a pile of napkins. It looked like we were ready for our road trip, but then Mac spied the candy bar section and added two Snickers bars. The bill came to just under twenty bucks. Mac paid cash but took time to scrawl something on the receipt, which I assumed to be notice that this was a government expense.

We carted the dietary essentials off to the SUV and buckled in for the half-hour drive from downtown to my spot. As we pulled out, the clock showed a few minutes past noon. In theory, we'd get there right around the same time as the boat.

*

During the drive we had a chance to chat. Mac was driving slowly. The winds had picked up, and leaves, branches, and vines were beginning to clutter the roads. Also, he had one hand full of his massive sandwich. Between periods of studious silence, and as we worked through our lunch, we talked about our diving history, which added to my comfort level. It also put me in a familiar zone and provided a pleasant reprieve from the past thirty hours.

"How do you like working for the law clerks?" He barely masked his grin. I was guessing lawyers weren't high up on his list of potential buddies.

"It's a rotating crop. Some better than others. I like the current group."

"Seems like you know the business a whole lot better than they do."

"Yeah, that comes with the territory." This aspect of the business both appeals to me and makes me chafe. I like the freedom of the lifestyle, but I answer to many masters. I like to keep things fresh and have flitted across the globe several times, as my whimsy led me, yet I have responsibilities I don't take lightly. I can't just up and leave. I'm somewhat of a renegade and contrarian, so senseless rules and control freaks make me twitchy. But recklessness and irresponsibility make me crazy. "They know their limitations, for the most part, and let me make the decisions when it comes to safety. And they gave me time off and paid for my training when I decided to become a trimix instructor. Smart move on their part—we've gotten a great return on that investment." But he was right, none of them had ever been dive professionals and they were often out of their depth when it came to most aspects of the business. I had to do some major arm twisting to get them to step up with the bucks for my training.

"So," asked Mac, glancing my way but turning his attention quickly back to the road, "if I might ask, and this isn't official, so you don't have to answer, what's the deal with being named Riccarda?"

"You want the full story?"

"Well, if you're offering. It's not covered in any of the reports I've read."

"My parents are Japanese and Swedish. They met at a track meet. He was competing for UCLA and she for UC Berkeley. Since he had flamed out early in the meet, Dad had time on his hands and decided to watch the "leggy high jumpers" as he is wont to say.

"As he tells it, it didn't take long to pick out his favorite, and he wasn't alone. Mom was, by all accounts, never at a loss for male suitors. Dad somehow won out. Admittedly, he has an intoxicating personality. He's brilliant, but odd, and percolates with joy and an absurd sense of humor. Many people don't get it and think he's a bit mad. Mom got it."

"Mom and Dad married as soon as they graduated, and I was born five months later. Don't ask. It's always been a sore subject. Dad went on to get his PhD at the University of Hawai'i Manoa campus in Oahu and then on to a career in astrophysics."

"A legendary career, according to his bio." Uchel's research, it seemed, had gone deeper than my unfortunate run-ins with the law.

"Yeah, so he says."

"So, I spent most of my early and teenage years in Hawai'i, when Mom was employed for an uncomfortably long time as a crossing guard at my elementary school. In later years, she would periodically pull me away to California or Colorado, where she had a reasonably long stint as a gardener and sometime lover for a well-heeled socialite. That's where I was shuttled off to when Dad decided Hawai'i was no longer safe for me.

Later still, she made her living as a yoga instructor, and a life guide. Ersatz shaman. Pilates instructor. Aromatherapist. Numerologist. Host of an organic gardening show on basic cable. When asked her profession, she usually says, "A lifelong student of spirituality."

"But the name Riccarda?"

"Oh, yeah, that. Sort of a tribute to his friend Riccardo—Nobel Prize winning astrophysicist and beer buddy. And, as dad tells it, for a wrestler named Rikidozen—you could think of him as Japan's Hulk Hogan. Riccarda is on my legal documents, but that's about it. By the age of two, I was Ricky."

Mac seemed to take a while to process that flood of information. After a while, he just grunted, which I figured it was an opening for me to take my turn.

"What's the deal with all your dive training, but being a cop?"

It turned out, he did have some impressive training, even beyond what I'd seen in his certification cards. As he plowed through his bag of chips, washed down with the soda, he became what, for him, constituted gabby.

Mac had spent almost an entire year in Florida, participating in a joint training program between Palau and the US Navy at the Navy Diving Salvage and Training Center. That's where the best of the best go, and most wash out. He was the only one of three from Palau who made it all the way through. The word among the dive community was that when the US government needed someone to assist in sensitive wreckage recovery or mine defusing, they'd get an NDSTC grad. I was pretty sure the spooks used them too, but I didn't ask. Or at least not directly.

"I must have missed that certificate on your trophy wall. Some sort of 'I could tell you but then I'd have to kill you secret?'"

He grimaced slightly. "They don't give out sheepskins for that type of training," was his clipped response. "It's not the sort of thing where you need to show your card." He was probably the only graduate in the country, but if there were more, I'd never know it.

Even so, this, it turned out, was his first deep body recovery. Mine too, so we were in the same boat.

13

12:45 P.M. – NORTHWEST COAST OF BABELDAOB ISLAND

THE PLAN SEEMED straightforward. I'd offered to let Mac join me in the cliff jump, but he had a different idea. We'd swim out, just beneath the surface to avoid the roller coaster of the increasingly severe waves, and meet up with the boat. They could pull in fairly close to shore, given the site's dramatic drop-off, even at the point where there was beach. The boat would then run us just up-current to my marker buoy and drop us in the water along with the cable. We'd follow my line directly to the bodies. Our descent would take seven or eight minutes, and they'd play out the cable as we dropped. Our timing was well-matched with the slack tide, which translated to almost no current, so one less complication.

We waited about fifteen minutes for the boat, which gave us time to review and map out the scene as best I could remember it. Time was of the essence, so being able to immediately and precisely begin the recovery was key.

"Walk it out one more time," Mac said. He had pulled some washed-up branches, coconut shells, and a small log onto a flat space on the beach and had me assemble a miniature facsimile of the scene. Then we discussed navigating it as if coming with the current. I made some adjustments to the spacing, and we did it again.

Uchel insisted on one last review of the dive plans. "Once we get to the bodies, it's my lead," he said. "No freelancing. This is a crime scene, and I'm accountable for preserving it as best as possible. For the most part, you stay out of the way and hold the light."

"And," I replied with no less authority, "I'm the lead diver. If I think conditions warrant it, I modify the dive plan. If I call the dive, you follow my lead."

"Sorry, no can do. This is my recovery. You're here to assist. If anything goes south or we hit our time limits," he placed his hand heavily on my forearm to ensure I was focused, "then I am taking us up. You've been deep twice in the past thirty hours. You know what the tables say. If anyone's at risk, it's you, so I want you sticking within the plan. If you need to go up, so will I. By the book. Ishikawa can wait. We don't need to add to the body count."

This was a new twist, and I yanked my arm away. "That's fine with me," I said, although I bristled at his automatic assumption of that critical responsibility. "I want to put this behind me as soon as possible." In a sense, I was relieved to have that agreed upon. My training ran counter to that, but on this dive, I was playing a different role. For one of the rare instances in my life, I was not necessarily the most proficient diver; I was just showing the man where the bodies were. I reconciled myself to that limited role. I could handle that.

*

After swimming out and meeting up with the boat for the short ride to the surface marker, we handed off the two backup tanks for hanging below the boat, did one final gear check, and stepped off the back about a hundred feet up-current from where the orange tube bobbed with the increasingly angry waves. Dropping below the surface, we kicked slowly over to the line to begin our descent. I had described the terrain to Mac in fairly precise detail, so the descent held no surprises. He handled the quarter-inch thick cable like a pro. The plan was to play out three hundred and twenty-five feet of cable at a rate of sixty feet a minute, allowing us to work our way down my buoy line. We kept up eye contact and checked each other's gauges as we neared the seafloor. Everything seemed copacetic.

The sun was high in the sky, so even with the cloud cover, we had fairly good light for the first one hundred and fifty feet. We kept close to the wall for orientation, and watched as our computers read off the increasing depth. Our eyes adjusted as we dropped, but we both turned on our big spotter beams as we approached a hundred and seventy feet. By simply following the line I let out the day before, we were soon floating ten feet over the boulders. Even from that distance, I could easily make out the scene. Bachelor #2, still a mystery man, was where I had left him—chained to the axle. And there was my light from the day before. Down between two other boulders was Ishikawa.

Mac handed me the cable. We'd discussed this during our walk-throughs—I grabbed tight and nodded, the signal that he could let go. Even thought it was slight, the pull of the current on the cable yanked me right into him, and bubbles poured from my regulator as I grunted. The current had only just begun to pick up, but it was pressing along the full three hundred and twenty-five feet of played-out cable. I was stunned at how much resistance it produced. When Mac was handling it, he didn't appear to be exerting any effort, but clearly, he had wrestled it all the way down. I pushed myself off him—easily done since he was built like a truck—and tucked myself in between two small boulders for added support. I hunkered down, wary of the ebb and flow of the pressure on the cable, and watched as Mac moved around the scene. The space we had to work in was about twenty feet by thirty, between two boulders and about fifteen feet high.

Today's visit reached the same depth as the day before, but we'd taken more time to descend with the cable, so we had twenty-three minutes of bottom time. We had allotted no more than two minutes for the video. It was pure guesswork, figuring how long it would take to wrap the bodies, but we had wanted to give as much time as possible to the job. Mac worked quickly but also very precisely. He was almost balletic underwater for such a big man. He would pivot and drift, using the current to his advantage as he moved about the scene, shooting from the periphery of the small space. Every once in a while, he would make a note on his dive slate. I stayed out of the way. He shot the scene from every angle and took the time to play back and check his footage. He even swam back and forth over the bodies in a tight up-and-back pattern. There are no redoes when you're about to disrupt an entire crime scene—or secondary crime scene.

He finished quickly and clipped his camera to his belt. That added one more bit of complication as the bulky housing bounced off his legs, but he didn't seem to notice. He looked like a rather intimidating Christmas tree, dripping with tanks, bags, computers, and his Glock, which he had strapped to his calf. He signaled it was time to retrieve the bodies. I checked my watch. The video had taken nearly four minutes. Nineteen remaining. He looked at his watch as well and made a note on his slate. I remembered he said we would both ascend if we ran out of bottom time, but my stubborn side was telling me he was going to have a fight on his hands if he tried. I wanted to be done with this.

*

Gliding over, he reached out to relieve me of the cable. I had almost forgotten I was holding it, but my hands were clamped tight. He took possession, turned, and let the current pull him away. Gliding down to the axle, he wrapped the cable once around and hooked it off. His body rotated as his momentum pivoted him over the axle and down-current from it. To ensure the hook didn't separate from its load, the cable had a clip; we called them suicide clips in diving, because more than one had unintentionally gotten hooked and led to tragic results. In this case, it made sense, but it still raised a red flag in my brain when he first handed me the cable.

One of the bodies, and its weight, was now connected to the topside world. Once we were done, with the bodies bagged and the cable set, Mac would deploy his surface-marker buoy, the signal to start reeling in the package.

Once he tested the cable connection, Mac pulled out the first pair of stockings. As he let the packaging drift away in the current, I made a mental note to chide him about the environment once we were on shore. Right now, I just kept the spotlight on his hands or, when he pointed at something else, on whatever he needed to look at. He got stockings on both arms with surprising ease and then moved up-current. He had to wrestle a bit with the body, which was tightly wedged between a small boulder and the axle, but he freed it and gently guided it down-current until the chain pulled taut. Bachelor #2 was now floating just above the seafloor, still chained to the axle. As the beam of my light illuminated him, his shadow performed a macabre dance on the down-current boulder. My stomach did a little dance of its own, but I was getting used to that. I avoided looking at his face.

Pulling out the first net from his gear bag, Mac swam to me and extended his hand. I took the net. We hadn't been sure when we planned the retrieval, if he would wrap the axle and the body together—that detail was to be worked out on the fly. At this point it was obvious that shouldn't be necessary, since the key was to wrap the body and make sure it and the axle rose together. The chain looked as if it should accomplish that.

We had agreed that I would position myself

up-current from the body by about five feet and hold one end of the net. Mac would do the rest. Of course, that meant both my hands would be in use and I couldn't operate the spotlight, so I clipped my light to my utility belt—no need to repeat my earlier error. With just a nod, he signaled for me to switch to my alternate, and we both turned on our head-mounted lights.

Then came the part that we had to improvise. I'd had no clear picture in my head of how much chain there was or how accessible the body was. This was a bit like folding sheets with another person—we had to choreograph our moves. I had never been good at that little launderette dance, though I attributed that to discomfort with the whole domestic-bliss, Cosby Show thing. I took the rolled-up net and, holding one edge, released it into the current, which caught it and pulled it out to its full length. In one fluid motion, Mac caught the other edge, spread it out to the full width of his wingspan, and guided the net under the floating body.

The work, though unpracticed, went smoothly. I let out enough netting for him to wrap the body, in sort of a porous funeral shroud. We exchanged a few signals, but mostly worked independently. He positioned himself and began to roll the body.

There was a little uptick in the current and Bachelor #2 rotated around. This time I wasn't prepared, and I saw the face again—the same face that had shot past me screaming for help. By my best guess, a crab or some such had been snacking on his eyeballs and lips. I didn't need that. I fought the surge of nausea and tried to get my breathing back under control. *Steady. Focus.*

I must have flinched because Mac looked up from his work but quickly returned his focus to the task at hand. I appreciated that. The last thing I needed was to hold up the job because I was going all Jell-O inside. By the time I composed myself, Mac had finished a complete rotation. Bachelor #2 was now looking like a trussed-up roast. I also noticed he had retrieved my spotlight from last night and placed it in the netting with the body. *Yuck. Oh well, I guess it is part of the crime scene.* I was going to need a new light. With a few additional turns, he rolled the body and the light over until they were well wrapped. Holding the netting with one hand and finning gently against the current, he then pulled out one of the bundles of rope from his dive bag. With unusual grace and dexterity, grasping the netting and bundle with one large hand, he threaded the rope through the netting with the other, and with a flourish, he tied it off and released.

I went to a rodeo once when a local promoter brought a Western-style roping and riding competition to the Big Island. Mom took me there as part of an animal-rights protest. I was ten-years-old and dressed as a dead baby seal. What that had to do with the abuse of cattle I'll never know, but I got my picture in the paper. (We also reused the costume for Halloween that year, and I came home with almost no candy.) The point being that Mac trussed that body with the skill of a rodeo cowboy taking down a calf. I was duly impressed.

*

One down and one to go. I checked my watch. "Ten minutes remaining" I signaled. Mac nodded. We were ahead of schedule and had already completed the more difficult of the two. The stockinged and trussed body of Bachelor #2 floated in the current at the end of the chain like a Macy's parade float. Mac had been wrestling with the axle to remove it from where it lay wedged. Finally, he got it to move, released his grip, and rode the current around the next boulder to where Ishikawa floated. I pushed away from where I had wedged myself and followed. Drifting past Bachelor #2, I felt an involuntary shudder.

The anchor that secured Ishikawa looked to be fairly substantial—maybe a hundred pounds, which was more than enough to hold down a body that was barely buoyant. At that point, the body was slowly pivoting in the current, his wrist attached to the anchor by the handcuff I had noticed the day before. *Yep,* I thought, *definitely fur-lined.*

Mac pulled out the next pair of stockings. It looked like it took a little effort to roll the first one on underneath the handcuff, though the fur lining provided a bit of leeway. Mac looked surprisingly relaxed as he worked it up the tattooed arm. Then he applied the second one. In other circumstances, this might have seemed perversely erotic. Not this time.

Having secured the evidence, Mac set about with the second net. Again, I held it out from up-current, and he did the rest. We finished just before the twenty minute mark. He had Ishikawa trussed and tied off to the axle with about ten feet of five-hundred-pound test line. The anchor was also tied off to the axle with another twenty-five feet. Mac deployed his marker and, with grace that suggested he had done this often, sent it to the surface, tying it off to Ishikawa's anchor. Three minutes remaining.

*

From a distance, the marker might have been easy to miss, but the crew had obviously been watching their own clock and were at the ready. Within a minute of releasing the marker, we saw slack being taken up as the angle of the cable slowly became more vertical. Mac did a few quick passes of the area looking for any additional items, then he signaled that we were done, and it was time to prepare our ascent. I checked again—two minutes left of our planned thirty. The cable tension was enough to start pulling the axle, so Mac pulled Bachelor #2 to the side so the axle wouldn't collide with him. The cable was nearly vertical; the boat had been situated perfectly. The axle hit the boulder and then, stubbornly at first, began to slide up the face of the rock, breaking off scabs of sponge and ripping a path through a colony of mussels. In less than a minute it was clearing the top of the rock, a scar marking its path. Mac still held Bachelor #2.

Unexpectedly, the axle began to bump along the top of the boulder, pulling the two men with it. The boat wasn't directly above us, so there was still some down-current force. The axle swung off the far edge of the boulder and arced past Ishikawa before the lift was sufficient to start pulling it up and shallower. Through all of this, Mac held onto the Bachelor #2 package, just like that rodeo cowboy. As the line finally went taut, the axle rose, and the anchor followed—then Mac and Bachelor #2. We hadn't thought of that. I think we'd both imagined they would lift directly off the bottom, which Ishikawa finally did. Once Ishikawa was about fifteen feet off the bottom, Mac released. The two bodies hung from the axle like a pair of sausages jerking about in a clumsy ballet, but now the axle and the rest of the package were moving slowly upwards. The weight overcame any drift the current might be influencing.

I checked my watch. We were thirty seconds into our ascent time but still near the bottom. We had a generous margin of safety built into the plan, but I didn't want to start using it up so soon. I took out my slate, did a quick mental calculation, and added a few minutes at the end of the dive.

"Overtime," I wrote on my slate, "add deco 5 min/20 ft."

I showed him my revised slate. He read it, paused, nodded again, and made the changes to his slate as well, handing it to me for a final check. All this while slowly rising toward the surface.

The next few minutes would be tricky. We needed to keep the package in close proximity but could stay above or below it. We'd gone over this with the boat crew by radio as we waited for them on the beach. Our ascent rate was pegged at no more than thirty feet a minute; the cable would be drawn in slower than that. We would proceed with our ascent, using the cable as a guideline until we were at a depth of twenty feet. We'd be met there by the other officer to hand off responsibility for the package. "Chain of custody" as Uchel described it, apparently unaware of the irony of using that term in this case. This gave us some latitude in timing our ascents to the winch's pull rate, and the additional five minutes would be after the hand-off, so wouldn't be a problem.

Things quickly started getting trickier. The cable began bouncing up and down, first gently, but then with increasing violence. We'd already experienced a gentle rise and fall as the big boat rode out the surface swell, but this was more rapid. At first it was just two or three feet, but then it became more pronounced. The packages started rising and plunging as well. Soon the changes were five or six feet. Mac and I didn't have a signal for it, but we both knew the storm was hitting up top. As we got shallower, with less line and less slack, the bouncing became more extreme. I was thinking the lift bags would have been a superior idea. Mac wrote on his slate and handed it to me—"nxt time. lift bags"—as if he had been reading my mind. Nice to know he wasn't too proud to admit a mistake. I promised myself there would not be a next time.

We had both released our grip on the cable when the bouncing began, and just kept an open hand on it. We didn't want to get separated from the package, but I also didn't want to go through the agitation cycle in the washer. Thirty feet beneath us, Ishikawa and Bachelor #2 whipped up and down. Mac's wrapping job seemed to be holding up well.

As we reached fifty feet, we were met by the other police diver—a bit deeper than planned—I suspected he took pity on us. He and Mac shook hands, which I interpreted to be the official signal for an underwater exchange of chain of custody. He signaled for a readout on our remaining breathing gas, aware that we had two spare tanks hanging nearby, but we were both well within our safety margins and let him know we were ok. He waved us off. As we turned, I waved goodbye, hoping I was done with the two bachelors for good.

*

The coroner would have had us drawn and quartered if he had seen the last ten minutes of the recovery. Mac and I finally swam away when the package reached a depth of fifty feet. We could see the boat hull rocking and rolling above us, and Mac signaled that we should put some serious distance between them and us. Besides, we still had some significant decompression time before we surfaced—another thirty-five minutes, including the minutes I added on for the extra bottom time. But after swimming off a short way, Mac turned to watch. It was probably best to do our decompression stops in deep water—I was expecting a severe pounding once we neared shore—so we watched as the Ishikawa and Bachelor #2 packages continued their underwater dance. I was relieved Mac did such a good wrapping job. I would have hated going back for dislodged body parts.

As we began our ascent, after the near fiasco of the bouncing axle, Mac had the foresight to adjust the rigging so that Ishikawa, the anchor, and Bachelor #2 were tied to the axle by an equal length of rope, about five feet, so everything was above water quickly after the axle broke the surface. We could only watch from below. The fishermen plunged their gaffs below the surface to snag the ropes and pull our two friends onto the boat. Watching with a bit of anxiety, ready to perform a rescue if necessary, we watched the police diver grab a hold of the bouncing ladder and pull himself out of the water.

I'm sure, after two and a half hours of bouncing around in the boat, even veteran fishermen got a bit queasy when they pulled in their catch. Watching the two corpses swinging in the wind as they hung from the twelve-foot-tall crane must have ratcheted that queasiness up a notch or two.

With the package and cable finally above the surface, the boat props churned up the water as they made a hasty retreat, and for the first time in an hour, it was just the two of us in an increasingly angry sea.

There's not much to do during a decompression stop, other than think and monitor your depth and gases. My mind wandered to the business of the shop and their enthusiasm for my discovery. It was, to say the least, a bit macabre to see their excitement, but it also made sense. If they knew much about the business, it was marketing. And a successful recovery meant good press for the shop.

We finished our decompression stops in deep water and made our way to shore. The churning sea, compressed in the shallows of the beach, thrashed and pounded. Timing our exit carefully, we rode the current in and finally crawled up onto the beach with waves breaking over us. The trails we left as we dragged ourselves and our extra tanks up the sand looked like small amphibious vehicles had landed. I thought it was like a scene out of a war movie.

*

I plopped unceremoniously on my butt in the sand. Mac walked to his SUV, pulled out his radio, and called the coroner to tell him his package would be in port in about ninety minutes. Dropping down onto the sand beside me, he released what could pass for a sigh of satisfaction. "Good work out there. You were really quite smooth. A regular Rikidozen with some of those moves." His wink was a little less creepy this time. As if to seal the deal, we shook hands, mine disappearing into his.

"Thanks, I've trained a lot."

The wind was really kicking up the surf, and we both squinted as the spray struck our faces. The sky looked much darker and angrier than it had when we began the dive. "Hey, the lady at the desk..."

"Ms. Embry."

"Yeah, Ms. Embry. She said you were busy preparing for the storm. How'd you get roped into that?"

He gave me a quizzical look. "I didn't. She must have made that up. She takes her job quite seriously and feels compelled to provide a buffer between us and the lunatic fringe."

"Being me?"

This time, he gave me a sly smile. "You and about half the island. But, yeah, you. At least that was her assessment. From my perspective, the jury's still out."

14

4:15 P.M. – NORTHERN KOROR ISLAND

DETECTIVE UCHEL, LOST in thought, drove far too slowly for my taste, particularly as he crossed the Koror-Babeldaob Bridge connecting the two most populous islands in the nation. I was eyeing the water, which had become increasingly choppy as the day wore on, and the wind, which was whipping angrily at the trees and plants along the shore.

The official name given to the bridge was the Japan-Palau Friendship Bridge. The nation of Japan donated it to replace the original bridge, which had been an engineering marvel right up until the day it collapsed.

"Is there much talk at your shop about whaling and finning?"

My mind was elsewhere, so I had to take a moment to process the question.

Whaling and finning? Politics in Palau were a wrestling match. The US still had some military and legal roles from the days when Palau was a US territory.

Japan, however, had contributed generous amounts of money to the Palauan economy since the split. For most of that time, Palau had, for reasons subject to much debate, sided with Japan on the issue of the continued harvesting of whales. The more cynical among the locals suspected a long-standing quid pro quo arrangement, but the tide had recently shifted, inspiring a lot of speculation. It didn't surprise me that the topic of Ishikawa had led Uchel to think about the whale and shark industries. There'd been a lot of discussion over beers, certainly among the expats, on whether Palau's reversal and vote against Japan's whaling interests in the 2010 vote would have any impact on Japan's investment in the tiny island nation. *Does this have something to do with Ishikawa?*

"Not so much with the customers. We like to keep things upbeat. But yeah, frankly, there's a lot of talk questioning the commitment of the government to make a difference. Some folks think officials are getting paid off."

His only response was a grunt, and he stayed silent for the rest of the drive.

Regardless, the topic inspired a lot of passion among the professional divers. All of us had dived with sharks, and most of us had been in the water with whales. Yeah, the country had passed impressive shark finning legislation, but enforcement was limited.

Historically, the harvesting of the ocean was ingrained in island culture, while the conservationist movement was quite recent. Plus, all the rumors about the inflow of money from Japan into the pockets of local politicians drew strong conclusions. I asked Ruluked about it once.

"Honey," she replied, "you haven't lived here long enough to come close to understanding the relationship between us and the ocean. The sea provides and we reap the harvest."

*

Main Street was almost deserted, so we made good time through town, slowing only for detritus blown into the road. Uchel stopped once to drag a stray Ben Franklin's cart to the sidewalk. The doors of the department store were shuttered, dashing any thoughts I might have had of food shopping before the storm. By the time he finally pulled up to drop me off at my Jeep, double-parking in front of the police station, it was almost five o'clock.

Another day shot, I thought, unbuckling my seatbelt. I opened the door to jump out and realized my muscles were slow to respond, having tightened up during the ride. Slinging extra tanks, cables, and bodies around had really taken a toll on me. I considered for a moment whether I was getting too old for my line of work, but quickly rejected the notion. I figured with a good night's sleep and the resumption of my regular routine, I would be back in the saddle. I eased out of the SUV and went to my Jeep.

Stopping as I got to the driver's door, I shot a look at Detective Uchel, who had just gone around the back to get my gear. I lifted my windshield wiper, removed the pieces of paper from underneath it, and held them in the air. "Hey," I called as four new tickets fluttered in my hand. Suddenly, whatever spell he had been under was broken. He slammed the rear gate of his SUV, turned on his flashers, slammed the door closed, grabbed the tickets from my hand, and started toward the front door of the police station.

"Follow me," he barked. I trailed after him, obediently.

Taking the steps two at a time, Mac (though once he got in the vicinity of the police station he seemed more like Detective Uchel) clutched the tickets tightly in his ham-sized fist. I trotted behind him, trying to catch up, my muscles complaining with each step. He opened the double doors to the lobby, displaying an impressive wingspan as he spread them wide. I thought he was going to hold them open for me, but he let go and they slammed shut in the wind. I pried one open and followed, finding him standing just behind the alleged yellow line where he seemed to be composing himself.

After a brief pause, he slowly walked up to the receptionist's desk and said, in a surprisingly gentle voice, "Miss Embry. Mildred. I'm hoping you can do me a favor. This young lady, Ms. Yamamoto," he said, pulling me forward, "is assisting us in a high-priority investigation. I've just now spoken to the Minister of Justice to apprise him of the investigation, and he would greatly appreciate our extending every possible courtesy to Miss Yamamoto. In light of that, I'm sure we all find it quite embarrassing to discover her car—which remained here while she was aiding me—was ticketed repeatedly for being parked in a two-hour zone. Now, I would appreciate it—and I'm sure the minister would as well—if we could make sure this doesn't happen again. I notice you have a clear field of view to those parking spots. Could you please be so kind as to bring this to the attention of any officer who might errantly try ticketing Miss Yamamoto's Suzuki Samurai again? I'll be sure to mention your assistance to the minister when we next speak."

With that he handed her the crumpled tickets, turned, and strode back in the direction from which we'd just come.

I looked at Miss Embry, who suddenly looking like she had just sucked on a lemon, and I shrugged my shoulders. "Thanks. But it's a Jeep," I said in my perkiest manner before scuttling across the lobby in pursuit of Detective Uchel.

As we walked down the stairs, he looked at me and winked. "That should keep the old biddy in her place. She just loves to mess with people. Often, she picks right. She picked wrong this time. And, for the record, it's a Suzuki Samurai with the word Jeep painted on the side."

I liked the support but had a queasy feeling he meant it when he said I was assisting in the investigation. I was definitely looking for an end to that relationship, not an extended engagement. "Thanks. I've got to get back to the shop."

*

Mac ignored the minor traffic jam that had built up behind his SUV. Being close to five o'clock and the changing of shifts at the police station, it probably wasn't the best idea to double-park, but these were his co-workers. No one seemed to be giving him grief as they slid by and checked us out. He helped me switch the considerable amount of gear into my Jeep and was polite enough not to mention the stench that seemed to permeate every crevice and cubbyhole of the passenger compartment.

I had resisted taping plastic over the broken window thinking that might air things out, but the odor lingered.

Just for good measure, before stepping into his SUV, he made clear to the lead car in the line behind him that I was to be allowed to pull out before they moved on. Giving me that wink again, which I still found a bit unsettling, he climbed behind the wheel, turned off his flashers, and eased his large, white gas-guzzler down the street. I pulled out behind him and waved to the cars waiting in the lane. We minor celebrities have to remember the little people.

I noticed that Mac had not pulled into the secondary police station parking lot, but rather continued down the street. Of course, this close to five o'clock, even diligent cops in Palau recognized quitting time. And, in a mobile society, who needed to be at their desk anymore? As if proving my point, I noticed he had his cell to his ear when he turned right onto Main Street, slow-rolling and talking on the phone. I turned left.

*

It took me about five minutes to make it to the bridge leading to Ngerkebesang Island, home to several upscale resorts, the local hospital, and our dive shop. From there, it was slow going along a road littered with debris.

Our dive shop was a tad unique – it was owned solely by American lawyers with no formal experience in the diving business. As a former United States Trust Territory, Palau adopted what was essentially an American-style legal system. In fact, the Palau Supreme Court staffed itself with American law school graduates who served one-year terms as law clerks, and who sometimes stayed in other capacities once their time was up. Former clerks could be found in the Supreme Court as justices or staff counsel or in private practice, working in other capacities for the government, captaining fishing boats, and tending some of the gloomier bars on the island.

They also invested some of their money in-country. That's where the dive shop came in.

As the law clerk pipeline became established, the court realized they needed to ease the complication of transitioning from the US to Palau. They took on long-term leases for several apartments and houses in the area, filled them with what—by island standards—passed as modern furniture and appliances, and provided them rent-free to the clerks as part of their "expat" package. When each clerk ended their term, they handed off the apartment to the next clerk, often adding to the package various odds and ends they acquired during their stay.

And, from that, the idea for the dive shop was born. You see, for most US law school graduates, the opportunity to live in a tropical paradise for a year was attractive, but not as attractive as the six-figure salaries being handed out by American law firms. Add to that the suspicion with which law firms viewed lawyers whose first choice was not corporate law, but a backwater island nation, and you immediately limited the number of motivated applicants. It was safe to say that ninety-nine percent of all applicants to the Palauan positions had one thing in common: they either already were or they planned to become certified scuba divers. And they planned to do a lot of diving once they hit the island.

Life in the court made that possible. Palau court calendars weren't as demanding as those in the States, and there was a relaxed attitude toward time off. A motivated diver could get in a dusk dive every day and ten dives over the weekend—an expensive endeavor until an opportunistic attorney by the name of Barry Cohen took advantage of a temporary tourism downturn. He bought a failing dive shop—lock, stock, and barrel—and even kept on most of the staff. Barry's family had been in the retail business for generations, and unlike most dive operators, he'd picked up a few tricks of the trade. He cornered the more predictable market by providing nominal discounts to the other expats and court personnel, and built up a steady business. They shifted their hours of operation so that their boats left an hour after all the others, which meant they got passengers who missed boarding times or hadn't planned in advance. His out-of-pocket costs were minimal, and he was able to delay paying out for upkeep during slack periods, as the operation had been well maintained during prior profitable years.

The plan was simple: use POS as his private service, make enough money to cover costs as opportunities fell to him, and sell it to his successor when his year was up. It was brilliant in its simplicity. During the day, they had enough customers to pay the bills. Barry and his partners (his two fellow clerks, who quickly came on board) dived every weeknight, and on weekends he shared the boat with paying customers. A year later, he sold the business for a slight profit. And so it came to be that every year the leased housing, an increasing number of random items of furniture and appliances, an aging fleet of compact cars, and Palau Oceanic Scuba (including an eclectus parrot named Ralph) transferred to a new set of owners.

This had been the model for the prior twelve years. I had been at the shop for the past four and a half, which made me the longest-tenured employee in the short lifespan of the company, and far more experienced at running the business than any of my bosses. Sometimes that made our relationships bounce between friendly and awkward, depending on which way the wind blew.

*

Arriving around 5:15, I found the Palau Oceanic Scuba shop battened down, noticing that the speed boat and both open boats had been trailered, covered, and parked in the customer parking lot. At thirty feet long, the open boats weren't exactly toys. It must have taken some teamwork to get them out of the water. I pulled around back where a sign hung on the back door. It read:

Diving suspended for at least the next two days due to weather

- *prepaid diving will be refunded*
- *we're at the Rock Island Café, meet us at the bar to get your refunds*
- *Ricky, come join us, we want all the details. You and your secret site made the news*

It was signed "the Benthic Barristers," a name that one merry prankster of an owner had hung on the group a few years back and it had stuck. I think the lawyers actually liked the comparison to bottom-feeders. I sighed. These were the country's best and brightest. Heaven help us.

The reference to the news concerned me, but I didn't have to wait long for the answer. Below the note a print-out from the local paper's website had also been taped to the door.

Police Confirm Criminal Investigation at Ngarchelong Beach

A source within the Koror police confirmed that operations sighted off Ngarchelong Beach were, indeed, a police action. Witnesses reported seeing a large axle, perhaps from a truck, being hoisted from the water.

Illegal dumping in the area has reached epidemic proportions as of late, reports local farmer Yale Remengesau. Officials at the Division of Marine Law Enforcement were not available for comment.

Crap. The byline, Stephaliza Rengulbai, was unfamiliar – not that I read much in the local fishwrap or noticed who wrote it, but you get to know most everyone in a place this small. I would have thought I knew her or at least know of her. Still, all things considered, the article was not very specific and lacked the most important details, so maybe it would all end there. Probably a one-time piece that would die on the vine. It was, after all, the *Island Times*.

15

5:30 P.M. – NGERKEBESANG ISLAND

ALTHOUGH I OFTEN avoided happy hour at the Rock Island, somehow the idea of cold beer and live people seemed appealing. I figured I could finish up quickly if I cut a few corners – actually, a lot of corners. Unlocking the door, I propped it open with a handy wedge of wood, pulled a flat cart out the back door, loaded the gear onto it, and pushed it into the workshop. *We'll have plenty of time tomorrow to put it away*. Before locking up, I tore the article from the door—no sense in calling attention to it.

As I worked my way through the parking lot, now littered with an increasingly odd collection of items that couldn't or hadn't been tied down, I stepped around my neglected floor mat, which had stiffened in the afternoon heat but lost little of its stench. It may very well have become one with the asphalt, having not moved an inch despite the high winds. As I drove through the front parking lot, I passed our two neighbors, who appeared to be shuttered as well, and saw that a sign similar to what I had found on the back door had been posted on our front door as well.

Turning on the radio to get the weather report, I located the local news channel just in time to hear, "...in breaking news, Associate Crime and Weather Reporter Stephaliza Rengulbai from our print and online affiliate, the *Island Times*, joins us in the studio with an exclusive live report regarding the double gangland slaying involving local crime boss Masura Ishikawa. Stephaliza, what can you tell us?"

Criminy. I turned the radio off. The whole mess was spinning in the wrong direction. *Why can't people just mind their own business?* We'd only pulled them up two hours earlier. *How the hell is this happening? And who the hell is Stephaliza?*

*

Bouncing over the curb and into the Rock Island Café parking lot, I found a space right in front. That was a rarity, and I took it as a good sign that my luck was changing. Sore and angry, I just wanted to catch a few breaks.

The windows were boarded up and sandbags walled off the front door, but the noise from within told me business was booming. As if by divine guidance, the pungent wind from offshore pushed me toward the building. Climbing over the sandbags, I pried the doors open. The crowd was deeper and more vocal than I expected—it was a full-fledged typhoon party. On the TV screens was a rugby scrum, but judging by the noise level, few in the crowd cared that it was a tape delay. I appreciated the ability to suspend disbelief, both in treating last week's match as new and in thinking that boozing it up was the best way to prepare for a storm. At least if Stephaliza started appearing on broadcast TV, we wouldn't see it for another week.

I wasn't much in the mood for socializing and, frankly, didn't like being the topic de jour, so I veered away from a familiar group—a bunch of local pilots who split their time between private aviation, tourist flyovers, government work, and medical evacuation flights. Pretty much any size plane and any size job. They weren't bad guys; as a matter of fact, they were all quite good by reputation. Almost exclusively ex-military. One of them had evacuated a local dive guide who'd gotten bent. He had taken him "fast and low" to Guam, keeping the altitude down to avoid adding to the decompression affect. They yelled an indecipherable greeting my way, and I managed to respond with a grin and a wave.

After spotting my gang near the rear exit, I worked my way through the crowd, getting groped twice. My luck was holding steady. They picked the wrong day to have wandering hands. I figured I left a broken finger or two in my wake. When I got to the table, a glass of beer was waiting for me, and I realized that our gang had expanded. In addition to Sarah, Dmitri, Roland, and Justin, the sisters had joined us, and they seemed to be enjoying themselves quite thoroughly. I hoped they weren't driving.

"Here she is! Here she is!" squealed one of them. I'm not sure if I ever knew which one was Karen and which one was Kate, at that point I certainly had no idea. "You've got to tell us all about it."

"Oh, yes!" cried the other. "Please do!"

In the soft light of the Rock, they didn't look half-bad, and Justin appeared to be fairly deep into his first pitcher of beer. Perhaps by the end of the evening, they'd have that Justin sandwich. On the other hand, Justin, who was squeezed between the two of them, looked relieved to no longer be the subject of their attention.

"Oh, I'd love to, but I've been cautioned against speaking about an ongoing criminal investigation," I said, pleased that I had spent so much time watching American police TV shows. That dialogue can come in handy sometimes.

Sarah, it appeared, had gotten quite a head start on the beer. She was louder and a little more brassy than normal. "Give it up, Rick. People die. It's someone else's problem. Don't insert yourself into the situation. Trust me. I'm a law clerk." Dmitri patted her on the head which normally would have resulted in a twisted arm, but merely elicited a squiggly smile.

As I grabbed an empty chair from a nearby table, I spotted Ryan beginning to work his way through the crowd. That would be a rarity—all the bosses relaxing and spending downtime together. Ryan was older than the rest and a little more sedate. Besides, Rock Island was beer and pizza, and he was more sushi and chardonnay. Nothing like a typhoon to nurture tight bonds. Ryan paused to exchange a few words and handshakes before he squeezed his way past the pilots. After all those years as a civilian, he still considered the military to be family. The camaraderie, given his history of prosecuting miscreants during his time in the military justice system, may not have been shared by all expats on the island. Another group of former pilots, more raggedy, and with reputations of playing fast and loose with the rules, not only ignored him but went so far as to turn away as he passed.

"Well," said Karen or Kate, returning to a conversation I would rather end, "that doesn't seem to stop that Elizabitha—"

"Stephaliza," corrected Kate or Karen.

"Yes, Stephaliza... that doesn't seem to stop her from talking up a storm. She's been all over the radio... it's really quite an exciting story. And to think, we're right in the middle of it."

I was feeling no love for this Stephaliza person. *What is she doing talking about gangland murders?* Maybe, though, she knew more than I did. Maybe, I thought, Mac wasn't as forthcoming as he seemed. After all, a gangland execution certainly made sense. I had read about the yakuza, and they seemed to be a pretty ruthless bunch. And a truck axle didn't seem like the run-of-the-mill passion murder weapon. You had to really want to make a point and do some planning to send someone to Davy Jones' locker shackled to an axle.

Crud.

I hadn't really stopped to think about what led up to my encounter with Bachelors #1 and #2, but as I listened to the sisters going on about the reports, I redoubled my commitment to get away from it as quickly as possible. There were people who were paid to deal with that kind of stuff, and I was not one of them. Now the police had their proof and I wanted a lot of distance. Maybe it was time to find a new home. Four and a half years was an awful long time to be in one place.

Ryan finally made it to the table. I hoped he would distract the sisters as I let him wedge another chair in beside me.

"As a matter of fact," I said, putting my hand on Kate's and Karen's forearms, or Karen's and Kate's... whatever, "The authorities would appreciate it if you didn't mention my role or even the role of the business in any of this. It's quite hush, hush. I'm sure you understand. When we were talking with the Minister of Justice today," I whispered, giving Ryan a wink, "he expressed great concern that anybody who knew any details might be at risk. I'd hate to see you get caught up in this, so—for your sake—please, let's keep this to ourselves."

"The Minister of Justice? Oh my, but of course. Not a word." And then Karen or Kate made a zipping motion with her hand, applied an imaginary lock, and threw away the key.

Ryan nodded sagely. He likely had no idea what the conversation was about but was smart enough to know I needed a little backup. He tended to be the herder and babysitter for our youthful group, although at times he could be a bit more controlling than I liked.

"So," I said, hoping to change the subject, "how were the dives at Peleliu? And the land tour?" The girls had insisted on heading out to the most distant dive sites after hearing Justin wax eloquent about them. I'm sure he regretted that after the day's winds.

"Well..." said Justin, "we experienced a bit of weather out there and had to cut it short. But the first dive was fantastic, right, ladies?"

"Oh, yes, quite!" exclaimed the K girls in unison, back to their usual giddy selves. "It was like Disneyland underwater," said Kate or Karen.

It seemed Justin could do no wrong.

He wasn't that different from dozens of expats I'd worked with: sufficiently good-looking to charm the customers, gentle in nature, and quick of wit. Like most of us, he kept himself reasonably fit and was more than capable of handling anything that came up during a dive. The years, though, were showing. His six-pack was short a few, and his love handles a bit more pronounced; he was certainly not the young stud I met in the Maldives ten years earlier when we were the wild ones, but then again, I wasn't a spring chicken anymore either. He'd been talking about hanging up his gear more frequently in the past year. Probably just talk—Justin was one of those guys who would die with his fins on.

"It took two hours to get back. Justin, who was piloting the boat, had to wear his mask and snorkel the whole time because the spray was so heavy."

"We took the fast boat," Justin said with a wince. "In retrospect, that was a poor choice." Our fast boat—which, though speedy, was also small and used a lot less gas—was nearly perfect when we had only a couple divers. And we could get in and out of sites quickly. We usually took one crewman to take care of the boat on the surface during the dive, but sometimes left the boat unattended. But, because the thing bounced like a beach ball on the waves, I only took it out on smooth days, extra crew or not. It sounded like Justin rolled the dice and lost, but still made the best of a bad situation. One of the most scenic views in the Rock Islands, and one of the most requested photo ops for our customers, was a feature called The Arch. Apparently Justin took advantage of high tide to race through at full throttle, the sisters' screams reportedly drowning out the whine of the engine.

If I had taken a group of divers on the hour-long boat ride to Peleliu, and then a rough two hours back, and they'd only gotten one dive, I would probably be swinging from the yardarm by the time we got back to the dock, arch or no arch. But then, I wasn't exactly known for my people skills. A cold beer or two usually helped, so I ordered another pitcher.

*

We amused the sisters and ourselves for the next hour with stories of dive mishaps and foul-weather nightmares. They seemed to have survived what must have been wretched conditions quite well, and I was gaining a measure of respect for them. I had not, however, given up on pinning down which was Kate and which was Karen.

They were excitedly making notes in their journals—I'm sure to provide fodder for their e-mails home and discussions around the coffee machine at work. "I can't get the hang of how to say, or even spell, the island name," exclaimed one of the sisters, as she wrote in her leather-clad notebook. "Is it Ngerb... Ngerba?"

"Ngerkebesang," said Justin. "A lot of names here, both places and family names, begin with Nger. The 'ng' is a sort of nasal sound. We just treat it like the 'ng' at the end of 'bring.' For all intents and purposes, the G is silent like the P in swimming."

They looked confused by the joke Justin had told a thousand times before, until one lit up and said, "Ooooh, *pee*..." They both squealed, and Justin beamed.

Ultimately, the crowd quieted, which probably meant the rugby match was over. I glanced at one of the TVs and saw a live weather report was on. The typhoon was predicted to make landfall in the coming twenty-four to thirty-six hours, but even before then, winds were expected to bump up from forty-five to more than sixty miles an hour. With that announcement, a cheer went up through the crowd.

Dmitri pushed himself away from the table. "Well," he said, with a forced effort at clarity that underscored how much he'd had to drink, "I'm the designated driver, and I think it's time for me to go. Sarah? Somebody's got to open the shop in the morning. Roland? Shall we go? Dinner perhaps?" Sarah and Roland both took about two seconds to assess the situation and, with appropriate thanks and apologies, said they'd be sticking around for a while. "Drive safe," said Sarah, her tone heavy with concern.

"No worries," said Dmitri, and he navigated himself through the crowd with a gait worthy of a seasoned sailor. Impressive, except he was on dry land and the floor wasn't moving. As he made it through the door, we all exchanged fearful glances.

I just was getting up to see if I could catch him and offer Dmitri an alternate way home when we heard an enormous crashing sound. The crowed seemed oblivious to the sounds as I wiggled through towards the entrance. Pushing through the double doors to the parking lot, I was astonished to see that one of the two palm trees that graced the front of the restaurant had blown over and smashed three cars. Amazingly, it had missed mine by less than a yard. *Gee, maybe my luck is changing.*

Dmitri, on the other hand, sat ashen in his driver's seat, staring at the two-foot-thick trunk that had pan-caked the front of his car. It looked like he would be open to a suggestion of alternate transportation after all. My luck was definitely turning to the positive.

16

SOMETIME AFTER SUNRISE – AIRAI, BABELDAOB ISLAND

DAY BROKE WITH a bang. I bolted up from bed, thankfully not hungover, but still a bit sore from two days of intense deep diving. Unsure of what I heard, my mind raced back to poor Dmitri and his Toyota pancake. It had taken us a while to get him out. First was the issue of getting his brain back to a functional level. Despite our knocking on the window, waving our arms in front of the spiderwebbed windshield, and calling out in what my EMT training referred to as "a calm and reassuring manner," Dmitri had sat frozen, hands on the wheel, eyes fixed forward.

Finally, he blinked. And then a spasm that threatened to break the seat back wracked his body. He yelped—a pathetic little yelp, perhaps more of a yip. Turning to look at the rest of the team staring at him through the driver's side window, he pointed at the tree that rested across his and two other cars and cried out like the master of the obvious, "Do you see that? Do you see that?" Then he uttered a string of Russian obscenities that would make my mother blush.

Having determined that the front doors were pinched tight by the twisted chassis and body, we extracted Dmitri through the rear of the car and took him back into the Rock. Some patrons, bless their souls, remained glued to the TV, watching network television news, which was always interesting. Like the sporting events, it was on a seven-day delay, something contractual I was told, so those of us lucky enough to get Internet service and, thus, current news, were able to relive the experience seven days later.

I often wondered if, given the tape delay, the end of the world would give Palau a seven-day reprieve so we could catch it on the evening news.

*

But the morning after the palm tree crash, I was more curious about the sound that had stirred me from my deep sleep. I rolled out of bed and pulled on Roland's Capri shorts and oxford shirt, which I was still wearing when I went to the Rock the night before and now formed the closest pile to my bed. I made a mental note to clean them before returning, especially since it appeared I had sat in something foreign at some point during the evening libations.

My house in Palau was a bit off the beaten track. Over the years, I had upgraded several times through the hand-off process that we expats developed, and each house was more remote and distant than the last. Leases and rental agreements are not exactly formal on an island where property lines are often described in terms of tree trunks, abandoned tractors, and high-tide marks. Many property rights go back hundreds of years and the inevitable legal disputes provide endless entertainment to all who have the luxury of watching from the cheap seats.

I had been living rent-free in a house owned by a high-tech refugee from California's Silicon Valley. Having comfortably profited from stock sales, he decided to retire and move to Palau. He dived with us almost every week, in between fishing trips and beach days along the eastern coast. He lasted about eighteen months before the cravings for fancy restaurants, first-run movies, and twenty-four-hour grocery stores got to him. He went back to the States for a visit and seldom came back. His last visit was more than two years ago.

Unwilling to give up his island dream, he decided he needed a caretaker, a decision that coincided with the end of my failed attempt at cohabitation with my boyfriend. Make that ex-boyfriend.

There was only one rule. "No parties," he said before giving me the keys. I agreed, knowing that a single visit from any of the bosses or folks from the shop would lead to a virtual home invasion. So, as far as most of them knew, I lived in a small shack that I was too embarrassed to let them see. Roland was an exception, and to this point, he had only seen the "public" areas. And the rain gutters.

As far as any other male companionship, I had so far managed to convince them to use their place or, in more desperate times, the workbench at POS. Although I seldom had visitors, I was never without companionship, as I did have a pet that required my attention. "Pet" may be a bit of a misnomer. It was a small bonsai Hawaiian umbrella tree. *FICUS BENGHALENSIS* according to the label on its base. It travelled with me everywhere I went. My grandmother gave it to me when I was seven, saying it would teach me responsibility. (Actually, it's not really a tree; it's a ceramic replica of a tree. I would have killed a tree.) I treasured it. Kuku (that's what I called my granny, while Mom called her Kuku too, although she spelled it "cuckoo" in her letters) used to take me to Honolulu for shopping (the bribe) and museums (the real destination). I loved the Bishop Museum and its massive banyan tree. I would sometimes spend so much time climbing on it that we had to race through the museum just before closing time. Kuku is gone now, but I kept the tree statue and named it Kuku in her honor. I've done a reasonably good job of keeping it dusted.

Below the lowest corner of the house was a carport jammed with boy toys, including a small speedboat that had been parked there ever since I arrived, and last served as the home to a family of chickens that appeared to have fled a neighbor's coop. So, I parked out in the driveway by the front door.

Anyhow, it was to this sanctuary I retreated after we trundled Dmitri off to bed in his little Koror apartment, the sight of which reminded me that I lived far better than my bosses. But that bang I just heard had me on edge. The wind had picked up even more, and the windows were rattling, the leaves flying by on a horizontal path. If the talk was right, we were going to be hit by the edge of a typhoon sometime in the next day or two. At that moment, Mitag (as the storm had been named) was sitting about a hundred miles away, lurking and picking up strength. With luck, the weather service reported, it would miss us, but its westward path meant it would likely batter the lower islands.

I eased open the front door, which was then caught by the wind and yanked from my hand. The water catchment tank from the roof of the carport lay crumpled on the lawn at the foot of my stairs amidst a giant puddle. The little remaining water that poured out of it was turning to spray in the wind. I wasn't about to climb up on the carport to assess the damage caused when the tank tore away, but I knew with a quick glance it was going to exceed my monthly maintenance budget. I made a mental note to add one more item to a long list of problems I didn't need at that moment.

*

Going back inside, I noticed it was already eleven. *Geez, that was a tough night... I really overslept.* I also noticed my telephone message light was blinking. That was not unusual. Sometimes it blinked for days before I picked up. There were a variety of ways to get in touch with me, with mixed levels of reliability. Some of that could be credited to the intermittent availability of Palauan communications. Of course, I had the cell phone, with which I had a fairly poor relationship. I didn't really like the prospect of being interrupted anytime, anywhere. Besides, service areas were spotty enough that "anywhere" was a joke; it always seemed that when I actually wanted to make a call, I was in a dead zone. And the whole charging thing was incompatible with the way I lived life. I tended to drop my knapsack at the dive shop counter and head to the deck, as I wasn't programmed to unpack and hook the phone up to a plug. My dad on the other hand seemed to have seamlessly integrated every new aspect of technology into his life. He had attempted to contrive ways to keep my phone charged but had generally failed.

Most people in the know contacted me through work. We had a good Internet connection, and someone almost always answered the phone during work hours. Otherwise, we had an answering machine that somebody would check at least once each day. If a message came in, I usually got it quickly. Whether I would answer it quickly was a crapshoot, but you can ask only so much from technology. The other choice was my home landline, which went to an answering machine. I eventually listened to those messages. Emphasis on "eventually".

That message machine was showing two new messages. The first, with the familiar Hawai'i area code, was from Dad. The second was from Ruluked. I saved the first message. Before I had a chance to listen to the second, my phone began to ring. Unused to it ringing while I stood next to it, it took me a minute to realize it had nothing to do with my messages. I was also unused to answering, but given the past twenty-four hours, I reluctantly picked up.

"Hello?"

"Ricky, this is Ruluked. Is that really you? Answering a phone? Will wonders never cease? Woman, I don't know how you managed to do it, but that pit bull

Stephaliza Rengulbai is on your case and that can only mean trouble."

"Who the hell is this woman?" I asked, a bit too stridently. "I've never even met her."

"Well, you might as well have peed in her cornflakes because she certainly seems to know you. She came strutting into our offices today with one of those smug, self-satisfied smiles, and a fancy coffee from the take-out place that sells five-dollar cups to tourists. She was yacking about how her big story had a prime spot on page three. And how the editor had held the press until 3:00 p.m. And she was dropping names of this anchor man and that radio personality. I wanted to puke."

"What's her deal? Why is she doing this?"

"Stephaliza only knows one style, and that's grab hold and don't let go. I know her from back at the university." Ruluked had, by virtue of a scholarship, gone to the University of Guam. "She joined the soccer team my senior year. I was assigned to be her mentor. Not a highlight of my college career. She was a sight. Not good enough to start but the coach would put her in sometimes near the end of the game. Seemed like every time she got in, she either stole the ball, got red-carded for penalties, or went down with an injury. I heard she tore up her knee her sophomore year and had to give up the game. But she's tenacious, Ricky, tenacious."

"I've noticed."

"She's been parked on page nine of the paper forever, writing the weather and that police log section. Every few days she comes sniffing around the office for a tip, reminding me of our "good times" back at the U, but usually doesn't get anything. Definitely not from me. No sir. I hear she's been quite friendly with the holiday gifts, if you get my drift. Now, with her newfound celebrity, people's lips may start loosening up a bit. That can never be good."

"Was there something else? I hate to cut this short, but I'm running late."

"Yeah, I know. I called the shop and they told me they were expecting you in soon. No, that's it. I just wanted to warn you. You do not want Stephie on your tail. You may want to just give in and tell her what you know. It's just a thought. Or you could tell me and I could leak it. You know, 'unnamed sources in the government'? I'd do that for you. It's not healthy to keep secrets."

"I'm not sure I can do anything like that. I've been told not to talk. But thanks for the warning."

I hung up. Ruluked had spent too much time among the politicos. She was wrong about this one. Quid pro quo would not work in this situation. All I wanted was to go back to the way things were before I ran into my two bachelor buddies, but that couldn't happen if the local media kept pulling back the sheets. And I sort of resented that she was pushing me for information—I wasn't holding anything back. I closed my eyes and tried some deep cleansing breathing, but I couldn't get my mind off that Stephaliza woman.

The *Island Times* used to only be the primary source for local items, want ads, and the big world news items. Readership of the print version had plummeted as customers began getting reliable Internet connections. CNN. CBS. Google. The *New York Daily News*. This was the new competition. An afternoon daily no longer provided the timely information the local populace needed. The paper had introduced a new format and added online publishing in the past year. Each morning at six, they published the online version. This was the news that couldn't wait. World news. Breaking stories. "Blood, lust, and noise," as their new editor put it in one of her editorials. Dmitri was a big fan. He usually went online as soon as he got to the front counter.

The afternoon printed edition, which was better suited to my schedule and temperament, had become the resting place for news that might be of interest but didn't need immediate attention. Petty crime and weather were always favored topics of the locals but not the stuff of true journalism. Apparently, those low-brow topics had been Stephaliza's domain. As best I could tell, I had become her ticket to the big time.

Crud. I lay down on the couch and considered the sorry state of my affairs.

By the time I completed the inventory of how badly my day had turned out, it was almost noon. We'd cancelled diving for the day, but I had left unwashed gear—gear that had been in close proximity to two corpses—in the shop. I made a note to myself to tell the bosses we should get a new spotlight. I was not touching the last one. I pulled on a pair of running shorts and a fairly unwrinkled purple blouse, then ran out the door and into my Jeep.

Geez, I'm going to have to hose this thing or leave the top down during the typhoon. Where's the smell coming from?

17

NOON – KOROR AND NGERKEBESANG ISLANDS

THE ROADS WERE fairly empty, other than the leaves, branches, trash, and a solitary lawn gnome that blew across my path. Most people seemed to have the good sense to stay inside. Although they were rare, some bad typhoons had hit the island in the past, and fortunately, most people do learn. I'd heard the water surge could be far worse than the winds. Sitting as low to the water as Koror did, I understood why people were heading for higher ground. Even downtown was quiet—I ran into almost no delays. Because my Jeep was a bit on the light side, I had to muscle the steering wheel to keep on track. There were times I wished I had a real Jeep and not a flimsy wannabe with the name and logo painted on. Others seemed able to navigate through the wind as well. Judging by the number of cars parked in front of the local bars, it seemed the locals, including the fishermen, were taking the day off.

I got to the shop and stopped in front. For good

measure, I checked the small boats that had been trailered. Whoever had done it, Justin probably, had taken the care to chain the trailers to the concrete car stops in front and had put a number of sandbags inside the boats as ballast. I walked around each, checking the chains, tarps, and ropes. The tarps rippled in the wind, but they seemed ready to ride out the storm.

Driving around back, I parked and went to check the big cabin cruiser. It had been acquired before I arrived for handling large groups. Though we didn't use it much, we often rented it out to other operations that needed replacements while theirs were out of commission. It was actually quite lucrative, and the bosses didn't seem to mind that we didn't fill it with customers—that's not why they bought into the business.

The boat seemed secure. Justin had used standard storm protocol—extra lines in case the primaries failed, some slack but not much, all windows covered. He had even removed loose equipment and stored it inside the working area. But he'd also missed a lot. I spent the better part of an hour checking lines, duct-taping vents and exhaust pipes, draping additional fenders, and sealing doors. I probably could have done more, but that seemed sufficient.

Justin was getting sloppy. The gear problems were as much my fault as his, but he knew better than to leave vents and ducts open.

The prior evening, Sarah had explained her typhoon readiness preparations: she had printed out all the insurance coverage details, in triplicate, and secured them in various safes on- and off-site. "Done. Ready. Bring on the storm." Each of us contributes in our own way.

*

Ours was the longest of the docks in our section of the island, extended to eighty feet to handle our "fleet" of the small speedboat, two thirty-foot open boats, and our cabin boat, used for the more complicated technical dives and, more often, for VIP trips. I suspected that my inclusion on the advisory board for our national shark preservation organization came less because of my grassroots activities and more because of my access to a large boat on which we could hold get-togethers. Our neighboring properties gave their smaller, sixty-foot docks fairly constant use. The neighbor immediately to the southwest of us was a fishing and kayaking service. They ran a few boats, either rigged for deep-sea fishing (but no longer for sharks) or with a rack of kayaks destined for cruising about the blue waters and white beaches of the Rock Islands. They did a modest amount of business, and once in a while we lost guests to them. Folks sometimes got nervous when we gave them their legal waiver and described the dive conditions. They would step outside to discuss it and never come back, opting for something that kept them on the surface. The neighbor seemed to have been equally diligent in securing their boats.

As an import-export business for ship and boat parts, the other neighbor was the only one using their warehouse for its original purpose. They supplied businesses throughout the islands, which was a captive market with limited options. For a businessman with the right contacts and limited competition, it was a seller's market. Big markup, banker's hours. They had no direct customer business that I had seen, though pleasure craft were occasionally tied up at the dock, so they were the perfect neighbors: no traffic, they didn't complain about noise or a mess in the parking lot, and they kept to themselves.

Their dock was packed. They must have invited friends to find safety in our little harbor. Sailboats, run-abouts, a small cabin cruiser. They were all jammed in—not a formula for successfully riding out a storm. And they definitely weren't rigged for big weather. I thought about warning the owners, but both shops were shut up tight. I left a note. It wasn't our responsibility, but their flying gear could become our problem.

Once inside our shop, I saw that all six of our out-board motors had been carted into the workshop on our custom wheeled stands. The smaller ones were manage-able by anyone in the shop but the four massive 250 horsepower models, weighed five hundred pounds each and really had to muscled around. I questioned how much thought had been given to this decision. Clearly in a hurry, Justin, and whoever he had wrangled into helping, had placed them side by side right inside the entryway so that they now blocked access to one half of the workshop. They laid smack between me and the corner where I dumped all the gear from the day before. I decided I could get in there by climbing up on the shelves, or I could wheel the things outside and then back in when I was done. That would take time, though, and it was too much hassle to get the gear out and wash it.

Bailing on the washing, I unlocked the door from

the workshop to the retail area and let myself in. The place was closed and dark. If you're not running boats in Palau, you're not opening the doors. The amount of business looky-loos bring, buying T-shirts, hats, and postcards, just doesn't make it worthwhile. The bosses had obviously given Justin the day off, and Dmitri had either never shown up, or he'd left early. Someone had been there when Stephaliza called, but they were gone now, which also meant no one was answering the phones.

Despite my generally negative attitude toward phones and answering machines, I decided the responsible reaction was to check. Two calls. The first was from one of the sisters—Kate—who wanted us to know that if we decided to change our plans, both she and her sister were anxious to dive again. She left her phone number at their resort. And her room number. The message had probably been left about two minutes after they got back to their hotel. As I said, blind optimist. But I dutifully texted the message on to Justin just in case he was feeling particularly bored. The second call was from the other sister, Karen. She just wanted to make sure we had the right room number. The number she gave was different from the one Kate left. *Sheesh.*

*

Dealing with the company phone reminded me I should locate my own.

My knapsack was sitting under the display case in the same place I left it days earlier. It seemed like it had been a week—a lot had happened in the past forty-eight hours. I emptied the bag out on the counter near the cash register with a flourish that would have been impressive if anyone had been there to see it.

Cell phone, check. Charger? It was a pretty fancy cell phone, one of those Apple iThings. My dad had given it to me when he visited me a few years ago. He did all the setup so, as he said, "All you have to do is keep it charged, and answer it." I guess he set the bar a bit high for me. I found the charging cord, which could work off a computer or an outlet, further reducing any argument I might have for not being able to charge it. In fact, he had given me four charging cables so I could keep one at the office, one at home, one in my knapsack, and one designed to work off the cigarette lighter for my Jeep. That lighter hadn't worked in years, but I didn't feel the need to point this out to Dad.

I plugged it in, and the picture of a battery came up... showing a red bar. I had almost been surprised it hadn't been programmed to say, "Ricky, what did I tell you?"

It isn't that I don't like technology—I really do. I love working on the computer, and even had a hand in creating some of the handouts and signs for POS. But over the years I've become accustomed to the solitude of diving. Even when others are around, floating within a few body lengths, intrusions are fairly subdued. People move more slowly, sound doesn't travel as far and is quickly muted, and even the occasional collisions are buffered and gentle.

Cell phones, on the other hand, are intrusive and overly complex. They long ago ceased to be phones. Now they are calendars and direction givers and food advisors. They have all sorts of settings—and God forbid you press the wrong button. Worst of all, though, they're demanding. They demand that you constantly feed them. They keep demanding to be updated. Their irritating bells and buzzes demand that you pay attention to missed calls, batteries in need of charging, and appointments you had a year ago. That last one might be the result of operator error.

The battery picture on my phone switched to green, and a notice popped up indicating I had messages and missed calls. I had twenty-two messages. Scanning them, I decided most were so old they probably no longer mattered.

Several from Sarah. Based on the receipt time, those were left when I was out hunting for bodies.

Seven from an unknown number.

Two from Pascal. Probably apologizing for missing the bodies. Those could wait.

One from the library. I was sure I returned that book. *They'll find it if I just keep ignoring their calls.*

I looked back at the call log. The last one had been at one this morning from my unknown caller. This could be a telemarketer. Worse yet, someone I owed money. Even worse, an ex-boyfriend thinking that maybe I'd changed my mind. What the heck, I wouldn't know unless I checked. Another coin-toss decision. I pulled a one-dollar coin from the till and gave it a flip. Heads—listen to the messages.

"Hello, my name is Stephaliza Rengulbai and I'm the senior crime correspondent, online and print, for the *Island Times.*" *Correspondent? Another new title? She was rocketing up the org chart.* "I'm working on a story regarding the murder of Masaru Ishikawa and his associate Riku Koga. My sources indicate you are the primary witness to the murders. I am calling to request confirmation before we go online with the morning edition. I apologize for the late call, but I've tried your cell number several times and get no answer. Please call me at..."

At the same moment I hung up, someone rapped on the front door. The glass door. I looked up to see a short, stout local woman waving at me and holding up a laminated badge she wore around her neck. It read "PRESS."

Crap.

*

I was trapped. She had seen me. She knew I had seen her. I went to the door and yelled, "I have no comment. Please leave me alone." She held up the laminate again, as if it were some powerful shamanic talisman that would compel me to open the door. "I've got nothing for you. Write the story without me."

She smiled. An arrogant, troubling smile. "I already did. It's online. I just wanted to see if you had any comment." I did. It involved my middle finger. She shrugged and walked back to her car, a relatively modern, unblemished American sedan. I waited until she pulled away, then I did what I should have done in the first place.

I ran.

*

As I dashed into the small back office, I swept past Ralph, who squawked in recognition, "Ricky's in the bathroom. Ricky's in the bathroom."

This fine display of language skills was a gift from one of our previous owners, a particularly bored, playful soul who spent the majority of his stay on the island scheming up ways to embarrass me. Quickly latching onto my well-earned reputation for an active bladder—hey, I like to stay hydrated... what's the crime in that?—he strenuously argued, with a puckish gleam in his eye, that Ralph's new catchphrase would preserve my feminine pride, lest someone inadvertently enter the bathroom while I was in it.

Having been lavished with praise whenever he issued this report, Ralph eagerly awaited my departure through the rear hallway. It mattered not whether I was going into the office, the workshop, or actually going into the bathroom, Ralph was always happy to be the town crier. In fact, there was no way of knowing which room I was heading for. They were all connected to the same hall. If you went straight, you went into the workshop, turned left you were in the office, and if you turned right, you were in the bathroom. The fact that most everyone in earshot laughed and smiled only further cemented in Ralph's tiny brain that this was a trick to be performed whenever possible.

Sitting down at the office computer, I pressed the power button. As I waited an eternity for the piece of crap to power up, I checked the rest of my messages. I made a mental note to call Sarah as soon as I was done with this.

Glancing at the computer, I realized it was not doing any of its normal chugging or whirring. *No blinking lights.* Nothing. I pressed the rocker switch on the power bar. *No light there either.* The office lights were on, so we had power.

It eventually dawned on me that the power strip was unplugged. Sarah was a bit anal about storms and power plugs. Something about an exploding TV set when she was a child. She would have unplugged the power strip in case of a power surge. The wall outlet was behind the desk, which was wedged up against the wall, and you had to really maneuver to get the plug in. The chair scraped across the floor as I pulled it away. Liberal use of marine grease and some TLC had repaired four of the five wheels on the relic, but the fifth only moved begrudgingly. Shoving it aside, which was a challenge in the six-by-eight confines of the office, I crawled under the desk. This was one place where my freakishly small hands really came in handy. After a minute of angling and wiggling the plug, the prongs slid in.

I hit the power button again, and all the appropriate blinking lights and whirring sounds began. Once the computer was warmed up and the screen had loaded, I pulled up a browser, searched for the online version of *Island Times*, and clicked on the link for the most recent edition. Two stories occupied the entire page. The first screamed, "Typhoon Mitag Coming Ashore." The second bellowed, in identically large print, "Local Expat Eyewitness to Murder." The byline for both was none other than Senior Crime and Weather Correspondent Stephaliza Rengulbai.

Despite the urgency of a typhoon hitting our island, I went immediately to the other article:

> Ministry of Justice sources today identified local dive guide Ricky Yamamoto as the sole known witness to the ruthless gangland slayings of Masaru Ishikawa, and his associate, Riku Koga. Authorities investigating the murders believe that Yamamoto, a resident of Airai and an employee of Palau Oceanic Scuba, may hold the key to the crime. According to sources, further interviews will be conducted when American law enforcement, including the FBI, arrives on the island. Ishikawa has been a longtime target of the United States Justice Department, dating back to prior his June 1986 arrest in a sting operation jointly run between FBI and Palau Ministry of Justice operatives. Yamamoto did not respond to repeated requests for comment.

Holy crap. Holy crap. That bitch. How could this possibly get worse?

*

While I was cursing at the screen, my cell phone rang, playing the *Star Trek* theme. It was Dad.

"Hello?"

"Finally. Don't you ever charge that thing? I left you extra cords."

"I know, but reception's bad. I don't stay in any one place long enough to charge it. And it doesn't work underwater, but I do." I blushed a bit, but not much. I was only slightly embarrassed by my infamously poor phone maintenance skills.

"A reporter from the *Island Times* called."

God, I hate her.

"She says you're mixed up in a prostitution ring—I think that's what she said. I was at the beach, so it was hard to hear. I'm over on the north shore with Falstaff and Waxer. We're getting some great waves. Something about a storm down your way. Do you need money?" Two things I could say for Dad: he was seldom judgmental and always practical.

"I'm not mixed up in prostitution, that damn storm shut down our diving, and I don't need money. I found two freaking corpses on a dive, that's all. Well, one corpse and one who was quickly on his way to becoming a corpse. The FBI says they're mobsters from Japan who ran a lot of the gambling in Palau and dabbled in prostitution. I think the prostitution was more of a hobby. But it's the FBI, so what do they know?" I knew as soon as I said it, I had taken the discussion in the wrong direction.

"Be respectful. Remember last time. These are people you want on your side. Like their poster says, they can be most helpful when you help them help you."

I knew it! They're programmed to repeat company mottos.

"And," he continued with his nag, "if you kept your phone charged, you could have told me that and I wouldn't have to hear about it from a stranger. She had a nice voice. Is she cute?"

"Cute? This woman is making my life miserable. She published a story saying I'm the key witness. That I saw the murders. And I do remember the last time. Very well, thank you. It seemed to me I was more right than they were."

"You were also wrong, and almost got yourself killed. And it sounds like what she's reporting is true. Good reporting. She's a bulldog, I like that in a journalist." He was good at deflecting. We'd never really recovered from that summer. Not me, for sure. Him, maybe. Definitely not "us."

"Great. I'll give her your address. Maybe we can get the Japanese mob to come visit you."

"You know I love yakuza movies. You saw the tattoo? That must be so cool."

Eye roll.

"Was there any other purpose for this call? I have a few other messages to return."

"Your mother says hello."

"Mom? Is she there? Again?"

"What can I say? She can't get enough of me."

"Oops, incoming call. Gotta run. Love you."

I disconnected before he could hear me wretch.

It was eerie. He always seemed to know when to reach me. Mom says he and I have a psychic connection.

*

My parents have a complicated relationship. Divorced for more than twenty years, they seem to have a common goal to drive me over the edge. It's a bond that doesn't weaken over time.

My relationship with them is equally complicated. It's no accident that I chose a profession that keeps thousands of miles of open sea between them and me. But that's not enough.

Take, for example, the last time I went to visit Dad.

I was passing through Hawai'i on my way to Palau, and arranged at the last minute to stop for a day. I decided I would make it a surprise and take him out for lunch. I found him at his front porch as he was locking the door. It seemed like perfect timing.

His reaction said otherwise.

"Wow... this is great. Stellar. Really cool. I'm... overjoyed to see you, but I had lunch plans and it's too late to change them, so if you don't mind... it may be a bit awkward, but you could join us."

Oh, no, I thought, *I'm the third wheel on a date.* I mustered my best nonchalant daughter voice and said, "No, of course not... I wouldn't mind, if you don't mind. I mean, I just popped in unannounced and all."

"No, no... as a matter of fact, it's long overdue. Let's go, loco moco for everyone. My treat."

Crud, I thought, *he's got a girlfriend... how did I miss this?* But at least I was getting a free lunch of loco moco, which can go a long way toward curing what ails you.

"Here she comes now."

Crap, MOM?

"Mom? Wh-wh..." I was stammering. I hadn't stammered since I was eight. "What are you doing here?"

"Oh, I just came over for a quick visit. Things were rather slow on the other coast and I thought I could use a little excitement."

"In Hilo?"

"Wherever your father goes, that's where the party is."

"You? Sumo? Together?"

"Honey, just because the marriage didn't work doesn't mean we had to stop sleeping with each other."

Mom shot Dad a look that suggested his interruption was unappreciated. His mimed hara-kiri self-disembowelment suggested he understood.

"How did I not know this?"

"I don't know, dear. We just thought you might find it confusing. You were always so easily upset by the evolution of our marriage. You liked consistency. And you have never seemed to embrace the spirit of our emotional growth as life partners. Like that time you locked yourself in your room for two days..."

I looked at my plate and sighed. Sitting before me was the perfect meal: chili, nice greasy smoky sausages, four slices of grilled spam, two eggs sunny-side up—the whole mess laid over a bed of rice and covered in gravy. Perhaps my favorite meal in the whole world, and suddenly, with this turn of events, I lost my appetite. *$4.99 down the drain.* I saw a guy at the next table eyeing my plate as if he might want seconds... I figured I could give it to him as we left.

Looking up, I said, "Locked myself in my room? You chased Sumo, naked, through my eighth birthday party with a ping pong paddle. How would you expect me to react?" They remembered me locking myself in my room. I remembered it as the day the stammering began. Took almost a year to get past it.

"See, you're already getting agitated. This is why we keep our sex life private from you. We're just fortunate you've never taken to web surfing. There are things out there in cyberspace you probably would not want to know or see."

"Oh, God, you don't post photos, do you?"

"Instagram, YouTube, Facebook... your father is quite an active source of content for the web. Of course, most of it is strictly professional."

"I have to keep my peeps up-to-date." Dad beamed then studied his plate of loco, seeming to be developing a plan of attack.

"Your peeps?"

"Dear, your father tweets."

"Yep, I tweet to my peeps," he said proudly. "More people follow my tweets than those of Howard Stern. Asteroids, space shuttle, Hubble pix, star sightings, new things... voices from outer space. It's an amazing tool. I think of something and within seconds I'm sharing my thoughts with the world."

"Unfiltered thoughts," said my mother with a playfully withering glance.

"Yes, well, there is that. But I've gotten much better. The character limit actually helps keep me under control. It's when I start going on and on that I get into trouble. Sometimes, though, it forces me to use comparative descriptions for the sake of brevity. And, you must admit, some of those nebulae do take on rather erotic forms."

I vowed at that moment to never get a Twitter account.

18

2:15 P.M. – PALAU OCEANIC SCUBA

AFTER THE CALL with Dad, I flipped the phone over so it couldn't nag me. I was wound tight, so I went outside to distract myself with one last attempt at destinking the Jeep. I forced the rag top closed and rolled down the windows to take advantage of the winds, which had to be pushing sixty miles an hour. I'd been through the interior three times, hosed down the floor mat (learning very quickly to keep the wind at my back), wiped the console, and scrubbed under the seat, but as soon as I rolled up the windows, the smell hit me again. It didn't just linger – it was more like it had taken up residence. I had no idea what to do next, except perhaps drive to a cliff in Ngarchelong in the far north and give it a good push. Of course, Stephaliza would probably be there with camera and notepad to get the scoop: "Plastered Expat Pollutes Palauan Waters." Until then, I'd just let Mitag give it a once over.

I had options about what to do next. I considered

completely blowing off anything to do with the bodies, by working on balancing the store's books. But that would be irresponsible and I sucked at accounting. Then I thought about finally dealing with the dive gear in back that needed cleaning, and though I had been the last one to use it, I didn't think spending the time elbow-deep in an aromatic blend of salt water, cleanser, and whatever microscopic critters had hitched a ride with me to the surface was the right way to prepare for a meeting back at police headquarters. Besides, it was still blocked with the engines. No matter what options I considered, it kept coming back to talking to Mac. I also had to find out how that reporter got my name. As it was, I was going to spend too much time in a smelly Jeep, picking up a bit of the essence. I would get to the gear later. I'd leave the accounting to someone else.

But I wasn't ready to talk to Uchel, so I decided to kill some time by taking a few minutes to catch up on the news, rationalizing there might be new information about the murders. Besides, the weather was getting worse, and it wouldn't hurt to know the forecasts. There hadn't been any typhoon warning sirens yet, but those would probably come in a matter of time. I certainly was not going to consult the *Island Times* or the radio. *No and no.* The last thing I needed was more Stephaliza. I'd been away from the shop's computer long enough that the security settings Sarah insisted upon had logged me out, so I logged in again and opened the CNN website. Thank goodness for current news. This was far better than watching the soaps. Corporate greed. Celebrity meltdowns. Political warfare. I clicked on the World

News page and then the Micronesia section, and there it sat, like a steaming pile of donkey dung. She was going global with her story:

> **Pacific Isle Paradise Pursues Gangster Probe**
>
> The idyllic Pacific paradise of Palau was rocked this week by reports of at least two gang-land-style murders. Stephaliza Rengulbai, Crime Editor, Online and Print, for the *Island Times*, and CNN contributor, reports that...

Editor? Another day, another promotion. But the article was just a rehash of what she had written for the *Island Times*. I closed the window. I was running out of reasons for putting off my discussion with Mac.

I reached for my phone figuring I might as well take all my lumps at once. Four messages from Sarah, the most recent one coming in a half hour earlier. *Do I have my ringer on?* I wondered. I pressed "play."

"Rick, omigosh, your name's in the newspaper. And our name too. This could be great for business. Thank you. How can we work this into our website? Call me."

I fat-fingered the screen. Instead of deleting the message, I accidentally hit call back. I realized too late what I had done as Sarah answered on the first ring. Who are these people who answer their phones like that? Do they just wait, staring at the phone, chanting, "Ring, ring, please patron saint of the cell phone, make my phone ring"?

"Rick. Omigosh, you're a celebrity. That rocks," she gushed, "Everyone in the court is asking about it. This is so much cooler than any of the stuff that gets handled around here. This will put us on the map."

"Sarah."

"I got a call from CNN. CNN Micronesia, but still it's CNN."

"Sarah."

"Should we update our website? Crime scene management? Investigation support?"

"SARAH. Stop. This does not rock. This is not cool. There's a killer out there and he knows my name and where I work. And the yakuza are involved. I'm kind of freaked."

There was silence on the other end.

"Sarah?" More silence.

Finally, Sarah replied in a much more sedate manner. "I hadn't thought about that, Rick. That's horrible. You have to find the killer. Then we can update the website."

"No, Sarah. The police have to find him. I have to let them do their job. WE have to keep a low profile. YOU have to refuse to talk to CNN. I need to find out why my Jeep still smells like puke. And we all need to make sure the boats don't blow away in the storm. The waves are really kicking up here. They seem fine, and there's really nothing we can do if we get hit, but I'm going to shutter the windows before I leave."

"Rick? You sound a bit off. It's ok, I have the insurance covered. Do you think the killer's going to come after you? I mean, you're the key witness, and that reporter seems to think you may know more than you're saying. And they're sending in guys from Japan to clean up the mess. I remember a case in law school where years later somebody finally realized they'd seen the killer as they drove past the crime scene. Did you see anyone before you began your dive? This could be huge."

"NO. No one before my dive and nothing after. And yes, I was a little freaked. Now, thank you, I'm a lot freaked. I saw raining bodies. I'm in the middle of a yakuza gang war. There's a typhoon coming. And my boss thinks it rocks that I'm a key witness, and the entire world knows my name, where I work, and the general area in which I live."

"I rescind my rocking statement. This definitely does not rock. Do you want me to come stay with you?"

"Sarah, no offense, but you're five feet tall when standing on a Bible. The only good you could do if things go south is confuse them with legal mumbo jumbo."

"To the contrary! You've never seen me in a bar fight. I'm actually quite an asset."

"Sarah, go back to work. I have to talk to the police."

"Ok. And if CNN calls back, I'll just deny everything."

"Sarah, what did you tell them?"

"Almost nothing. Gotta go."

*

I really needed to talk to Mac. Someone was talking to the media, and now it was impacting my mental health. But a repetitive banging coming from the back had my attention. Heading past Ralph, who faithfully announced I was going to the bathroom, I returned to the workshop only to discover the outside door wide open and banging against the outside wall. The wind was more powerful than I thought, and I must not have closed it tight. I pulled it closed, bolted and padlocked it. I would have to leave through the front. I turned to go back into the store just in time to see a shadow darting toward the back of the workbench.

Shit.

I wasn't alone. I grabbed a rubber mallet, the first available tool I saw, and oriented myself. I was about ten feet from the door leading to the front of the store. It had a lock. If I could get in there, I could buy some time. *Maybe call Mac. Crap, this mallet won't do any good.* I threw it in the direction of the shadow and ran to the door. Before I could get there, the biggest damn rat I had ever seen scurried past my feet.

I hate rats.

I ran into the public space, slammed the door closed, and locked it. A rat. That was all it was. Probably just looking for a safe place to ride out the storm. I told myself to hold my imagination in check, but just in case, I went to our spear gun display and picked out a JBL Woody Sawed-Off Magnum. If I needed to shoot, I needed a compact spear gun with great accuracy. The Woody fit the bill. Good to about twenty feet, which was about half the distance from one side of the room to the other. I didn't think I would take anyone out, since I had never used one, but I would certainly scare the shit out of them and definitely slow them down. I thought about practicing on the rat, but I wasn't taking a chance of letting it into the public portion of the shop. For good measure, I grabbed one of our display dive knives and strapped it to my thigh.

I called Mac, who answered on the first ring. I realized this was a trait I appreciated in certain circumstances. "Miss Yamamoto," he said, as soon as he answered. It was oddly formal. I thought we were "Ricky" and "Mac."

"I've got you on speakerphone," he continued, "and in the room I've got Special Agent Ben Perez from the FBI. Your timing is great."

"M… Officer Uchel, this is not great. Nothing about this is great. My name is plastered on the Internet and the killer is still on the loose. And there's a yakuza convention forming here."

"Miss Yamamoto, Ricky… calm down. Where are you?"

"The office—just getting ready to leave."

"I'm sending a police cruiser to pick you up. We need to talk to you at the station."

"I can drive. I'm fine."

"Ok, but head out right now. The cruiser will leave in just a minute, so it's likely to intercept you before you get here. Let them escort you back to the station. I'll tell them to look for your Suzuki. No speeding."

Jeez, speeding? Does he just keep my file open on his desk?

"Got it. I'll be out of here in two minutes. And it's a Jeep."

I hung up and turned to go, bumping into something—or someone—as I did. I jumped back and fell on my ass. It was a *someone*, and he was between me and the front door. In the darkened shop all I could see was his silhouette. He was big. Giant, from my perspective on the floor. I grabbed for the spear gun on the counter, and he grabbed for my wrist. We both reached our target at the same moment.

"Whoa there, cowgirl. You don't want to be poking me with that." It was Ryan.

"I could have shot you."

"I doubt it. I saw the spear gun when I came in. I was ready in case you got spooked. On the other hand, I didn't know you had that knife." I hadn't even been aware of the blade in my hand until he mentioned it—instincts again. "Sorry to have scared you like that. I didn't want to interrupt your conversation... it was the police, right? Why can't they just do their job and leave you out of it? I swear, they're desperate. You've told them everything you know, haven't you? Rule one: don't withhold information. That could have saved some of my clients significant jail time. You've been helping, right?" His right eyebrow rose as if to form a question mark while he grabbed my arm and pulled me to my feet. "Maybe you should get a lawyer. Want me to hook you up?"

Having been around the island for quite a while, Ryan had seen more of the upside and the downside of island life than most. A former military attorney from the Judge Advocate General's Corps, Ryan had retired after twenty years in the service. Instead of going corporate or becoming a sole practitioner, he decided to stay in the area and settle down in Palau working as a staff attorney for the government. He handled landlord/tenant and domestic disputes, employment law... immigration. Simple stuff.

After all those years in the military, I think he was looking for a bit of a respite. That was twelve years ago, and not much had changed. Despite his military accomplishments, ambition and kowtowing to the authorities didn't seem to be his strong suit. He did seem to favor regimentation, however. He wore a tie and dress shirt to work, which no one else did, and he could probably still pass the military physical. He had a flat stomach, a straight back, and a firm grip. For him, the dive shop had always been more of an investment than an excuse for diving. I had seen less and less of him over the past few years.

I smelled the aroma of an old, familiar friend and looked around the room, finally spying a four-pack of the high-end coffees over on the counter by the door. Ryan sometimes liked to treat, and we never pointed out that the coffee was tepid by the time it got to the office. "Did you bring those? You can definitely hook me up with one of them." I was running on adrenaline, but somehow a coffee buzz sounded good.

Tracking the movement of my eyes, he finally let go of my arm and retrieved two of the cups. "I guessed the team might need a pick-me-up. I didn't count on them all being AWOL," he said, glancing around the empty store. "So, what's up with you?"

"If you've read the paper, you know most of it. It's not good, and that's why I need to skedaddle. Can you lock up?"

"Sure, that's why I'm down here, just looking after my investment." Handing me the coffee, he said, "Extra sugar, right? Mind if I put away your spear gun?"

"Actually," I said, "I think I'll take it with me."

"Ok," Ryan said with an indulging smile and a sigh of resignation, as if I were a child with a security blanket, "but next time, in case it really is a bad guy, have the bands ready. We may teach that you don't load above the surface, but you need to know when to bend the rules and when to break them. And no taking the coffee. I've seen your one- and no-handed driving technique and it scares the crap out of me. Drink up." I gulped down the coffee, thankful this time for the barely warm temperature. Ryan began puttering around, cleaning up after the various messes we'd left behind. He used a wet wipe on a coffee cup ring while Ralph the parrot watched—probably supervising.

"Gotcha. Thanks."

As I drove out of the back parking lot and past the shop, I saw him looking out the glass door at me. I had never really appreciated his paternalistic attitude, but that sort of thing came out in these situations. It was good to know he had my back. I was starting to think his idea of getting a lawyer might be a good one.

*

There are essentially three roads on Ngerkebesang Island: one runs the length of the island, and two branch off from it. The lengthwise road leads to the bridge. Once you get into town, there's really only one route to take to the police station. If the police cruiser wanted to intercept me, it wouldn't be difficult.

Normally there's very little traffic on the road, and from our location, even less. With the storm coming, I expected almost none. Most hotels had suspended shuttle services for the duration.

As I left the store, I noticed the winds had died. That wasn't a good sign. That old cliché about the calm before the storm often holds true. The big storm of 1967, according to the old-timers who seemed to dredge up the story every time the wind blew, went from winds of something like ten miles per hour to sixty in three hours. Within another hour they were eighty-five. And then things got bad.

With my attention primarily focused on the road ahead to make sure a tree didn't decide to jump out in front of my car, I noticed only one other car after I passed the marina. I initially thought it was Ryan's, but he drove a nice—albeit old—Range Rover. This was one of the local Japanese economy models with more rust than paint. The guy came up on me fast and seemed to be in a hurry, so I slowed to let him pass. As he swung beside me, though, I realized I had misinterpreted the situation. The driver had a scarf wrapped around his face so only his eyes showed. As this was registering, I saw him jerk the steering wheel to the right. I had no time to prevent the collision. My Jeep shook as his car ground against me. To my right was a culvert with no shoulder. Ahead was a light post. I had nowhere to go. And then he swerved back away from me. *Did he flinch? What a freaking chicken.*

I hit my brakes like I was trying to push the pedal through the floorboard. Half the maneuver worked perfectly: he shot past me, but my Jeep started to slide, the back end coming around left. I tried to correct but overreacted, and I shot across the lane toward the other side of the road and the rocks that lined it. I turned hard right—again, way too much—and the Jeep began to slide sideways. I felt a rollover coming but, surprisingly, stayed upright. We—the Jeep and I—were still sideways when the passenger side wheels came off the ground. I tried steering to the left, but we slid like a drunken tortoise for what seemed like a lifetime and a half before the tires dropped down and I shot into the culvert. Tree branches slapped at the hood and windshield, turning it into a series of spiderwebs. I heard the undercarriage of the Jeep grinding on the edge as my hands gripped the wheel. The smell of hot oil and powdered concrete rose in my nose as the Jeep ground to a stop. A wisp of smoke rose up through my open window.

When the world stopped rocking, I sat askew in my seat, taking stock. My arms and legs seemed to work. I didn't appear to be bleeding. I could see and hear. At that moment, the concept that someone may have just tried to murder me didn't come close to registering. But then, as I stared out my shattered windshield, I saw the other car had stopped about a hundred feet ahead of me and reversed. It was coming back in my direction. I slammed the Jeep into gear, but the wheels just spun. I was grounded. Stuck. Nowhere to go—at least nowhere the Jeep could take me.

I pushed on the door, but it wouldn't budge. The force of the crash must have wedged it shut. My spear gun was leaning against the door on the passenger side. I tried to stretch for it but couldn't reach it. I was still belted in. As I grabbed my seat-belt release, I looked up to see the piece of shit had stopped his car not twenty feet from me. Before I could consider my options, the car lurched forward, down the road, and away. A few seconds later I saw the police cruiser pull to a sliding stop. *Good timing.* Great timing would have been getting there about thirty seconds earlier.

*

The cruiser came to a halt in the lane closest to my Jeep but facing the wrong direction for traffic—not that there was any. The officers jumped out, and even though I tried pointing them in the direction of the fleeing piece of shit in his piece-of-shit car, they were clearly only concerned with my immediate wellbeing. It appeared my guardian angel Uchel had made their task simple and unambiguous. After forcing me to lie down, they got on the line to the hospital.

No way. I did not need this drama. I was fine. I kicked and yelled like a banshee until they both stopped and mutely stared at me. I was sure I was a fine sight. I tried to calm down and explained that I was an EMT trained in Hawai'i. I knew the typical injuries and symptoms to look for: I did not have a concussion or whiplash or a herniated disk. I had no internal bleeding. My tires had blown, and my Jeep was beached high and dry on the culvert, but other than that, I figured we were both fine. The Jeep had a skid plate, and I had that Yamamoto blood coursing through my veins. We were both pretty impervious to serious damage.

"I'm fine," I protested, "so call off the ambulance and let's get to the police station." I did concede that they could call Uchel. After a brief exchange, they handed the radio to me. I quickly reassured him that the incompetence or lack of total commitment of the hit man, combined with my Evel Knievel driving skills, had led to a happy ending.

I handed the radio back to the officers, who did their best to set Uchel's mind at ease. It was clear that they now considered my safe arrival at the police station to be their sole mission in life. They shyly asked me to remove the knife that was still strapped to my leg. Then they eased me into the back of the cruiser, again inquiring about my health, before reversing and making a K-turn, taking me over the bridge into downtown Koror. Apparently, they were not fully at ease with the situation, nor convinced it was sufficiently under control, because they peppered me with questions the entire way. I believed that, had a divan chair been at their disposal, they would have carried me to the station.

On the way, I stretched a bit. Maybe I had tweaked a muscle or two in the crash, but I certainly wasn't going to show it once I entered Mac's office.

19

3:30 P.M. – KOROR POLICE STATION

THE TWO OFFICERS who met up with me on the road refused to leave my side until they delivered me directly to Mac. Instead of heading to his office, they stopped short and guided me into the fancy conference room. I shuffled in, still dazed from the crash. Mac sat near the door at one end of the table; FBI Agent Ben Perez sat at the far end in a pressed suit, his jacket still buttoned, a white Oxford shirt and a striped tie. Generic cologne. It all screamed FBI. He really needed to cut back on the styling gel on what hair he had left.

The officers transferred me to Uchel in a manner similar to the way we handed off Ishikawa and Koga—like a package. He dismissed them with a thank you and guided me to the other end of the table, where Perez had parked his briefcase and now stood leafing through a file folder.

Mac introduced me: key witness in the murder and body disposal and, since the attack on the road, it appeared I was also the target of a campaign to derail the investigation.

Mac introduced Perez by title only: FBI Special Agent with the Criminal Investigation Division (CID, because everyone needs more acronyms). Agent Perez added some detail. His job was, he said, almost robotically, "multi-jurisdictional investigations into organized crimes, public corruption, drugs, and sex slavery." He added, "At least, with regard to my interest in you, that is the relevant scope of my role."

Perez shook my hand. His grip was viselike, though unlike Mac's, his skin was soft. His fingernails were short and smooth, as if they'd been manicured. So far, he was like field agents I had met before, favoring image over performance. I hoped he would operate to a different standard. I didn't appreciate depending on the undependable.

"The FBI has offered their assistance," Uchel said, and I caught his emphasis on *assistance*. "They believe their experiences with the yakuza might help shed light on our investigation. Please consider Agent Perez a member of my team. But, before we begin, let's take care of those cuts."

*

I hadn't even noticed them before, but I'd gotten a split lip and a cut on my forehead during the crash. Miss Embry brought the medical supplies but merely slid them in my direction and then handed me a small makeup mirror. Pink, with seashells. I guessed it wasn't hers.

I cleaned myself up as best as I could, but Perez

insisted that Mac bring in a doctor to make sure the inside and outside of my head were ok. Mac put in the call. Then Perez invited me to sit, and they began to grill me.

I most definitely did not like the situation in which I found myself embedded, but I did find these two men, and the way they went about their jobs, fascinating. Uchel kept his inquiries to the details of the assault, but he seemed to also be concerned for my wellbeing. He asked very precise questions, took lots of notes, and often paused to ponder what I said. Perez spent most of his time staring at the ceiling, jumping in at random times with a line of questions, interrupting either one of us at will. He was neither invited to join in the questioning nor did he ask. This was the FBI I had come to know and loathe.

Likely in his late forties, Uchel was maybe five to ten years older than Perez and a few inches shorter (maybe an inch shorter than me), but he was built like he could play linebacker in college. He carried a few extra pounds to be sure, but nothing you would call fat. Perez looked like he had always been lanky and not particularly muscular, more like the captain of the debate team than the captain of the basketball team. He had a bit of a belly and some paunch, and he was showing more scalp than hair.

Uchel, whose broad face always seemed to be smiling, had dark hair, skin, and eyes and a mouth full of teeth. He might not grace the cover of *GQ*, but he had a face you could look forward to seeing. In the animal world, Uchel would be a bull, both in form and action.

Perez was getting a bit jowly and, if I had to compare him to another animal, he sort of looked like a donkey.

After getting as much detail from me as I could provide, which was very little, Perez closed his folder and put it back in his briefcase. Uchel got the not-so-subtle hint.

"Ricky," Detective Uchel said, after a short pause, "Agent Perez and I need to discuss a few details. Can you wait in my office? If you need anything, just go ask Mildred at the front desk." He smiled. I figured my odds of getting any cooperation from Mildred had improved with Mac's gentle scolding, but I didn't anticipate it had improved to the coffee-with-extra-sugar stage.

Leading me to his office next door, Uchel unlocked the door, sweeping his hand to suggest I had the run of the room. "Make yourself at home... and don't forget to ask Mildred if you need help." He smiled again.

*

I deposited myself in one of Mac's comfy chairs and pulled my knees up until I was tucked in. My stomach was gurgling, but I didn't have a plan for dealing with it. With nothing immediately obvious to entertain myself, I studied the walls and bookshelves, discovering I had missed one of the certificates: Detective MacArthur Uchel had been to Israel for "security training."

I had soon scoured the walls and resisted snooping in the "out" box, having already noted that the "in" box was again empty. As I sat in quiet contemplation, I noticed I could just barely make out Uchel and Perez's conversation through the wall. Uchel had a naturally deep, resonant voice, which vibrated through the drywall and plaster. Perez's was getting more demonstrative as the discussion progressed. Both raised their volume as the intensity increased.

At first, I tried not to listen, but with my head near the wall, it was difficult not to. When I pressed my ear against the wall, it was completely impossible. I didn't need to be in the same room to have a front-row seat.

Though I missed most of what they said, I heard enough. The argument seemed to center around jurisdiction, procedures, and a mutual disdain for each other's motivations. Apparently, the FBI had stepped all over the local inquiry, but had gotten results. I heard Perez reference some sort of toxin—a long name I didn't recognize—and the yakuza. Uchel was railing about the FBI and their lack of cooperation.

Uchel must have moved closer to where Perez was parked, nearer to our common wall, because the voices seemed calmer, but I could hear more of the conversation.

From the volume and rhetoric, it seemed the two had finally achieved some level of civility and were reviewing one or more reports. Mac was going on about Ishikawa and "signs of recent injections." Perez interrupted with some questions about a "cocktail of toxins" and seemed disdainful of the local coroner.

The two didn't stop jousting, however. It sounded like Mac believed Perez was using this case for career advancement and that the agent was withholding information. Mac seemed to have a simpler agenda. He didn't like people being killed on his turf, and he wanted the time, room, and resources to solve the case.

Apparently, the national police had searched Ishikawa's estate in the Mechang Lagoon area and come up relatively clean, with one major exception: steroids. Mac ran through a list of names I couldn't understand, but it sounded like he had quite a medicine chest.

*

His chair slid noisily on the conference room floor as Mac excused himself for a restroom break, although his phrasing was a bit indelicate. Shifting my position in the cushy chair away from where I had been pressed against the wall, I sat cross-legged with my head on one knee – just in case he came in to check on me. He didn't.

I needed a break as well. I began to unfold myself to stand, but I never got a chance – Perez opened the door and strode in. He was carrying his briefcase, which he laid on top of Mac's "in" box, before easing himself into the comfy chair next to mine. He grimaced. I guessed Palauan standards for office furniture, like their policies and processes, didn't match the FBI's.

"So," he said, "you're a diver?" I nodded, unsure where this was going but assuming it wasn't just small talk. "Ever been to the Chicago Museum of Science and Industry?"

"No, I spent time in Michigan, but never made it to Chicago."

"I grew up in the suburbs. When I was a kid, we went to the museum. They've got an entire Nazi submarine in there... really, an entire submarine. You and me, we couldn't serve on submarine crews—too tall. How tall are you anyway? Five ten? Five eleven?"

"Yep, exactly."

"Surprisingly tall for your heritage, if you don't mind me saying."

"Yeah, it probably would be if my heritage were Japanese. I'm not one hundred percent. My mom's Swedish. I'm what you call a Hapa. Half and half."

He seemed to be trying to wrap his brain around that one. "I'm one hundred percent American. But both my parents were born in Mexico. Moved to Illinois and became citizens."

I eyed him cautiously. As best as I could tell, this was his way of making a connection. It wasn't working.

"Your friend, Pascal. What can you tell me about him?"

That was a turn I hadn't expected. What had Pascal done this time?

"Excellent diver. We hang out sometimes, but I can't tell you much about him other than diving—that's about all we talk about."

"Can you think of any reason he might not want to talk to us about the bodies? We've tried reaching him."

"He didn't find them. What else is there to say?"

"Your co-workers said you were angry when you heard he hadn't found the bodies. Was it unexpected?

They're talking to the bosses?

"I wasn't mad at him. I was mad at the circumstances. Why the interest in Pascal?

"He left last night on the last flight out. Destination appears to be Egypt."

"Well, that's the way we roll. He was always going to be a short-timer here, for sure. My guess is he found out about a job opening and jumped on it. You have to be opportunistic in this business."

"He called you. Twice. Care to share?"

Sigh.

"I have two messages from him. I didn't listen to them when I was in the shop."

"Shall we listen now?"

I had no idea if this was protected by some sort of law, but I had nothing to hide and was pretty sure Pascal didn't either, so I rooted around in my pack until I found the phone, which was still charged and despite the hard landing we had in the Jeep, seemed to be in operating condition.

I clicked on the first message—eight seconds long: "Ricky, it's Pascal, can you call back when you get this? It's important." Nothing more.

The second message was longer: "Ricky, it's Pascal. Sorry for leaving the message but I'm off for the airport. You know how I feel about police and groups like Interpol. Pretty much like you do—a bunch of liars and players. Palau is going to get too hot for my tastes. You know what they say—"Un malheur ne vient jamais seul"—misfortune never arrives alone. My friend Sasha says he can find me a job in Dahab, so I'm off. You should come. There's nothing here to keep you."

Mac appeared in the doorway, seeming amused by whatever part of the conversation he had caught. He slid past Perez and stepped over my now extended legs. Settling into his office chair, he seemed oblivious to its slight groan as he nodded at Perez, who didn't appear disposed to provide a recap of what Uchel missed. He looked my way.

"Dahab?"

"Egypt. Great tech diving. I would have jumped at the chance too." Except I wouldn't have. Not right now. Pascal was right, I did consider police, and the FBI, to be a haven for charlatans and con artists but I wouldn't bail in the middle of an investigation. Not that I wanted either Uchel or Perez to have heard that part.

"The man you call 'Bachelor #2,' the one whose demise you had a front-row seat for, was Ishikawa's right-hand man." Perez seemed willing to leave the whole Pascal issue behind, at least for the moment, as he tapped a large file he had just pulled from his briefcase. I was good with that. "A lower-level yakuza who followed him from Japan in 1986 and spent the last thirty years providing some degree of intimidation, and sometimes some gentle persuasion, but mainly serving as a flunky and runner for Ishikawa's modest enterprise." He handed me a photo. "Before yesterday, had you ever seen him?" I glanced at it and recognized him instantly, but had no recollection of ever seeing him before he showed up at Ricky's Rocking Spot. "Nope. Not that I remember."

He searched through the file for a moment, though when he spoke, he did so without looking at the page. "His paperwork identified him as Chobei Banzuiin, but that's probably an assumed name. The real Banzuiin was a revered Japanese Robin Hood of the seventeenth century. Seems like he was yanking our chain a bit with his phony passport. Our best information suggests his real name was Riku Koga."

"I've heard that name before," I said, before stopping to think about how I was just digging myself deeper into this mess. "That was the name the reporter from the *Island Times* used when she called me for confirmation."

The web was getting more complex, and I couldn't hear him over the chatter in my head. *How did she know this stuff so quickly? Is someone leaking information, like my address? How did the guy in the head wrap know I'd be on the road?* Unfortunately, I didn't trust Perez enough to raise the subject. It was déjà vu all over again.

"Ms. Yamamoto," said Perez, "I need you to pay attention." I straightened my back, assuming that would convey a greater sense of involvement on my part, and tried to shut down my inner dialog. "We're not sure what the situation is with the *Island Times*, but we are monitoring it. Until then, we're working up a plan to keep you out of harm's way."

Monitoring it. I slumped again. *Working on a plan.* My stomach churned again. *Harm's way.* I felt a belch coming on. I knew enough about the FBI to know I didn't know enough to trust them.

"Detective Uchel and I agree that you deserve a better understanding of what's going on. In return, we expect full candor on your part. I expect you will keep our information in absolute confidence. There are legal ramifications if you don't."

Criminy. I was being threatened by the good guys too. I should have just stayed in bed.

*

"Ricky," said Uchel, "solving this case is our number one priority and protecting you is the most important part of our plan. On the plus side, the attempt on your life was clearly amateurish. We're hoping whoever tried will now be scared off, but we'll prepare and act as if they're still a threat. And we'll find the leak. When we do, we'll close it and prosecute to the fullest. You have my word on that." The words seemed sincere, but my stomach was doing flips. The idea of moving to another locale was starting to make even more sense. Tahiti had good diving and no mafia. I would have to check to see if they had typhoons.

"We're still tying together the threads, but we expect," said Perez, "to close this out quickly."

"As Officer Uchel said, a lot of this seems amateurish. Koga's cause of death, as you no doubt surmised, was drowning. He had also suffered a blow to the head that appears to have taken place before he hit the water."

He continued, a precise cadence to his speech. "Koga's role was as both aide and minder—keep Ishikawa out of jail and out of the news. Are you sure you've never seen him before?"

Big fat F on Koga's part, I thought, managing to keep it to myself. "No, no, he's not at all familiar."

"He still had strong ties within the Japanese yakuza—maybe stronger than Ishikawa's. A good foot soldier, though he messed up at least twice. You saw the stubby fingers. That's the result of a yakuza ritual called *yubitsume*. It was likely self-inflicted as a form of repentance. You have to admire the yakuza for their sense of order and discipline." *No, frankly, I do not.* And I wasn't exactly comfortable with Perez thinking so. "But we're not sure they're involved in this. We've been keeping tabs on the yakuza situation here in Micronesia and have seen no evidence that they're escalating their activity. We're keeping the possibility on the table but hoping this is a local skirmish."

Despite their apparent calm, they also were clearly aware of the recent arrivals of two yakuza who had, Perez reported, headed directly to the coroner's office to inquire about Ishikawa. One presented paperwork indicating he was Ishikawa's nephew, here to return the body to Japan for burial at the earliest possible opportunity. He was told that the coroner was not prepared to release the body, which he took with what was described as "grim determination." Neither seemed interested in Koga. They parked themselves on a bench outside the coroner's office and sat. No one who saw them reported any conversation. They merely sat and stared at the door.

*

Koror is a small town. I could have guessed who they'd send, and she was not surprised to see me in need of stitches. Dr. Eden Tmetuchel had sutured me before, shortly after a festive-turned dangerous evening when another divemaster and I decided to try our hand at topiary. The experiment involved a borrowed speedboat, a chainsaw, a ladder, and a pint-sized island covered with foliage. The stability of a ladder lashed to a floating speedboat was the weak link in the equation. We retrieved the chainsaw from the water, but it never worked again. The ladder was none the worse for wear, but when we returned the speedboat, we discovered it had been missed. The boat owner declined to press charges after we paid a "rental" fee and filled it with gas, but the police refused to forget. On a small island, reputations have a life of their own. I ended up with a clean cut right at the hairline that required seven stitches, which served to remind me—and others—of my somewhat reckless past. Dr. Tmetuchel had the good graces during the visit not to mention that incident.

This time she worked on a nearly matching cut on the other side of my forehead and a cut lip. As she sewed, she talked—an endearing trait that only made me a bit nervous.

"You'll have some swelling and tenderness for a few days, longer for the lip. I would stick to liquids for the next twenty-four to forty-eight hours. Call tomorrow and make an appointment for five days from now so I can check the stitches. I can probably remove them then. No diving. I don't want to have to redo the stitches and treat you for an infection. If you behave yourself, the lip should heal with no visible scar, and that new scar on your forehead should make you appear more balanced."

"Mentally or physically?" I asked, though Eden and I had enough of a relationship, I was fairly sure she fully intended to leave that one hanging.

"I can give you some pills for the pain and a couple to help you sleep."

"No pills." Perez was quick to insert himself into the conversation. "We need her to be sharp in the morning."

Mac thanked her and counseled her, unnecessarily, on the need for absolute secrecy. As she left, she slipped me the pills.

*

Mac stood behind me and put his hands on my shoulders. I was sure he meant to be reassuring, but it only made me slump lower in my chair. He said, "Agent Perez and I agree that you require increased protection. We've ruled out the jail both for comfort and security reasons."

He was right. The Koror jail was infamous for breakouts. The walls were paper-thin, there were only two guards, and safety protocols were virtually nonexistent. Besides, I had been inside one of those cells, and I was taller than the bed was long.

"Agent Perez has arranged for a room at the Palasia, courtesy of the United States government. He's got an agent who will stay in an adjoining room, and we'll have uniformed officers watching your room around the clock. You should go get some rest. We may need to talk more in the morning."

He was right. It was not yet seven in the evening, but I was exhausted. Normally, the Palasia would not top my list of places to stay on someone else's dime, but it had several redeeming qualities. It was close by. It was away from the water. And it was built like it could withstand any storm Mother Nature could throw at it. Uchel spent some time going through the process for transferring me to the hotel and finally shrugged, as if to indicate there was nothing else. We stood to go.

Perez was standing in the doorway. I wasn't sure how long he had been there—he had left for a while to make some calls, and my powers of observation were at an all-time low.

"I've gotten some additional security measures in place. The agent on-site—her name is Nancy—will go into more details. What's important is you do what she says. It's probably overly cautious, but we don't want you going outside without an escort or eating meals that haven't been checked out. This is just a precaution and will likely last just a day or two, but as I said, we like to play it safe."

"Play it safe" was an understatement. After making some arrangements for the following day, Mac handed me a bag. He had someone from the force bring some clothes and essentials from home since Ben Franklin's was closed and my house was too far away. That was nice, although whoever supplied the clothes must have thought my hastily assembled combo of running shorts and slightly wrinkled purple blouse represented my standard taste. Inside the bag were two bright purple blouses and a pair of dress shorts. One of the blouses was enormous. If I actually filled that thing out, I would look like a giant grape with long arms and freakishly small hands. I started to put it back into the bag when Perez stopped me.

"Wait. It goes over this." He handed me a heavy black nylon vest.

"Bulletproof?"

"Reportedly."

It was the first time I'd heard him joke—at least I took it be an attempt at humor.

"Remember these are just precautions," Perez said, handing me a floppy hat in a style popular with the locals, usually to block the sun. In the middle of a storm, it just looked foolish.

All the camouflage seemed just a bit silly since I was

probably the tallest woman on the island by several inches and no disguise was going to hide THAT. But I did begin to worry that this seemed to be going beyond prudent behavior. *Did they know something I didn't?*

I dutifully donned the vest over my blouse and then covered myself up with the big purple muumuu blouse, pulling the hat on last. I felt like a dork. A giant purple dork standing under a neon "Pay no attention" sign. As we huddled before leaving the room, I noticed that, for the first time since I had met him, Uchel was wearing a holster and pistol.

20

4:30 P.M. – KOROR

At some point, Mac must have moved his SUV because I was escorted out a back door of the station and immediately into the back seat where I was told to lie down.

"Merely a precaution," was Mac's explanation. "Certainly no reason to worry." *Right.* Mac and Perez climbed in front, and two uniformed officers followed us in a cruiser. Mac tried to keep it light with small talk.

"By the way, I can get my brother-in-law to help with your wreck. He's got a truck and a shop—he'll give you a good price for replacing the tires and straightening anything that should be but isn't." At some point I should have told him his bedside manner needed some work. The mention of my Jeep just brought back vivid memories of the guy in the scarf. My only response was to burp.

Our destination was only a few blocks away, and with the empty streets, we arrived in only a couple minutes, even though the wind—now carrying horizontal sheets of water—made it rocky. We didn't pull up to the fancy entrance but went around to the rear loading dock instead. Mac and Perez, joined by the two uniformed officers, led me to a freight elevator and pushed the top button for the seventh floor. When it opened, we stepped in. One uniformed officer stayed behind at the loading dock, his hand on his holstered pistol.

When the freight elevator stopped at the seventh floor, the doors opened to reveal two more uniformed officers who joined Mac and Perez. The uni who had ridden up with me stayed behind at the elevator door where he reached inside and fiddled with the controls. I noticed that the elevator indicator lights that normally showed the floor number were now showing dashes. I guessed that meant the elevators were not in service. This was major security. This was like dignitary-level security.

We walked down the hall toward a room watched over by yet another uniformed officer. I was doing the math. Palau had around one hundred and eighty officers. They worked three shifts, so sixty officers worked each shift, not counting vacations. I now had at least five officers assigned to me—at least eight percent of the on-duty police force. I considered the possibility there might be more in the lobby and watching the stairs.

Sadly, my room was not the presidential suite, but it was nice. I assumed it had an ocean view, but the curtains were closed, and Perez told me to keep them that way. Judging by the rat-a-tat banging coming from outside and the lack of light coming from the window, I figured the curtains were just window dressing—plywood already covered all exposed glass. I suspected the room was picked for security and not to show me the striking horizon; storm preparations merely added to the bunker atmosphere. The room was basic—a bed, dresser, two chairs, a coffee table, and a floor lamp in the corner. The bed had been moved away from the window and into the far corner of the room. There was no phone.

Perez's other FBI agent was waiting for me. Her jacket said Fraser, and she was my height or a little bit taller, and probably carried thirty more pounds, little or none of it excess. Probably an extra-large if I was sizing her for a wetsuit. Her red hair was tied back but loose, and her freckled face was round but not flabby. She was broad-shouldered and big-boned. I might have put my money on her in a fistfight against Perez. She greeted me curtly and with reservation, but she invited me to call her Nancy. Then she pulled Perez aside for a quick chat followed by a survey of the room and hall. She moved with an efficiency of effort as she reviewed with Perez the plan for my visit.

"I need your signature. Standard protocol. It helps avoid finger-pointing when things go bad."

"You mean 'if', don't you?"

"You would be surprised how often it's a 'when' if local law enforcement insists on being involved."

Perez signed off on the checklist and dropped it on the table, then he signaled for Mac and me to join. Among his own, Perez—and Nancy by proxy—was clearly making sure there was no uncertainty about whose operation it was. Mac seemed quite put out by that posturing.

The protocol for me was simple: don't answer the

door, and keep it locked and chained, no outside phone calls, no texting, no e-mail. The bureau would notify my bosses and family with any specific messages. I could not indicate where I was or why I was there. Nancy would supply all my food and drink. Essentially, I was in prison with a queen-sized bed and down pillows.

Perez and Mac disappeared into Nancy's room and left us "girls" to chat. I was exhausted and ready for sleep, despite the early hour, although I kept thinking a pizza or burger would be nice. Of course, Ben's had battened down the hatches, and who knew when they would be operating again. I was tired and cranky. And a bit pissy.

"So, do you do this babysitting often?"

"Witness protection is one of our greatest responsibilities. The bureau trusts it to our best officers."

Ok, can we deviate a bit from the company script? "Do they always have women protect women?"

"This is a team exercise. I'm your point of contact, but there are a number of agents and local law enforcement officers tasked with your safety. Many of them are men. Is this going to be an issue?"

"Hey, how about some beer?"

"I'm not allowed to drink on duty."

"I assumed that—I was thinking for myself."

"I'll check with the national police officers. Do you have a preference?"

"A pitcher of draft. Red Rooster. It's the local brew. They have it downstairs."

"No draft and no bottles. They can be tampered with."

"Red Rooster comes in cans. They have it for sale down the street at WCTC, but they're probably closed. Closer to the police station is a Shell Station, I'll bet it's open. They have it. Six-pack, please."

"I'll see what I can do. Anything else?"

"Some spam and bread."

"Spam's ok. Bread isn't."

"Spam it is. Can I have a fork?"

"Sure. Spam and fork."

"And a six-pack of Red Rooster. From a cooler, if possible."

"Got it."

I wanted to check the storm progress, but plywood not only blocked any view, it also dampened the sound. That was the other thing... no TV or radio. *What the hell is that all about?* Nancy had picked up a pile of magazines on her way to the hotel, so when the scintillating conversation had run its course, I started thumbing through the latest copy of *Star Chaser*. It was nice to see that Brad Pitt was still sufficiently fit. He looked good sprinting away from the camera.

The food and drink arrived fairly promptly, the Spam slightly warm, the Red Rooster as cold as beer got in Palau. Mercifully, and surprisingly, the meat had not yet reached its "best by" date. I suspected this was a plum assignment for the uniformed officers, so they were eager to please. They might have picked up some treats and beer for themselves, if I knew the local constabulary (as Roland would say).

The Spam was greasy, and the chairs seemed to have new upholstery, so I sat on the floor with my back against the wall and forked the spicy meat straight out of the can. Nancy watched as I ate and drank. She may have been looking to see if I suddenly succumbed to a sinister poison, or that might simply have been the job she had been told to perform. I was rather pissed the bureau had removed my TV and radio. I was not in a good mood, but the Red Rooster helped. I tried to avoid thinking about why I was there.

*

While I ate, the door from my room to the hallway had been blocked off with still more plywood, and the dresser was pushed up against it. Nancy insisted we leave the door between our rooms open, which was probably bad news for her. I suspected agents assigned to babysitting detail were light sleepers, and since I was on my fourth beer, I was pretty sure I would snore up a storm.

She spent the next hour trying to pull more information from me with increasing frustration at what she characterized as a flippant attitude on my part. Fair enough. It was. The FBI had come in huffing and puffing, and the only progress made was me almost getting killed. Now they wanted me to do their work for them and I had nothing more to give.

She finally gave up and suggested I get some rest.

The reading lights were affixed to the wall where the bed had been, so I had no light with which to read. I pulled the floor lamp over beside the bed, and grabbed the latest issue of Star Chaser, so I could make sure I was up to speed on Mr. Pitt's latest alleged pratfalls and dalliances. I fell asleep sometime after sunset. The pills helped.

*

I woke up to sirens and—I swear—dogs howling. I was a bit disoriented. Ok, I was a lot disoriented. My watch told me it was just past midnight. A traffic jam of images packed my brain. The open mouth and begging eyes of Bachelor #2, Koga. The scarf guy jerking the steering wheel as he ran me off the road. Horrible flashbacks from long ago and a few thousand miles away. The accusing eyes of the parents who would never see their daughter—my best friend—again. I curled up as yet another wave of nausea washed over me. Storm warning sirens were blaring, and I couldn't understand why. I shuffled to the window. The plywood blocked my view, but I could feel the storm pounding away from outside. The sirens seemed redundant.

*

As the T Bone Burnett song goes, "When day breaks, I'm in pieces." The next time I woke up, I woke up slowly, and though still slightly drugged, the mash-up of memories hit me all over again. It was only after enduring a full-frontal assault of the images of the past few days that I began putting all the pieces together. The more I remembered, the more pissed I got.

The plywood on the window was still being pounded like a big bass drum, which dispelled any hope that the storm had come and gone quickly, but that bore little importance to my life. With no diving to be done, a general ban on activities that were even remotely interesting, and my FBI-enforced solitary confinement, I had nothing to occupy my mind other than the wreck of the past seventy-two hours. I was frustrated and definitely out of my comfort zone. I just wanted it all to go away. And I wanted people to stop judging me.

Nancy – Agent Fraser – was awake, dressed in her standard FBI garb and working on her laptop. Breakfast was already on the table: toast and fruit for her, two cans of breakfast supplement for me. I shuffled to a chair pulled near the table and lowered myself into it. She handed me a straw, which reminded me of my lip. I checked out my reflection in her bureau mirror. I looked like I lost a bar fight.

"So, what do we do?" I asked. I lacked direction but felt a need to do something.

"Sit," she replied without looking up. "Preferably quietly. Unless you have additional information you would like to share."

"Agreed. About the quietly part. I don't have any more information. Old car. Scarf wrapped around the face."

"That does not help move us forward."

"Understood, but I've got nothing."

"Then try harder. You would be surprised at how much data you take in every second of every day. Did you see his hands?"

"No, he was wearing gloves."

"Eyes. Any exposed skin above the scarf?"

"Wraparound sunnies. No visible skin. Couldn't tell if he was local, Japanese, or white. You want me to tap dance or something?" My previous dealings with the FBI had clearly left me with some unresolved frustration.

"We need to meet with Special Agent Perez and Detective Uchel around ten. I'm sure we would all appreciate it if you could approach the meeting in a professional manner."

"You can count on it."

"We're the bureau. We only count on ourselves. We approach everything else with skepticism."

"I'll try to earn your trust."

"Please do. You'll find we can be most helpful when you help us help you."

There was that saying again—I'm sure it was printed on a poster somewhere at the academy. Or maybe it was a Barbra Streisand lyric. My mother would know if it were the latter. Whatever, it was delivered robotically.

*

Mac and Perez arrived shortly after ten. Although unscarred, they both looked like their night had been tougher than mine. Neither appeared to have changed clothes, and Perez had a five o'clock shadow that was definitely not standard-issue FBI. They did not mention my injuries.

Agent Fraser had crafted a small meeting area in her room by assembling her chairs and one coffee table and appropriating the chairs from my still unusable room. It made for tight conditions, but it provided enough workspace for Mac and Perez to conduct a briefing and revisit my interrogation.

"Last night two additional incidents occurred that may be related to the Ishikawa case," said Perez, taking the lead. He made eye contact but, unlike Mac, at no point registered any reaction to my bandages.

"In the spirit of cooperation, I'm going to share some details," said Mac. "This is, of course, confidential. First was a firebombing of a local karaoke bar." He mentioned the name. I knew the bar and its reputation. The owners provided services to their clientele that extended beyond adult beverages. The women who provided these services had been brought to Palau from China, Taiwan, and the former Soviet Union with promises of jobs and opportunities, but their passports were taken, and they were forced into service as prostitutes. "We suspect Ishikawa may have had strained relations with the owner of this bar, and there may have been a turf war. Shortly after five yesterday afternoon, the owner of the bar received a telephone call advising her to evacuate everyone in the building immediately, which was packed with a private storm party. Fortunately, she took the call seriously. Shortly after she got the last drunk into his car, the bar burned to the ground. There were no injuries, but the building was a total loss." I guessed this was still a local matter, hence Mac's job to tell the story.

"Then," Mac went on, "at ten fifteen last night, an explosion destroyed a local tattoo parlor and parts of two adjoining buildings. The owner of the tattoo parlor was killed in the explosion. There was no advance warning, and at this time we have no link between this explosion and either the fire or the Ishikawa murder. Are you familiar with the bar or the parlor?"

"Nope. Never been. Never heard of them." I wasn't completely forthcoming, but I didn't know anything that they didn't already know. "I don't make it my business to snoop around the underbelly of Koror."

"Ricky," interrupted Perez, "I've spoken with the Honolulu office. I know you've got your own ideas about how we work, and I can't tell you that the agency hasn't had screw-ups in the past. But this isn't the same. We're going into this with an open mind. What we need you to do is work with us. Help us help you."

If I never hear those words again...

He continued talking, but I had stopped listening. Mac's comments had just registered, and my head was buzzing like a chainsaw. *Five last night? Around the time I ordered dinner. They suspected a gang war was spinning out of control, and they didn't tell me.* That meant they didn't trust me. Even worse, they thought I was a loose cannon. This was the Surf Slayer all over again with a new cast and an even more screwed-up script. That's why they took away my TV and radio. *Sons of bitches.* My ass was on the line, and they were keeping information from me. The bastards who tried to kill me—and succeeded in killing Koga and Ishikawa—were running rampant in Koror, and these guys were helpless to stop them.

"Assholes. What else haven't you told me?" I jabbed my finger at Perez but my eyes were shooting daggers at Uchel. I was sputtering. The spittle that hit his shirt was unintentional but satisfying.

"Ricky," said Mac, "it was a judgment call. We're taking every prudent precaution to protect you. Telling you would not have made you any safer but would have made you more nervous. You needed to rest. We didn't have sufficient details last night."

"Ms. Yamamoto," Perez jumped in, "it wasn't

Detective Uchel's call. This is a bureau investigation, and we followed protocol. You are a witness in protective custody. You may still have relevant information that we might not yet have uncovered. To expose you to the gossip and speculation of news reports, or even our own early investigations, could unduly influence and color your recollection. We need to preserve the integrity of your memory, and it would serve none of us to have it tainted by TV and radio 'journalists.'" He actually used the double-finger air-quote sign when he said it. Perez paused and cleared his throat. It was so unnatural and out of place that both Uchel and I looked at him quizzically. "You know, I read the Surf Slayer file."

Here it comes. "I figured you might."

"I can't defend the way things went down. You want to talk about it?"

"Not really."

"It might be relevant."

I looked at Uchel for assistance, but he seemed blindsided by the turn in the conversation and content to let it play out. "It's not."

Perez drummed his fingers on the coffee table but never took his eyes off me. "I sent your section of the file to someone in the home office. He thinks it might be."

"I don't see how."

"He's a psychiatrist. He thinks you may be..."

Geez. "That was then, this is now. It's not relevant."

"Not the cases, but perhaps the way you're reacting."

"I know exactly what you mean and it's not relevant."

"I'll let it go for the time being, but we may need to talk more."

"I look forward to it."

"If we do —just to be clear—it will be on my terms."

"I figured. That's how it was last time and you saw in the file how that turned out."

21

11:30 A.M. – KOROR

As THE WIND continued to pound the hotel, the uniformed officers standing guard had to shout to hear each other, which meant I was able to pick up bits and pieces: the worst of the storm pummeled the island for about seven hours as it brushed by. As the morning grew late, we were just experiencing the edge.

Mac and Perez headed out after it became clear I had nothing more to give them. They said they needed to get in touch with FBI sources back in the States and couldn't do that from the hotel. After that, it sounded like Perez was going to start chasing down leads. They'd gotten quite a few Ishikawa leads for the day leading up to the big splash. People seemed to notice when he showed up. He had been to a couple restaurants, a few bars, a construction site for a new government building, and the marina.

"Kick a few stones," Perez said, "and see what slithers out."

Water stains had appeared in the ceiling of the room

Agent Fraser and I now shared, and I could hear workers on the roof, pounding and sawing. No effort was made to clean my room or make it more habitable. I still couldn't see outside, but it seemed like repairs were increasing in proportion to the wind decreasing. Palau knew how to dig out from one of these things.

I was still in a media lockout and had scanned all the interesting articles in the magazines Agent Fraser had brought. I found a Bible in our room and looked for the racy parts, which kept me busy for an hour, but I was really just turning pages and staring without reading.

One of the unis, a new one who had arrived for the morning shift change, had assembled lunch for me from the hotel kitchen. The shift change left me uneasy—one arrived but three left. So, it was just me with one officer and Agent Fraser, and I wasn't sure she'd be willing to lay down her life for me after last night. I heard a rather heated exchange between Mac and Perez, and assumed that was the topic. It seemed that I became a lower priority for local authorities as the storm receded. The Department of Justice gives, and the Department of Justice takes away.

It might have seemed like the island would pull together at times like this, but the workers were talking about looting going on and the WCTC being stripped bare before the police were able to get men there. I guessed the uniforms were needed elsewhere, and politically, I was just one pawn in a much larger chess game.

Lunch was ok. He provided only canned goods, nothing that could be tampered with—green beans, peach slices, and tuna. And a can opener. And a fork.

The peaches were how I remembered them from my childhood—syrupy sweet and slippery. Actually, it was probably better than I would have eaten at home.

I picked at my lunch. I did some stretching. I even did some push-ups. According to what Perez had said before leaving, the bureau was sending additional agents on a company jet as soon as the skies cleared, which seemed to have happened. So far, all we'd done was wait. Agent Fraser was anxious to get the reinforcements, and she was expecting additional police. When she tried the hotel phone, she could reach the front desk, but they could not get her an outside line. She left to use the radio in one of the police cruisers.

Throughout the morning, she adamantly maintained the ban on media. No radio, no cable TV, nothing. She wasn't worried about my cell phone because all the cell towers on the island were down. Besides, the battery was dead again. She wouldn't talk. The cops barely talked. I was beginning to climb the walls.

As she left, she chastised the uniformed officer on duty for reading a printout of some sort, instead of monitoring the doors and elevator. As he tossed it onto the chair outside my door, I realized it was the early morning online edition of the *Island Times*. I waited until he walked away, then I opened the door and grabbed the pile of paper. It was almost fifteen pages long, stapled in the corner. I automatically started to flip past the first page, expecting anything about Ishikawa to be buried behind the storm news, but that wasn't necessary. There it was, sharing page one with the storm story—that horrid woman was becoming a fixture. Cute title though: "Expat Central Figure in Island Mayhem." I guessed that meant me.

> Sources in the Ministry of Justice have confirmed in an exclusive interview with the Executive Online and Print Editor for Crime and International Relations for *Island Times*, LLC...

Did she just give herself these promotions? Executive Online and Print Editor for Crime and International Relations? She had to be kidding. Two days ago she was the page nine girl.

> ...that Ricky Yamamoto of Airai...

Bitch. I vowed that when I had more time, I was going to apply some serious thought to making her life miserable.

> ...that Ricky Yamamoto of Airai is a central figure in the rash of murders and bombings that have swept this peaceful island nation. As of last night, the death toll has reached at least three, with the bombing and death of local tattoo artist Max Urapa.
>
> Authorities have so far been unable to determine if Yamamoto is related to infamous yakuza leader Kenichi Yamamoto of Kobe, Japan. If she is, she has brought to this island a long history of intra-yakuza battles. Police have thus far refused

to release her criminal record, though sources do confirm she has a history with the national police.

Kenichi Yamamoto—who? *And, please, stop bringing up my piddling little run-ins with the law.*

Ms. Hasinta Regulbai, Spokesperson for the Ministry of Justice, provided the following statement: "The investigation into the reported gangland killing spree is still preliminary. The coroner has yet to release his report, and final toxicology results may not be available for several weeks."

A copy of the coroner's initial report has been acquired by this reporter. The report reads, in part:

She got the autopsy report? That meant either she had better sources than Uchel, or he was keeping information from me. So much for the spirit of cooperation. My immediate thought was that I wanted to stomp on Uchel's toes, though I settled for rolling up the printout and smacking the hell out of the table. By the time I was done, the printout was quite mangled, and a number of pages were lying about the floor. I collected them and put them back in order so I could finish the article.

Initial assessment suggests death by asphyxiation. There is no apparent physical trauma typically found with forceful asphyxiation, nor does the stomach or throat contain any object that might have caused accidental asphyxiation.

She quoted large chunks of the report with no apparent attempt to interpret the coroner's comments. It included vague and non-committal references to Ishikawa having an empty stomach, and whether that provided any clues (not so far). Apparently, the FBI had taken over toxicological testing in Guam. Ishikawa had a number of hypodermic punctures. Though the reason behind them was unknown, steroid use was mentioned. It ended with some comments suggesting the local coroner had been benched in favor of the FBI experts.

The article went on for more than a page, with a note on the two yakuza pit bulls camped out in the coroner's lobby, vivid descriptions of the burning karaoke bar, the smoldering ruins of the tattoo parlor, and wild speculation about the pervasive role of the yakuza in the very fabric of Palauan society. I tried to get through it, but my vision blurred and my mind was racing.

Intra-yakuza battles. Who the hell is Kenichi Yamamoto? I hope to hell we're not related. What wasn't Mac telling me? My history with the cops—will they never let that go? And who's feeding Stephaliza this crap? I sat down hard on the floor, and then just as quickly decided I couldn't sit on the sideline anymore.

The officer was outside in the hallway, wearing a path in the carpet back and forth between the elevator shaft and the stairwell door. I waited until I heard him pace past my door and then stuck my head out. Security had been set up to keep people out, not in. I could see that the elevator was still shut down and the stairwell had a simple knob and bolt lock. I closed the door and considered my options. Agent Fraser had left her purse, but it contained little of use. No gun—not that I would have known what to do with it. No mace. No handcuffs. A roll of dimes. That would have to do. I figured I could use a little something I had picked up during my time in college.

*

Going to the door, I listened for the uni to pace past me and then peeked out. He was heading toward the stairwell. I closed the door and waited some more. The next time he passed, on his way toward the elevator shaft, I slipped out of my room and through the stairwell door. Closing it, I slowly released the knob to reset the bolt. Pressing my foot against the bottom of the door, I pushed a small stack of dimes in, then wedged in a few more. I repeated the process near the top of the door. The pressure of the dimes pushed the bolt against the frame to the point I could not turn the knob. Nor would the uni be able to. It had worked on dorm room doors too.

I started to take the stairs two at a time. It was only a few blocks to the police station where I might find a sympathetic soul. Anything would be better than being penned up at the Palasian. As I rounded the fourth-story landing, I realized I had figured wrong. There were two guys... wearing stockings on their heads. Both had Tasers.

22

SOMETIME – SOMEWHERE

I NOTICED THE pain in both shoulders first, then my dry mouth and thick tongue. My head was foggy and pounding, like Charlie Watts had used it for rehearsal. In my confused state I thought I heard a riot of children's voices, but as the cobwebs cleared, I realized they were birds. Terns. *Maybe the storm had passed.*

Opening my eyes, I tried to focus, looking at my feet and my hands. My situation quickly came into fuzzy but obvious clarity… I was tied to a large patio umbrella. The kind that sits in a big concrete stand. Expensive. Fancy. My arms were out and up and tied to the thick wooden ribs of the umbrella. My feet were tied together at the base. I couldn't figure out how long I had been out, and I couldn't see the sun, but the shadow of the umbrella suggested it was high in the sky.

I couldn't see anyone, but my field of view was limited, what with me being tied up in a crucifixion pose. Sonofabitch. I was thirsty. I was cranky. And I needed to pee. I was so going to make those guys in the stocking masks pay. But, right then, there was the little matter of my being trussed up like a pig being taken to market. I looked around, trying to assess my situation and develop a plan. The umbrella was too well made for me to break it by myself: thick wooden ribs and, I assumed, high-grade metal brackets. Although the wind still whipped wickedly over the rooftop, the umbrella barely moved.

I was in an interior courtyard of what looked like a very expensive house. Nice imported tiles. White stucco. Copper fixtures. No exposed wires or pipes. I was in a small section of the courtyard set off by a three- or four-foot-high patio wall topped with spikes. Beyond the wall I could see a deep pit that featured a run-down pool. To my right was a doorway, and across the patio was another. The base of the umbrella was about four feet away from the half wall. I hoped that if I rocked back and forth enough times, I could make the umbrella fall and either totally smash my ribs on the wall or, if I was lucky, break the pole and the wooden ribs to which I was lashed. It was worth a try. I couldn't imagine the punks letting me go, so this might be my only chance.

I started to rock the umbrella back and forth. At first, I just got a little movement from the pole, but I quickly got a cadence and some momentum, and the umbrella stand started to rock. It was only a few inches at first, but then I really started to get some lean. That's when I heard the bloodcurdling screech.

I stopped moving—except for my shaking, which was as bad as it had been over the past few days. *What the hell was that?* I looked around. Nothing in the doorways. Nothing in front of me. And then I saw it.

A monkey—one of those that ate crabs—was swinging back and forth through the support bars for the patio roof. It seemed quite agitated and kept looking from me to the pool and back again. I didn't know if it was a Palauan burglar alarm or what, but I couldn't stop at that point.

I resumed my rocking, and soon the monkey resumed its screeching. Rock, screech, rock, screech. I got the umbrella to the point where I was leaning at least fifteen degrees before lurching back. Once I got past forty-five degrees, I could just let gravity do its thing. My one risk was falling facedown, which would smash my ribs while protecting the pole and likely break the wrong ribs on the umbrella. Unfortunately, my weight kept rotating me so that I was facing the wall. I would have to work in a twist at the end—one more practical application for my circus school training. I was up to thirty degrees and had managed on two of my swings to rotate my body sideways. It was going to work. On my next swing, with the damn monkey still screeching bloody murder, I rocked to the point I was almost suspended over the wall. That's when I met my next-door neighbor.

*

A crocodile.

There was a freaking crocodile sunning itself deep in the pit beside the pool. The entire center of the courtyard was like a gladiator pit with a prehistoric relic instead of a lion. And the thing was huge. As I hung over the wall, it raised its head and lunged upwards, snapping its jaws. Missing me by a good three or four feet, it let out an ungodly hiss of putrid breath. This all took just a few seconds before the weight of the base swung me back away from the wall. I froze, and the umbrella settled down. So did the monkey.

Off to my right, someone laughed.

Crud.

"So, you met Oscar," said one of the two guys standing in the doorway.

They were still wearing their stockings. That was a good sign. If they were still hiding their faces, maybe they weren't going to kill me. At least that's the way it worked on TV.

"Welcome back to the land of the living. You conked your noggin pretty good there after I zapped you. Made life easier for us, you being unconscious and all."

My attention was split between them and the crocodile. I wasn't sure which was a greater threat.

"Yeah, Oscar's a big'un, ain't he? Scared the fuck out of me the first time I saw him. Crazy dude, that Ishikawa. Great party pad he got here. Kept a pet monkey and a saltwater croc. What sort of fucking joke is that? Thing must be fifteen feet long. I don't think that wall would really hold him if he got inspired. Looks like he ate well though—crazy Ishikawa fed him whale blubber and shark fins. We found refrigerators full of the crap. Brought the whale shit in from halfway around the world. Fancy wrapping paper with Norwegian stuff written on it. And the dude ate that shit himself too. It's in his fridge along with bottles of vodka and 'roids. We've been searching for something for lunch, but *nada*. Freaking millionaire and the guy had no food except for fish parts and vodka. Crazy. The world is a better place with him gone, that's for damn sure. Shame about Koga, but he brought that on himself."

He was talkative. But I figured the more he talked, the better chance I had of finding a way out of this mess.

"Whales aren't fish." *Ah, the other one can talk too.*

"What the fuck you talking about? They live in the ocean."

"They're not fish. They're mammals. And it sucks that people kill them." *Oh my, at least one of my captors has some degree of ethics. Nice to know.* "Slimy bastard made his living greasing the skids for whale and shark killers. Makes me want to puke. Damn straight the world's better off without him."

Crude, but right on. "Aren't you his partners? Why did you bring me here? You tased me."

"That we did. And then you toppled over like a mighty redwood and smacked your head on the steps. Now that you're talking again, little lady, we need to chat. It seems a friend of ours has a problem not of his making, and you may be part of it. We've volunteered to help him fix it." The shorter one, the gabbier one, was clearly in the lead. The other seemed a bit of a mental lightweight with a hint of loose wiring. A real Butthead. He nodded a lot, and giggled, but didn't bring much else to the party. I did, however, have to give him bonus points for having an anti-whaling stance.

*

No way these guys were yakuza. Nothing about them fit. Neither one sounded Japanese, they weren't dressed in that funky '50s style, and they were way too informal. And rude. American? Maybe the short one. The tall one sounded like he had been local for a long time. The short, talkative one, though, was American through and through.

"Newspaper says otherwise. You're the key witness and have all sorts of info about the Ishikawa murder. Our friend would like to know exactly what you know, and who you've told. Cuz it's not true."

I thought I might actually be ok. If they were still concerned about what I might know but hadn't said, which was nothing, then maybe they'd let me go. If there was nothing more to hide, then I wasn't a threat.

"I really don't know anything. I was diving," I pleaded. "I found Ishikawa's body. Koga's body went flying by me. Well, not his body—he wasn't dead yet. I helped the police recover the bodies—I'm a dive guide. I do technical diving. I'm not with the police. I don't even like them and I'm pretty sure they've been using me as bait. Did you notice they pulled away all my guards so you could get me?"

"Actually, we left two of them in the trunk of the cop car. I'm pretty sure they were trying to protect you."

"Oh God, a woman?"

"Yeah, she was the easy one. We'd already gotten the cop when she came out. I tased her while she was talking on the radio."

"She's alive?"

"Yeah, both of them should be. What? I look like a killer?"

"I don't know. You seem like a nice guy. And you

guys like whales and sharks, which makes you cool in my book. But you're wearing a stocking over your head—"

"Great. Now that we've gotten the mutual admiration society meeting out of the way, sweet cheeks, we need to get back to our little situation here. So, you found the bodies. Did you see anything else? Maybe the guy who tossed them in the water? Maybe, for instance, a truck you passed on the way to your dive?"

Oh, geez, was that what this was about? They thought I'd seen the killer?

"No, I've been over this with the police. First thing I saw was Ishikawa and I didn't even realize then that anything was wrong. By the time I figured that out, Koga went flying by. I was a hundred feet deep. I couldn't see surface light, much less somebody standing on the cliff above."

"That's certainly not what that newspaper chick's saying. She's been on TV saying that you're the feds' star witness and you saw it all. Our friend is quite concerned. People who know people say you had a lot to tell the FBI. This was all a very unfortunate accident and it would be a shame if you tried to pin things on him that shouldn't be pinned. Now, from the top, what have you told the cops?"

"MB said we should wait."

"Shut the fuck up. MB wants us to help and I'm helping. If he'd trusted us in the first place, maybe there'd only be one dead body. And a good excuse."

I had no idea what they were talking about, but the more I told them, the more they seemed willing to talk. "I'm telling you: one body on a ledge, another body shooting past me. I didn't see anybody or any truck."

"Why do you say *truck*? It could have been a car. What did you see?"

The pounding in my head intensified. "You said *truck*. You asked me if I saw a truck. I didn't see anything. I drove to the site and dumped my gear. I parked near the beach. I walked to the jump-in spot and went for my dive. I'm not a cop and I wasn't out looking for killers."

But as I said it, I realized I had seen something. There had been a truck pulled way off the side of the road in the trees. I saw it as I walked back up the hill and figured it was abandoned. But that was the first time I had seen it, and come to think of it, there was a tarp in back. Crap, I *had* seen the murderer's truck. But there was nobody there. *Oh God, I can't tell the guys this. They'll kill me. This sucks.*

"You do understand that we can't just, you know, take your word for it?" said the gabby one. "So, we've arranged a test." He elbowed his partner. "But where are my manners? You asked me a question about why we brought you here. We brought you here because we may have to kill you. The feds assume the yakuza is taking care of their own problems. If we do it here, it closes the loop. Two birds, one stone. We get rid of the witness and we direct attention to the most obvious suspects. But whether we have to do it is up to you. You can tell us everything you've forgotten to tell us, and then we have options – options that might even include you going home intact. Or, if you stick with this story, we let Oscar do some interrogating." He gestured in the direction of the pool. "You see, our friend believes you saw more than you're saying, and we need to know what you've told the cops. Since you're not being—shall we say, forthcoming—my associate and I are going to have to get a bit creative in our interrogation."

I wasn't buying it. They weren't going to let me go. On TV, this was where they'd take off their stockings.

*

He nodded at Butthead, who grabbed the umbrella pole behind me. The short guy grabbed the waistband of my shorts with one hand and put the other one on my boob. *What a scum bucket, he's threatening to kill me but he's copping a feel first. There's a special place in hell for people like that.* They started to lean me over the pool. Oscar saw the action and got quite excited, working his jaws open and closed and holding his head up high in anticipation.

"How's your memory now? Any epiphanies?" I did have one recollection—these were the jerks hanging outside of the police station when I first reported the murders.

This guy liked his big words, and I swore I was going to make him eat a few if I got the chance, and add in a little whooping for the catcalls at the station. I decided there was no advantage to sharing that recovered memory. "No, I swear on a stack of Bibles that's all I remember. That's all I told. Anything I know, the cops already know."

That caused them to pause.

I pushed the point. "Why would I hold anything back?"

"Maybe you want to shake our friend down. Make yourself some nice spending money. Buy yourself some nice dresses. I'll bet you dress up really nice."

Slime mold still had his hand on my boob, and now he was mentally undressing me. He was so busy getting his jollies he hadn't noticed I'd worked one of my feet free of the ropes that bound them to the pole, nor that I was well on the way to getting one of my equally small hands out of its bonds as well. The burning sensation told me I was leaving a bit of flesh behind as I worked out of the ropes.

"We just want to talk. Make you understand it was all a misunderstanding. Why should our friend be made to pay for a simple mistake?" said the short one, leaning me even closer to Oscar, who rose up and snapped his jaws just inches from my face.

That was when my infamous bladder kicked into action. I peed in my shorts, producing a flood of biblical proportions. It flowed down my leg, stinging the raw flesh on my ankle, and splattered on the floor, forming a puddle and setting in motion an unexpected string of events.

Short guy bent over laughing, releasing his grip on my boob and shorts. The umbrella and I rocked back toward the taller stooge, giving me the perfect opportunity to let loose with a kick, catching boob-grabber flush in the face and standing him up—just for a moment. Even through the stocking, I could see his eyes roll back in his head just before he hit the ground, his pantyhose-encased face landing in a big yellow puddle of pee.

The force of my kick rocked the pole back even farther, knocking me into Butthead. I heard a thud as he smashed against the wall. The pole rocked forward and crashed down onto the ground just as I heard a scream and a splash. I had one foot and one hand free. I needed to get the others out before either of the men regained their senses. The rope that had held my feet was now loose, so I tugged my other foot out and twisted, breaking the already cracked tent rib and freeing my other hand. Short guy was still down and out.

Jumping to my feet, I did a quick turn to deal with Butthead, and saw the pool. The water had turned pink and was being whipped into froth as the crocodile, which was almost as long as the pool itself, relentlessly rolled near the surface, a struggling Butthead locked firmly in his jaws. I'm pretty sure I saw a body part separate and sink to the bottom.

Having just wet myself, I worked hard to avoid vomiting as well. I had to focus on my next step. It occurred to me it would help to know who I was dealing with. I pulled off boob-grabber's stocking and realized I knew the face. *But from where?* I knew I had seen him around the island but had never talked to him. Then it hit me. He was the weaselly kid who had spent years hanging around the marina doing odd jobs. One of those Americans who would just show up in Palau without enough initiative to make anything of himself, or even to leave. He had the reputation of doing pretty much anything for a buck. Last time I saw him, he was gutting fish in back of the sushi restaurant and tossing the innards to a stray dog. *A real animal lover.* Or one stray taking pity on another.

His eyes began to flutter. My kick hadn't put him out as much as I had hoped. I kicked him in the head again. And then again. This was probably the sonofabitch who ran me off the road. I kicked him in the ribs and heard some cracking sounds that definitely made me feel better. I think he whimpered.

And then I heard a louder, more ominous sound from outside. Like a car door. *Oh Jeesus.* Their friend. The guy who killed Ishikawa. I looked around for a place to hide, struggling to orient myself. The courtyard was surrounded on all four sides. The two lackeys had come in from the space to my right, so I figured that was the main house, or at least the entrance. Whatever, my money was betting that was where the next guy was coming from too.

The doors to the room immediately in front of me were clear. It appeared to be a gym, and it was lined with mirrors—not a good place to hide.

The room to my left was darkened and had blinds. That was an immediate plus, and it also had the closest set of doors. But it was also immediately opposite the doors the bad guy would come through, so it would be the first thing they'd see... other than the dimwit lackey lying on the patio with his face in a pool of pee. Too likely a hiding place—if he even thought I was hiding. As far as he knew, I was long gone.

But I couldn't go, because I hadn't found a way out. My last choice was a set of double doors on the other side of the enclosure. It was the farthest and least visible if they entered from my right. Likely the last place he'd check. I heard a door open. I had two choices if I was going to that room: Run around the enclosure, which would take time, put me closer to my adversary, and require me to run through a gravel and cactus garden. Or run through the enclosed pool area. With the crocodile.

Prehistoric beasts be damned, that was what I did.

Thinking the enclosure was four feet high and about twenty-five feet long, I leapt over the wall, clearing the spikes with a high hurdle move that would have made Mom proud, took four giant strides to cross the enclosure, and used one last leap to mount and vault the opposite wall. I dropped over the side, took another big stride, and skidded to a stop in front of the door before quietly turning the handle and sliding into the room, easing the door behind me.

I had no idea whether the croc even reacted—I was too busy running. From the sounds behind me, I was pretty sure it was still enjoying its death roll.

*

I found myself in the middle of one hellacious room. Ishikawa certainly knew how to build a party location. Thirty feet across, at least sixty feet long, and two stories high. At one end was a stairway that stretched almost the entire width of the room. Most of the space on the stairs was used as shelves for CDs, DVDs, lava lamps, a Hello Kitty electric guitar, and samurai swords. He had pachinko games, video games, and the biggest damn big-screen TV I had seen that wasn't hanging in a football stadium. All of this, but almost no place to hide. And I had to find one. Fast.

I heard the doors to the patio slam and a whole lot of yelling. There were two voices, so either there were at least two more bad guys, or the boob-grabber was sufficiently recovered to talk. I knew I should have stamped on his head again. It wouldn't take them long to check out the mirrored room. I guessed mine was last on the list, which gave me a minute, maybe more.

The only door out of the room that didn't lead to the patio was at the end, opposite the big stair/shelf structure. Logic told me it led into the front room. If the two bad guys were on the patio, I might be able to make it through there, but they might see me, or there might be others. That seemed like a fallback position at best. At the top of the stair structure on the right side was what looked like a pulpit and, beyond that, a set of windows. I had no idea what lay past the windows, but I had run out of choices. At least from there, I could better scope out my options. I took the first three stairs in one stride. My shoes squeaked a bit, and the raw skin from the ropes stung, so I slowed down and took them two at a time. I tried not to think about what was making the shoes squeak, but the smell of my own pee rose every time I took a step, giving me a fairly good idea.

I made it to the pulpit and the windows. *Perfect.* They were large, had removable screens, and put me out onto the roof where I could see in two directions. I knew where the courtyard lay, so I had only one blind side. Popping out a screen, I laid it gently on the floor. The voices had gotten quieter, so I figured the boys were searching the room opposite the entrance. Hopefully there was more to it than the others and would take a while.

I had to move gently because the pulpit was crowded. Evidently, it was the karaoke stage. There were amplifiers, microphones, and stands. And a life-sized Michael Jackson mannequin, complete with one of his military-style outfits of black pants and a jacket of red wool and gold braids. Sequin socks and black shoes too. I recalled a rumor going around that Ishikawa bought the original at auction a few years back for something north of a million dollars. It seemed a bit sacrilegious, but I needed a new set of clothing, and Ishikawa wasn't going to need them again.

I found a nylon bag filled with cables and dumped the contents, then quickly relieved Michael of his shoes, socks, pants, and jacket. I shoved them into the bag and pushed it out the window. I followed immediately, sliding the window closed behind me. In the pulpit, Michael stood stripped down to aviator glasses, lavender tank-top undershirt, and matching banana-hammock underpants. And a single glove.

*

Slithering across the tiled roof, I tried to put some distance between me and the window so that I wasn't there when they searched the pulpit. I heard voices from the courtyard. A loud curse told me they'd chosen to go through the cactus garden to get to the party room. They'd be there soon, and I didn't think it would take them long to find the pulpit and its window.

From my vantage point I could barely see the lay of the land. The wind had masked the sound of the waves, so I hadn't realized the house stood on a small hillside near the shore. Jungle surrounded it though, and even from the roof I could barely see the waterline. A section of mangroves had been cleared away to make room for a large boathouse and several docks. I had seen them before from the dive boat. It took me a minute, but I realized I was on Peleliu.

Talk about being out in the boondocks. The place was obviously Ishikawa's hideaway. I had been out to Peleliu dozens of times for dives and had always come ashore for a quick tour of World War II sites, usually to take guests through the honeycomb of caves and tunnels the Japanese had dug throughout the island. But I had never been to this remote part of the island, other than to pass by. It was at the northernmost tip, closest to the main island, but being mountainous and exposed, it was the least habitable part of Peleliu. That might have been part of its appeal.

The cove was marked with a buoy that identified it as private property, so we'd never entered. Funny thing about those docks and the boathouse: they were really tucked away and looked derelict from the water, but I could see now that they were new and must have been made to look old. Tied up at the docks were several boats, including one of those high-speed offshore monsters. *Probably good for meeting up with shark-finning boats to get your payola and dinner delivery. In and out quick. Scum.*

Only one road led in, and blocking that road was an old Toyota four-wheel drive. An FJ40. My mom had owned one back in Colorado. I did some wild driving in that during my exile, and it was about the only thing I missed when I left the state a week after I turned eighteen.

This one had massively oversized tires, a rack of overhead lights, and a full-on winch. I couldn't see if anyone was inside so I had to play it safe and assume so.

I wouldn't be using it for my escape. At least I couldn't plan on it being available. Three sides of the house were backed by jungle, and from what I remembered of the island's geography, there was at least a mile of jungle between us and what passed for a main road in Peleliu. My only option was to go by sea.

I heard the guys in the party room. They sounded panicked. I had obviously seen one face, and they had to expect that I could identify the weasel. The equation had changed, and the stakes were now higher for both of us. Releasing me was no longer an option. I had to go for broke.

I slid down and across the roof past the corner, pushing my bag ahead of me so that I was out of view of the window. I was on the side with a straight shot to the boats. I edged down. I could barely hear, what with the wind and the fact I was on the far side now, but I could tell at least one of them was running up the stairs. I heard the window open and some shouting, but as far as I could tell, no one came out onto the roof or had figured that I was out there. Then I heard, "She's on the roof," and realized I'd messed up; I'd left the screen inside when I made my exit.

My options were limited, so I jumped and landed on an old oil drum, which fell and banged into another. If they hadn't yet figured out my location, I'd just given them a very good clue.

23

A BIT LATER – ON THE RUN

I WAS UP and running withiin a few seconds. Mom had been a part-time sprinter, using those long legs that Dad loved so much and that I inherited. I had tried to follow in her footsteps, dabbling in sprinting in high school, but I never had Mom's success. I think my small feet held me back. Even ten years later, though, my legs still worked pretty well and did look damn fine in shorts (even better, I'm told, out of shorts).

It was about two hundred yards to the dock, and I had covered about a hundred when I heard the Jeep behind me. There was no way I would make it to the dock, so I cut right and started running through the jungle, hoping that might level the playing field a bit. The sutured cuts in my lip and forehead throbbed. *Has that really happened in the past twenty-four hours?* I couldn't recall, but I suspected running was on the list of things I shouldn't be doing for the next few days.

As I considered my options, which were too few, I

remembered an open patch I had seen from the house. If my guess was right, I could turn this fight in my favor.

I found a small but clear trail leading away from the shoreline through the jungle, and I took it. I had no idea if they had seen or figured out my maneuver, but I had to assume one or both were following me. I kept up my sprint as I lurched through the jungle, tripping over roots and vines and scraping my knee more than once. Worse, I was beginning to doubt my sense of direction and—worse still—my theory.

There was no turning back, so I pushed on... to a fork in the path. *Crap!* Without stopping to think, I took the one sloping slightly upward, and almost immediately burst through the jungle and into the clearing. Halfway down the cliff wall that formed its eastern border was a cave opening. I knew enough to figure that somewhere there was another. Beyond the cave was a road leading back into the jungle that appeared to drop downhill toward the shore.

I had never been in this particular cave system, but I'd been in enough of them to know it would be complex. Hiding wouldn't be a problem. Finding my way out might be. One problem at a time.

I ran through the clearing and up to the cave entrance. As I looked back, I saw the first of my pursuers, a little guy but not the boob-grabber, race out of the jungle. We both froze, then he broke into a sprint directly towards me. About a hundred and fifty yards separated us. The clearing was flat, and had at one time been paved, but it was littered with old machine parts and war detritus, plus stacks of industrial drums, metal tubing, and wooden pallets. Running in a straight line wasn't possible.

By the time I got to the cave, the pounding in my head was constant and painful. My vision seemed a bit hazy as well.

I didn't give him a chance to catch up, dashing up the slope and into the opening. It began as a large cavern, but after about fifty feet I came to my first tunnel—on my left, *north*—and took it, hitting my head on the low ceiling. My plan had at least one flaw. I was five ten, the guy chasing me was probably no more than five five, and the cave had been dug out quickly with four-foot ceilings and little respect for comfort or maneuverability. That was ok while leading a tour: you would walk slowly, duckwalk when necessary, and keep one hand over your head to keep track of the noggin-knockers. But when you were running for your life and being chased by psychopaths, the low ceiling was a problem.

I tucked myself into a crouch and tried running but hit my head again. The other problem was visibility. There were lights in the tour tunnels, but not this one. As I put distance between myself and the cave entrance, darkness began to envelop me. Taking the next branching tunnel I found on my right—*south*—I continued on... in total darkness. I pressed the button on my dive watch to see if the illumination provided enough light to see in the tunnel, but all I got was the time, day, and date.

I started to hyperventilate. I hadn't thought this part through. I sat down, simultaneously jabbing my butt with a sharp rock and scraping my back against the ragged walls of the cave. It was humid, and the cave smelled of mold. At least I wasn't twitchy about spiders, but I had no plan, and my eyes were barely adjusting to the faint residual light seeping into this branch of the cave.

That accounting made me hyperventilate even more, so I tried to focus on the good parts. Good part one: I knew that these systems were almost always laid out in a grid. Almost always. Good part two: I was a great navigator. I had done hundreds of night dives in very similar conditions—jet black with no landmarks to guide me. I was great at tracking changes in direction. Good part three: I was in great shape and capable of running for miles. I couldn't think of a good part four, and I was still hyperventilating.

Then I heard a voice echoing behind me, and I froze, instinctively holding my breath. Noise carried well in the caves, which meant I would hear them long before I saw them. Unfortunately, it also meant they could hear me.

"Loosey... Looosey... I'm hoooome..." Funny boy. His singsong voice echoed through the cave. I couldn't really pinpoint where he was or how far away he might be. But he was between me and the cave opening.

"Come on, Lucy," he sighed, "this isn't going to work. I've got my guy outside. Even if you get past me, you're going to have to come out at some point and he'll be waiting for you. All I want to do is talk.

"I promise I won't hurt you," he continued. "This has all been a terrible mistake."

I wasn't about to get into a discussion around the nuances of the word *mistake*, or the likelihood that he wasn't going to kill me, but if he wanted to talk, I would let him. I could hear his feet shuffling as he came closer. I began to move slowly but purposefully down the tunnel, keeping one hand on the ceiling and the other on the right wall. When I found the next tunnel, I took it. If I figured correctly and didn't hit a dead end, I would reconnect eventually with the main tunnel and come out behind him. I would still need to deal with the second guy, whoever he was, but I had some degree of confidence that I could take him. I didn't have a choice.

"Really, I'm not the bad guy here. Ishikawa croaked himself. All I did was get rid of the body. Koga was an accident. All I need is a chance to tell you my side of the story. Really."

Right. Accident. Like an accidental smack on the noggin before accidentally chaining him to an axle?

I wasn't about to stick around for his tale and kept moving. The floor was slick, so I took small steps, which also helped minimize the squeaking of my shoes. At times it seemed like the tunnel was rising upward, but then I noticed a slight downslope. Any variation in elevations seemed random and not a sign of something to come—a lot like the seafloor.

"I can hear you breathing, Lucy... you're making this too easy."

Not quite buying that, I nevertheless tried to regulate my breathing and step even more quietly. I was still carrying the nylon bag, and it was slowing me down. And my shoe kept squeaking.

"Talk, face-to-face, that's all I want," he said.

I took my next available tunnel. *West.* He was talking again. Rambling. Maybe nervous, and probably going slowly to make sure he took the correct tunnel. If he checked out each option, I would likely lose him. I changed the pace and took two more turns—south and west, heading back toward the clearing. I was banging my way along in the dark, but I was putting distance between us. Every so often, I turned down a tunnel with slick walls and floors. I slipped more than once but kept my grunts quiet until I got to a junction with five spurs. No longer a grid. *Crud.*

His voice was getting a bit distant. I could tell he had stopped. "Geez, Lucy, I can smell you. You really did pee yourself, didn't you? The bloom's off the rose now, honey. I don't think I can go through with the wedding."

He was right. I really did smell. I had to get out of my clothes—they were leading him right to me. He had stopped, so I had some time. Reversing my direction, I took the northish tunnel then unzipped the bag and took out the clothes I had liberated from Michael. Stripping down, I piled my clothes on the ground, hoping they might delay him a bit. I squeezed into the purloined clothes and thought I had misjudged his height a bit. The pants were a little short but serviceable. The lining of the jacket felt quite nice against my skin, but it was a bit tight in the chest. I wasn't sure about the shoes when I grabbed them, and sure enough, they were enormous. At least there were when sitting beside my freakishly small feet. Still, I pulled them over the sequined socks and laced them as tight as I could. I was just happy they weren't loafers and thanked Albinus of Angers, one of the few saints I remembered, who was the patron saint of avoiding pirate attacks. Albinus seemed legitimately appropriate for this situation. All this while, the guy had been talking. Wisecracking.

I had been too busy fighting to really take it all in, but there in the dark, dressed up like a character from the march of the wooden soldiers, I suddenly felt exhausted. And petrified. I sat down again, in the middle of a puddle, and hugged my knees to my chest. The tunnel was hot, but I shivered uncontrollably, the pee fumes replaced by the smell of my own sweat.

The slacker was on the move again. I heard a clatter of metal on rock and some choice swear words—he was getting close. I really only had two choices: let him come to me and fight it out or keep moving and find a new option. Fighting wouldn't work. He was short and better able to move around in the tunnel. I forced myself out of the tunnel and back down the west tunnel as quickly as I could. Then I hit a wall. Dead end, no exit. My hope now was that he had gone past this tunnel following the smell of my pee, and I could go out the other direction after he passed.

I was about ten feet from the tunnel junction leading to my clothes when I realized the tunnel was getting lighter. Sonofabitch. He had a flashlight. It was so not fair. But he must have had the nose of a bloodhound and taken the bait because he was moving faster, passing my tunnel without a glance.

Judging by the dimming light, he had gone about thirty more feet and into the other tunnel, just like I hoped... but I hadn't planned on the flashlight.

"Everything would have been fine and dandy if it hadn't been for you." He paused, neither walking nor talking. "Oh, Lucy, did you get naked just for me?" He found the clothes. "Are you going to make this a happy ending?"

He kept rambling. Perfect. It had distracted him and bought me time. "Lucy, this isn't going to turn out the way you want. It's bigger than you and me. Ishikawa had his hands in a lot of pies and a lot of people want this to go away. People you can't beat. Trust me on this."

The jabbering stopped, and I could tell by the sound of his footsteps he had turned to stalk back toward my tunnel. He must have realized what I had done. There was no way I could get away from him with a thirty-foot lead and him with the flashlight. I saw the beam of his light as he approached the junction. I had run out of options. All there was left for me to do was fight—but nothing said it had to be a fair fight.

Among the cans and bottles and other remnants of war life scattered around me were large cast-iron grills on which the soldiers would have cooked their meals. Big, thick chunks of metal. Probably ten pounds each.

With a quick final step, he turned the corner, just three feet from where I stood. I hesitated to make sure he was within striking distance, long enough for him to see me but, luckily, not enough time for him to react. I was coiled in a crouched position, and like a hammer thrower, I started low and spun up into the swing, the metal grill clenched in my fist. I almost lost my grip with my sweaty hands, but my timing was just right, and I caught the kid square in the jaw right at the apex of my swing. I definitely heard breaking bone.

He went back against the wall and bounced forward,

dropping down hard at my feet. I pulled back my right foot and kicked him in the head for good measure. And then, for screwing up my life in more ways than I could count, I curled around, lined up like a soccer player on a penalty kick, and let him have it, right in the balls. Then I grabbed his flashlight—which turned out to be attached to a Taser and his keys—and started back down the tunnels. I thought about using the Taser on him, just for good measure, but I wasn't sure how to operate it.

I went ahead and took off his mask, not that it mattered, I already knew who he was.

*

I had planned to backtrack, but with the spinning and kicking, I'd lost track of which direction I had been pointing. I did a quick mental coin-toss and picked the tunnel to my left. I took no more than three steps before I began to second-guess myself. Something felt wrong. I couldn't put my finger on what it was, but I backtracked anyway and took the tunnel to my right. With the flashlight, the going was faster. It might have been my imagination, but the floor seemed less littered and the ceiling higher.

I was about to turn around yet again when I came to a door. A solid, modern door. Beyond it I heard a low hum, and the metal on the door slightly vibrated. With an uncertain path back to where I started, and the very strong possibility of crossing a pissed-off adversary along the way, I took a deep breath and tested the handle. It turned smoothly and quietly. Easing the door open, I pointed the beam of my flashlight through the crack and found myself staring into the largest cavern I had ever seen on the island. The room was humongous. Big enough for a hundred men.

I gently pushed the door shut and went to lock it, but there was no lock. Whoever built this place must have had a lot of confidence in their security, or nothing to secure. I panned the light's beam around, looking for an exit. The room was a lot more modern than the tunnels filled with Japanese relics that I had been stumbling over. The floor was actually flat; in fact, it was concrete, and the room looked like it was still in use. The air was dry and no longer smelled musty. Plastic sheeting covered the ceilings and walls, and folding worktables were laid out in several rows. Several heavier tables held what looked to be lab equipment. Large drums sat on the floor and the tables, and an entire wall was lined with wooden crates and pallets. Along another was a simple assembly line. Electrical cables snaked out from a large group of marine batteries. Two large industrial ventilation units, the source of the hum that I heard, labored away on another wall, connecting the room to the outside world through six-inch aluminum tubes that appeared to rise up through the cavern ceiling some twenty feet above.

Several desks—the blocky, featureless ones you see in police stations or cheap offices—held stacks of papers, folders, and boxes. Other tables were littered with the stuff of everyday life—empty bottles and lots of trays, plates, and boxes from one particular restaurant on the main island. No surprise there, given Ishikawa's line of business. Not that knowing who he was helped. I still had no idea what that meant in the big picture. The humidity was lower, but I was sweating even more than I had been in the tunnel.

I also had no idea what this room contained, but I was hoping that whatever sort of operation this was, a gun was part of their equipment list. I'd have to figure out how to use it, but gun would be better than no gun. It was probably wishful thinking—gun possession was almost nonexistent in Palau, given the harsh penalties.

Swinging the beam across the room, I scanned the walls until I found a light switch. I flicked it up, and the room was bathed in bright light—too bright. While I took a minute for my eyes to adjust, I stopped and listened for a sign that I was being followed. I had hit him hard in the head twice but had no idea how long he would be out. Hopefully, the kick in the balls would slow him down as well.

I began rifling through the boxes. No gun. No knife. Nothing. I dumped them out on a table and still found nothing. No racks on the wall, no gun cabinet or secret door with enough weapons to outfit a small army. The room smelled like chemicals, so I added anything volatile, or at least a tool that I could use to maim or gouge, to my list of potential weapons.

As I searched for a weapon, I noticed the whiteboard on the wall. Scrawled in messy but organized notes was a list of boat names, dates and times, IDs. *Hercules*, *Galaxy*, *Globemaster*—US Navy planes. I recognized the names from my time in Hawai'i when we had nothing better to do than hang out by the naval base and watch the planes take off. There was a map of the Palau region marked with grease pen—like a navigation chart, with lines and arrows, but a lot more complicated. They had scrawled times and destinations all around the Pacific.

I was trying to sort it all out when I heard a dull thud behind me in the caves, followed by cursing. He must have come to. He sounded close. I could only hope the door was well sealed and he hadn't seen light leaking out from inside.

I abandoned my weapons search. It was time to move on. There were two tunnels—the one I had come out of, and one at the opposite side of the room. I went to the opposite side and tested the door. Also lockless and well lubricated. There was a light switch on the wall. I turned on the flashlight and pulled the Taser off the key ring so I had the light in one hand and the Taser in the other. I reached for the light switch and my arm brushed against a stack of magazines piled on a desk pushed up against the wall, sending them sprawling across the floor. A stack of muscle-builder magazines featuring greased, abnormal-looking men in contorted poses. *Gross.* I hit the light, closed the door behind me, and headed for whatever or whoever was waiting for me at the opening to the tunnel. After a couple of turns I heard a door bang open.

*

"Bitth!" was the first word out of his mouth; he wasn't trying to mask his voice anymore. I could figure out that word, but it was hard to understand anything else he was saying. I guessed I had managed to at least break his jaw. Even with his mask on, I had figured who he was—one of the least likely characters on the island—and I was pretty sure he didn't care if I knew his identity. He knew I knew it. There was no way he was letting me walk out of here alive. Knowing who he was, however, made me a lot more confident. And totally pissed me off.

The path out was a lot easier than the path in. Not only did I have the flashlight, but this tunnel, unlike the one I first chose, had been upgraded since the war. The floor was flat and uncluttered, the ceiling raised, and it was strung with lights, I took it on faith that they led to the opening. I took the time to break each of them as I passed. No sense providing aid or comfort to the enemy.

As the ambient light increased, I knew I was getting close to the cave entrance. Finally, at a last turn, I could see the entry chamber. I also realized that the floor was again uneven and littered, and the ceiling was low. I had to crouch again for the last thirty feet, but I was able to stand up as I reached the cavern. The entrance sloped down, so I had no view of the clearing. Neither did I have a clear idea of what was waiting for me outside—hopefully just the boob-grabber.

I knew there was at least one more obstacle out there between the boats and me, but I also assumed I would have the element of surprise. I thought the flashlight beam might lull the lackey into complacency, and I might be able to get pretty close before he realized his error. As soon as I could see the natural light up ahead, I started walking down the slope. Once I could see the beginnings of the clearing ahead, I accelerated my pace. The shoes made accelerating and turning a bit of a challenge, so I just headed straight out and hoped I'd be able to close the gap in time.

*

"MB," came the call, "did you get her? No one's come out. MB?"

As I trotted down the slope, I could see his feet and then his knees. That meant he could see mine. I had only a few seconds before he realized the sequined socks didn't belong to his boss.

The cave opening was larger than the tunnel. I was able to stand straight up, but had an awkward starting point. I had a taser, but he probably did too—and he knew how to use his. Deciding that surprise was my best option, I started running. I hit full speed on my fourth stride, and from the shocked look on the boob-grabber's face, he had not been expecting Michael Jackson to come running toward him at full speed.

I hit him full-on, and we both went down, our Tasers flying. I'm not a fighter, and figured I couldn't duke it out with this guy, so my strategy was to keep close and fight dirty. I head-butted him, and his nose exploded in a spray of red. Totally gross, but effective. Grabbing his hand, I bit as hard as I possibly could and suddenly my teeth clicked together. Something rolled around on my tongue. I spat his finger out onto the ground.

He stopped fighting and began screaming. I stopped fighting, continued spitting, and began gagging. I stood up while he remained on his knees, holding his bloody hand and looking at me like a wounded bird hoping for salvation. "Never, ever, grab a girl's boob... or whatever... without permission." I was tired and pissed off, so I added an exclamation mark by kicking him in the head. I was growing to like this fighting thing, especially the head kicking.

I dropped the flashlight, picked up both Tasers and the keychain, did a little moonwalk, let out a Michael Jacksonesque squeak, and took off running.

24

AFTERNOON – PELELIU

I MADE IT to the boats in less than four minutes. I may have looked good in my new garb, but those four minutes definitely proved that the shoes were not made for running. I probably should have retrieved my squeaky sneakers from the cave, but I wasn't thinking too clearly.

There were three boats at the dock. I guessed two of them were Ishikawa's and one belonged to the boys. I could tell that one had been used recently—the engines were still putting out a lot of heat. It was a fast boat, a Nor-Tech 3900 Super Vee. I knew this because on the side it said, "Nor-Tech 3900 Super Vee." I also knew a bit about it because the boys at the shop had built a shrine to the Nor-Tech line of offshore racers. One of the guys had put up a poster over a bare patch of wall, and over time, various offerings had appeared. In the past few years I had seen one around, perhaps even this one, a number of times. I think the boys said it could do over a hundred miles per hour.

It had to have been Ishikawa's ride—those things

cost some hefty coin. I guessed that was the one they were going to steal, and the guy they called MB had been joyriding in it. Top dog in the kennel!

The wind was heavy, but nothing like it had been the day before. It looked like the southern islands got off easy. The waves, however, were still bouncing the boats around like corks. I started up the Super Vee's engines. A pelican that had been observing from the top of a piling took to the air as the engines belched smoke and roared to life. I made sure it was in idle, jumped back onto the dock, and ran to the other two boats. Disabling them would buy me time to get back to the main island. Like the big boat, these had keys in the ignition, which I pulled out and threw into the water. For good measure, I yanked some key wiring and pushed them away from the dock. It wouldn't permanently disable them, but it would slow boob-grabber and MB down. I'd seen no sign of them yet and hoped they'd be slow in arriving. With any luck, their injuries would keep them from a flat-out run.

There was the issue of the boathouse, which I figured was used for long-term storage. I had to go on that assumption because it was locked. I returned to the big boat, cast off the lines, and pushed off from the dock.

I'm not what you would call a master boater, but you don't get far as becoming a dive guide without learning to run zodiacs and tenders in some gnarly waters. I had even taken the helm of a sixty-ton boat during a long transfer between islands. How hard could a recreational boat be? I sat down and pushed on the throttle, and the boat jumped like a bronco. *Holy crap*. That thing was pure power. I reset myself in the captain's chair, put on my seat belt, and pushed the throttle a bit more. Within a minute I was screaming along—literally, I was screaming—at something past fifty miles per hour, cutting through the waves like a pro. Or so I imagined.

Ishikawa's house was in a cove on the northwest side of the island. The waves were more manageable there, but I knew I would get beaten up once I reached more exposed waters, which took all of thirty seconds. Thanks to the fringing reef around Peleliu, the waters were usually calmer than in the open ocean, but the wind was kicking up a lot of chop. I knew I would also have some tricky navigation as I exited the cove, watching out for lots of small outcroppings and pinnacles. I would have to slow down. My hope was that if the men were even able to start one of the other boats, they would have to go slow as well.

The trip from Peleliu to Koror normally took an hour—an hour of eye-popping displays of lush tropical jungle islands. At the speed I was going, I estimated I would be at the dock within thirty minutes. We had a short-wave radio at the office, and I had some calls to make.

It was tougher than I expected. I was dealing with a lot of power in the Nor-Tech, and it required a gentle touch on the throttle. A look back, though, told me the boys either hadn't been able to start the other boats, or maybe they were still seeing stars.

I had no idea what their plans were, but I was hoping they would choose flight over fight—unlikely, since I now knew their identities. By the time I was a few miles north of the cove, there was still no other boat in sight, so I cut the engines to idle and took a moment to assess my situation. The boat was tricked out, and I figured that if it was one of Ishikawa's, it might have a few bonus items. Of course, the others might as well, so I decided to do an inventory and assume they had the same.

There was a VHF radio built into the dash. I gave it a try. Nothing but static. Peleliu was pretty isolated, and the VHF tower was up on a high ridge. I found a pair of binoculars in the dashboard storage, scanned the ridge, and couldn't see anything. It stood to reason that the tower was an early casualty in the storm and would probably be one of the lower-priority fixes. I might not have got radio contact until I was a lot closer to Koror.

Since I didn't have a clue as to who was on what side, calling in the cavalry was a risk. I needed to figure out my self-defense plan. I had two possible places to dock—our shop or the marina. The shop was closer, but the boys knew I worked there. The marina provided a more public space, if anyone was out there yet, but more hiding places for an ambush. I decided I would prefer to do battle on my home turf. If the boys guessed I would head for the shop, they might have someone waiting for me. I needed to be prepared.

*

Guns are illegal in Palau. Period. You get caught with one and it's fifteen years in the hoosegow carving storyboards for the tourists. In all the time I had been on the island, I had only heard of a few people getting caught, and gun crime was almost unheard of. The island was safe that way. I would have been surprised if Ishikawa had one. His reputed style was intimidation and maybe some strong-arm if need be. He was too smart to get caught with a gun. But, for only the second time in my life, I wished I had one. I searched the boat, hoping to find one. No joy, but I turned up a lot of other firepower.

The man liked his spear guns. I didn't recall him ever buying any from us, but he had quite a few. And most were the compact type... probably better for his uses. He even had a Woody Sawed-Off Magnum, my favorite for getting big fish in close quarters. I'm sure they're not as effective as a gun, but if someone were pointing one of these at me from twenty feet or less, I would pay very close attention to their instructions.

I kept looking through the built-in storage. The rear bench sat on what looked like an aftermarket backup gas tank that probably held 200 gallons. Under one long bench I found two complete sets of scuba gear, including tanks. I did a quick check, and they both had air, though one was only half-full. It was probably used for quick checks under the boat or to get the evening meal. In the side lockers I found several flare guns and waterproof cases filled with flares. The man was a model of boating safety.

The cabin didn't look anything like I expected. Where there should have been couches and a coffee table were industrial metal racks with tie-downs. There was still one small couch, but that was it for luxury. The bow, which was probably designed for a bed, was filled with stacks of empty plastic tubs like you get at Ben Franklin's. I checked the few closed storage bins but found nothing in the way of weaponry, unless you counted the rather excessive set of kitchen knives in the galley drawer, including a damn big cleaver and a sashimi knife that looked like it could slice through most anything. I figured they could be very effective persuaders in the right hands. But when you had a fifteen-foot crocodile, why mess around with knives? Next, I came across lots of booze and some good snacks. I grabbed a can of peanuts and a jar of Nutella and flashed on that crocodile's last meal. A shiver ran down my spine. That was way too close for comfort. I'm a lover, not a fighter, and I was way out of my element. I wolfed down the nuts and several big spoonsful of Nutella—just enough to abate my hunger.

I may not be a fighter, but I wasn't going to be an easy mark. I climbed back up out of the cabin, tossed the three best spear guns into the back seats, laid two flare guns in the passenger seat with a case of flares, then tucked one of the Tasers in the driver-side cup holders. I checked the other Taser. It seemed pretty simple: a red light indicated it had power (I assumed), and a safety was set to "armed." I switched it to "safe." It looked pretty much like a gun, so I figured when it was set to "armed," I had only to aim and pull the trigger. Hopefully I wouldn't need to find out if my guess was right.

I slid into the seat, buckled up, touched the throttle, and took off. The whole stop had probably taken two to three minutes. I guessed I had a minimum five-minute head start on the boys, maybe ten, and maybe they weren't even going to follow. If they did, I definitely had the best boat, but anything could happen in a race. I slowly pushed forward on the throttle until I was skipping across the waves with the RPMs just below redline.

*

I was bouncing across the wave tops and taking a bit of a beating in the post-storm waves, but making good time. In open water, I had the luxury of time to think, and played out the scenario as I saw it. I needed to get into the shop and didn't have my keys. The cove had been crowded with boats when I checked out our cruiser, and I didn't know what condition it might be in. I realized I might be dealing with a whole mess of boats and ropes. I might need the knives from the galley.

I set the throttle to idle, and the boat settled down quickly. I was in a slow drift but there were no obstructions, so I jumped out of my chair and dropped into the cabin. I grabbed the big cleaver and the sashimi knife and tossed them up onto the passenger seat. The sashimi knife stuck in the padding, and the cleaver cut a long tear in the seat back. I climbed back up, put the knife in the passenger-side cup holder, and wedged the cleaver into the gap between the armrest and the seat cushion.

As I finished, I looked back and thought I saw some spray kicking up from back by the cove. It was at least a few miles back, so I couldn't be sure. I picked up the binoculars. *Crap! A damn boat.* Judging from the rooster tail it was spitting up, it was a fast one, and they had the throttle pushed to full-on boogie.

I sucked in a breath, took the Nor-Tech out of neutral, and started to apply power. The boat took off, and within a minute I was up to full speed. With each bounce on the waves, the throbbing in my head got worse, and keeping my eyes focused became harder.

I looked in the side-view mirrors (the boat really was truly tricked out) and thought the other boat might be catching up with me. *Crap. The boathouse!* That was where Ishikawa would have kept the best and brightest. They didn't need to deal with either of the boats I disabled—they had a better one. I realized I might actually have a race on my hands.

By my estimate, I was about twenty minutes from base. The clock on the dashboard indicated it was 2:15. If they were five miles behind me, and I was going at least eighty miles per hour, I should have had a good margin for beating them to the dock. I was a dive guide, though, who liked healthy margins, so I pushed forward on the throttle and uttered a few improvised prayers.

Whoever was following was good, but I was good too. They were clearly gaining, but not much. I wasn't going to fool myself—we were still thirty miles from home, and a lot can happen in that space. I knew I should have kicked both of them a few more times in the head. Sometimes I was just too much of a softy.

I kept it at full throttle as I prepared to enter the area known as the Rock Islands. For many, the Rock Islands were the essence of Palau. They covered the space between Peleliu and Koror with a random pattern of small dome-like islands, the remnants of an ancient reef that was thrust above the surface by shifting plates and continents. They were covered with thick jungles of growth. To some they resembled mushrooms. Others thought they looked like turtles.

I passed a few small ones that signaled the beginning of the labyrinth. Some were only a hundred feet across, others much larger. Each rounded island, with no gaps in its canopy, perched on a limestone base that had been undercut by the relentless buzzsaw of tides and sand. The result was almost like a pedestal—faded yellow and tan rock bases carved out as much as five feet or more, depending on the level of the tide. From above, the islands looked like perfectly polished emeralds tossed onto a deep-blue felt pool table, but as you race by in a boat, they look more like something out of Dr. Seuss or a Hollywood computer-graphic studio. It was on one of these smaller islands that I attempted my ouzo-fueled topiary project, which, by now, had probably been exposed by Stephaliza as some macabre attempt to recreate the Texas Chainsaw Massacre. The only good part about the last few hours was I hadn't seen a paper. Normally, I would slow down to enjoy the scenery, but I leaned into the throttle to keep it screaming. I was tempted to keep pushing when the needle approached the redline, but I forced myself to keep it just below.

The exposed gaps on the islands told me it was low tide. I made a mental note to keep that in mind while navigating, but then I looked back. The other boat had closed the gap substantially. I had been running at top speed, and they were still catching up fast. In that part of the islands, it was hard to hide, but as long as I had some distance between us by the time I got to the northern islands around Ngerkebesang, then I figured I should be able to lose them. I tried to avoid thinking about what would happen if I didn't, but the prospect kept creeping into my brain. After one particularly gruesome thought, I realized I'd eased off on the power, so I compensated by pushing beyond my comfort zone. At that point, comfort wasn't an option.

Navigating through the Rock Islands was like skiing a slalom course. There were over two hundred of them, scattered about willy-nilly, and some had narrow passes just a boat-length wide. In a few cases, what looked like a channel turned into a dead end—I had to make sure to avoid those. I could have taken an outside tack and stayed at full throttle, but I figured I could mask my position if I went into the maze. Besides, I went through these islands five to ten times a month. I knew the best routes, and I knew where I could get lost. In a boat race, I could outfox just about anybody. I turned toward the densest section of islands. It was time to turn the chase into a game of skill instead of pure horses.

They were still more than a mile back when we got to Ngerkebesang Island. I shot through the narrow gap that led into the wild mash-up of islands and backed off the throttle. I knew those islands well, but not at a hundred miles per hour. Despite my misgivings, I decided that risking a spectacular crash was better than letting them catch me. I nudged the throttle and started cutting my turns a bit shallower. My eyes were stinging from dripping sweat. More than once, I thought I was going to clip an outlying rock, but I never eased back on the throttle.

It was impossible to tell if I had lost them. As I crisscrossed though the islands, visibility was only three hundred to five hundred feet. They could have been that close before they'd be in view. The two hundred Rock Islands are spread out for almost twenty miles, and the trip seemed much longer than that. Toward the north where the clusters were denser, I could no longer run at full speed, so I worked the throttle and constantly checked my mirrors. To that point, I hadn't seen them. Once I was out of sight, it would be virtually impossible—and only through dumb luck—for them to find me again. I said a few more prayers as I approached the end of the northernmost islands. Once I was past the islands, I had a quick shot to Koror. All I needed was enough of a gap to beat them to Kgerkebesang Island. Once I was out from the islands, I would be in radio range. I'd be able to call the Port Authority and have them call out the Marines. Or national police. Whoever. And then I would pray that they were the good guys.

As I reached the end of the pack, the islands started thinning out and I had a better view behind me. No sign of the other boat, but there was still less than a half mile between islands, so they could be a mile back—or less—and I wouldn't be able to see them. That might be the difference between success and failure.

I had gotten increasingly comfortable working the throttle as the slalom course opened up, and for the last couple islands I was back to full speed, or at least close to it. I shot out into the open and looked back. Nothing.

*

Then I scanned to my left. *Crap*. They were off to the side and slightly ahead of me, less than a half mile away and coming fast. I froze. They stood between freedom and me. I had been an idiot. They'd never even followed me into the islands—they'd just run up the open waters to the west and waited for me. So much for cunningly trumping their power.

I took a deep breath, veered right, and pushed the throttle until the gauges showed I was redlined. The scream of the engines was incredible... metal-concert mosh-pit loud. It sounded like a drag racer in my back pocket. I was skipping across the tops of small waves and taking a beating, and they were still closing on me, the beast getting airborne as they banged through and over the waves. They were a few hundred feet away, and I could see that their boat was even bigger than mine. The hull was knifing through the waves. Through the spray I could see "Nor-Tech 5000." *Five Thousand? Crap.* No wonder they could catch me. Their boat was enormous. Fifty feet long, easily.

Maybe I could work that to my advantage.

They closed to within a hundred feet, but I needed them to be a bit closer.

Within moments, the flaws in that decision became obvious. Sounding like a car wreck, the left quarter of my dashboard blew apart. I instinctively backed off the throttle, and at a hundred miles per hour, they flew past me in an instant. Then the left side of my windshield shattered into shards, making me instinctively jerk the wheel to the right. They had a gun and were shooting at me. *Where did they get a gun?* That asshole Ishikawa. They must have found his secret stash. I wondered if I'd missed one in my boat.

I didn't have time to find out. Another shot smacked

into the side of the boat. They'd slowed and were no more than a hundred feet from me, but luckily the bouncing of the boats made aiming difficult. I had no idea how many shots had been fired, since the engine noise covered up any reports, but at least three shots had found the boat. I glanced over at the flare gun and spear guns but couldn't imagine either was going to help me at that point. I wasn't going to get into a shooting match, and I wasn't going to offer myself up for target practice.

Throttling back about a third, I cranked the wheel farther to the right. The boat slapped and bounced on the waves as it muscularly leaned into the turn. I had braced for a pummeling and an extreme lean, but it handled beautifully—more carving than battling. I straightened out the wheel and pushed on the throttle. The boat shot forward and was back to full speed in less than thirty seconds.

I looked back. I probably had three hundred yards on them. The surprise of the maneuver, and the wider turns their big boat had to make, gave me a little room, but I didn't want too much of a gap. I wanted them close. They were up to full speed even faster than I had been. I had boat envy. But I also had a plan, and them being bigger and faster was part of it.

The Arch. It sat almost like a massive stone entry at the northern part of the islands. I had passed it just before running into the boys. It was a hundred feet wide and forty feet high, its center empty, forming a dramatic frame of the view beyond. The gap was big enough to get our dive boats through, but only at certain times. The feature was made when erosion undercut the base of the island, and much of it collapsed, leaving the uppermost portion behind. What had crumbled, though, littered the seabed and formed a shallow ridge at a depth of just a foot at low tide, which was why we always timed our visits for high tide, when it was safely navigable. I could tell by the waterline on the islands that it was currently low tide. I doubted the boys knew any of that. I was counting on it.

We were both racing toward the Arch at a hundred miles or more, and they were closing. Another shot hit the boat, this time ahead of me on my raised bow. *C'mon boys, just another five hundred yards, maybe a bit more.* We covered two-thirds of that distance in less than twenty seconds. I was aiming right for the Arch, and so were the boys. I eased off the throttle just a bit, not so that it was noticeable, but enough that they closed the gap. They were now right on my tail, a hundred feet behind at most. I kept one hand on the throttle and one on the wheel.

Just when it looked like I was going to shoot through the arch, I cut my speed and forced the wheel hard right. I skittered across the waves and thought for a moment I had cut it too close and would broadside the rocks. The boys didn't anticipate the move, so they didn't have time or space to turn and went straight toward the Arch. I was sure they figured they'd go through and then resume the hunt. I knew better.

I was still wrestling with my boat when I heard the bang of their hull hitting the shallow rock reef and the screech of their props biting into the air. I couldn't chance taking my eyes off my own path as I fought through my turn, but the crash and explosion that followed were catastrophic. I could feel the heat on my back as I shot off to the right.

Cutting my power as I turned, I looked back. All I could see were floating bits and pieces of burning boat. The thing had literally disintegrated when it hit the Arch, which was now on fire, thanks to the fuel from the boat, like a ring at the circus. Except, these daredevils hadn't made it through.

25

2:45 P.M. – ROCK ISLANDS

FOR THE FIRST time since I regained consciousness at the hideaway, I had both reason to be optimistic and time to panic. Barely able to catch my breath, I let the boat drift. The screaming sound in my head continued, even though the engine was now just purring at idle, competing with the pounding for my attention. My heart was racing. I was covered in sweat. My mouth was dry, and I couldn't stop the shaking. But I was alive. And the killer was dead.

I continued to let the boat drift. The current was moving me slowly toward Koror, and I was fine with that. As I slumped into the captain's chair, I noticed that the corner of the backrest was gone. *Fuck. Too close.* My stomach started doing flip-flops, and for what seemed like the hundredth time in the past few days, I felt like I was going to vomit.

I had been at risk before, but I hadn't known at the time. In fact, I had probably been closer to death during that horrible summer in Hawai'i, sitting in a car with a man I thought I could trust. I barely had time to figure it out before the locals had the Surf Slayer in handcuffs, and the FBI had taken their stupid profiles and theories and slunk away with their tails between their legs. This time was different—I had been face-to-face with death and could have folded, but I didn't.

The wind was blowing me along at a decent pace, so just to play it safe, I dropped the anchor. It felt like the bottom was around twenty-five feet. Once the boat was secure, I let out a big breath. The shaking had stopped. I dropped down into the cabin, which was really quite nice, and searched the fridge. Ishikawa had lots of booze, but at least he had some mixers. I pulled out two cans of tonic water, powered one down, and set the other aside.

I needed to catch a break. The winds were still kicking up quite a bit, but I guessed they were now down to the low thirties. Plopping myself onto the sole plush couch in the cramped cabin, I helped myself to the second tonic water.

Within minutes, my bladder began to make itself known, so I checked out the facilities. Though designed for luxury, the cabin lacked headroom. The head was worse—not exactly luxurious and not at all appropriate for someone who stood five ten. After I wiggled out of my tight pants—damn, that Michael Jackson had narrow hips—I folded myself into the small space and had a very pleasing pee. Then I unfolded myself from the seat and wriggled back into the cabin where the short, silk-covered couch called out to me. I had to resist the temptation to take a nap. There were probably still more bad guys back in Koror.

The situation was totally messed up. Of course, there were more—at least one in the government. There'd been leaks, although MB wasn't smart enough to have figured that out. The reporter was getting information too. I had been freelancing for the last twenty-four hours, and it had gotten me nothing but trouble. I really needed help. Whoever was out there would be monitoring the radio, so I couldn't use the open marine band. I did the only thing I could do: I pulled up anchor and headed to Koror. Slowly. I needed time to think.

Even at reduced speed, it took only ten minutes to reach our side of the island. I was home, there were fewer of them than before, and I had what might be called a plan—none of which made me feel very safe.

*

Nearing our shop and its small cove, I cut the engine and let the boat drift before coming to a stop about two hundred yards out. The waves were minimal, the wind had dropped to somewhere around fifteen miles an hour, and water slapped at the side of the boat with a pleasant beat. The air, though, was heavy with humidity and the stench of rotting flora and fauna. A line of pelicans flew by, probably confused and frustrated by the debris that covered the normally clear waters bordering the island. I realized that, for the first time in days, I could hear birds singing.

Through the binoculars I could see that the storm had done its share of damage. The big boat was still floating, though it had damage to some of its rigging and had lost its dive platform. The water was fouled with trees and plants and floating junk that probably was not junk just a few days before.

During my trip from the Arch to Koror, I had tried to figure out who the leak was. I was pretty sure it was Ben Perez. It fit. I couldn't figure out what his game was, but he was the most motivated to bust the yakuza; maybe he had seen me as his chance to stir up some trouble and force the issue. He had been running the operation at the hotel when my security got messed up. He was the one who kept pointing us toward the yakuza and away from any other theory. He had access to all the information. He made sure that Mac kept him up to speed on what the police knew. There were a lot of bits and pieces that fit. I didn't have the whole puzzle assembled, but I was pretty sure. Besides, he was FBI—historically, that meant bad news.

During the summer before my senior year in high school, my best friend had disappeared after a beach party. She was a problem child. A partier. Barely making it in school. The popular theories were that she either ran away or had taken a drunken swim and never returned. Either was possible but not likely. Then another girl disappeared. That one seemed less sinister. She had argued with her parents and left during the night. It happens. Kids split and never return. But then a third girl disappeared. She was from the other side of the island, and although she wasn't a problem child, she had something in common with the others. Surfing. It was the easy answer. Ninety percent of the kids on the island hung out at the beach and knew surfers.

The FBI rolled in, and the beach scene went into

hibernation. The parties stopped. Parents imposed curfews. I got sent to Colorado. In the end, it turned out the FBI were completely wrong. They had blinders on. Once they'd figured out the truth, they kept their mouths shut, almost costing another girl her life.

Me.

It happened the day I returned, eight days after my eighteenth birthday. It wasn't a surfer but a pillar of society. A respected member of the community. A serial killer who'd left a trail from New Jersey to California to Hawai'i. And the feds never had a clue. Now, here they were, bumbling around again with their yakuza gang-war theory.

Whoever it was—Ben Perez or someone else—might have been in with MB, or at least knew he had me. That probably meant they weren't looking for me or expecting me. By my reckoning, that gave me a major advantage. I needed to get back to the shop and reach out to the few safe contacts I could rely on, but I wasn't sure if the place was safe. I needed to approach quietly, just in case somebody I didn't want to meet was inside.

There was nothing for me to wear for the dive. No wetsuits, swim trunks, or even a t-shirt. Michael's jacket and pants were all I had, and I wasn't about to be caught (dead or alive) sneaking naked into the shop. I'm not saying that never happened before, but it was never planned.

A full set of scuba gear was prepped and ready to go. Whoever it was rigged for, it wasn't Ishi—he would have needed an XXXL. The bench had taken a hit from a bullet, but I checked the gear, and it was fine. I hoisted it up onto the bench, opened the valve, checked my gauges, and strapped myself into the buoyancy compensation rig. I pulled on a mask and fins, put my regulator in my mouth, and backrolled into the water. I held the Woody spear gun in my right hand and had strapped the sashimi knife to my leg. I looked like a badass. I felt more like a scared cat stuck up in a tree with no fireman around to rescue me, and all I could think to do was walk farther out toward the tip of the branch.

26

3:15 P.M. – NGERKEBESANG ISLAND

RECENTLY, EACH OF my plans seemed to be missing the mark. The hotel escape had not gone as expected. Running into a dark cave with no flashlight was, in retrospect, not a clever move. My inspired boat-chase scheme, though it ended fine, had assumed the boys would follow me into the maze. They hadn't. And my coin tosses were doing no better.

As I sank into the dark, confused water, surrounded by the mess the storm had left, I felt unsettled. The salt water stung not only my face where I'd been cut, but also the abrasions on my wrists and ankles from the ropes—and my knee, which I must have cut in the cave. The mental agitation, though, was worse than the stinging pain. By my count, I had killed three men in a single day. Technically, I didn't kill any of them, but that's not how it felt. I'm not a killer. I'm not even a good fighter. And I had never wanted to do either. The Woody seemed less and less like a weapon and more like a burden. I wasn't even sure if I could make myself pull the trigger.

For what seemed like the hundredth time in the past few days, I suppressed the urge to puke, but nothing would stop the flood of doubt that wracked my brain. I dropped toward the sandy bottom and hovered motionless for what was probably only five minutes, but it felt like an hour. I floated and thought, second-guessing my most recent plan—reaching shore on scuba. It hadn't taken long to figure out I had run out of options. With a few swift kicks, I drove myself away from the bottom and toward the shore.

It wasn't just the surface of the harbor fouled with rubble. As bad as that was, the underwater scene was even worse. Ropes and cables hung down from boats. Broken masts, with loose and detached rigging, lay about like jackstraws. A sign from Ben Franklin's lay on the bottom of the harbor, while a tattered sail hovered in the water like an oversized ghost. Navigating through it was dangerous and slow. Twice I got snagged on clear monofilament line trailing from fishing gear that had ended up in the water, proving the knife to be handy. Thankfully, and true to form, Ishikawa—or one of his lackeys—had kept it as sharp as a samurai sword. On top of dealing with the snagging lines and the wave-strewn debris, my mask kept flooding. Clearly bought for a larger face than mine, it was a bad fit for my narrow Nordic-influenced features. Water leaked in through the entire dive, and I had to repeatedly stop to clear it.

Finally making it to the rock rubble that formed the shoreline of our man-made cove, I took off the gear while still in the water and let it float away. It would fit right in with the rest of the debris, and I saw no reason for making noise by pulling it ashore.

I left Michael's shoes in the boat so I could put on my fins, which meant the only things protecting my feet as I scrambled up the rocks were the sequin socks. The jacket was a little worse for wear, some of the gold braiding having been snagged and torn during my exit from the cave and again during the dive, but I didn't look half-bad, especially given the day I'd had. I suspected no one would bat an eye if I walked into the Rock Island Café looking like this.

*

Crossing the empty back parking lot, I moved toward the back wall. Debris was everywhere, but the building appeared intact, though a lot of the boards we'd secured over the windows were missing, and some of the glass was gone. The place looked empty. I got up on my tiptoes and looked in through what remained of the high windows that provided the only natural light for the repair shop and equipment room. No sign of activity.

In fact, the island as a whole was oddly silent but for the wind and the clatter of debris as it skittered across the tarmac. No cars on the road. No bicycles. No pedestrians. A few birds. It was a ghost town. The streets remained flooded and strewn with all manner of trash.

I worked my way around the side and looked into the office, which was intact, just as I left it. I crept around the corner and checked the front lot. Empty except for the boats that had been secured there earlier.

And an old Willy's truck. World War II vintage—more rust than paint.

I had seen that truck before but couldn't remember where. *Crap!* It was the truck by the side of the road at Ricky's Rocking Spot. MB's truck that he was worried I had recognized. He must have left it here when they took the boat and me to Peleliu. I scooted between the truck and our small boats. We'd be replacing at least one of them, judging by the looks of things. Hard to maneuver with a stop sign shoved through the side.

I peered into the front window and saw no movement. Checking the front door, I confirmed that everything was locked up tight and the glass was intact. The building had survived the storm relatively undamaged. I picked up one of the rocks from our ornamental rock garden and smashed the glass panel. I always knew it was a vulnerability.

Letting myself in, I stepped carefully over the broken glass in my now dirty sequin socks, went over to the gear case, and pulled out a pair of rubber booties. Until I could get some proper shoes, these would have to do.

Ralph the Parrot was staring at me anxiously, unusually silent. I'd been told that, although they were intelligent, eclectus parrots do not handle stress well and often appear to be quite stupid. In fact, they just freak out easily. Poor Ralph. I pulled out a particularly tasty-looking sugar cane from the storage portion of one of our displays and pushed it through the cage. I didn't open it or try to touch Ralph, who was, in reality, a female. Whoever first got him named him Ralph, and we didn't know why. He had been handed down with the business over the years, and that part of the history was lost. But "Ralph" stuck as a name, and it confused everyone if we referred to her as "she," so we'd all gotten in the habit of calling her "him." Anyhow, the female eclectus parrot was a vibrant ruby-red color and, like many redheads, quite aggressive. So, I kept my fingers to myself. Wouldn't want to lose a fingertip like one of the yakuzas.

That thought sent another spasm through my body. The first time I saw Koga, when he shot past me following the truck axle, he reached out to me and I saw that two of his fingers had been partially amputated. Nothing like his final fate, but still a nasty punishment.

Ralph lustily grabbed the sugar cane and started chewing. Probably not the best dietary choice for a parrot that might not have eaten in a few days, but he seemed to enjoy it. I poured a scoop of millet into his feeder then took his water bottle and went to refill it.

"Ricky's in the bathroom. Ricky's in the bathroom."

"Yes, Ralph, I am. Glad to see you've found your voice."

"Ralph is pretty. A pretty girl."

"You know it Ralph." I rehung his now full water bottle.

Ralph had taken me out of my game, and I had let my guard down. I grabbed the Woody and cautiously opened the door to the equipment room. It was dark... appearing empty. An unpleasant aroma reminded me I had left wet gear in need of a washing there. I returned to the retail space where Ralph was merrily working his way between the millet and the water. *Good choices, Ralph. The sugar high can wait.*

I went down the hallway to the office.

"Ricky's in the bathroom!" cried Ralph.

I knew I needed to get in touch with Mac, not that I completely trusted him. He had the facilities I needed, though, and at some point I needed to take a leap of faith. The solo route hadn't served me very well. The phones were still out, though power was back on, so the trouble must have been with some central equipment. Not good. The telephone company wasn't very good at redundancy and sparing. It would take them a few days to get a major piece of equipment back online.

My cell phone was... *where was my cell phone? Probably back at the hotel.* My God, the day had started there so long ago.

Thankfully, the shop kept cell phones that the crew took out with us on dives. We seldom got strong connections, but there were times when cell worked better than radio. I went back into the repair area, and there they were, still plugged in. Sarah hadn't unplugged them as she'd prepared for the unlikely possibility of a surge. Bless her obsessive brain—for once it had failed her. My good luck. They were charged, and based on the three bars showing, it looked like the cell tower had been repaired. *Give thanks for small miracles.*

Using a cheat sheet I kept in the office explaining how to check voicemail from an outside line (I often lost my phone and needed to use a different line to check messages), I dialed the numbers. Best to find out what had been going on before I started sending up my signal flares.

Since the phones had been down and cell connections

just recently restored, I wasn't expecting many voicemails, but I had a lot. Well, three from Mac, one from Ben Perez, one from PalauCel, four from that Stephaliza woman, one from Dad, a couple from Sarah, and one from Ruluked. *Ruluked.* It was nice to see her name pop up. No reply from Justin, which was odd.

*

Ruluked was essentially an ombudsman at the AG's office, which was perfect for her. When somebody got frustrated with the endless bureaucracy or was totally baffled by the cryptic rules and regulations, they got handed to Ruluked. It didn't matter if you were a minister in the government or a pauper trying to hold onto the family land, she would make your cause her own. She might have been the only person in the government I trusted without question.

I listened to her voicemail first. "Sister, I know your phone is lost, has a dead battery, and is out of range, but if you get this message, call me. You have no idea what sort of trouble you've gotten yourself into this time." She left her cellphone number, as she always did. She had no faith that I had her in speed dial, that I had access to speed dial, or that I knew how to use speed dial. Wise woman.

Well, Ruluked, I think I actually do have a fairly good idea, but I came by the education the tough way.

I called her, and she answered on the first ring.

Get a life people, I thought. *Any answer before the third ring just smacks of desperation.*

"This is Ruluked."

"And this would be Ricky," I replied.

Ruluked let out a hearty laugh. “Oh my goodness, Ricky, I’m glad you’re ok. I was getting desperate. What with everything going on with the storm, and at the hotel. Where did you go off to? The officer who let you sneak out is in a lot of trouble, you know. Did you really tase her?” The words had gushed out, and more followed. “I’ve been frantic. I’ve tried reaching your cell, and I notice you’re not calling from it, so I assume it’s dead or lost or both. I tried your bosses. I even called your dad.” *Oh, great, thanks.* “You have no idea what trouble you’re in. Can you talk?”

“When you stop to take a breath, I can.”

“I mean now. Are you in a private place?”

“I’m at the shop. I’m the only one here, unless you count Ralph, who’s a bit of a blabbermouth.”

“She’s a lovely bird.”

“He, we call her ‘he.’ It keeps the need for explanation to a minimum.”

“Honey, you have bigger issues to deal with. There are people out there who want you dead.”

“I know. They tased me and took me to Peleliu. It was crazy scary, Ru. They had a crocodile and were going to kill me.”

“You got away? Are you safe? Where are they?”

“Yes and yes, and the last time I saw them they were floating face down near the arch. I killed them. They’re dead.” I hadn’t spoken the words before, and my knees went weak as the full force of the statement hit me. “I killed them.”

“You what? All of them? Do I even want to know?” she asked quietly. “I am a government official.”

"No, you probably don't. Not now. I met three of them, now they're gone. But there's at least one more. These guys had inside information. And no, I didn't tase the agent—they did, right before they grabbed me."

"Uh uh, sister. There's more than that. I count at least two more. And at least one of those works for the government and has spent a lot of time with you recently. I work with some people who are working with people I don't work with, who seem to know an awful lot that we don't know. They say, at best, it's a stool pigeon. At worst, somebody with an agenda."

That actually made sense. "So, who is it? I don't have time for coy." I was starting to feel uncomfortable. I pulled the Woody toward me and turned to face the door. I was done with surprises. I hoped.

"That's the problem. No one knows. Whoever it is has close access to the case. They're probably assigned to it. They've got information that goes back to your first police report about the bodies. They think you know a lot more than you've told. Do you?"

"I do now. My next call is to Detective Uchel."

"NO. I don't think that's wise. What we have here is a horrible mess. I'm not the best at reading the tea leaves, honey, but I think this is a lot bigger than Ishikawa and cathouses and tattoo parlors. I think this is the beginning of a scandal that will rock the entire government. We don't know who to trust. That's why I have a plan."

"A plan?" I'd had mixed success with plans so far—they'd all gone south before heading north. "What's your plan?"

"Get you out of the country. Put you in touch with

someone we can trust outside the government. Here's the deal. Commercial flights are still shut down. The winds aren't too bad right now, but the data the NOAA guys are getting is that the storm may turn back this way." Leave it to Ruluked to have all the latest intel at her fingertips. "So," she continued, "I got you a seat on a government plane. A storm chaser. It's landing in about an hour at ROR." That made sense. Palau International Airport handled military and government traffic in addition to commercial. "Wheels up in about two. Can you get there? It'll take you to Guam. They're on a working mission, so it will take about eight hours. I'm thinking I can hook you up with some bureaucrats," a term she used as a label of honor, "who can be trusted. The Americans still have a vested interest down here and are still on the hook to provide military support. I know some very motivated people."

"Ruluked," I interrupted, "I love you, but I don't think this is a military matter."

"It is if we're having a government meltdown. Perhaps you've forgotten but the US of A is in charge of our national security. If this is as big as we think it is, the US military definitely needs to be involved. Have you been reading the *Island Times* website? Stephaliza has been spot-on with every report—too spot-on. She's been arrested."

"That bitch published my name and almost got me killed."

In her soothing, calming, "don't you worry, honey, Ruluked is on the case" voice, she said, "Stephaliza overstepped the boundaries of appropriate journalism, but she's got sources we don't even have, and she's already implicated three ministries. Just today there have been six high-level resignations. During a typhoon. People don't typically resign during typhoons. But they do get killed and I'm worried you might be one of them—and not by an act of God. I'm guessing there are three more out there, but it could be worse. And if you now have new information, they have even more incentive than before. Do not—I repeat, DO NOT—call Detective Uchel. I know you're thinking about it, but don't. And not that FBI agent, Perez, either. I think one of them is neck-deep in this, but I can't figure out which. My brain tells me it's Uchel, but he's so handsome I'd like to think it's not him. As a matter of fact, don't tell anyone about this. No one. Anyway, can you make it to the airport?"

"I don't have a car. My Jeep's being repaired by Mac's brother-in-law. I sort of have a boat, but the airport is a distance from the shore. I do have a truck I can borrow." I had left the keys back on the boat, but I was sure I could hotwire the old truck MB left in the parking lot. Wouldn't be the first time.

"Perfect," said Rulukod. "Now get thee to the airport. I sent you an e-mail with a letter of introduction and a government pass. Cable and Internet are up. I'll stay on the line while you confirm. Print them out. Go to the NOAA office. Tell them you're meeting up with the weather plane. They know what to do. And don't get yourself killed. I need a running partner. I get bored listening to Lady Gaga as I run. And after this all gets tied up and you get back in town, have someone else check your Samu... Jeep. I don't trust Mac, so I definitely don't trust his brother-in-law. And don't kill any more people unless you really have to."

"Yes, ma'am," I replied, and I meant it. Ruluked was wise. One of those Libras who are great at making decisions for others but not themselves. If she had been giving herself advice and following it, she would be president, and we wouldn't have a government in crisis.

As we talked, I had turned on the computer, but nothing happened. Then I saw the note: "Ricky, you left your computer plugged in. I unplugged it (again). Better safe than sorry. Love, Sarah."

"Criminy," I said to Ruluked, "the computer's unplugged. Sarah has this obsession about doing that before storms to avoid power surges. Give me a second to plug it in."

I climbed under the desk and found the dangling cord. Holding it between my index and forefinger, I slid my hand behind the desk. I had just gotten it in when I heard breaking glass.

*

The sound of the glass, likely the last remnants of our front door, was followed by a familiar, rumbling voice calling from outside. "This is Detective MacArthur Uchel of the national police. Identify yourself."

I was about to answer when I remembered Ruluked's strict instructions: "DO NOT" contact Uchel. *Crap.* What if he was crooked? A crooked guy who definitely had a gun. And my spear gun was on top of the desk, I was folded like a pretzel under the desk, and the shop wasn't all that big. He'd find me soon enough.

"You are trespassing. There is evidence of looting. We are under executive orders that looters are to be detained—shot if necessary. I have a gun and I'm prepared to use it." *Yep, a gun.*

"Ricky's in the bathroom. Ricky's in the bathroom."

Damn it, Ralph.

I heard Uchel stepping on the broken glass as he entered the front space. He was sliding his feet. I envisioned him with the gun out, in a shooter's stance, edging toward the hall. I hadn't been able to reach the spear gun, which remained in plain sight on the desk. I had, at least, pulled the chair up against the desk so that a casual glance might miss me, though it wasn't a large chair. I had campaigned over the years for a big executive chair, but the lawyers, who didn't have to sit in it—and who were tightwads with an affinity for historical legal artifacts—had purchased and kept a heavy oak chair, officially a banker's chair, on stubborn wheels. It was heavy as hell and very uncomfortable, but at that moment its main failing was that it was small and had a back made of staves. It didn't hide me very well.

As Mac came by my door, he was facing the bathroom with his back to me. Poor form for searching an area—based on the TV shows I had seen—but fortunate for me. He was indeed in a shooter's crouch and had his gun out.

"Ricky," he said, "it's Mac. Can you answer?" He reached out with his free hand, turned the knob, and inched the door open. Then he leaned back, raised his foot, kicked the door, and raised his gun. "Freeze!" he yelled.

Using the opportunity of his focus and noise, I made my move. I had one chance. Mom had talked about these moments: Third jump. Fouled on the first two. If you don't make it, you're out of the competition. You reach down inside and find a handful of confidence and a handful of fear. You use them both.

As Mac stood in the bathroom door with his back to me and gun raised, I tucked my legs back into my chest and then let them explode out, launching the chair with surprising force. It skidded out the door and across the hall, hitting Mac in the butt and the knees and knocking him into the bathroom sink and mirror.

I unfolded myself and followed in one relatively fluid motion. I couldn't give him time to recover, but I didn't have a particularly sophisticated plan. The mirror was spiderwebbed, so he must have hit it with his head as he flew forward. He was slow to react and just starting to turn when I reached him. I briefly considered a classic Rikidozen flying kick, but because I'd never actually tried one, I just drove into his back with my shoulder. His head hit the mirror a second time, and we both tumbled to the ground.

I struggled to get up, but he was lying on top of me. Mac was down. And out. I squirmed out from under him, pulling myself up on the sink. I was tempted to kick him in the head a few times, but I wasn't sure he was the bad guy. Besides, he was already bleeding from an ugly gash on his forehead.

I was confused and frustrated. *Had he kicked in the door because he thought I might be in trouble? Had he seen MB's truck there and assumed I needed help? Or was he planning on killing me, claiming he mistook me for a looter?* I couldn't take any chances. I rolled him over onto his back, wrapped his arms around the base of the toilet, and used his own handcuffs to secure him. No way he would get out of that. *Shame they weren't fur-lined.*

*

"Oh crap!" I shrieked as I realized I had left her hanging. "Ruluked?" I picked up the phone—she was still there. And hysterical.

"Ricky. Oh my goodness, are you alright? I heard all the noise—what happened? Who was in there?"

"Everything's ok. It was Mac," I said, trying to catch my breath and sound calm, which was far from the case.

"I don't think you should be there alone with him," she said in a whisper. "I don't trust him."

"It's ok. I knocked him out and handcuffed him." I left out the part about the toilet. I had to let the man retain some dignity. "He's bleeding a bit, but I think he'll be ok."

I could almost hear Ruluked's smile over the phone. "Ricky, you're beginning to get scary. You go, girl. Make Ruluked proud. Now get to the airport. And remember—tell no one."

"I will. I just have to print out the documents and tie up a few loose ends. I'll be there. Thanks bunches. I owe you. Now hold on while I print the documents."

By the time Mac came to, I was ready. The documents were printed, and Ruluked had repeated her instructions before signing off. I checked his phone and voicemail but couldn't find anything that would give me a clue as to whether or not he was dirty. I went through his pockets, his wallet, and finally his SUV. He had obviously switched to other food sources once Bem Ermii closed for the storm—his floor was littered with a new layer of trash, and it was almost all empty Pop-Tarts packages. His notebook was indecipherable.

Anyhow, I was in a hurry but had taken the time to go online and print out the web pages whose links she had sent me. Since I was already online, I went to the *Island Times* and printed out Stephaliza's latest articles. I might need reading material on the plane, and fiction is always good to pass the time.

I also took the time to check the rest of my messages. No, Stephaliza, you would not be getting a comment from me. Sorry, Dad, Ruluked is out of your league. I would have to get back to all of them later. I got my passport and $2,000 of cash receipts out of the safe. Thank goodness for sloppy banking habits. I kept my passport at the office because I had no security at home, and sometimes we traveled to other nearby island nations with our customers.

So, with no other tasks at hand, it was time to get some closure with Mac. I threw a glass of water in his face like they show in the movies. Surprisingly, it worked. He sputtered and blinked his eyes. It took him a minute to assess the situation. He seemed pissed but in control. I guessed that was the best I could ask for.

"Mac," I said, "I know this looks bad. And, what with my history with the force here in Palau, I might be considered a bit unreliable. But things are going to shit here, and I don't know who to trust."

"Rick—"

I kicked him in the ribs. "Listen. Don't talk. Either you or Perez is a leak and maybe worse. My security vanished. I had two bad guys find me way too easily. They almost killed me. Somebody's screwing with me. And you came in with your gun and kicked in the door after Ralph told you I was in there. I trusted you and now I don't think I can."

"Are you done?" he asked, clearly doing a controlled burn. "Because I would really like to get past this. I'm not at all comfortable. My head hurts like hell. And if we were to be discovered now, or if you leave me here like this, my career prospects might become severely limited. So, let me take a shot at this." His voice was weak. Between the smack on the head and being trussed on his belly and hugging the toilet, he had to work to get words out.

"One. If I'd wanted to push this under the rug, I could have. I was the only one who would listen to you. You still smelled like puke, by the way. My bosses wanted me to make you go away. You have a reputation with the force, you know.

"Two. If, after your return, I'd really wanted to get rid of you, I could have done it at two hundred feet. Accidents happen. I could have offed you and no one would have been the wiser.

"Three, the FBI was in charge of your security. They had the agent on scene. The rest were resources I requisitioned—again, against great resistance. I have no idea how the bad guys found you, but they were clever and outsmarted one of my men and the female agent. I'm on your side, Ricky. I'm the only one who's had your six the entire time.

"And four, I'm going to share some information with you now. Toxicology is back. Ishikawa was killed with a toxin. Could have been manufactured. Could have been natural. The coroner hasn't yet announced any of this—Perez has him sitting on it. I did some checking without them. I'm guessing the FBI wants this to be an international yakuza war so they can come in on their white horses and save the day, but it's local.

"Hideo's owner went missing. He's the link to Ishikawa and Koga. You saw them boarding up the door, remember? I checked the restaurant video. Old system. Doesn't automatically record over. The last night it was on, Ishikawa got in a drunken argument with Michael, the owner, then he came back later, kicked in the door, and tried to make himself an order of fugu. Grabbed the damn puffer fish right out of the fish tank and butchered it on a table. Wolfed down half the liver and washed it down with a bottle of sake. Passed out and never woke up. The owner came down in the early morning and found him. End of tape.

"I was the only one who knew about the tape, but I'm telling you—a Michael Jackson look-alike, no less. That's got to count for something. And now his truck is outside your shop. Out in the parking lot. So, I came in thinking you needed help which, clearly, was misguided. Now let me out of here and let's get you someplace safe."

"I know about Michael Braxton," I interjected. "Braxton and Koga dumped Ishikawa and then Braxton killed Koga. Braxton and his buddies kidnapped me to find out what I knew and who I'd told, then they tried to kill me, but they're dead now." The thought of the crocodile and the lackey made my stomach convulse, but the peanuts and Nutella stayed down. "Want to tell me something I don't know?"

"Dead? All of them?"

I didn't know if I was telling him anything new. If he was in on this, he already had the backstory. Except maybe the dead guys.

"Yes, dead. Some of them. All that I know about. That's on me. But I'd really rather not talk about it. I want to believe you, Mac," I said, trying to remain calm, though I was incredibly pissed off and confused. I should have just left a "Dear Mac" note. "But I've got things under control and I'll be safe. Safer than any of you have left me. And, because I'm pretty sure I believe you, I'm going to leave now without kicking you in the head."

"Fair enough," sighed Mac. "Be safe. And can you leave the key to my cuffs on the desk? With any luck the next person through that door will be a looter and I can convince him to let me out. And, by the way, you really need aviator sunglasses to pull that outfit off."

27

4:30 P.M. – BABELDAOB ISLAND

I HAD PLANNED on hot-wiring MB's truck for my ride to the airport, but Mac's SUV came with keys and a warranty that hadn't expired during the Eisenhower presidency. Plus, there were two packages of Pop-Tarts left in the passenger seat, so I was able to get some much-needed sustenance.

I also had flashers and a siren if I needed them. I had eaten up about an hour at the shop, what with messages and printouts and doing battle with Mac and all, so I had sixty minutes to make what should be a twenty-minute drive. I wasn't anticipating much difficulty once I got to the airport—it was all but shut down.

In fact, I made the drive in less than twenty minutes. There was limited traffic, and I wasn't bashful about running over trash and branches in the road. I parked in the White Zone right in front of the terminal. The SUV had national police plates, so I figured it wasn't going to get ticketed or towed. I left the keys under the seat to make life a bit easier for Mac. I had begun to feel a bit guilty about the way we'd left things—the gash on his head and the toilet-bowl thing in particular. Stealing his SUV would probably also not look good in the report, so hopefully he would get it back before anybody found out. I would call him before I left and leave a nice message.

*

The folks at NOAA were expecting me. They were almost all expats, and a couple of them dived, so I had at least a passing familiarity with a few. Plus, Ruluked had greased the skids for me. They were tripping over themselves to help me, offering me drinks and sharing their lunches with me. It was nearly six o'clock, and I hadn't eaten well for the past few days, so I was starving. Within minutes of arriving, I was pigging out on taro leaf soup, mangrove crab, and some fried chicken. And a big glass of caffeinated soda. With ice. They not only fed me but gave me some toiletries. I hadn't showered in a while, and I was still wearing the outfit that I wore in my swim to shore, so the deodorant helped mask my rather rank odor. No offers of replacement clothing had been made, but I was taller and thinner than all of them, so nothing would have fit. One of them had even been kind enough to point out that I had a fishing lure stuck in my hair.

I decided to pass my time tucked into a relatively plush chair in the small anteroom in the front of the office. Instead of skimming the assorted scientific journals on the side table, I tortured myself by reading copies of the *Island Times* I had printed out before leaving. Stephaliza had been busy.

Soon after I was kidnapped, she'd posted a follow-up

online article that might have been her best in terms of sheer gall. It wasn't the lead; it followed a notice from the *Island Times* that due to the storm there would be no print edition for the next day or two. Stephaliza's article read:

> **Gangs Using Storm to Mask Agenda?**
>
> Speculation has sprung up throughout the Island Nation of Palau that warring gang factions are using Typhoon Mitag as a cover for an escalation in violence.
>
> Overextended and exhausted national and local police are investigating a slew of "atypical" events that have occurred over the past 24 hours.
>
> A fully clothed man was found dead in the pool of the Palasian Hotel with trauma consistent with torture. Police are also investigating the discovery of a local islander, a known patron of the recently burned Lily's Karaoke Bar and suspected bordello, naked and chained to one of Palau's famous stone monoliths at Bairulchau. Investigations continue into the arson at Lily's and the explosion and fatality at the Kinky Ink Tattoo Parlor.
>
> Federal investigators have been seen in the Airai area searching a storm-damaged private residence. The coroner has not yet released the final report on the slain yakuza warlord, Masura Ishikawa, or his henchman, known by the alias Chobei Banzuiin.

Federal investigators? Storm damage? Private residence? In my neighborhood? None of that sounded good, but I didn't have time to consider the possibilities.

Stephaliza's article, which wasn't at the very top of the online page, but was bordered by red lines, continued: "Police remain silent on reports that local expat Haole dive guide Ricky Yamamoto may be related to, and still pursuing the interests of, the famed Yamamoto yakuza clan."

BITCH...

There was more rehashing of old rumors and speculation before she ended with: "News agencies across the globe continue to follow this story. A Google search of the words "Palau" and "yakuza" yields over 15,000 hits as of midnight."

Yeah, most either posted by or quoting you. Was there no journalistic integrity anymore?

Ruluked had also provided some URLs for international media that had picked up the news: Reuters, the AP, even something called *Meridian Magazine*.

I looked up from the printout. I wasn't sure if I had actually been voicing my responses or if it was just my body language, but a couple NOAA team members were staring at me through the big plate-glass window separating the anteroom from the lab.

*

One of the NOAA scientists came to tell me that the flight would be leaving in about fifty minutes. He pointed to an older plane that he called the *Orion*.

Although I wasn't sure it was part of his job

description, the scientist said, "I thought you might have needed assistance of some sort. The reason I raise the subject is that I noticed you seemed a bit distraught. You're clutching that paper a bit aggressively." It was only then I realized I was crumpling the printouts of the latest articles in one of my clenched fists.

"No," I said, smiling, "I'm alright. Just a bit stressed. I found some bodies the other day and there are a lot of issues to be closed out."

"I understand. I've been reading the articles. We're honored to have you as our guest." Jeez, I was a celebrity. "Sorry," he said, reading the look on my face. "If I may ask, have they determined who did it?"

"I can't really talk about it, though, you know? Minister of Justice, FBI... they're pretty rigid about what I can say. I should probably stop there." I was getting used to offering those excuses—they came in handy.

"Yeah, word is that it's international. At least that's the word on the street."

"Like I said, I'm really not allowed to discuss it."

"Very well, Ms. Yamamoto. If there's anything else you need, just knock on the window. I'm Dr. Lester. You can call me Les."

I was about to sit back down when I realized I did need something else. I went over to the window and knocked. Les was back in a flash. I think he had been keeping an eye on me, given my somewhat erratic behavior.

"Les, do you have anything to drink here? Do you have more soda? And where's the head?" My bladder seemed to be back to normal performance.

"That we do, Ms. Yamamoto. It's the local so it's sweet, but cheap and plentiful." He was back shortly. He had failed to mention it would be barely below room temperature.

Although I had been avoiding it, I knew I should calm down a few worried people, and I needed to get more help. I banged once more on the window to get his attention, then borrowed Les' cell phone, since I had no idea where the shop cell had gone. Before leaving, I had jotted down a few numbers I might need and brought them with me. I dialed Sarah's cell, figuring she could pass word on to Roland. She could also notify Justin and Dmitri, which might make them feel neglected, but I didn't have time to worry about that right now.

Sarah answered on the fourth ring. "Hello? This is Sarah Harmon."

"Sarah," I said, "It's me, Ri—"

"Ricky, Ricky, Ricky. Hold on. I'm putting you on speaker. ROLAND. It's Ricky. Omigosh, Ricky, where are you. What's happened? The police and the FBI are asking around. We thought they were with you. And somebody called about your car. It's going to cost more than they thought, and the parts still aren't in." I waited, knowing at some point she would either stop to take a breath or faint. "And that wretched reporter. Where does she come up with stories about you? I don't believe them, but Roland—"

"Lies, lies!" Roland shouted. "I didn't say I believed them, only that it would be cool if some of them were true."

The interruption stopped Sarah's nonstop gabbing, but I missed my chance to cut in.

"She's been calling here and at the shop, looking for you. And did you hear about the guy in the swimming pool? And the naked guy out at the monoliths? Your house... omigosh, your house. This place has gone mad. I think it has to do with high-pressure systems. Back in Michigan, just before a tornado would hit, the cows would stop giving milk. I think we just aren't aware of the way these things impact us. And..."

At least the monologue gave me time to wolf down the last of the fried chicken. When I was done chewing, I cut in. "So, I'm ok. I'm not going to be in town for a day or two. I figure we're not running trips tomorrow."

"Hell no, the viz has gone to shit." That was Roland. "We're not in diving condition for at least a few days. And none of the boats will be ready to go anyway. Did you see the stop sign that went through the six-pack? That was outstanding. Sarah's working the insurance. She's masterful. The alarm company called a few minutes ago. The phone lines just came back up and they got an alarm signal from the shop. They're thinking it's broken glass but they're sending a security guard right away. By the way, have you spoken with Justin in the past day? He's not returning calls.

"Call the alarm company back. Tell them to hold off and let the police handle it. And don't go over there until the police tell you it's clear. If you check the safe, don't freak out that the cash is all gone. I didn't have access to my ATM. I'll pay it all back. Anyway, I need to run. I'll be in touch in a few days then, if you won't be needing me. Justin's a big boy. He's probably found a typhoon party that's still going strong. Gotta go. Bye."

I delayed hanging up until the chorus of byes died down. Great bosses. I hoped I would get paid for the days I wouldn't work. But something was nagging at me. What had Sarah said about my house? What had the article said? Storm damage? And where the hell was Justin? *Crap.*

*

I went back to my printouts. Stephaliza was a writing machine. I did have to admit that, for someone who had previously been restricted to a quarter page next to the cartoons in the afternoon print edition, this had to be nirvana. Now she was using the online page for a running blog, posting several times a day. Her post from later in the afternoon was almost professionally done... a new tack for her:

> **Coroner Issues Ishikawa Report – More Mayhem Expected**
>
> An advance copy of the coroner's report for the Ishikawa slaying has been obtained by Co-Editor In Chief, Senior Crime Desk Editor, and CNN Contributor Stephaliza Rengulbai. Precise details of the report may not yet be disclosed, however, the following details have been culled from the report and accompanying e-mails:
>
> Toxicological testing has isolated the fatal agent. Secondary testing confirms the cause of death to be asphyxiation as a result of tetrodotoxin poisoning, but neither testing nor physical inspection

> could isolate with certainty the means by which the tetrodotoxin was introduced.
>
> Lack of stomach content is consistent with forced regurgitation pursuant to accidental ingestion of pufferfish, though none was found at his home, and no restaurant on the island appears to serve it. The owner of the local sushi restaurant was not available for interview, but sources indicate he does not serve fugu. Sources within the Koror Police and Ministry of Justice reject this theory as unsupported conjecture.

It went on for pages. If I hadn't grown to hate her, I might have respected the quality of the journalism. I read the report twice. It gave a mixed message: he had dozens of new and old injection sites in locations not used by doctors, which meant he was into self-injecting drugs. But apparently injection of tetro-whatcha-callit was now a popular form of murder for the yakuza.

He also had high levels of toxins in his body fat, a mix including over forty different kinds of PCBs. Information from the few people on the island who both knew him and were willing to talk to reporters, indicated he had recently experienced changes in the pitch of his voice, fatty pectoral growth, and loss of hair. Multiple possible causes were under consideration, not least of which was steroid use. Apparently, at least according to Stephaliza, the prevailing theory was attempted murder by long-term exposure to toxins and then a more immediate murder by injection of poison drawn from the glands of a deadly blue-ringed octopus. According to her alleged sources, he and his henchman were then ritualistically sent to the ocean depths in a manner consistent with one previously used by the yakuza on behalf of the Korean CIA.

I knew for certain that some of it was dead wrong, and didn't know how much of the rest could be believed, but I needed to get to someone who could help me put it all together. He had always been a great resource for all sorts of information and had connections up the wazoo. Besides, he was Mr. Reliability. I knew things that Stephaliza didn't, and pieces of the puzzle were falling into place. I was in more danger than I had thought, and he knew people in Guam who could help. It was just before five in the afternoon, so he was probably still at the office.

"Ziegler," he answered. Maybe it was the connection, but I didn't think I heard it ring even once.

"Ryan, it's me, Ricky."

"R... what the hell? Wait, let me go someplace quiet—it's pandemonium around here." I heard some scuffing of feet and a heavy door banging shut. "What's going on with you? The FBI said you'd been kidnapped. Did you get away? Where are you? I'll come get you. I can get a gun."

A gun? What happened to our perfect gun laws? "No, Ryan, calm down. I'm fine. The kidnappers won't be a problem anymore. This is a big mess, bigger than anyone thought. I don't have it all sorted out yet, but I know a lot more than I did before, and need to talk to someone I can trust—someone who has no connections to Palau. Ruluked arranged for me to meet with some people who can sort this out. I just need you to research a couple things and reach out to a few of your contacts."

"Ricky, I'm not sure that's a good idea. The Ruluked part. She's tied into everyone of any significance on this island. If this involves half the people whose names are being thrown around, she will have to have known about it. Don't trust her network. Wait for me and I can keep you safe." He really was rather fatherly. Ryan wasn't all that emotional or sentimental, and I wouldn't call him a close friend, but I liked knowing I could count on him. The others sort of lived lives of chaos, while he liked order and predictability.

"No, no, these people are way out of town. I'm flying to Guam. I don't know who to trust here, so she arranged a flight. I'm on my way to your old stomping grounds. Do you still have connections with the JAG group there? And the military police? I need some cavalry."

"Who's with you? FBI? National police?"

"No, I'm going by myself. I'm fine. I'm not sure I can trust either of them."

"Agreed. Are you alone right now? Can you speak privately?"

"Yeah, I'm in the lobby. Everybody's getting ready for the flight or monitoring the storm. What's the deal?

"Ricky, there's an arrest warrant out for Ruluked."

"Ruluked? By whom? Why?"

"The FBI. Perez didn't tell you? A new group that just flew in. Not Perez. They said she was interfering with an investigation as a person of interest in an international smuggling operation. Came right into the office with a warrant. She's not around so I can only assume she knew they were looking for her and took off. I'm not sure how deep she might be into this. That could just be what they have for now. She's been very secretive lately. They were tight-lipped.

"Ricky, I wouldn't get on any plane that she arranged. This whole thing stinks. I'm heading out to the airport. Just stay put and act as if you're still planning to get on the flight. If I don't get there in time, stall."

Ryan had been out of JAG for a number of years, but I figured he still had good instincts. And connections. *Crap. Ruluked?* Was I that much of an idiot? It made sense. She had her fingers in every pie on the island, which I had always seen as a good thing. But it added up. She knew that reporter. The reporter seemed to have a source within the government. She seemed overly pushy about my dive site. She had been trying to guide my moves. On the other hand, she was Ruluked, my most trusted and loyal friend on the island. Whatever the reality, nobody seemed to be interested in solving this case, and I was likely to end up dead if I waited for someone else to act.

As bad as it seemed, the final article took the cake.

Primary Suspect Missing – On the Lam?

Following the disclosure of the coroner's report for the Ishikawa slaying by Co-Editor in Chief, Senior Crime Desk Editor, and CNN Contributor Stephaliza Rengulbai, it has been determined that the primary witness, and perhaps the primary suspect, has gone missing.

> Riccarda ("Ricky") Yamamoto, originally identified as the sole witness to the murders of yakuza crime chief Ishikawa and his henchman, has escaped her FBI guards and disappeared from Koror. Attempts to reach her have failed. The FBI has issued an all-points bulletin identifying Palau and associated territories and nations of Japan, Guam, Australia, and the Solomon Islands as potential landing spots. Australia has issued a related KALOF (keep a lookout for) bulletin as well.
>
> Yamamoto disappeared while under the watch of both FBI and national police, several of whom appeared to have been disabled through the use of stun guns.
>
> Her present location is unknown, though police are scouring the countryside in search of her.

Crap. Double crap. Triple crap. This chick should have been buying me drinks for all the stories she'd squeezed out of my life. Instead, she took a dump on me.

*

My head was spinning. I had gulped down two glasses of caffeinated, sugar-laden soda and was beginning to regret it. I was pacing and sweating. The fried chicken in my stomach seemed to want to come out for one last day in the sun. Ryan called and made it worse.

"Ricky. How are you holding up?"

"Actually, I'm feeling a bit shaky. I think I ate some bad chicken. I think I might get sick."

"That's perfect."

His enthusiasm for my deteriorating condition was both confusing and aggravating. But then he continued.

"Ruluked's on the run, but she may still be turning the knobs. It's likely that one or more people at NOAA have been involved. We think she's been using them to run some sort of smuggling operation."

"Ryan, the guys who kidnapped me took me to Ishikawa's house. They had a whole drug lab out in Peleliu. There were crates with official-looking stuff stenciled on them. They had maps and flight times and ship schedules on the walls. I think they were US Navy. Maybe Coast Guard. They had fast boats that were rigged for business." I gave him the short version of what happened, including my adventures at the shop.

"Ricky, that confirms part of what the FBI was willing to say about Ruluked. The warrant included smuggling." *Crap. Ruluked was up to her eyeballs in this. And wasn't Mac getting free rides on Navy planes with his buddies from Guam?* I should have kicked him in the head when I had the chance.

"We need to get you into real protective custody. Here's the deal. We're going to tell the NOAA folks that you've been exposed to a disease and may be contagious. I've arranged for a medical transport plane to Guam. Your job is to sell it. Now follow my lead. I want you to be sick and disgusting and incoherent in that way you uniquely own. Be the sick girl you can be. Now let me speak with one of the NOAA people. Whose phone is this? Let me speak to him."

I banged on the window and pointed at the cell

phone. Les trotted out. I handed him the phone and said, "Health issue."

"Dr. Les Lester," he said. "PhD. Meteorology," he replied with a grin.

He nodded as Ryan spoke. Several times he repeated a word or two. I definitely heard him say "contagious" and "fatal." His eyebrows shot up at one point, and he frowned. He looked at me and mouthed something about "exposed to raw sewage?" I nodded bashfully. They'd never fixed the problem, and the harbor probably contained lots of spillage. I hadn't thought about it until that point, but it explained the smell. I had already realized that the deodorant I had used was not up to the task of masking the fumes. As he talked, Les slowly moved to the far side of the room.

"You do that," he finally said, "and send your best. I think I'm in love." I didn't know the context, but I liked the line—and the smile that went with it. For a nerd, he wasn't bad-looking. My stomach gurgled, and I let out a burp. He took a final few steps toward the door, said a couple parting words, put the phone on the table, and excused himself. Back in the lab, behind the glass wall, I noticed that he was aggressively applying antibacterial gel to his hands and face. I assumed the phone would get similar treatment.

28

5:30 P.M. – BABELDAOB ISLANDS

TWO VEHICLES ARRIVED twenty minutes later. For the entire time I waited, the NOAA team stayed behind the glass wall but kept glancing my way. I wasn't exactly sure what they'd been told, but it was clear they were happy I wasn't going to join them on their flight.

Ryan pulled up in his old Range Rover immediately behind an ambulance that had driven right up onto the curb, lights flashing, siren blaring. As the EMTs fussed around in the back of the ambulance, he came in wearing a gauze mask, playing his part to the fullest. He nodded hello to me, banged on the glass, pointed in the direction of the far end of the runway, and yelled loud enough to be heard, "We're taking her to the air ambulance, down past the terminal." At that end of the field were several jets, and it looked like two of them had FBI emblems. Turning, he crossed the room to where I sat, still belching and sweating from my greasy lunch and soda. I actually did look the part of a modern-day Typhoid Mary.

Shaking, I stood up, and Ryan let me rest on his arm. I had never noticed how strong he was. He might have been meek, but his military career had left him fit and toned. As dramatically as possible, we exited through the office door where the paramedics met me. I was impressed to see them decked out in surgical masks, gloves, and goggles. Perhaps Ryan hadn't let them in on the ruse.

The two medics immediately leaned me back into a gurney and strapped me in. They introduced themselves, but I couldn't really make out the names, what with the masks and the howling winds that continued to batter the island. They asked me my name and social security number. I got the name correct, but I had no idea without looking what my social security number was. So, I made one up. I think I used the right number of digits.

They asked me my name and social security number a second time. Again, I nailed the name part of the quiz, but I was sure my made-up number was not the same one I gave before. Their exchanged glances suggested they had come to the same realization. "Ricky" might also have confused them.

"I totally made that up. I don't remember my number. Ask me something else like... who's the president?"

As they finished strapping me in, they asked several more questions. I admitted to the raw-sewage swim, added details about the crocodile and monkey, and then volunteered that I had been in some sort of illicit drug lab.

They immediately loaded me into the ambulance.

As I was lifted in, I was facing out and able to take

in the scene back in the NOAA lab—one of the scientists was spraying cans of what I assumed to be Lysol throughout the waiting area.

This was a full-on ambulance, not one of those van conversions. A truck cabin up front—a big Ford F350 with a monster engine. Big ass tires—four-wheel drive. A large rear compartment providing enough room to stand and move about. Quite tricked out. The compartment had no windows, and I recalled from my EMT training and limited employment that these things were pretty much self-contained. In the worst possible cases, you might be quarantined inside the truck. I was feeling increasingly worse, and though I assumed I was just having a bad reaction to something I ate, going through the list of items to which I had been exposed had me thinking it might be something a bit worse.

During my brief stint with the Hilo Fire Department, I had played their role of medic, and one of the prime commandments was to keep the patient immobilized and settled. I wouldn't be much trouble. I didn't have the energy to do much and I felt increasingly lightheaded.

"Ryan, Ishikawa had a lab. Steroids. In Peleliu. Using boats. And..." I paused, remembering the whiteboard filled with dates, times, and some coded number and letter combinations, "Navy flights."

That was about all I could get out. The paramedics placed me on oxygen, which made it harder for me to talk. I started to reach for the mask to take it off, which I knew I shouldn't, so they did exactly what I had been trained to do—they held my arms down and started to apply additional restraints. I instantly calmed down, hoping my changed attitude would make them back off. They clearly didn't care and strapped both arms, which only made me resist more. One gave me a patronizing pat on the shoulder and said something about not worrying and that I'd be "fit as a fiddle." It was elaborate theater.

There was a narrow passage between the driver's cabin and the back. With Ryan in the chair normally occupied by a medic, they both went up into the truck cabin. It was only then that I realized there was another person in the ambulance. A slender Japanese woman. I knew her face from around town but had no idea who she was.

"Ricky," said Ryan, "meet Primrose. She works on the island and is going to take your place on the air transport. Anyone who's watching will think you got on the plane." *Hopefully*, I thought, *they won't be watching closely*. From what I remembered, Primrose stood about six inches shorter than I did.

The ambulance bumped twice as we pulled off the sidewalk and back onto the deserted access road. The private aviation area of the airport, from where medical transport operated, was at the far end of the runway. The ride back was a bit bumpy, the restraints on my wrists tugging as I bounced. My rope burns throbbed. The ride took about two minutes with a quick stop for what sounded like a sliding gate. Another quick run and we jerked to a stop. The EMTs opened the back door, and Ryan hopped out. Through the open door I could see we were on the runway, and barely in view was the wingtip of a small plane. He grabbed Primrose—who was even smaller than I remembered and seemed to weigh almost nothing—in his arms. The doors slammed shut, and strapped down as I was, I couldn't see what happened next. After what seemed like only a minute or two, I saw one of the EMTs climb back into the front. We pulled away as rapidly as we'd arrived.

We stopped for another moment and then took off again, the stop once more accompanied by the sound of a sliding gate. The driver was focused on looking forward, and I wasn't able to communicate with the oxygen mask on, though I tried. We made a few quick turns, then some strap-straining acceleration told me we had made it to the main road. The thing had power to burn. Oddly, it felt like we turned north just before the acceleration, which would take us away from town.

*

I tried to get the driver's attention but I was feeling increasingly nauseated and lightheaded. Maybe I really was sick. Then I realized that the NOAA people had given me food. NOAA people that Ruluked had spoken with. NOAA people that may have been in on whatever this scheme was. The flight numbers on the whiteboard… they all began with N. I had assumed N was for Navy, but now realized it probably stood for NOAA. I started to struggle—right around the moment that the driver quickly but smoothly brought the truck to a halt. Then he turned around in his seat and looked at me. It was Ryan.

"The others are following in the police SUV. Nice of you to bring it along." I noticed flashing lights through the rear window and heard the police siren blaring. Ryan hit the ambulance siren. "We're going to make good time with a convoy like this!" He turned back around, pulled onto the road, and jammed on the gas, but he kept on talking.

"Looks like you're not going to make it to the hospital after all. And with the antifreeze I've been giving you, plus the dose Les was able to slip you, a hospital is probably where you should be. All I wanted to do was make you more erratic than usual. Less reliable. I guess I should have given you larger doses. Les assured me that last batch was a doozy," he said.

Crap... all that sweet coffee and soda.

"We don't have time for subtlety anymore—we have a new plan. I'm going to disappear. But first, I'm going to get rid of this ambulance, and you along with it."

Nobody knew I was still on the island. I was still strapped to the stretcher. I didn't seem to have many cards to play in this game and wondered if anyone at NOAA had figured it out or even cared. At least one of them was in on it.

"The plane will go off radar near the edge of the storm. As far as anyone will know, I went down with you. Hell, eventually they'll figure it all out, but I'll be out of here."

I tried to say, "Why?" but it came out like, "Www?" He got my drift.

"I really wanted to prolong this a little more, but you... you just wouldn't stop. No. You just had to keep on pushing. Little Miss Can't Let Go. You know, that's your fatal flaw, and this time, fatal isn't figurative. You always think you're smarter than everyone else."

I tried to talk, but my tongue and lips weren't cooperating.

"We all know you think you're better than us. Especially the short-timers. They come and go. They let you run the place, not because you're better but because they don't want to be bothered. They have real careers. We indulged you. You know, the petty cash NEVER balances. You leave the office a mess. And what the hell is your problem with cell phones?"

I couldn't really argue with that. Even if I had a counter to it, I was incapable of talking. I tried pleading with my eyes.

"You always seem to forget that I've been an owner of the business longer than you've been there. You just think I'm Mr. Early Retirement, handling petty civil cases, employer-employee disputes, and dodging the big cases. Well, honey, I had other things going."

"Ishikawa?" It came out slurred, but Ryan figured out what I was saying.

"What a joke! He didn't know it, but for all intents and purposes, he worked for me. He was nothing. Put out to pasture with a little stipend. Let him think he's running the whale and shark-finning trade when he's little more than a runner, fulfilling deals the guys back in Japan had been working. He thought his petty threats influenced policy? It was millions of dollars from Japan in the right pockets and coffers. Vote-buying, plain and simple. But Ishikawa got to save face."

My tongue wasn't working, but my brain still was, and the pieces were falling into place. "Mmby."

Ryan laughed. "Yeah, MB. The punch line to the joke. What happened out there?"

I figured it was best to leave that question unanswered.

Besides, it would come out sounding like "bmoogle." And it couldn't hurt to know something that Ryan didn't.

As he slowed for a turn, I was pretty sure I knew where we were. I had driven this road enough times. I just closed my eyes and felt the tilt of the truck and the shudder when it hit the ruts. We were on the road to the west, heading toward Ricky's Rocking Spot.

*

Once we hit the dirt road, Ryan killed the siren. A minute later, the guys in Uchel's car did the same.

"Good thing Koga thought to call me after finding Ishikawa dead," said Ryan, "or I'd have never known. Good old Koga, he was a good foot soldier. Both he and I were needed to make sure Ishikawa flew under the radar. Shame I couldn't have insinuated myself in there sooner—it would have been a much cleaner operation." He was talkative. I didn't like the implications of that.

"Kooza?" My tongue still wasn't working.

"You don't get it. This was my deal. No, the yakuza were minor actors. Hell, the yakuza of today is more like the Kiwanis Club than they are the Mafia. Those five guys who flew in right after the news leaked? The two who parked themselves at the coroner's office were just pit pulls sent to drag Ishikawa home for a respectful funeral. He may have been shoved to the sidelines, but he was still one of theirs. The other three? Two accountants and a lawyer. Essentially, anything Ishikawa had was corporate holdings. It was all yakuza money. They're here to protect their interests. Very sharp guys. But none of those guys were killers. They just have that mystique, and they work it.

"The yakuza were two-bit players in Palau. The money was in the 'roids, and they were scared to touch that business. I got the raw materials from their neighbors to the west—China—delivered by shark-finning boats."

I could tell that Ryan was proud of himself. He wasn't confessing—he was bragging. All these years pretending he preferred being on the sidelines, even with Ishikawa... now was his chance to show what a big man he was.

"Bts?"

"Yep, quick runs out to meet the fleet. I even parked a couple times on a dock right next to ours. You guys never rolled in until seven or seven-thirty in the morning, so I could pull in before work and you'd never know." *The picture of the 3900 up on the wall.* I'd figured Justin, but it was Ryan. "You guys were clueless."

I guess we were. It was a pretty amazing story. He was enjoying taunting me with it.

"Koga got that. He had balls. Beauty of using finning boats is that they're sort of an accepted pirate fleet. Everybody looks the other way when they pass through, sometimes with a little cash to grease the skids. They never guessed that inside the illegal cargo was cargo that was even more illegal. Honor among pirates, I love it."

"Ruluked?"

"Nothing. Nada. She wasn't involved. I just made that up. She's nothing more than a glorified paper-pusher and gossip.

"We," he laughed, "had it nailed. Have for twenty-five years. My last thirteen in JAG and the twelve I've been here. Foolproof. Then you stumble into wrong turn after wrong turn, and each time you seem to kick over the right stone. A lot of people want you gone, and I get the pleasure of doing it myself."

An involuntary shudder shot through my body. All the rest—the sushi chef, the boob-grabber, butthead—they were just amateurs. Ryan seemed to have this dialed in. I didn't like my chances, and panic began to kick in.

"After this, no more. I'm going to dump this ambulance and you with it. I'll get picked up in a few minutes and then I'm heading to another island. Who knows, maybe I'll get a little diving in."

*

I knew the road, although the ambulance was much smoother than my Jeep, so I couldn't judge how far we'd gone. We had to be close.

Ryan had fallen silent again. I could tell by the movement of the ambulance that we'd gotten onto the worst part of the road, which meant we were minutes away. I had been working at the restraints and made good progress. When really compressed, my hand wasn't much thicker than my wrist. I had worked one restraint almost all the way off and the other about halfway. With Ryan looking forward, I could make better progress, but with him quiet I had to avoid making noise. If I got my hands free, and then removed the other restraints, I had a chance of finding something to turn into a weapon back here. I knew he had a Taser, but I wasn't sure if he was carrying anything else.

I felt the van easing to the right. We were definitely getting close.

I got one hand completely free, but I didn't want to move too much and draw attention to myself. I stopped and let my breathing fall back into a slow, measured pace.

"You like cliff diving, right, sweetness? I was thinking there would be a great synchronicity to having you meet your end by flying off a cliff strapped down and helpless. Sort of a tribute to poor Koga. You didn't even try to save him, super diver? I've seen you do some pretty dramatic stuff with those super fins of yours. I haven't been able to figure out if you couldn't or just wouldn't save him. Unwilling to risk your life for a stranger, perhaps? I hear that cliff of yours is very dramatic. This thing was made to go pretty much anywhere, though I suspect not underwater."

"Eat me," was the best I could come up with. Not my usual witty repartee.

"Aha, she has regained the power of speech. Such a mouth on you. And here I thought that 'crap' and 'sonofabitch' were as vulgar as you got."

*

I heard waves. We were close. My next thought was that the current at this time of day was ripping. I had done this dive a few times during high-octane currents and just flew along the wall. I had always sort of hoped that, when my time came, it would be on a dive. It was a shame that this time I probably wouldn't even feel its pulsing force as I sunk. I knew if I didn't do something right now, I would never get another chance. After everything I had been through, after each victory was snatched away from me, I was feeling a sense of inevitability. I had one hand free, but what the hell good was that? I started feeling around the ambulance for a scalpel or something to cut myself free. Reaching behind my head, I felt around and realized I still had a chance.

The van began to slow. I had no time left for subtlety. I thrashed back and forth, finally getting one leg free. Being able to pivot gave me leverage, and I pulled my second hand free, leaving some skin behind. One leg remained tangled in the restraints as I felt the ambulance come to a complete stop, but I was able to pivot my body into the passageway and behind Ryan, who had eased the ambulance down the slope to the cliff. As I stretched out to reach him, he turned to look my way. That's when I pressed the fully charged defibrillator paddles against his neck and cheek.

I should have anticipated what happened next.

29

8:15 P.M. – BABELDAOB ISLAND

ABOUT TWO HOURS later, the helicopter pilot announced his intention to land as he hovered above us. Not surprisingly, given the surreal events of the previous few days, the arrival of a large military helicopter, lighting up the beach and sending sand cutting into our skin, did not seem at all out of place. As a matter of fact, the only surprise was that the first man out wasn't Captain America or Iron Man. Instead, it was Mac, followed by Perez. And Doctor Tmetuchel.

Agent Fraser had arrived an hour earlier with a pair of commandeered national police vans and a gaggle of agents. With the help of another agent, she rolled a very resistant Ryan Ziegler onto his belly, untied the golden braids I had torn from my jacket to restrain him, and applied a pair of handcuffs in their place. Ryan had been perp walked to the van, but Fraser stayed with me. We said almost nothing but achieved some level of uneasy peace.

Mac pulled me to my feet, but I struggled to walk on my own as he guided me to the helicopter. I was too sick and exhausted to put up a real fight, and he didn't seem in the mood. If they were part of this, I didn't think I had much of a chance. I huddled on the bench in the helicopter, trying to sort things out, unwilling to relinquish trust so easily again, but as I played back all the conversations, I was pretty clear that neither of their agencies had been mentioned. As much as MB and Ryan had bragged, they would have mentioned the police or the FBI if they were involved. I was pretty sure we were copacetic and was almost ready to accept that the ordeal was finally over. I slid off my seat, leaned over to Mac, and gave him a hug, which caused him to wince a bit. I shook Perez's hand. He seemed ok with that.

During the ride back, a pair of Navy EMTs took over, with unofficial supervision from Dr. Tmetuchel, poking and prodding, force-feeding me fluids, taking fluids, asking about my ability to pee, which gave me my first laugh in days, and then settling in for the flight. Perez and Uchel huddled on their seat, but once I was on an IV and resting like the model patient I was supposed to be, they filled me in on what had happened since I disappeared. I filled them in on my end as well, as best as I could with thick tongue and fuzzy brain, though it seemed that they already knew Ryan had gone rogue. Apparently, the pilot had second thoughts when Ryan didn't return, leaving him with an increasingly panicked Primrose. He had been quite cooperative with the authorities. Neither Mac nor Perez knew about the guys who followed the ambulance in the SUV, but I guessed they were long gone.

"By the way," added Perez, as he pressed a small

device into my hand, “you left your phone at the hotel. Your dad called while we were checking it for clues—interesting guy. That Pandora’s Cluster sounds fascinating. Filled in a few details about the Hawai’i events from when you were a kid—I wish you’d shared your side of the story with me. It explained a lot. Asked me to charge the phone and see that you got it.”

Jeez.

*

Back in Koror, I spent two days in the hospital, with a lot of time on dialysis, where a number of different agencies put me through multiple debriefings. I got to shower and eat, which boosted my spirits. When I was released, Uchel provided a pair of Palau Police Department overalls, which fit better than the big purple blouse. I was still fragile at that point, but it seemed like every loose end had been tied off and life would be returning to normal. Things weren’t too bad at the shop, and it would be open for business in a day or two. I called the bosses… I needed a favor.

“Sarah, Sarah, Sarah… hold on. Please, give me a second. You’ll get all the details, I promise. We can have a beer. I’ll let you paint my toenails. We can do all that bonding stuff. I’ll even let Roland and Dmitri paint my toenails. But I need a few more days off. I’ve got some pieces to pick up back home. Hey, did Justin show up? Get out of town!” Sarah got in a burst of questions and comments as I paused to take a breath. “No,” I told her, “home, in Hawai’i. By the way, what was it you were saying about my house the other day?”

Well, it appeared I needed to add looking for a new place to live to my list of post-storm activities. That section of the island took a beating, and not much was left of the house. It would be hard to find one rent-free, but heck, I was about to become a local celebrity. First things first though. I needed to spend time with some friends and family.

30

LATER – BABELDAOB ISLAND AND BEYOND

UCHEL AND PEREZ had me lined up for one final set of interviews, and the sun had set and risen again by the time we were done at police headquarters. I had gone through several burgers and split a large pizza with Mac. The FBI and the Navy had literally fought over who would have the honor of giving me a lift over to The Big Island. It took a while to find a coin for tossing, but the FBI's Gulfstream V won out. Unfortunately, I slept almost the entire flight and failed to take advantage of any of the amenities.

Dad was waiting on the tarmac for me. He had gotten dressed up—no bathrobe and Jams shorts. Mom was on her way back from India where she'd been for another ashram visit. She'd meet us at the house.

Even when we were still twenty feet apart, Dad was already talking up a storm. I managed to shut him up by giving him an uncharacteristically long, warm hug. I clung to him like Velcro as he led me to his car. For perhaps the first time, I wasn't embarrassed to be seen in his VW Thing.

It was just after eight when we got home, and I realized it had been a long time since I thought of Hawai'i as home. Back in that awful summer. Before I had been exiled to Colorado.

By the time we'd cleared out the collection of old friends, including Falstaff and Waxer, who were polite enough to take the hint, it was almost eleven. I was exhausted, hungry, and frazzled.

"Hungry? Comfort food? I can whip up some musubi."

That did it—I started to cry. "Musubi? I love musubi."

He smiled. "I thought maybe it was too... I don't know, old school."

"No, no. Please, some musubi. Just exactly the way you used to make it. With real Spam, not one of those low-sodium or hickory-smoked or—God forbid—turkey."

"Nope, nope, Spam classic or nothing at all. I have more respect for the musubi tradition than to change the recipe."

Within minutes he had gotten the cold sushi rice from the fridge, prepared the seaweed wrappers, and sautéed up the Spam. It was musubi time.

"Root beer?" he asked.

I love my dad.

*

Sumo seemed to have a pretty good grasp of what had gone on. Apparently, Mac had gotten in touch with him.

Yikes—Mac! I made a mental note that I still owed him an apology. That was a nasty cut on his forehead, and Dad said I had broken two ribs, which would explain the wince when I hugged him. Anyhow, Mac had called and given him a lot of the details that morning while I slept. A form they'd e-mailed had detailed, among other services, something to indicate the government was offering me some counseling services. I was a bit chagrined that everyone felt that would be a good idea.

But Sumo just had to keep pressing. "Ok," he said, "so let's see if I got this right: steroid-abusing sushi chef accidentally offed customer with bad fugu."

"Bad fugu, right," I said. "But it was self-inflicted. The sushi chef didn't do anything wrong, cuisine-wise. I liked the sashimi there. And it was the customer who was on 'roids."

"Dumped body and threw in the bodyguard for good measure."

"Yup."

"You found the bodies and immediately envisioned a sinister plot."

"Yeah, it seemed to make sense at the time," I said.

"Your spotlight-seeking journalist friend concocted a paranoid vision of a multitiered conspiracy involving all levels of Palau's government—"

"Hey, she was no friend of mine. She's the one who ratted me out, but I'm not sure I'd call it paranoid. Turns out, she wasn't that far off."

"And you swallowed it hook, line, and sinker and decided to call in the Marines."

"Technically NOAA," I admitted, "but close enough."

"It's a figure of speech. Naked guy at the monoliths—kidnapping?"

"Vengeful wife."

"Oh, yes, the one who torched the bordello."

"Yes, he was spending too much time there," I told him. "Apparently, he just took his business elsewhere, so she had to turn up the pressure a notch."

"And the tattoo parlor."

"It was a front for a meth lab. Apparently, the guy was worried about police raids, so he was taking it down. The lab exploded."

"Dead guy in pool?"

"Security camera got most of it," I said. "He had to take the stairs because the hotel elevators were shut down. He looked drunk. Accidentally ended up on the roof, and the door locked behind him. Storm came. Couldn't fly, so he died."

"But your violent behavior," interrupted Mom, who had remained silent until this point. "You knocked two men out, fed another to the crocodile, bit another's finger off?"

"First, they were kidnappers, Mom. Second, the whole crocodile thing was an accident. Third, I think just the tip... it seemed like a lot at the time, but I don't think it was the whole thing."

"Horrific boat crash. Damaging one of Palau's most photographed icons," resumed Dad.

"That one's on me."

"You punched out a cop built like a linebacker and chained him to a toilet."

"Handcuffed, not chained. Not fur-lined though. Again, that one's on me. My bad."

My mother made a clucking sound that suggested she did not approve of my newfound ability to court mayhem.

"You don't have time to return my calls," continued Dad, "but you made time to call one of the bad guys to tell him where you were and where you were headed, then you got kidnapped and misused medical equipment, which—by the way—could cost you your paramedic's license."

"Yeah, that wasn't the plan, but things went squirrely. And I didn't know I was calling a bad guy. He was a lawyer. I thought I could trust him. I'm an EMT, not a paramedic—why can't people keep those two straight? But yeah, I expect some review board to ask me questions about that."

"What about your friend, Pascal, the fugitive?"

"He has had some issues back home and gets a little tweaked if he has to talk to the authorities. He panicked. He's in Egypt and says all is cool."

"Justin?"

"Turns out he was shacking up with the two sisters. Don't ask for more details, it makes my stomach dance. And how is it you always seem to call when things are getting crazy?"

"Can we get back to the arc of the story?" he said, clearly not liking being on the receiving end of the interrogation. "The lawyer, who was your boss, has been running most of the crime in Palau. And the business is being investigated by the FBI, the DEA, the FDA, and State Department."

"The shop will be fine. We needed time to repair the

boats anyway. Did you see that picture of the stop sign? It was on CNN."

"Yeah, that was pretty cool," Dad said, smiling slightly before getting serious again. "The yakuza? What about them?"

"Totally innocent. Complete pussycats. Didn't cause a lick of trouble. Apparently very good tippers, and quite charming once they let their hair down. Just in town to close the books on their business interests and take care of their own. Took Ishikawa and Koga home to be buried in honor."

"Honor. Yep. What about our good family name? That reporter told the world we were yakuza."

"She's crafting a retraction. I think we'll be fine. You might want to worry more about your Facebook posts if you're interested in preserving the family reputation."

Dad ignored the jab and said, "So, you zapped him, the ambulance rolled into the ocean, and instead of just swimming to freedom, you stayed in a vehicle that was sliding down an underwater slope so you could get him out of the van and rescue his murderous butt."

"Yeah, I probably should have waited until he turned off the engine or at least put it in park. He went stiff as a board when I hit him with those paddles. That ambulance jumped like a bucking bronco as he jammed on the gas. I didn't really think about not saving him—I just did what I was trained to do. Instincts took over. Besides, it helped clear things by actually bringing him up alive. The current was running fast, so I knew I didn't even have to swim, just ride with it and keep his head above water. I was pretty sure I'd have him on shore in no time.

Besides, I also grabbed an O2 tank. If he'd come to, I would have hit him on the head."

"And the fancy duds?" He nodded his chin at the pants and red jacket hanging from the doorknob.

"Perez is going to try to get the braided cords back. I'll get the stuff dry-cleaned, I swear. Ishikawa doesn't need them anymore, and nobody seemed very interested in taking them, so I figured I could just leave them here. If that's ok?"

"Sure. Can we talk about Surf Slayer?"

"Nope. You were wrong. Don't go there. Try me again in ten years."

"Fair enough. Yeah, we'll talk about it in ten years. So, you brought down a smuggling syndicate, and a whaling operation, made buddy-buddy with cops and the FBI, and then decided it was time to come back home and chill with good old Dad?"

"That about sums it up. I realized how much I missed hanging out with you. Despite... you know."

Mom raised her eyebrows.

"You too, Mom."

"Honey, have you ever heard of chaos theory?"

"Yeah..."

"You're the poster child. I love you, but I worry about coconuts falling on my head when I'm standing next to you. I'd love for you to hang out, but can we avoid trees?"

EPILOGUE

Ishikawa was taken back to his birthplace in the city of Fukuoka, in the Hakata ward on the island of Kyushu. Nearly 1,100 members of the yakuza, from over two hundred gangs, showed up to pay their respects. Flowers, from small orchid displays to large wreaths, arrived from all around the country. At the dinner following the funeral, shark-fin soup was served. The Norwegian blubber sashimi went essentially untouched. A Michael Jackson impersonator performed a moving rendition of "Beat It" to close out the evening.

Koga was cremated and his ashes honored in a private ceremony according to Buddhist tradition.

Sarah, Dmitri, and Roland hired locals for most of the repairs and pocketed almost half the insurance money from the storm, using a bit to upgrade a few features on the boats. They also replaced the glass front door with a more substantial wooden door. By maritime salvage law, Palau Oceanic Scuba is now the proud owner of a Nor-Tech 3900 Super-Vee that came to rest against their dock after the storm and went unclaimed.

Mildred Embry, the receptionist at the police station, was arrested and tried for "disclosing active criminal investigative or intelligence information with intent to obstruct, impede, or prevent a criminal investigation or a criminal prosecution."

Ricky does carry a cell phone, but she seldom checks it and continually forgets to charge it. She still doesn't know that her dad rigged it to send him a signal every time she turns it on.

En route to Egypt, where a job was waiting, she stopped in Japan. She boarded a southbound train to Tottori City where she was met at the station by a man and woman she contacted before leaving Hawai'i. Her father's cousins greeted her with a warmth and familiarity that took her by surprise. A generation and thousands of miles separated her from this side of her family, people whose names she barely knew and whose faces she had never seen. They took her to the sand dunes where her father played as a child, and she lay there into the night, listening to stories of young Otori and watching the stars.

While she was in the area, she spontaneously paid a visit to Koga's family home in the town of Fukuoka where she burned an incense stick at his altar. When asked if she knew him, she paused, then replied, "*Hitowatari*. Only in passing."

DISCLAIMER

This is a work of fiction. Any similarities to actual people or events are purely coincidental.

The places mentioned, for the most part, exist. In many cases I have changed distances and features to fit my story. The Rock Islands of Palau are quite possibly the most exotic and overwhelming landscape I have ever seen. I have never been able to do justice to them when trying to describe them.

Many of the political and social issues discussed also exist, though they may have been exaggerated or otherwise altered to fit my story.

Palau, like most countries, has its share of fine people and its share of less-than-fine people. I enjoyed my time there and hope to go back. Hopefully nothing portrayed in this novel will make my next visit unwelcome. The Palau National Police Force appears to have a very clean, corruption-free presence. Their politicians also appear well above average. Events and people were created for purposes of storytelling, not to paint a picture of how I truly view Palau.

Whaling continues to be a contentious issue. There is a substantial amount of content that suggests that Japan does, in fact, use "benevolent" donations to influence countries to support their ongoing efforts. Norwegian whale blubber does in fact contain high levels of toxins as described in the book.

Palau was the first country in the world to establish a shark sanctuary. Their efforts received global acclaim and have served as the model for other countries. Sadly, both legal and illegal shark finning continues. There is substantial evidence that illegal finning continues to take place in the waters around Palau. Enforcement on the high seas is difficult and far from absolute. Hopefully someday that will change.

Professional dive guides are a zany bunch. I'm sure their stories, if told in total candor, would make this one seem quite bland.

Beyond these items, please take this tale in the spirit in which it was written.

The End

Read more...

Read on for a preview of DERELICT, book #2 in the Divemaster Ricky Series, available on Amazon, June, 2022.

Keep up on the latest from Ricky by following her on Twitter @divemasterricky.

And, please, take a few moments to drop a review into Amazon.com. Feedback is a gift.

DERELICT

1

EARLY MORNING, LATE DECEMBER — DAHAB, SINAI PENINSULA, EGYPT

WE'D BARELY SPOKEN that day. As a matter of fact, we'd barely spoken for a week. We went about our business with grim determination. He had his group and I had mine—we briefed them separately, went to our RIBs separately, and dropped in on different parts of the reef.

Sunrise is late that time of year. The sun was still low in the sky, but we'd chosen a shallow reef—the reds, oranges, and greens were warm, and the light patterns played across the sandy bottom as the waves rippled above us. The reef life was awake and alert.

The dive should have been pleasant, if not downright joyful. It was anything but.

My group splashed in first, well up-current of the other group. The water was tepid—I wore a thin full-length wetsuit, mostly out of discretion and sensitivity to local custom. I'd have been happier just in a swimsuit, but when in Egypt... The reef was fishy, with a mix of small baitfish, larger vegetarian tropical, and even larger predators. Occasional flashes of silver told me the breakfast buffet was open for business. I led the group through several dramatic cuts in the reef, zig-zagging along for maximum activity in a small space. I made a point of avoiding a meet up with the others.

My customers spent ten minutes playing hide-and-seek with an octopus—every time they gave up, he'd pop back up from his hiding place in the reef and entice them back. He put on color and texture displays, flashing black and white... blue, then tan, brown, pink, and gold – smooth and then covered with bumps, the two photographers among them madly shooting away. Three enormous turtles had lazily munched on sea grass while my group floated only a few feet away. A ray had cruised up over a sandy ridge and parted our group as it calmly slalomed among us. A free-swimming eel repeatedly lunged at his own image reflected in the dome of a photographer's camera. A turtle swam by, heading up-current, just as the ray headed in the opposite direction. I chased after two stray divers and gestured emphatically that they had to stay with the group. I'd been very clear during the briefing—we require you dive with your buddy from splash-in to re-boarding the boat. And the buddy teams needed to stay with the group. It was a great dive, and I was miserable. I was pretty sure my customers thought I was a bitch.

They were probably right.

I was punishing them for situations that had nothing to do with them. Pascal was hiding something.

Something important. Maybe he thought he was protecting me. Maybe.

I can handle the unavoidable void—no information, only my wits and senses to guide me—and I can handle drama in the light of day where I know what's coming. I'll take on either of those any time. It's the deflection, misinformation, rumors created or passed on by fools—worse yet, maliciously by liars—that makes me want to kick someone in the head. You don't want to or can't help me? Fine. But do not—*do not*—get in my way.

*

Pascal's team was late getting back to the main boat, which only served to sour my mood even more. My group had already stowed their gear and were finished with the outdoor shower. I was preparing the briefing for the second dive, this time to Napoleon Reef on the far side of Dahab's famous lagoon. But now that would have to wait, throwing off our schedule. As soon as Pascal's team was had gotten up the ladder, we'd begun to motor through the flocks of windsurfers who came from all around the world to play in this windy mecca. Pascal had just dropped below deck when we heard the explosions. We *felt* the explosions. We saw the smoke. Something catastrophic had just occurred. That much we knew. The deluge of misinformation that followed merely created confusion.

*

It was a few months into the fifth year of the Arab Spring and the population was becoming numbed to, if not comfortable with, gun battles and grenade attacks. But this was more than just a grenade; it was an explosion that would reverberate for a long time to come.

As the percussions reached us, our attention immediately focused on the shore—we couldn't see where the explosions came from through the forest of sails, but we did see the smoke streaming down the coast.

Pascal was on deck and in action before I even had time to assess the situation. He started monitoring multiple channels, all crackling with chatter. The first reports were of a bomb located in a hotel region south of town. Maybe multiple bombs at multiple sites. We knew the area well, our shop was in an industrial park that bordered, and served, the handful of luxury resorts that had popped up in the newly developed area. It wasn't the first time they'd been subject to an attack, but it was being described as the biggest.

Then the reports changed. It was a single site. Somewhere in the area of the hotel district. It wasn't a hotel. Yes, it was. No, it wasn't. It was a warehouse nearby. There were multiple bombs. There was a car involved. It was a fire, not a bomb. The bickering and rumor-mongering were fueled by hysteria and that perverse need some people have to appear to be in the game, even though they can't even see the sidelines. Pascal held up his hands in surrender. I got on the radio and started asking questions of the few sources I trusted. None of the answers were good.

Over the past few years, the locals had become, if not accustomed, then at least familiar with bombings. Most had heard them or seen the immediate aftermath.

Many knew someone who had been in the immediate vicinity of one. Some had been victims.

The friends and loved ones who lived with a pain of loss that was long and unflagging claimed that the lucky ones were those who were killed instantly.

When we finally got a clear, definitive report, it was the last thing I needed to hear. The boat had a PA system, which we never used—it was far better to speak directly to our customers—but it was designed for moments like that. I yelled for the dive guides to secure the dive deck and to drop the line we'd connected to the buoy marking the site. I told the customers to sit down, make sure they and their gear were secure and hold on. Once Pascal gave me the ok, I jammed the throttle and headed to shore in the straightest line I could manage. The boat had a siren and I put it to good use.

We were back at the dock within five minutes, having violated several marine laws and cut off a few very pissed sailboarders. The fire department was already there, but they had lost the battle. Our shop, what was left of it, was pulsing with flame. The heat was melting buoys piled twenty feet away. The boys jumped out and grabbed the saltwater hose, not only a futile effort but also one that diluted the effort of the fire crew to dump foam on what was likely a chemical fire. It took the fire captain and one of his lieutenants, armed with a very retro pike, to convince them to stop. Even if it had been a good idea, they couldn't get close enough to put the water where it was needed. In the first few minutes after we arrived, three more tanks stored in the shop blew.

The witnesses said there had been at least thirty

explosions before we got there. We had somewhere around 120 tanks in the shop so, as far as we knew, there were still dozens of potential explosions to come. Everyone kept their distance. No amount of heroic effort was going to save the building.

My focus, unlike that of the boys, was not at all about the shop, but all about the people. I grabbed the nearest gawker, a man who ran the gas station down the road.

"Have you seen the girls?"

"Girls", he repeated, parroting my word as if he'd never heard it before.

"Jacqui and Sarah!"

"Blondies?"

"Blond. Red" I tried to mime frizzy.

"No red. Two blonde babes. They came, they left."

The Barbies. Two of our customers. Bossy, bitchy and of questionable moral standing. They were the companions for the unsavory Russian, and part of the group that had chartered our team for the next few days. They'd been dropping by the office almost daily to go over petty details and ratchet up the requirements. Sometimes they were accompanied by a couple of the Russian's goons. My nicknames, though lacking in originality, stuck. The too good-looking sculpted one, was Natasha. The pudgy one was Boris. The monster, barrel chested and big armed, but with a round, soft, smiling look, was Baby Face. Not everyone embraced that name—Baby Face had the look of a boxer who had never learned when to fall down. His otherwise pleasant face featured a nose that was mashed and angled to the right, his left ear a mangled cauliflower and his eyebrows were webbed with scars. The thick forehead, though, was built for taking blows and was, as of yet, unblemished.

I checked with each of the dozen onlookers hanging back in the parking lot. No one had seen Jacqui or Sarah. They weren't found until later. Unlike terrorism victims—for whom at least there is an answer, however insane—for Jacqui and Sarah there had been no closure. No clear and definitive explanation. No villain to whom we could point. It was a stupid accident. Or it was intentional. By whom, and how, we would likely never know. And because of that, each of us hoisted onto our shoulders some degree of guilt. What could we have done differently? What had been our contribution to the situation? Why them and not us?

At least, for the victims of bombings, there was the ability to map out the convoluted logic of the event, to trace the steps and understand how it came to be. That the logic was twisted and horrible, born of hatred and bigotry, didn't mitigate the fact that it provided some degree of certainty.

Now, in addition to Sasha, I needed to get closure for Jacqui and Sarah.

ACKNOWLEDGEMENTS

I owe thanks to a veritable village of friends and professional associates who devoted their time to helping me improve this novel, step by step. Despite their best efforts, some residual errors may remain—these are completely my responsibility.

Many thanks to Robert Woodruff, Tony Jonick, and Rick Kelly for the first early read and feedback. I didn't realize until working with you that creating a novel in a one-man silo was a fool's errand. Thanks for your patience.

To Jon Tomashoff, Peter Van Scoik, and Tom Winegar. You were my first readers, and you heavily influenced each draft as I revisited your comments as a litmus test for my progress. There were many others who took the time to provide me with additional guidance. I appreciate your assistance and value your friendship.

Sarah Lovett and Michael Carr provided extensive developmental guidance and editing, helping me evolve FLOTSAM from a confusing jumble of thoughts to a less confusing jumble of thoughts. And to Sharon Honeycutt for a final edit after extensive revisions—you helped propel me to production. Victoria Brock, thank you for the final proofread to help me appear to be literate.

Simon Pridmore, a pioneer in the world of deep technical diving, provided invaluable advice and amplifications to all aspects of diving safety and protocol. Any remaining errors are mine and were introduced during subsequent edits.

Finally, to Dana, who had faith in me even when I was lacking, and who provided enough kicks in the rear to propel me over the finish line. Thank you. I love you. Please tell your friends to buy the book. (And leave reviews.)

ABOUT THE AUTHOR

This is Tracy Grogan's first novel.

In creating Ricky Yamamoto, the protagonist in *Flotsam*, Tracy drew upon his travels through Papua New Guinea, Indonesia, Borneo, Micronesia, and a half dozen other South Pacific dive destinations. During those voyages, he has spent hundreds of days in the company of quirky, passionate, funny, bull-headed expats.

Among them were a number of kick-ass women who more than held their own in the testosterone-fueled environment of non-stop diving. They live in a small community where they are subjected to challenges to their skills, unwanted advances, and frequent stereo typing. If they show weakness, they are marginalized, so they have to be better than their male counterparts, below and above the ocean surface. In addition to all of this, their unique take on life, and the marine environment in particular, provided a perfect lens to view the collision of modern civilization with noble and more traditional cultures.

Two of Tracy's advanced scuba certifications were awarded after training and testing by women dive-masters. Some of his favorite dives and post-dive conversations were with women. His best dive buddy is a woman. Ricky is an aggregation of all of them with a little Stephanie Plum thrown in for good measure.

Tracy is originally from Berkeley, California, but now resides with his dive buddy Dana in Ann Arbor, Michigan.

Made in the USA
Las Vegas, NV
27 December 2021